CANARY CLUB

BY: SHERRY D. FICKLIN

WHEN LIFE MAKES YOU A CRIMINAL,
ONLY LOVE CAN SET YOU FREE.

Canary Club
Copyright ©2017 Sherry D. Ficklin
All rights reserved.

ISBN: 978-1-63422-250-1
Cover Design: Marya Heidel
Interior Typography by: Courtney Knight
Editing by: Cynthia Shepp

FOR THE GRIZ
STILL DIRECTING THE CHOIR, I'M SURE.

BENNY

ONE

MANHATTAN, 1927

I'VE NEVER KILLED ANYBODY.

Maybe that's a silly thing to take comfort in, but having just spent three months sharing a dank cell with someone who couldn't say the same, well, it puts things in perspective.

Not that my innocence of that particular crime makes me virtuous. In my seventeen years on this earth, I've done more than my share of wrong. But not murder, never that. Lying, cheating, coveting, hell, I've got most of the list covered and then some.

But a fella's gotta draw the line somewhere.

Pushing the thought away, I focus on the rain beating against the tin roof across the street, the melody of it urging me forward with the promises of better things. This is the land of opportunity, after all. And here, on the tiny island of Manhattan, anything is possible—or that's the sales pitch. Glancing back over my shoulder, I offer a farewell wave to the stone fortress. It might be considered beautiful, architecturally speaking, if not for the misery seeping from the walls like moss on stone. Eight-stories high with a deceptively ornate chateau façade, the Tombs is where the worst of Manhattan's criminal element are sent to rot. A high stone bridge connects the jail to the

1

police station, which boasts tall, arched windows and Roman-style columns, all topped with rows of stately gargoyles looking down on the street below with menacing eyes. The Bridge of Sighs, they call it. A fittingly gloomy name for those crossing from independence to incarceration.

I wish I could be more like the other Joes, beating the streets with wild dreams of striking it rich in the market or becoming the next Broadway darling. They flood in by the train full, with stars in their eyes and holes in their shoes. But dreams are for suckers and con artists, and this city has more than enough of both.

The rain falls in fat drips on my head and shoulders as I stand on the corner of White and Elm, turning my back on the Tombs. It's early on a Sunday morning, a normally bustling time of day, but the streets are eerily still. Perhaps it's the weather that's keeping folks inside, or the fact that Miller Huggins is, right this moment, leading the Yankees against the Washington Senators minus one very ill Babe Ruth. No doubt the majority of folks are sitting on their hands, listening to the radio broadcast of the game. Most of the guards had been—I'd strained to make out the announcer's voices as they offered the play-by-play of the top half of the second inning through the crackling speakers. The guard doing my release papers had been annoyed at having to take the time away from the game to process me, which earned me one last backhand before he opened the final doors. I touch the corner of my eye with soft fingertips and hiss at the lump I find there.

Small price to pay for freedom, I suppose.

Ma has no idea I'm coming home today—though I've written to her a dozen times during my stay in the joint. Bad enough she'd had her oldest son shackled and tossed in the back of the paddy wagon. No, I'd rather spare her the humiliation of having to pick her child up from jail—it's the least I owe her.

I'm a disappointment, an embarrassment to the family, even if she would never say as much out loud.

2

Turning down White Avenue, I head for our tenement building. It's not close, just on the outskirts of Queens, but I don't have a nickel for a trolley, much less enough dough for a cab. Rummaging through the pockets of my pants, all I find is a ball of lint and a bubblegum wrapper. But the rain is warm with summer air and the sidewalk feels sturdy under my feet, each step more confident than the last, taking me further and further from my six-by-six cell.

The sound of screeching tires cuts through the pounding of the rain, and I jerk my head up, seeing the door fly open and a body hit the street. It rolls out of the dark car only a few feet before coming to a stop, one bloodied hand upturned and being washed clean in the downpour. It's followed immediately by a second body and more screeching. Then, as quickly as it'd come, the black sedan speeds off, its whitewall tires peeling down the road and zipping around a corner with a splash.

My first instinct is to rush to the bodies to try to help—if they can be helped. It's only the stern voice in my head that pulls me up short, my footsteps faltering.

Keep your head down, Benny.

My father's warning echoes inside my head. I cringe against the memory of the last words he'd ever spoken to me. Frozen in midstride, I watch the scene unfold before me, distant and partially obscured in the downpour.

Rumor has it several key players are scrambling since Joey Noe, one of the more prominent bootleggers in the area, was bumped off over a plate of minced beef and spinach cannelloni. I don't know anything first hand, but the Tombs buzzed for weeks with talk that one of the heads of the five families had taken him out after a dispute at a craps table in Jersey. Now, they're stuck looking for a new beer runner, making the smaller local importers battle for a foothold.

It's not the first time their secret war has spilled onto the streets. More and more violence eats at the heart of the city, and this is the result. Prohibition has turned good people into criminals, and criminals into modern gods.

Up the street, an elderly woman shrieks at the sight of bodies in the road, dropping a sack of groceries and clutching her pearls with one hand, barely keeping hold of her umbrella with the other. Behind me, footsteps splash through puddles. A glance over my shoulder reveals two uniformed police running for the street.

Good, let them handle it.

Looking away, I turn up my collar against the rain, though I'm already soaked through.

I walk swiftly, stopping only long enough to help the shocked woman repack her bag of potatoes before ducking into the next alley. Wiping my hand down my face, I brush my wet hair back before resuming my trek homeward.

By the time I arrive at my doorstep, I'm soggy, cold, and my stomach aches with hunger. I pause, my hand on the brass knob. Taking a deep, steadying breath, I turn the handle and step inside.

My brother rushes me immediately, wrapping his small arms around my waist, his head burrowing into my stomach. He's grown three inches since I've been gone, the last traces of childhood nearly wiped from his face. He's thin, too, not just lanky but borderline malnourished. A ripple of guilt rolls through me.

"Careful, Thomas, you'll get all wet," I say, rustling his sunshine-yellow hair.

He pulls away, "That's okay, Benny. I'm just glad you're home. I——I mean, Ma and Agnes missed you."

"Where is Ma?" I ask, peeking down the hall toward the tiny kitchen.

He shrugs. "She's at the cannery. It's a double-shift day."

"And Agnes?"

"In bed," he says, his tone deflating.

Stripping off my jacket, shoes, and socks, I drape them next to the radiator in the corner of the living room. Shuffling down the short hall, I stop outside my room—the small corner room I share with the twins—and push the door open. Curled in her bed, threadbare blankets piled high over her tiny form, Agnes sleeps. Her face is pink with fever, her eyes squeezed shut as if in pain. Her curly yellow hair is matted to her face and pillow, her lips thin and chapped. Not wanting to get the bed wet, I kneel next to her. Reaching out, I touch her forehead. Her cornflower-blue eyes flutter open, and she fights to smile through her cracking lips.

"Benny, you're home," she says light as a whisper before launching into a fit of coughing and spasms.

Soothing her as best I can, I take her small hand and kiss it. Her flesh is hot and dry.

"Yeah, I'm home."

She licks her lips. "Can I have some water?"

Thomas is already beside me, holding out a smudged, cracked teacup of clear liquid.

Taking it from him, I help her get a few sips before she falls back into bed, her eyes closing once more.

I grab some dry clothes from my dresser and leave the room, closing the door slightly behind me.

"Has the doctor come?" I ask, following Thomas to the kitchen.

He scoots a stool up to the sink and begins running water to scrub dishes. "Twice last week. I don't know what he said, though. Ma wouldn't tell me. I'm just supposed to look after Agnes while she's at work."

"What about school?" I ask. The twins are seven now, and in the second grade.

"It's vacation, for summer."

After waiting for this day for so long, I'd forgotten that spring would have faded away so quickly. With a nod, I say, "Let me go change, then I'll make us some supper, alright?"

Turning to me, he smiles widely. "Boy, that'd be great. I don't think I want sugar beets again."

Heading to the bathroom, I take a minute to look at the empty medicine bottles littering the dirty porcelain sink. Various concoctions and tinctures in glass bottles claim to treat everything from fever to gout, but every single one is empty.

Once I'm dressed, I take a minute to clean up the bathroom before going to the pantry. Thomas wasn't kidding. Other than a few jars of beets, some cornstarch, and a sack of beans, the cabinet is bare as a bone. I manage to scrounge up some bread, jam, and a few bits of cheese. It's a far cry from the chiffon pies and jelly rolls Ma had made nearly every night when Pa was still alive, but it will have to do.

Thomas and I sit at the table, devouring the humble meal, while he fills me in on everything I've missed.

The words pour out of him in a torrent, and I wonder how long it's been since the kid had anyone other than Agnes and Ma to talk to. Afterward, he takes a small plate of food into Agnes while I clean the kitchen. We listen to the radio for a bit, catching the last few innings of the game, then wile away the day playing cards and discussing the hundreds of things I've missed in my absence. When night finally falls. I tuck them both in and then continue cleaning up the tenement, gathering dirty laundry, washing the smudged glass of the main window, and even dusting the old oak shelf where Pa's family Bible sits, untouched since his passing.

It's a little after nine when Ma walks through the door, kicking off her wet boots and shaking off her brown cloche hat before tossing it on the coatrack. Seeing me, she warily walks forward, pulling me into her arms. At first, I think it's a half-hearted hug, then I realize she's resting nearly all her weight against me, almost as if she's fainted. I lift her gently from her feet, carrying her over to Dad's worn leather armchair before setting her down.

It's only then that I get a good look at her in the dim light of the electric lamp. She seems to have aged ten years in the few months I've been away. Deep lines penetrate her forehead and cheeks, dark circles sit under her eyes, and her lips are dry and cracked. Even her once-rosy cheeks are sunken and hollow, her normally fair skin tinged with green. Her hair is more silver than blond, pulled back in a fraying bun. Her hands are covered in small, angry cuts, no doubt from the hours spent shucking oysters at work.

"I'm so glad you're home," she says, barely getting the last word out before breaking down in tears. Kneeling at her feet, I pull her forward so her head rests on my shoulder as she sobs, her body convulsing with each breath drawn. "Benjamin. My sweet Benjamin."

As I rub her back, I can feel each of her rib bones under my fingers, and it's all I can do not to join her tears.

I'd abandoned my family when they needed me most. Never mind that it wasn't by choice or that I wasn't even guilty of the crime they accused me of. I wasn't here. That's all that matters. Dad passed, and it's my job to provide for them now, a job I've failed in spectacular fashion.

"No more double shifts," I say finally.

Sitting back, Ma opens her mouth to protest, but I cut her off.

"I mean it, Ma. Agnes is sick, and she needs you. I'll get a job tomorrow. I don't care what it is. I'll even sweep up at the cannery if I have to. I'm just so sorry."

She cups my face in her hands. "No, I'm sorry. You're a good boy. You always have been."

Her words send a sliver of guilt through me. Standing, I retrieve the last remnants of my dinner and hand it to her, sitting across from her as she eats.

"Is there nothing left?" I ask. I know Pa's savings had been small, but it should have lasted longer than this.

She shakes her head, swallowing the last crumb of bread. "When Agnes got sick, the doctor said she needed medicine. It was expensive, and it took everything we had. But nothing helped. He came back a few weeks later, and said she must have something else—he thought it was a chest infection, originally—but now he says we need to take her to see a specialist up in Albany. But the money is gone now. We're barely getting by. I had to sell your father's pocket watch for bread and milk this week."

She brings one hand to her quivering lips, as if admitting to a great crime of which she's deeply ashamed. I know the watch she's talking about. It was one of Pa's prize possessions. A gold pocket watch engraved with the image of a train. For him, it represented his trek out of Germany, his coming to America—to the land of opportunity—where my siblings and I were later born.

I shake my head. "You did what you had to. Pa would understand."

"We had a good life," she says, sounding completely defeated. "I just don't know how it came to this."

"I'll fix it. I swear," I vow, taking her hand and squeezing it gently. "Whatever it takes."

THAT NIGHT, I CAN'T SEEM TO SLEEP. BETWEEN MY HEAVY thoughts and the too-soft mattress, I toss and turn. Finally, I pull a thin blanket and pillow onto the hard floor and manage to drift off only to be woken periodically by Agnes' coughing fits and Thomas getting up to fetch her water.

Everyone is still asleep when dawn breaks, but I can't force myself to lie there anymore. I put on the kettle and have a cup of stiff black coffee before showering and dressing in my best slacks and blue shirt, adding navy-blue suspenders and a matching bow tie. I comb my hair back and scrub the grit from under my fingernails. By the time I'm done, Ma is awake, rummaging in the kitchen.

"I'll go to the market on my way home," I call out.

She holds up a box of corn flakes, shaking it victoriously. "This will hold us till then."

Coming around the corner, she tucks the box under one arm and reaches out, straightening my tie.

"Just be careful, Benjamin. You don't want to go getting into trouble again."

I grin. "No more trouble, Ma. I promise."

She sighs. "From your mouth to the good Lord's ears."

MASIE
TWO

THIS ISN'T THE FIRST TIME I'VE SNUCK OUT OF THE PENTHOUSE.
On the contrary, it's become a semi-regular occur-
rence as of late. Tony, my stoic and constantly frowning
guard-come-chaperone took me home after dinner, as per
Daddy's instructions, depositing me safely in the apartment my brother and I share before heading home for
the night. He told me to sit, to stay. *Be a good girl*, he
chastised me sharply without words but rather using a
cutting glance.

This is our dance. He commands me to behave. I
promise I will. It's a terrible lie, though. I don't want to
sit. I don't want to stay. The city, thick with beating drums
and screaming trumpets, heavy with sweat and clouds of
smoke, humming with dancing feet and billowing laughter, soaked with gin and glitter and unmitigated freedom,
calls to me, and I'm helpless against it.

But I pretend to obey and he pretends to trust my
word, taking his leave. Butler is already turned in for the
evening, and my maid, all too aware of our little routine,
already has a slinky little number draped over the back of
my vanity chair before I even open my bedroom door. The
only creature with wide eyes is the guard outside the front
door, one of an ever-rotating number of fellas my father

9

employs to keep the penthouse secure. I almost laugh at the thought. As if the wolves were outside our door and not already in our very hearts.

Thanking the maid, I wave her off to bed, quickly refreshing my rouge and lipstick.

The midnight air is brisk as I slip from the servant's entrance into the alley, my snappy t-strap shoes clacking on the pavement as I make my escape. I take a deep breath, my lungs filling to nearly bursting. There are no eyes on me now, no lies I must tell or smiles I'm forced to fake.

It's just the city and me.

I may have actually opted to bathe and turn in for the night—for once—but that plan had been shot to hell with one frantic call from June.

Now, I'm walking the street alone, clutching my beaded purse. The fringe of my maroon dress tickles the tops of my garters as I make my way toward a group of flappers lined up outside one of the smaller clubs, smoking their thins in long, black cigarette holders, laughing loudly at the two Joes making faces at them from the other side of the wide glass window, waving and begging them to enter.

I recognize one of the girls as Maggie Kurskey, daughter of Rabbi Kurskey, a man with whom my father has occasional dealings. The good rabbi likes to procure wine from Daddy's company—for religious use, of course. I wave and she grins, opening her arms and taking me by the shoulders, leaning forward to kiss the air next to my cheeks in French fashion.

"Getting into trouble, Maggie?" I ask, returning the gesture.

She shakes her head. "Who, me? Trouble? Never."

Her response elicits a fit of giggles from some of the other girls. Dropping her hand to her thigh, Maggie lifts her dress and slides a flask from her garter. "Though, I'm sure we can scrounge up something, if you'd like to join us?"

Normally, I might take her up on the offer, but tonight…

"Sorry, I'm going to have to pass. But come by the club tomorrow night after my set. First bottle will be on me," I say, the invitation a cheerful chirp.

She grins widely, exposing one chipped front tooth. "I will, for sure."

I make my way around the usual hotspots—stopping only briefly to offer a flirtatious wink or a quick hug to the usual faces—toward the garment district.

I should have known something was wrong when June didn't show up to the club to watch me sing. Instead, my brother, JD, had entered uncharacteristically alone, then spent the better part of the evening nursing two fingers of whisky. June's call a few hours later had been unexpected, her boisterous laugh and pronounced slur telling me she'd been out getting into some sort of trouble, and I may as well be part of it.

It's not until I run into a couple of JD's employees, all of them completely blotto and being roughly escorted out of the Scanty Nancy, a poker and beer joint in Hell's Kitchen, that I stop to ask about my friend, just in case her adventures had taken her elsewhere. The tallest boy, Dickey, throws one arm over my shoulder. His boldness surprises me, but only for a fraction of a heartbeat. I pat his hand once before twirling out of his embrace with an admonishing laugh.

"What brings you out tonight, princess?" he asks, the gin and lemon still fresh on his breath.

"I'm on my way to meet June." I hold up my hand, forcing a polite smile. "You know, yay tall, stick-straight black hair bobbed at the chin…"

"And curves that don't stop," another boy says, laughing loudly. He points down the road. "I saw her get into a car with that Brewer fella, maybe an hour ago?"

The forced grin slips from my face before I can stop it. There is literally no one she could have flung herself at that would have upset JD more. Not only is Lepke the number two of a rival crime family, but he and JD have a very personal beef that goes back to an ill-wagered boxing match that JD swears Lepke had fixed.

Of course she's with Lepke.

There's a fire in that girl that burns everything she touches. I know it all too well, because I have a similar flame in me. It's a deep, irrational desire to push limits, to test boundaries, and, when things are going smoothly, to take a match to it all. It's part of the reason we became such fast friends when JD introduced us—and why we end up in so damn much trouble together.

"How do you plan to repay me for that information?" the boy asks, wagging his thick eyebrows suggestively as I collect myself. "Cash or check?"

He chuckles, and Dickey slaps him on the back, joining in.

Taking one step forward, I grab him by the front of the shirt and pull him to me, pressing my mouth to his in a kiss so hard I can feel his teeth behind his lips.

He freezes, completely stunned by my move. I lick his bottom lip, fighting back my repulsion at the taste of stale beer and cheap tobacco, my eyes never closing, locked on his as they go wide with shock. When I release him, the poor boy nearly falls over, and another roar of laughter spills out of Dickey.

"Don't feel bad," he says, offering his friend a hand as he rights himself. "That dame's a firecracker. Fellas like us don't stand a chance."

Wiping my mouth with the pad of my thumb, I glare at the boy, shrinking him with my gaze. I can read the panic on his face as he realizes, through the booze-induced haze, what he's done. He just kissed Dutch Schultz's daughter.

For a fella like him, that's as good as a death sentence, especially given Daddy's tendency to run a little hot under the collar where I'm concerned.

I see the realization hit his eyes even as the flush drains from his cheeks. A question forms on his features— was the kiss a flirt or a threat? Would I tell my father that this boy with holes in his shoes—without two pennies to rub together—had dared steal a kiss from my lips? Honestly, I already know I won't say a word, but I hold my expression in a stern half smile anyway.

Having people fear you gives you power. Having them love you gives you influence. Having both, well, that's how you build an empire.

I wave as I spin on my heel, turning my back on the rowdy boys. "See ya around, fellas."

It's only a few blocks to Lepke Brewer's hole-in-the-wall speakeasy. It's hidden behind a tiny green door in a dark alley. If I didn't know where to look, I'd never be able to find it. It's one of the few perks of the family business—we know where every gin joint, dive, and dance hall in the city hides, and we are welcome at any of them—at least outwardly.

As I stand outside the door, my hand ready to tap out the secret knock, I already know what kind of stir my presence will cause. As a matter of fact, I have, in my room, a lovely brown wig I use for just these sort of occasions, something to hide my telltale golden waves. But I'd neglected to bring it tonight, a mistake I doubt I'll make in the future.

Oh, to hell with it.

I knock, three quick taps, two slow ones, then two more quick ones. The door swings open and the host rakes a quick look over me, ankles to eyebrows. It's only when his eyes meet mine that the recognition hits and he bows from the neck, waving me inside.

"Welcome to the Pennybaker Players Club," he says, hastily closing the door behind me and sliding the lock in place. "The table games are upstairs, speakeasy is down and to the left."

A young woman, barely covered in a dress made from faux rabbit fur, holds a silver tray of candies toward me. I accept one, popping the small chocolate in my mouth and rolling it around until it melts away. The small, brandy-filled confections are a delicacy served at the higher-end establishments, but now, they've somehow migrated even to places like this. The décor is gold leaf everything, from gaudy glass vases to antlers hung on the wall. A few round tables litter the small space, and people talk loudly over the music throbbing from the gramophone in the far corner.

"Where's June?" I ask, licking my fingers while holding eye contact with the host.

He blinks, his eyes darting from my mouth, to my eyes, then back again.

"I'm sorry, Miss, but I don't know..." he stammers.

I sigh. "Of course you do; she came in with Lepke. As a matter of fact, she probably called me from that phone." I motion to the black phone set into the far wall beside the coatroom.

His eyes flicker to it, then back to me. "I don't remember any such person, Miss."

My ire rising, I pull a folded ten-dollar bill from my purse, holding it between two fingers. "Where's Lepke?"

His eyes dart to the coatroom, then back at the money in my hand. A trickle of sweat rolls down his temple, and alarms sound inside my head. I stick the cash back in my bag, leaving it open but clutching it close to me

"Never mind, then. I'll just find him myself," I say, stepping past him. The bunny girl catches my eye, jerking her head just a fraction toward the coatroom, her expression souring.

I make it five steps before the host darts in front of me, cutting me off.

"That's just the coatroom—staff only," he says, looking down on me.

I step closer to him, so close we are nearly touching, and draw myself up to my full height, still a few inches shorter than him but tall enough to rise above his chin as I glare. "I'm not leaving here without either my friend, or some idea of where she's gone, and if you plan to stand between that objective and me, then I suggest you write down your suit size, so I can tell the undertaker how big your casket will need to be."

14

The threat is a risk, but it seems to hit home. I'm a Schultz, after all. We aren't exactly known for making idle threats, or for failing to punish people who anger us. Thank my father for that.

Truth is I will do whatever it takes to find June. An almost-electric humming deep inside me is demanding I do no less, warning me that something is very, very wrong here. Luckily, he takes me at my word and steps aside.

Brushing past him, I walk into the coatroom. There's a door on the far wall, only half obscured by a rack of suit jackets.

I push it aside, muttering to myself. "June, you better not be playing games with me."

It's then I hear it, my hand on the rusted steel lever. The muffled sound of screams.

Not playful, joking screams, but guttural, voice-breaking ones.

Without thinking, I hit the lever and the door opens inward, exposing a large study lined with bookshelves and a series of high-back leather chairs surrounding a round, stone table. But it's the table that holds me frozen in shock.

Lying across the table, stomach down, her screams and sobs intermingling in the cramped space, is June. Lepke is behind her, his meaty fist clutching her hair with one hand, his face red and glistening with sweat.

Seeing me, he freezes, even as I find my breath again. I'm moving toward them now, one hand balled into a fist.

I could kill him, I realize as he backs away. When he releases her, she falls to the ground in a bloody clump. I could beat him to death with my own small hands. The rage inside me demands I do it. I need to end his sorry existence in that very moment. It's only June's hand on my ankle that stops me from moving past her.

When I look down, I see her face. It's swollen and lipstick smeared. Blood from a badly split lip and bruises discolor her jaw.

I bend over, wanting to help her and cover her exposed flesh. But I don't get the chance to do either. Three of Lepke's men rush into the room, two guards and the door host.

Not waiting for them to advance on us, I pull the pearl-handle pistol from my purse and wave it in their direction. Not prepared for me to be armed, they hadn't drawn their own weapons and can do nothing but stare at me, hands upturned. One of them considers drawing his own piece, so I fire a warning shot, missing his hand by inches.

"If you think I'm incapable or unwilling to drop you right here, you would be gravely mistaken," I say, fighting to keep my voice even. Standing tall, I spread my legs just a bit, holding the gun with both hands as JD taught me. I hear something rustle behind me and glance over my shoulder to see Lepke slipping a suspender over his shoulder and buttoning his trousers.

"Come on, Masie," he says breathlessly. "You don't want to start something here that you can't finish."

I blink, turning my attention to the guards. They're still frozen, but their expressions clearly say they are thinking about rushing me.

"I didn't know she was armed," the host says by way of apology.

Lepke snickers. "It's fine. We can take out the trash."

At my feet, June snarls.

"Be a good girl and put the piece down," Lepke continues, taking a step toward me.

Now it's my turn to snarl. "You seem to have forgotten who you're talking to," I say, producing a smaller gun from my garter and leveling it at him, my aim just below the waist. I glance at him for only a moment, just to see that my intended target is clear. He pales and I turn back to the guards, motioning to the host.

"You, grab June a long jacket out of that closet." I wave the gun pointed at Lepke. "And you, move over here beside your guards."

As he passes, his hands still up, June struggles to her feet, leaning against the table for support. She lifts one leg, then the other, prying off her shoes and lobbing them one after the other at her attacker.

He dodges one, but takes the other in the shoulder, laughing with the impact. "What's the matter, June? I thought we were having a good time."

She lunges for him, fingers curled into claws, and I have to lower one arm to wrap it around her waist to keep her from putting herself between my would-be targets and me.

The host returns. He tosses the coat at me...as if I'd be dumb enough to try to catch it and lose my advantage. It hits the ground and June scoops it up, throwing it over her shoulders.

"Now, we're going to walk out of here, and so help me, if any of you try anything, I will shoot out Lepke's testicles like balloons at the fair, even if they are such tiny targets," I say, holding his gaze.

Finally, with a blustering laugh, he drops his hands. "Let'em go, boys. I've had my fun."

I want to hand my spare piece over to June to cover my back as we walk, but I don't dare put the weapon in her hands just now, fearing she'll shoot the scumbag dead and we'd have an all-out war on our hands.

But a voice inside me roars to life. It's unreasonable, adding fuel to the already-burning rage in my veins. The voice demands revenge, demands I fire straight into his head, then watch as the blood spills from his body.

He deserves it, the voice screams.

It sounds a lot like my father's. That is the only thing that stops me, the only thing that holds me back.

As we pass by Lepke, he puckers his lips, blowing a kiss in our direction. Without thinking, I step forward and slap him across the face, gun still in hand. He hits the ground, cradling his now-bloody cheek. His guards flinch, some moving toward him, some toward me. I wave the other gun, and they raise their hands once more.

As soon as we back from the coatroom, moving through the club with all eyes on us, I take a moment to breathe, to fight back my darker impulses. Once I'm out, I can breathe again. Behind me, June fumbles with the lock, finally freeing it and pulling the green door open.

"You come see me anytime," Lepke calls to June, smiling sadistically though my hit has done its damage and his teeth are pink with blood. "You too, doll face. We could have some real fun, you and me."

I step forward, closing the distance between us in the blink of an eye. Before his guards can even think to stop me, I press the barrel of one gun under his chin, the other into his groin. "Lepke, if you ever see my face again, you'd better make peace with the dear Lord because it will be the last thing you'll ever see on this earth."

I step back, tucking the smaller gun back into my garter. Motioning to the crowd, still seated but now staring at us, I wave the pistol around the room with a laugh.

"Relax, everyone. Drink up. Carpe noctem and all that jazz."

With that, I'm out the door, helping June into the back of a taxi as we speed off into the night.

BACK HOME, I SIT ON THE EDGE OF MY BED, GENTLY DABBING the peroxide-soaked cotton ball to the fresh cut beneath June's swollen lip, making her hiss and pull away. My hands are still shaking, the last of the adrenaline bleeding from my veins. I crack my knuckles, as if I can force the quaking to subside.

"June, what happened?" I ask, taking careful account of each bruise, each welt visible through the tattered remains of her party dress. "Why in the world did you go to Lepke's?"

I blink, tossing the now-bloodied cotton on the silver tray of bandages sitting on my bed. It isn't the first time I've had to nurse someone—though it's usually Daddy or JD—and our house is well stocked with first aid supplies. One of the few upsides of having a gangster as a father is at least the gauze and boric ointment are always on hand.

Lucky for us, neither JD nor Daddy had been home when we got back, since we had to take the main entrance back up. June was too banged up to take the stairs in the servant's entrance, and I'd given the elevator man a wad of bills to ensure his silence about the whole affair.

Daddy probably opted, as he often does, to rest his head at one of the many apartments he keeps for entertaining his mistresses. JD was who knows where doing who knows what.

Sniffling, June explains. "JD and I had a fight, as usual." She pauses, taking a deep breath, then wincing on the exhale. "I was upset so I went down to Chelsea, to that new place that just opened, and I had a few drinks. After a bit, Lepke Brewer came in and started buying. I figured we could go out, have a few laughs, and maybe make JD a little jealous in the process."

I frown, and she rolls her eyes.

"I know, Masie. *I know*. But I was so lonely and sad. JD just makes me crazy like that sometimes."

Yes, they have the very definition of an on again-off again relationship. Constantly waffling between passionate adoration and cold indifference. It isn't the first time she's used some Joe to try to make JD rethink her value. Normally, it works.

I say nothing, so she continues. "Anyway, we go to dinner at Marcolli's uptown. And maybe I let him get a little fresh over the entree. But the lights were on us, and I wanted to be sure word would get back to JD. So after dinner, we headed back to his club to dance and drink. Next thing I know, he's pulled me into the back room and he's got his hand up my dress. I..." Her voice breaks now. The next words wobble their way out of her mouth, her eyes filling with tears. "I tried to tell him no. I tried to push him away. He called me a tease, and he..."

She doesn't have to continue; I'd seen more than enough to fill in the rest. Gritting my teeth, I force the image from my mind.

"You have to help me; JD can't find out. He'd never have me back, not after this." She sniffles in earnest, her eyes wild with desperation. "I can't lose him, Masie. He's my whole world."

I hold her for a long time, letting her cry until her sobs settle. Running my hands down the sides of her head, I kiss her forehead gently. "Alright. I'm going to run you a bath, then we'll get some ice on that eye. You can hole up in here with me today, and we'll cover what we can with makeup. Write a letter to JD and tell him you've gone to your mother's place upstate to get some air and calm down. You can hide out until you're back on your feet."

"Do you think Lepke will say something?" she asks, her eyes bloodshot and puffy.

I wrinkle my nose. "And let the whole world know that some dame got the drop on him? Never. He's probably got the whole mess covered up by now. But that means there's no witnesses, no one who can confirm your side of the story except me. If you want to go to the cops, we will. I'll back you up."

"I can't," she says, grinding her teeth. "Promise me you won't say anything."

It takes me a moment to answer, but only because the whole thing is so disgustingly unfair. "I promise, June."

Nodding wordlessly, she curls up in my bed, her black, beaded dress rumpled and her fishnet stockings ripped beyond mending. I make my way down the hall to the large Grecian-inspired bathroom and run her a hot bath, pouring a full cup of lavender salts into the copper tub. All the while, rage continues to build inside me.

It's not like the police could do anything anyway; everyone saw them flirting, and it'd be his word against hers. And besides, a man like that probably has enough cops in his pocket to make any charge they might level vanish before breakfast. And even if JD did believe her, there's only so much he can do without going to all-out war. He'd strike back at Lepke somehow, sure, but at the end of the day, she's right. It wouldn't matter. JD couldn't take her back if this went public. She'd be damaged goods. Tainted. And all because that schmuck didn't understand the meaning of the word *no*. Hell, *dogs* understand what no means. And when dogs attack people, they get put down for it.

A sickening double standard to be sure, but there it is. *Lepke.*

I roll the name around in my head like a curse.

Glancing back over my shoulder toward my room, toward June, I know what I must do.

For the most part, it suits me just fine to let people think I'm just some silly girl, some empty-headed dame. Because what it means is they never see me coming, never suspect I'm capable of doing terrible things.

But I *am* my father's daughter.

I was born to violence like a fish is born to water. It's part of me, part of who I am. All my life, I've watched the people around me suffer—the women most of all. It's a fact of this life that oftentimes, shots are fired, grievances aired, and warnings sent through the women around the powerful men. They are soft targets. Disposable, but cared for enough to make a point.

In this business, women are nothing more than weaknesses to be guarded and fodder to be thrown when needed. Pawns in a game we aren't even allowed to play. It's one of the reasons I was so glad when Mother sent me off to private school upstate. For a few months, I'd felt normal. Safe.

Being called back to the life after losing her was like suddenly having an axe hanging over my head. I'd even considered running away for a while. But I quickly realized this is where I belong, even if I might wish otherwise. I know my part, and I can play it as well as any Hollywood starlet. I know I should be appalled, bereaved that things like this come so easily to me. But I let that grief, and the dreams of being anything other than what I am, go a long time ago. And so, I stay.

But Lepke isn't going to get away with this. Not this

time.

I drag my hand through the water, mixing in the salts as I cement my plan in my head. As soon as I deposit June in the tub, I steal away to the den to make a call.

"Hello?" Vincent Coll's groggy voice reverberates through the receiver.

"It's Masie. I need a favor."

"What's up, doll?"

I hesitate, biting my bottom lip. It's then I notice the smear of blood on my dress. "I have blood on me, Vinnie," I say, more to myself than him, but his tone heightens with his next words.

"Are you alright?"

"It's not my blood," I clarify. "It's the blood of someone I care about, though."

He calms again. "What do you need?"

"Lepke Brewer." I spit the name, unable to quite put into words how I want him to suffer. How much I want him to hurt.

On the other end of the line, there's a deep sigh, followed by the sound of a lighter flicking and Vinnie taking a long drag. Once a childhood friend, Vinnie is now a dangerously unstable man on a good day. But I know he'll do what I'm about to ask without breathing a word of it to anyone—not out of loyalty to me or sympathy for June and what had happened to her, but for the sheer opportunity to level some brutality on a rival.

Most people call him Mad Dog, thanks to his reputation for being about as well tempered as a rabid animal. But to me, he's just Vinnie, the young boy who'd come to stay with us after being expelled from the Catholic Reform School his mother had abandoned him at. We'd spent our formative years together, thick as thieves, until he took up the role as Daddy's enforcer and hit man. He'd changed after that.

Hell, we'd both changed. And neither of us for the better.

I roll the memory of him around in my head, biting

the inside of my cheek as I decide what to say next. We haven't been close in a very long time, and that's the way it has to be. He must be hard to do what he does. Must have no weaknesses for our enemies to exploit. And if I'm being honest, there's a darkness to him that terrifies me. Not because I don't understand it, but because I do. I know exactly how easy it would be to allow myself to be consumed by the violence of this life—and how good I would be at it.

But that's not the person I want to be.

Even so, here I am, about to ask him to do the dirty work for me, just so I can keep my hands a little bit clean.

"You want him taken care of?" he asks finally.

I suck in a breath before answering. Yes, I want him dead. I want him wiped from the face of the earth, so he can't ever hurt anyone again. I imagine myself saying yes. Imagine myself throwing a fistful of dirt onto Lepke's coffin as it's lowered into the ground. And then I imagine trying to look at myself in the mirror every day after that.

"I want him to hurt," I say after a moment. "I want him to be broken to the core of him. But leave him breathing."

Leave it to Vinnie to echo my own fears back to me. "You sure about this, Mas?" he asks, taking another drag and exhaling it slowly. "It's not going to keep you up at night?"

It's a barb from an accusation I'd leveled at him the last time we'd spoken, when I'd asked how he slept at night after all he'd done. His answer had been crude and aimed to hurt me. Mine would be much kinder.

"I suppose I will have to find a way to live with myself," I answer, keeping my tone indifferent.

He hangs up without even saying goodbye.

I hold the receiver in my hand for a few heartbeats before returning it to its cradle. JD is being groomed to take over the family business, despite Daddy's constant berating that he's too softhearted or slow-witted or whatever insult he feels like hurling in the moment for the job. I've never stepped in and asked for a place in the business. I'm just the girl, after all, to be coddled, protected, and mollified. If Daddy had seen me tonight, would he rethink the line of ascension?

And I can't help but wonder what life would be like for me if he did.

BENNY

THREE

THE STREETS HUM WITH THE RHYTHM OF THE CITY, MOTOR cars rolling down the boulevard, shops opening, people setting out for the day, their smart shoes clacking against the pavement. I take a deep breath, letting it all back in. The normally stale city air is fresh from last night's rain, the remaining puddles quickly evaporating as the sun rises, warming the air.

I'd hit the pavement at sunrise, a list of places looking for help scribbled on a scrap of paper in my billfold. Ma had gotten up early and swiped the neighbor's newspaper long enough to copy the wanted ads for me before returning it. I've already hit the cannery, the appliance store, and the local grocery, only to be turned away a split second after they found out I was a recently released felon.

As I step out of the deli, I pull the paper from my pocket and strike off the final address before balling it up and tossing it in the wastebasket near the door. The butcher, at least, had offered me a sad sort of apology before hustling me out of his shop.

A heavy noise makes me jump and turn toward the sound. I'd mistaken it for gunfire, but it was just a local newsie dropping a stack of papers outside the deli.

"Is that Bad Luck Benny I see?" a familiar voice calls

out, putting one hand on my shoulder and turning me around. "Finally outta the clink and back on the mean streets?"

"Dickey," I answer, turning to offer my friend a warm hug and a pat on the back. "I never thought I'd be so glad to see your ugly mug."

"Feeling's mutual," he says with a half grin. "When did you get out?"

"Yesterday," I say, looking him over.

"What brings you to this side of town?"

I shrug. "Trying to pick up some work. Ma really needs the help and Aggie's been sick, so we got lots of doctor bills." I swallow, almost hating what I'm about to do. But I'm out of options, and I need some cash fast. "I'm really glad I ran into you."

"Why?" He hits me with his elbow playfully. "I owe you money or sumthin'?"

Richard 'Dickey' Lewis has been my friend since elementary school. He's been living in a flop house since his old man tossed him out on his ear for losing his mother's good pearls in a hand of poker. He's easily gotten me into as much trouble as he's gotten me out of over the years, but he's as loyal as they come. And even better, he's always got some sort of gig up his sleeve, even if it isn't always on the level. I lick my lips, glancing back at the deli one last time before I speak. *This is it*, I decide. *I'm officially out of options.*

"Those are some glad rags you're wearing there, Dickey. You come into some scratch?" I ask, pretending to admire his grey tweed suit and two-tone brogues. He looks less like the scrawny pickpocket who used to work the crowds at the pier and more like a genuine fella.

He pinches his sleeves, showing off. "Got a few box jobs while you were gone."

I hide my surprise. Safecracking was never his strongest skill; he's far too clumsy and fat fingered for that. Normally, I'd make a crack about it, but I figure it's best not to stir the pot when I'm about to ask for his help.

"Listen, I'm in a tight spot just now. You know of any jobs I might step into?"

He wipes his face. "I might know of some people looking for a decent outside man."

I frown. Of course the first job he'd throw at me would have the potential to land me back in the clink. "Anything a little more on the up and up? I could use something on the regular, not just a one-time score."

He grins, his blue eyes dancing as he pulls a pack of Luckys out of his pocket and lights one, taking a long drag and exhaling as he talks.

"I can probably get you into the gig I'm working right now. It pays ten dollars a day. Better than you'll get at the docks this time of year."

I scratch the back of my head. "What's the job?"

He grins, jerking his head for me to follow him down the street. We turn a corner and see a handful of men unloading a truck full of crates into a small warehouse. "Shipping and delivery."

"What's in the crates?" I ask, not fooled for a moment by his calm demeanor.

He shrugs, tossing the cigarette to the ground and stomping it with the toe of his shoe. "Does it matter? It's a fair wage for honest work."

I swing my gaze back to him. "I didn't know you knew what honest work was, Dickey."

He slaps my back. "Relax, Benny. When have I ever led you south?"

"I can think of a few times," I offer with a grin.

He wags his eyebrows shamelessly and walks toward the men loading crates. I watch them greet him before lowering my chin and following. Dickey is many things, but he's not often wrong. Ten dollars a day is twice what Ma is making, and considering my recent troubles, I doubt I'll find anything else that pays even close—and that's if I can even find someone willing to hire me at all.

When I catch up, he leans over to a tall fella standing beside the truck. His clothes are nicer than Dickeys' are, a pinstripe suit with leather gloves and a stark white pocket square. His hair is combed back in a gentlemanly fashion, his jaw sharp and his face freshly shaven.

Dickey chats with the man for a few minutes, then waves me over.

"JD, this is Benny. He's the fella I was telling you about."

I hold out my hand, and he shakes it half-heartedly.

"Dickey tells me you're looking for work."

I nod. "Yes sir. I'm no rube. I'm a hard worker, and I can keep my mouth shut."

"Don't you want to know what kinda work this is?"

I take a breath, looking him in the eye. "No, sir. You give me a job, and I'll do it. Don't much care what it is."

He takes a notebook out of his back pocket and flips it open. After tearing off a page, he hands it to me. "There's a delivery being made at this address in an hour. You go, help Dickey and the boys unload, then ride back to the warehouse in the truck. I'll pay you a half-day's wage today, and if you're a good worker, there'll be more tomorrow. Alright?"

I nod, taking the folded slip of paper. "Yes, sir. Thank you."

He grins. "Don't call me sir. Name's John David Schultz." He pats the side of the truck that reads *Schultz Shipping*. "But my boys call me JD."

I glance at the address, then tuck the paper in my pocket. Dickey pats the truck twice before we cross the street and make a line for the street car that will take us downtown to the address he'd given me.

It's a long, backbreaking day. I'm not sure what's in the crates, but they're heavy enough to be headstones. By the time the truck is unloaded, the muscles in my neck, back, and arms ache. Dickey and I climb into the back of the now-empty truck and ride along to the shipping warehouse down by the docks. Once we pull in, we hop out and gather with the rest of the fellas as we wait for JD to arrive.

Some of the guys I'd seen at the first job are sitting around a rickety table playing cards when JD finally pulls in, the tires of his Lincoln sedan screeching to a stop. My jaw snaps closed as I stare at the car. It's gotta be a coincidence that it looks just like the car I saw dropping bodies on the street yesterday. There's gotta be dozens of them in the city, and I hadn't looked close enough to make out any details. Even as I think it, a shiver crawls up my spine that tells me otherwise.

"Dickey, who is this guy?" I ask under my breath.

Beside me, Dickey smirks.

"JD's the son of Dutch Schultz. He owns the shipping company and a club on the Upper West Side. I heard he just bought a new place in Midtown, too."

As soon as he says it, my mind makes the connection, and a chill courses through me. Dutch Shultz the only major non-Italian gangster in the city. Once in business with Joey Noe, his name had been bandied about as the next big player to hit the city. From what I've heard, he keeps low key—unlike the other notorious players in the ongoing turf war—and as far as I know, he's never been caught being anything other than above board. Of course, greasing the right palms can do that for a person. He also controls the largest fleet of trucks in the city and—if the rumors are to be believed—has a certain local police chief in his club every Friday night for cards and drinks.

I pinch the bridge of my nose with my thumb and forefinger. Of course it was his car I saw. I can only hope whoever was behind the wheel doesn't recognize me as a witness.

JD walks toward us and pulls a wad of cash out of his jacket, peeling off bills and handing them out. When he gets to me, he smiles.

"Ya did good work today. Come back tomorrow. I'm sure I can find a permanent place for ya," he says, pressing a folded bill in my hand.

Without looking at it, I crumple it and stuff it in my pocket. "That's swell. Thanks."

29

He nods, giving me one long look before turning his back to me and returning to his car.

Dickey pats me on the shoulder. "You're not thinking of swiffing out on him tomorrow, are ya?"

I shake my head. "Nah. I need the dough."

He grins. "Good. Don't wanna make your best friend look bad to the boss. Come on, I'm gonna go over to the Rattle and see what's what."

The Rattle, a burlesque club in Alphabet City, is the preferred choice for lowbrow entertainment. Bathtub gin, cheap cigars, and backroom poker all at a bargain price. Unless you lose, that is. Men have been known to drop fingers when debts couldn't be paid.

I wave him off. "Not tonight. You have fun. I promised Ma I'd hit the market on the way home."

Slipping his snap-brim hat from the pocket of his jacket, Dickey hits it once before setting it on his head. "Suit yourself."

We leave together and step out into the afternoon sun. It's only a bit after four, according to the clock in the steeple across the road, but I decide to take a street car to the market by our house. When I pull out the folded bill, I see it's not a five at all, but a fifty.

Unsure if it was a deliberate act or a mistake, I make change. I'm careful to only spend the five I earned, resolving to return the rest. I fill my sack with eggs, cheese, bread, and some vegetables for soup, as well as a packet of Agnes' favorite shortbread cookies, then head home.

It's a much shorter trip than it had been this morning, or at least it feels that way. When I step in the front door, I'm feeling pretty good about life, even though my new employer is the son of a mob boss. That might have bothered me more before jail, but being in there taught me that good people don't always wear badges, bad guys don't always wear shackles, and sometimes people have to do what they have to in order to protect what they love.

I've lived a crime free life up to this point, and I still wound up in jail, so I figure the system owes me one. Besides, most of the fellas I met in the joint were decent enough, law breakers, sure, but just doing what they had to do to feed their families. Maybe the law didn't allow for that, but I'm hoping other folks, the upstairs kind, take that into account.

By the time Ma gets home, the soup is on and the rolls are in the oven. Thomas helps me clean off and set the small dining room table. Agnes, still pale and weak, decides to join us. Ma wraps her up in a wool blanket and sets her in the chair to my right.

Pa had been a big, hulking man. When he was alive, the table was a tight fit for all of us. But now, with him gone, there's plenty of room. And yet, somehow, I miss the closeness.

"Should we say grace?" Agnes asks in a small voice.

At the other end of the table, Ma bristles. She's gotten out of the habit, and though she never said as much, I think she's still angry at God for what happened to Pa. After his funeral, we'd never stepped foot in church again, all prayers had quietly stopped, and the cross that used to hang over the door mysteriously disappeared.

I cover her hand with mine. "Sure, Aggie. You want me to say it?"

She shakes her head. In a voice both innocent and wise beyond her years, she declares, "No. Mama should say it."

It takes Ma a moment to respond, though there's no doubt she'll do it—if only for Agnes' sake. "Of course I will." We bow our heads and clasp hands as Ma stumbles over a hasty blessing. When I look up, I swear I see unshed tears glistening in her eyes.

"I got a job today," I say, hoping to ease us into conversation. "I'm working for a transport company."

Ma sits back, laying her napkin across her lap. "Transport? You can't even drive."

Beside her, Thomas giggles.

"Well, yeah. I'm not a driver. I just load and unload trucks," I admit. "But it pays ten dollars a day."

Ma's eyes flicker up to me, a flash of worry darting across her face. "That's a lot of money."

I nod. "It's a lot of work."

She frowns into her soup, and I know she disapproves. A silent ember of anger ignites inside me. She'd be happier if I were digging graves for eighty cents a day. At least that, in her mind, is honest work. I want to rage...to tell her it's all right to be paid well, remind her that pride is a sin and she should be glad I could even get a job at all.

But I bite my tongue. She'd lost Pa and me in one week, and she'd been thrown to the wolves with no one to look after her and the twins. She'd done her best, and I shouldn't be so hard on her.

It's then I decide that the less she knows about my work, the better.

I don't want her judging me for doing what I can to support them, and I don't want to fight about her moral objections. So I'll just keep quiet. I'll lie—if I must—and let her live in blissful ignorance of the fine grey line I'm walking.

The next day, I corner JD when he arrives, holding out his money. "I think you made a mistake yesterday. I was only supposed to get five. You gave me way too much."

JD holds up his hand. "You know, I've done that with every fella here on his first day, and you're only the second who has tried to return it." He snorts. "Keep it. I want you to go down to this address after shift and get a new suit. Can't have you looking like that if you're gonna be working for us." Opening his billfold, he hands me a small white business card with an address printed on the back. "Giuseppe's the best tailor this side of Paris. You tell him I sent you."

I stick the card in my pocket. "Yes, sir. I mean, thank you, JD."

He nods and I return the money to my pocket, torn between gratitude and shame as I wonder who the other Good Samaritan might be.

MASIE

FOUR

JD JOINS DADDY AND ME AT THE TABLE ON THE PATIO. OUR penthouse offers a breathtaking view of the city skyline, and we've taken to eating nearly every meal here, surrounded by the pots of flowers and topiaries lining the short wall around us. Butler brings a glass of scotch and the morning paper in on a silver tray, holding it out to JD with gloved hands.

"A bit early, isn't it?" I tease, taking a sip of my orange juice.

He winks, accepting the glass. "Hair of the dog that bit ya, little sister."

Daddy sets his stubby cigar in the crystal ashtray and takes the paper, shaking it open with a flourish. "That better not be from my private reserve," he chastises.

"Would you rather I imbibe that coffin varnish you're pushing down by the docks?" JD smirks, the corner of his mouth turning up behind his glass. "Just remember that if I die, you'd have no one to take the reins when you retire."

Daddy snickers. "Don't you worry about that, my boy. I plan to live to be five hundred, and I'm never retiring."

"If anyone could wrestle Father Time to his knees, it'd be you, Daddy," I offer, taking a bite of my omelet. "Anything interesting in the news?"

He lifts the paper so I can't see his face, and JD sticks his tongue out at me playfully.

"I did hear that Lepke Brewer got out of jail yesterday," Daddy offers, making my ears perk up. "Turns out the evidence against him was phony. Not a surprise. Everyone knows he had nothing to do with that casino heist. Not sure where the cops got that lead, but it was all trumped up. Shame, really. It was nice to have him off the streets, at least for a few weeks."

JD interjects, "Well, if it makes you feel any better, my boys say he took quite a beating in the clink. Might never walk again. At least, that's what I was told."

It's only been a few weeks since June's attack. She's dealing with it by trying to pretend it never happened. I'm dealing with it by replaying Vinnie's last call in my head over and over. 'It's done,' he'd simply said.

I take another bite, not looking up from my plate. "Isn't that a shame?"

"That reminds me, Masie," Daddy begins, making my head snap up. "I'm heading to Chicago in a few days. Alistair thinks we might have an investor for the new club."

I choke down my last bite, following it with a drink I wish was something stronger than juice. "That's wonderful."

Leaning across the table, he takes my chin in his meaty hand. "Just imagine it—you, headlining your own club. We'd bring in all the big producers and stuff, let them see how beautiful and talented you are. They'll be knocking down our door to put you in the pictures, maybe even the talkies. You mark my words, baby girl, your star is on the rise."

"And if it keeps the club filled every night, all the better. Right, Dutch?" JD adds, taking another drink.

Daddy pulls the linen napkin from his lap and points at him. "You listen here, this club is our family's future. It's going to be our cash cow. Bigger and better than any other in the city and so exclusive people will be begging to get in. I've got a new distillery opening in Canada next month, and we're going to be shipping the booze in right down the

Hudson. I've already had to set up meetings to negotiate some trade with the other bosses for union workers and permits. I've thrown every penny into making this happen for us, and your sister is the key to making it work. With her pipes and my brains, we're going to have the biggest operation this city has ever seen. And you are going to be right there, by my side."

"Doing what, exactly?" JD barks, practically slamming his now-empty glass on the table.

It's an old argument. JD wants a club of his own to run, but Daddy doesn't trust him on his own. Or maybe he's just afraid JD will do such a good job that nobody will need the old man anymore. It also could be because he suspects—not wrongly so—that JD is skimming from the existing businesses. Either way, there's not a chance he's going to back off and hand over the keys to the kingdom. At least not yet.

Butler interrupts before a full-blown argument can ensue. "Post for Miss Masie," he says, handing a letter across the table to me. Before I can put fingers on it, Daddy snatches it from him and scans the return address.

"Stanford College? What's all this now?" he asks, using his butter knife to slice open the envelope.

"I'm sure it's nothing," I stammer, shooting a glance to JD looking for help. But he doesn't look at me, rather stares at his hands entwined on his lap.

Drawing out the folded paper, Daddy reads, "It's our pleasure to inform you that you've been accepted to our early enrollment... Masie, what's all this about?"

I snatch it from his hands, quickly folding it away. "It's nothing. When I was in school, they required us to apply to colleges. It was before I came home."

He huffs. "Well, no need for college. You've got every-thing you could ever want right here."

I say nothing, tucking the letter beneath my plate.

"Besides, nobody cares how smart you are, Masie. You'll learn everything you need to know out here in the real world," Daddy continues. "And the rest your husband will take care of for you. You don't need to worry yourself with college. Don't want you to end up like one of those stuck up blue-blood debs anyhow."

I take a deep breath. There are so many things I want to say, so many demands I want to make, but I know that now isn't the time. At seventeen, I'm lucky he hasn't tried to marry me off already. Luckily, he doesn't want anyone else being able to lay claim to my time and talents so long as he can still profit from them. More likely, I'll end up a spinster, living in this house with him and JD until I'm so old no one will want me anyway.

The idea doesn't bother me as much as it probably should.

For some reason, Daddy has it in his head that college will turn me into some sort of snobby, elitist debutante. It's an old grudge—us versus them. New money versus old. Sure, we've got the cash to get in any door, but that doesn't keep them from looking down their noses at us once they know where it came from.

Not that he needs to worry about me. I mean, I'm no prissy deb, but I'm no blushing virgin either. I've had my share of flings and dalliances. None that either of them know about, of course, and none that have left me longing for more permanent relationships. Wild, that's what my mother called me. Her wild child. Though she always said it with a hint of envy rather than disdain. She longed for freedom, that much I could see. But my father kept her close and on a very short tether.

Perhaps that's ultimately what did her in. A flower cannot bloom without sunlight, after all, and her life was so very full of darkness.

And now, here I am, taking my small freedoms where I am able, all while trying to be the obedient daughter I'm expected to be. Trying to walk the tightrope of his expectations without being hung by it.

I don't fight the matter, because I won't win. Not today. Someday, a door will open. It will either be my chance to take over or my chance to break free, but whatever it is, I'll be ready to take the leap.

BENNY

FIVE

Two weeks later I show up for work in my new suit. It's double breasted in light gray with faintly contrasting stripes. Tailored to my exact fit, it has three buttons, peak lapels, and the inside is Alpaca lined. Beneath it is a matching vest, a crisp new blue shirt, and cuff bottom trousers. I'd even had enough left over for a pair of brown leather oxford shoes. It feels odd, dressing so dandy when I've been managing just fine in my old slacks and my one good shirt that I have to wash every evening. Going to the tailor had been an interesting experience. Just when I was sure the old codger was getting fresh with me, he'd stood, handed me a receipt, and told me it would be a few days for the alterations. I'd left feeling confused, and if I'm honest, a little excited.

Seeing me, Dickey whistles. "Who's this fine-looking fella?"

I hold open my jacket, giving him a glimpse of the inside. "I still think it's too fancy to load crates in."

Dickey waves me off. "Just set the jacket aside and roll up your sleeves while you work. That's what I do."

"Why does JD want us looking so fancy anyway? Why does it even matter?"

Dickey shrugs. "Far as I can tell, it's a status thing.

Shows they can afford to pay even the least of their crew well. It makes them look good, and it makes the guys working for their competitors want to jump ship and work for him instead. Make no mistake, JD never does anything out of the goodness of his heart, and he never does anything without a reason. He's a shrewd one."

Dickey gets into the truck, and I slide in beside him as he cranks the engine.

"You wanna drive?" he asks.

"Depends, do you want to make it to the club alive?" I ask, my tone heavy with sarcasm. He knows very well that I don't know how to drive, and he never fails to jab me about it.

With a sputter, the truck backs out of the warehouse and down the road. The sun is shining like there's never been a cloud in the sky, and the sidewalk is thick with people bustling this way and that. Dames in floral dresses and long scarves, and gents in spats and bowler hats. Signs hang on shingles outside office doors and motor cars are parked along the boulevard. A bright green trolley passes us, its bell ringing, as we turn onto Fifth Avenue. A copper on a motorbike passes us as we head down, swerving to avoid the occasional cab. When we turn down Broadway, a billboard sits above the Capital Theater depicting a mysterious man walking through the sewer. It proclaims in massive golden letters—*Lon Cheney in The Phantom of the Opera.*

This street is even more packed with people, in cars and on foot as they make their way down to the theaters and spill out into Times Square. We fight the crowds until finally parking outside The Green Door, Dutch Shultz's nightclub and speakeasy.

I've never been here before. Most of my deliveries go to warehouses across the city, but today's delivery is for the club itself. I open the back of the truck as Dickey taps on the locked door, waiting for someone to let us in since the place is shut during daylight hours. A short redheaded fella props the door open with a brick and waves us in.

Taking off my jacket and rolling up my sleeves as Dickey suggested, I heft the first crate off the stack and carry it inside. I follow the man through the empty room, across the dance floor, through another door, and down a set of stairs to the speakeasy below.

"You can just stack them there," he says in a thick Irish accent, pointing to the corner of the bar.

"Yes, sir," I say, doing as I'm told.

It's only walking back to the truck that I really have a chance to take in my surroundings. The ceiling is tin tiles, the tabletops covered in crisp, red linens, and the walls are papered in swirling velvet shapes. The dance floor is pale wood, while a massive brass-and-crystal chandelier hangs from above. In the periphery of the room, there are long bench seats with tables and high-backed chairs. An elevated stage sits off to one side. It's empty now, save for the voluminous crimson drapes in the back and a single copper microphone in a stand in the very center.

There's a stillness to the room, as if it's keeping a tight-lipped secret. I can almost feel it in my mind—the pulsing music, the heat building as people dance their cares away, the electric buzz as they sip their illegal liquor from pearl teacups. It's a spider web, waiting for and anticipating its prey. It will lure them in by the dozens, with its bright lights and melodic sounds, then capture and enrapture them.

It's as if the room itself is calling to me, a promise of wonder and excitement. *Come and lose yourself.* The bar is dark oak and shining brass, lit from above by lights dangling on chains. Behind it, there's a shelf and a row of mirrors stretching almost to the tin-tile ceiling. As I watch, a man tips a beer tap and the glass slides back, exposing bottles of booze in compartments below.

I'm so distracted I don't see the three men walk in the door until they take a seat at one of the empty tables. I recognize only one, JD, in a white suit and straw boater hat. He looks tidy, as always, like he'd spent the morning lounging in the sun to flush his complexion.

39

By contrast, the other two men wear sharp blue wool suits and swagger hats. They speak in hushed tones, one snapping his fingers at the Irishman, who vanishes behind the bar only to pop back into sight with three short glasses of brown liquor.

Turning away from them, I continue about my work, careful to keep my eyes cast downward. I focus my thoughts on the task at hand to keep from accidentally eavesdropping. We are closing the truck when the three gentlemen exit the club behind us. The street crowds have thinned and only a handful of folks still mill about, most oblivious to everyone and everything around them.

The truck door slams shut as Dickey cranks the engine. I'm latching the rear when I hear it…the familiar sound of tires screeching across pavement. My head snaps up, my eyes darting back and forth down the street.

I spot the oncoming car a moment too late. Too late to listen to my father's ever-warning voice in my mind telling me to keep my head down. Too late to shout a warning to Dickey sitting in the front seat. Too late to do anything but react on instinct.

From the corner of my eye, I see JD react, but in that moment between heartbeats, I know he's moving too slowly. I lunge to my left, my intention being to take him to the ground with me.

The first bullet rips through me. The pain is blinding. My ears ring with the sound of brass casings hitting the street, rubber tires digging into the firm roadbed, and my own frantic pulse filling my ears.

The force slamming into my body is enough to push me backward and on top of the man behind me just in time for another bullet to graze me. I don't feel that one as much as the first, which spreads pain like wildfire through my chest and up my neck in waves, stealing the air from my lungs.

Dickey shouts my name.

Around me, the daylight fades as I surrender to the fire, closing my eyes and drawing in a shallow, shaky breath before everything else slips away.

MASIE

SIX

"*Is the laudanum not helping?*" *Doctor Mackie asks*, shining a penlight in my eyes, momentarily blinding me.

I take a deep breath. Truthfully, I passed the last three bottles off to June for recreational use. Despite his assurances it will help with my insomnia, I can't bring myself to use it. After seeing Mother abuse it so often, and with such devastating results, just the thought of it turns my stomach.

"I don't like it," I complain. "It makes my mind foggy."

Putting the light down, he tsks. "That's the point, dear."

Far greyer than a man should be in his mid-thirties, Doc Mac has a surprisingly grandfatherly countenance. One stern look from him carries the guilt of a hundred nuns, and he gives me one now.

"I know you are under a great deal of strain, dear." He hesitates, choosing his words very carefully. My father is his employer, so he can only complain so much about my working such long hours, my frequent headaches from the smoke and lights, and my borderline high blood pressure. We both know the culprit behind my troubles, but we also know that nothing either of us says or does will change my circumstances. "But you must try to rest. You will put

41

yourself in an early grave otherwise."

"Better me than someone else, I suppose," I quip, attempting to lighten the mood, but failing.

"The laudanum will help you relax. Help you rest. You need that, at least."

Sprawling back against the white wing-backed chair, I wave him off. "Whatever you say, Doc."

He opens his mouth to speak, but he's cut off by Butler, who clears his throat behind him.

"What is it?" I ask, wearily draping one arm over the headrest.

"JD just telephoned, Miss. He and your father are on their way here. Doctor, they ask that you remain here until they arrive. There has been a shooting."

I spring forward, the bodice of my floral dress tightening around my middle, adding to the tension already growing there.

"Is everyone alright?" I demand, pushing to my feet and slipping back into my t-strap shoes.

"One assumes not," Butler responds, holding out his gloved hands. "But I gather that he and your father, at least, are unharmed."

My breath escapes in a low hiss. Is this my fault? Retaliation for the beating I'd personally ordered on the man who'd assaulted my friend? Or was this something else entirely? Father has no shortage of enemies on his own. Even so, I mentally curse myself for adding one more name to that list—even if he'd well and truly deserved it.

Doc nods to me. "I should go wash up and get ready to receive any wounded."

I nod, but say nothing. This is his real job, after all. Not looking after me—though Lord knows he tries to do that as well—but pulling out bullets and stitching up knife wounds. The sort of thing that can't be done in a hospital without having to answer too many questions. I motion to Butler, who stands in the doorway still.

"Fetch some clean linens and towels. Set them up in the kitchen. It will be easier to clean up blood from the tile than the carpet."

He bows stiffly and exits, leaving me standing in the study and wringing my hands. I should probably go, or at least hide in my room. That's what Daddy would want. He's very keen on pretending the violence of his world can't reach its icy hands into my life—though deep down, I'm sure he knows better. Perhaps this will be a good thing, a way to remind him that, despite his best efforts, he can't shelter me. He can't keep me safe, not really. Perhaps he'll be more open to the idea of sending me off to college then.

I roll the thought around in my head, balancing it with the silent prayer that whoever is hurt will be all right, while wondering if using this person's misfortune to my own advantage makes me a truly awful person.

I don't have time to debate it too much because the front doors open with a thunderous boom, and I rush toward the sound. One young man, his face pink with exertion and speckled with sweat, carries the limp body of another as JD ushers them toward the kitchen. Father enters last, followed by Vincent, who twists his cap in his hands. Daddy rushes toward me, planting a rough kiss on my forehead.

"You should go to your room, darling. You don't need to see this," he mutters, nearly pushing me down the hall. Then he points toward Doc, who is ushering the boys into the kitchen. "Take care of that boy. He saved my life."

I dig my feet into the long carpet. "No, that's alright, Daddy. I want to see if I can help."

Without giving him a chance to respond, I hurry to the kitchen, throwing open the door just in time to see Doc lean over the young man now laid across our antique mahogany table.

The one who'd been carrying him backs up against the sink, watching Doc work with intent eyes.

"What can I do?" I ask, taking a spot across the table.

Doc doesn't even look up; he simply hands me a towel. "Apply pressure here while I remove the bullet."

Taking the towel, I press it to the young man's side,

43

drawing a deep groan from the mostly unconscious patient.

Doc uses his light to check the boy's eyes. Though his face is spotted with blood, his skin paler than my fine bone china, there's something attractive about him in the cut of his jaw and the small, barely noticeable dimple in his chin. As soon as the thought comes, I shake it away, forcing myself to remain clinical as Doc cuts off his shirt and tie with a pair of medical shears.

No time for that now.

"Young man, can you hear me?" Doc asks as he sets to work. "What's your name?"

The other boy answers, "It's Benny. Benjamin."

"Alright Benny, this is going to hurt, but I need you to lie very still."

Doc motions to the other boy, then to me. "You two are going to need to hold him."

I almost ask why since he clearly isn't responsive, but the other boy takes one shoulder, just above where Doc begins to cut. As soon as the metal pierces his skin, the boy bucks, his eyes flying open. I struggle to hold his other side, pinning him to the table with all the weight I have.

Finally, there's a wet popping sound, and Doc wrenches the bullet free. Blood flows in earnest now, down Benny's arm and soaking his chest. The boy whimpers through gritted teeth. Doc wets a rag with some laudanum, pressing it over his nose and mouth for a few seconds. When he finally draws it back, the boy's head lulls to the side, his green eyes wide.

Leaning over, I lower my face close to his. "Are you alright?"

He opens and closes his mouth a few times, as if it isn't quite functioning.

Finally, he half grins and manages to slur, "I can't feel my tongue."

I let out a sharp laugh, and he smiles up at me. "Hey, you're really pretty."

"You aren't too shabby yourself," I offer with a grin. "I

44

mean, except for being full of holes and all."

He frowns. "Why am I full of holes?"

His face is so full of concerned innocence that it's hard not to smile. "Because you got shot, silly."

"I got shot?" His head jerks up in alarm. "Is everyone else alright?"

"Calm down," I say, soothing him as best I can with a hand on his shoulder. Then, realizing I'd almost forgotten to keep pressure on the towel at his side, I return to it. "Everyone else is fine."

He nods once, his expression relaxing again. "I feel pretty good, considering. Really good, actually."

"That'd be the laudanum Doc gave you. Takes the edge off," I offer, my eyes flicking up to Doc. He's slowly stitching up the hole in the boy's shoulder. The bleeding has mostly stopped; it's just sort of weeping now. "But you're gonna be fine, Benjamin. Just rest now."

His eyes flicker up to mine. "That's a shame."

"What is?" I ask.

"That I'm gonna be fine. I kinda like being here with you."

I sigh. "Oh, you like bleeding out on my kitchen table?"

He nods once, his face serious. "Whatever it takes." He hesitates, then continues, "But just in case I don't make it, do me a solid and look in on Aggie for me."

I raise one eyebrow. "Aggie…that your girl?"

But his eyes roll back and his face goes slack, his head rolling to the side once more. Alarmed, I tap Doc.

"He's fine. Just fainted. Probably for the best."

"Aggie is his baby sister," the other boy answers. I'd all but forgotten he was still in the room but when I look up at him again I recognize him as Dickey. He continues, "She's been sick. Did you mean it when you said he'd be alright?"

I look to Doc for confirmation.

"He'll be fine. Just needs some stitches and rest. Back on his feet in a day, two tops. Can you see he gets home and rests?" Doc asks.

Dickey nods, but I cut in. "Don't be silly. He saved my father's life, and we owe him a great debt. He'll stay here until he's recovered enough to go home. You'll let his family know he's alright?"

His expression tensing for a moment, Dickey nods firmly. "Sure thing. Just don't be surprised if his Ma decided to kill the messenger."

BENNY

SEVEN

I FEEL THE WARMTH OF THE SUN ON MY FACE BEFORE I EVEN crack my eyelids. Rustling under the sheets, I reach up to stretch myself awake only to be knocked breathless by the shooting pain in my right shoulder. Jerking my arm back down, I cradle my elbow in my hand and suck in a sour hiss between clenched teeth.

"Careful there or you'll spring a stitch."

Turning my chin toward the voice, I force my eyes open, straining against the light.

It's then I see her. An ethereal figure poised between the large window and me, sheer white curtains fluttering in the breeze behind her. The sunlight streams in around her, bending to caress her silhouette, making her hair shine. She takes a slight step toward me, and her face comes into focus. Her lips are full and the color of ripe strawberries, her nose perfectly sloped, her cheeks high and round. But it's her eyes that steal my breath, wide, deep set, and the most perfect shade of winter grey I've ever seen. There's a band of rhinestones stretched across her forehead, dripping down either side of her face and adding to her otherworldly appearance. My eyes slide down the length of her, my mind languishing between dreaming and wakefulness. Her dress is a delicate shade of purple with careful silver beads swirling in abstract flourishes across the fabric, a beaded fringe caressing her legs at just above the knee. Something inside me twists uncomfortably.

"It's not polite to stare," she says, her tone bemused as she picks up a martini glass from the bedside table and swallows the clear contents. "Or is your tongue full of lead as well?"

I clear my throat, struggling to sit up. It's then I realize two things. The first is that this is too soft to be my bed. The sheets are cool, white satin against my bare legs. But the second thing I realize is I've been stripped bare, not even my union suit separating my flesh from the linens. With my good arm, I quickly tug the bedding up around me, still unable to tear my gaze from my mysterious visitor.

"Am I dreaming?" I ask, shaking my head.

A slow grin spreads across her face as she answers. "Would you like to be?"

Her voice is as deep as dark water and honey smooth. I lick my bottom lip, forcing myself to look away from her face before speaking. "How did I get here? And where is here, exactly?"

Slowly the memory of the shooting blossoms in my mind, the aching in my shoulder finally making sense. "I was shot?" I say, though it comes out a question.

"Twice, in fact," she responds. "Though the second was more of a graze really, just above your right hip."

My hand involuntarily searches out the area she described. Sure enough, there's a wide gauze bandage. It's tender to the touch, but not overly so. I run my hand up my torso and to my opposite shoulder, finding a similar wrapping.

"And as for *where* we are, well, they couldn't just leave you in the street to die after such heroics. So they brought you back here, and our friend Doctor Mackie tended you. He says you're quite lucky."

My eyes flitter back to her, and I can't help but grin. "Well, that'd be a first," I mutter.

"They say you leapt right in front of a bullet. And because of that bravery, I'll forgive you the bloodstain on the kitchen floor, though the maids may not be so kind. They scrubbed it for hours to get it clean."

My mind finally clearing, I begin to put the pieces together. "This is JD's place?"

"And mine. This is one of the guest rooms." She grins again and nods, pointing to the high-backed chair in the corner of the room with a pile of clothes draped over it. "JD left you some clothes. If you'd like to get dressed, I will let them know you're finally awake."

"Finally?" A lump forms in the back of my throat. "How long have I been here?"

"About a day and a half," she responds, crossing the room.

"A day and a half?" I throw back the covers, intending to spring out of bed. It's only when she glances over her shoulder, then swiftly turns away, that I remember my state of undress and recover myself. "My family will be worried."

"Better they worry for a few days so you can return healed than to have you back immediately in a box, don't you agree?"

Her words are sharp and cut right through me. "Yes, of course. I don't mean to sound ungrateful, Miss…?"

"Masie," she says, risking another glance over her shoulder, one slender eyebrow rising. "Besides, your friend took them the news. Told them you'd be recovering here."

"Well, I'm Benny. That is, Benjamin Fleischer. It's nice to meet you." I motion to the blankets. "I'd offer you a more formal greeting, but I seem to have misplaced my underwear."

The corner of her mouth turns up in a way that makes me blush furiously. I'm not sure if it's because I've accidentally exposed myself to the dame who is probably JD's girl, or the fact I can't bring myself to stop staring at her, half wondering if she's some sort of merciful angel.

"Well, Benjamin, that is quite a problem, isn't it?" She smirks. "I'll let JD know you're up and have Butler fix you something to eat."

She steps out of the room, closing the door behind her. As soon as she's gone, the air chills like she's taken all the warmth with her. I slowly process our strange conversation as I dress. Sore and feeling a bit like a schmuck, I make my way out of the room and down the hall. Masie intercepts me, sliding one hand up my good arm and hooking her wrist through.

"This way, Benjamin."

I snicker, and she looks genuinely confused.

Taking pity on her, I lean over, whispering, "Only my mother calls me that."

Her expression melts into a satisfied smirk as she leads me out a set of glass doors onto a rooftop terrace. A table is set up, and JD and one of the other men from the club stand as we enter. Masie releases me and takes one of the empty seats as JD reaches out to shake my hand.

"Benny, good to see you up and about so soon."

His handshake is aggressive, overly so, and it shakes my arm painfully.

The other man speaks, his voice gravely, a cigar stuck between his teeth. "My boy, I want to personally thank you for your quick thinking." He holds out a hand as well. While his grip is firm, it's also more solid, genuine. "Please, have a seat."

JD waves to the older gentleman, who squats into his chair. "This is my father, Dutch Schultz."

The older man jabs a hand at me, the cigar now hooked below his finger. "You can call me Dutch."

Nodding, I take my seat, my mind spinning. Between the drugs they must have shot me up with, the shock from the wound, and the surrealism of the room around me, I feel as if I might slip into unconsciousness at any moment. Everything feels hazy, the edge of a dream I'm only now waking up from.

"And I see you've already met my sister, Masie," JD says, jerking his head in her direction. She smirks and lifts a champagne glass of orange juice, saluting me. The strange feeling inside me twists again, this time in a sense of something else, something eerily similar to victory or relief. Which is silly, because no matter her relationship status, this dame is so far out of my reach she may as well be a star in the sky.

"I have, thank you. And thank you for seeing to me. Masie says you fetched a doctor. I can't tell you how much I appreciate it."

"Nonsense," Dutch sputters. He's a slender man, a long narrow nose, grey-yellow hair, and a slim, flat mouth. Like JD and Masie, he's dressed to the nines, his double-breasted suit open to reveal a light mauve shirt with a tall white collar. "You saved my life, son. That's not something I take lightly."

His words strike me like a blow to the stomach. Saved…his *life*?

JD chimes in, cutting a chunk of sausage and holding it on the tip of his fork as he speaks. "If you hadn't stepped in like that," he points the fork at his father, "that bullet wudda taken him right in the chest, no doubt about it."

"Similar tragedy recently took a good friend of mine, Joey Noe. It would seem I have made some folks very nervous with my expanding business."

My eyes catch his, noting the only resemblance between him and Masie is revealed in their shape and shade. I nod once.

"You don't look surprised to hear this," Dutch says, his gaze hardening on me. "You work for any of the families before?"

I take a deep breath. "No, sir. I recently did a stretch in the Tombs. Word travels fast in there."

Seeming to relax, Dutch nods, putting his cigar out with a rough stomp. "What were you in the clink for?"

I stare down at my plate, mostly to avoid the weight of Masie's eyes on me when I speak. "Theft, sir. But it was a bad rap. I found a bag of cash behind the trash bins near my place. The cops caught me with it, but I didn't steal it—not that anyone believed me."

I leave out the part where the bag belonged to Dickey, who had ditched it there before running to my place to hide out when the heat came down on him. I don't mention it had been my intention to return it to the people Dickey robbed. None of that really matters to anyone but me, anyway. It doesn't pay to do good in this world. My father followed the rules all his life, and where did it land him? Six feet under when a hoodlum tried to knock over his watch shop. He'd taken three in the chest, and we—well, we'd lost everything.

"Figures. I swear the coppers in this city couldn't spill water out of a boot with the instructions on the heel." He pauses, pointing at me again. "But I bet you know who done the deed, don't ya?"

I swallow. "I might have some idea."

"But ya kept your trap shut. That's what people don't understand these days, loyalty."

Glancing over at JD, I see he's downing his food as if he were starving, hardly paying attention to us at all.

Dutch sits back. "Let me ask you something, Benny. May I call you Benny?"

"Of course, sir."

"Benny, back in my day, we took care of our own. We rewarded dependability, and we punished disloyalty. None of this calling the cops and going to court—none of this nonsense with lawyers and judges. We had our own justice. So let me ask you, do you think I should track down the people who did this? Would I be wrong to seek out justice for this slight done to us?"

I raise my eyes to Masie, who is watching me with sharp, grey eyes, her expression unreadable. Seeing a glass of water in front of me, I take a sip before answering.

"Yes, sir. I think you should find the people responsible. Not on my account or for revenge, but because, and pardon my bluntness, sir, you clearly have enemies. And it's best to know who your enemies are, so you can decide how best to deal with them."

"An eye for an eye, that's what the bible says." JD finally speaks up, and I catch a cold glare exchanged between father and son.

"That's true, it does," I interject, feeling like I've stepped in the middle of something I probably should have steered well away from. "But what do I know? I'm just a delivery boy."

When Dutch turns his gaze on me once more, a chill drives its way across my skin. "No, you aren't, not anymore."

The blood in my veins freezes at his words. Raising my chin, I stare him right in the eye, "I'm sorry if I've overstepped. But I do need this job, sir. Please don't can me. My father died a few months back, and I'm the sole provider for my family now. I can do the job, even with one good arm."

"Fire you? My boy, don't be silly. I'm giving you a promotion. I need someone like you in my organization. Someone I can trust. With what happened to Joey—what almost happened to me—I think having another guard at my side would be very beneficial. Someone with quick reflexes and a good head on his shoulders. And I think you're just the fellow for the position. Whadda ya say?"

What can I say? Refusing him, especially now as I sit at his table wearing his clothes, seems like a quick way to land myself in a pine box. "Of course, sir. I'm happy to accept."

"Good, good. Now that's settled, let's talk turkey. I want you to come by the club tonight. Let me introduce you to the rest of the crew."

It doesn't seem like a request, so I just nod.

Across the table, Masie stands, her chair grinding across the stone floor. "Well, if you boys will excuse me, I have rehearsals."

Leaning over, she gives Dutch a quick peck on the cheek, leaving a strawberry-red stain behind. It takes all the strength I have not to turn to watch her sashay from the room.

53

IT'S NEARLY SUPPERTIME WHEN I RETURN HOME. MA FLIES into my arms, her face streaked with tears. I clench my teeth against the pain as she squeezes me tightly. It's not until she releases me and steps back that I can draw breath again.

"Dickey said you'd been shot…" she begins, her voice trembling.

"I'm fine. It's not so bad. The doc stitched me up. Truly, Ma." I try to soothe her, but she steps away, her fear quickly turning to fury.

"I told you that job would be trouble," she says, poking a finger into my chest.

I hold up my hands. "It wasn't like that. There was somebody coming out of a building behind me; I was just in the wrong place at the wrong time."

She snorts derisively. "I'll have them put that on your tombstone." As soon as she says it, she flinches. "No, I didn't mean that. But Benjamin, I can't lose you again."

Thomas pokes his blond head around the corner from the kitchen. "Did you really get shot?" he asks, his eyes wide.

"I did, and it had nothing to do with my job," I lie, leveling a look at Ma. She waves me off, turning instead to Thomas.

"Come on, dear, let's take some soup to your sister, then you can help with the wash."

Thomas groans and disappears around the corner. Ma spares me one glance before doing the same. Pulling the last of my cash from my pockets, I keep a few bucks and add the rest to the coffee tin on the window ledge before letting myself fall onto the sofa, kicking my feet up on the table. I know I should tell her about my promotion, about every detail of what I've agreed to take on. But I can't. Partly because I can't stomach seeing the look of disappointment on her face—yet again. But mostly because I'm not entirely sure how I feel about any of it just yet. Nervous? Excited? Terrified? A combination of all three?

Forcing my eyes closed, I manage to fall into a light, restless sleep. When I wake, Ma has already left for her shift and Thomas is cooking dinner. Sagging with relief that I don't have to lie to her anymore today, I make my way to the kitchen to help.

The smell of potatoes and pot roast thickens the air, making my stomach grumble in protest. My shoulder is aching badly enough that it's making me sick to my stomach as I set out the plates. As I watch Thomas, I know what I should do. I should go to Dutch tomorrow and thank him for the opportunity, but politely decline the job. It's one thing being a nameless, faceless cog in the machine, but it's quite another to be standing beside the guy pulling the strings. And the difference could mean leaving Thomas, Aggie, and Ma alone again.

Just as my resolve begins to set, I hear the front door open and close from the other room.

"That smells heavenly," Dickey calls, stepping into view. "Glad to see you're back on your feet there, Benny."

Reaching out, I tousle Thomas' hair. "Why don't you see if Aggie wants to come out to eat?"

He glances between us, then takes the cue, ducking under my arm and out of the room.

"It was an awfully close call," Dickey says, plucking a carrot from the pot and popping it in his mouth.

I nod. "That's what JD says."

"What happened? Dutch insisted on taking you to his place for the doc. I didn't wanna argue. Besides, you seemed like you were in good hands."

"Well, I suppose he didn't want any cops asking questions. I don't blame him for that. But the doc did a good job. It hardly hurts." I hesitate to tell him the rest, but I suppose he'll find out anyway. "And he offered me a promotion. Wants me to work as one of his guards from now on."

Dickey whistles. "Guess the old man was pretty grateful you took the lead for him. Helluva way to get a better gig, though."

I shake my head. "It wasn't exactly planned. Just my stupid, normal bad luck."

He laughs. "Well, something good came out of it for once, at any rate."

When I don't respond, he pulls out a chair and sinks into it. "Let me guess, you're thinking of declining?" Withdrawing a Lucky from a tin in his pocket, he sticks it between his teeth. "Not a good idea, Benny."

I snatch the cigarette. "You can't smoke that in here. You'll set off Aggie's breathing problems. And I have to refuse the job. I can't risk going back to the clink, or worse… getting shot again. I might not be so lucky next time."

Snorting, he leans to the side, resting one arm on the table. "Benny, I hate to break it to you, but if you didn't have bad luck, you'd have no luck at all. I mean, you could get hit by a trolley tomorrow. Or struck by lightning. Or have a piano dropped on you. That's just the sort of luck you have."

"That doesn't mean I should invite trouble," I defend, tossing the Lucky back to him.

He catches the pack in one hand and stuffs it in his jacket. "At least this way you can earn some real scratch before you go." He snickers, but I don't join in. "I'm serious. Where else are you gonna make that kinda dough? Who else is gonna give a nobody like you—with a felony record—a job that pays well enough to take care of your family if something happens to you? Nobody. Not in this city."

I hate to admit it, but he makes a good point.

"I'm telling ya, just take the job. JD is good people. If something happens to you in the line of duty, he'd take care of your family. He's that sorta fella."

I rub my chin, considering his words. "You really think so?"

He raises one hand. "I swear. I'd take care of them myself if it came to it. But you can't let this opportunity pass you by. People wait their whole lives for this kinda break. You're morally obligated to accept on behalf of the poor schmucks stuck in nowhere gigs, grinding out pennies a day until they work themselves into early graves."

"I never thought I'd see the day where you were lecturing me about moral obligation," I retort.

Dickey grins. "The world is full of surprises, Benny."

I start to fill four plates. Dickey sits in Ma's chair as I gather the kids. Thomas continues to ask how I got shot, making little Agnes pale even more.

"Your brother's a bona-fide hero," Dickey cuts in, pointing at me with a fork full of roast. "He saved a man's life. And not just any man, but a very important one."

"Like the governor?" Agnes asks in her small voice.

Dickey opens his mouth to speak, but I cut him off. "Sort of, Aggie. But the important thing is that I'm fine."

I shoot Dickey a glare. He lets the subject drop until I get them cleaned up and into bed.

After dinner, Agnes wraps her waifish arms around my neck. I carry her to bed while Thomas and Dickey clear the dishes. She's warm again. Her mysterious fever has been up and down, despite the new medicine Ma bought. I give her a spoonful and she dutifully sucks it down, cringing from the bitter taste.

"How are you feeling, Aggie?" I ask, tucking the blankets around her.

She licks her lips before answering, as if carefully considering her response. "Mostly tired, I think. But better now that you're home."

Her eyes flutter closed and I stare at her face, brushing the hair back from her forehead and leaving a kiss there. She's not getting better—that much is clear. Her eyes are rimmed in red, her cheeks sunken. I haven't heard her laugh in weeks, not since I've been home. Not even when I'd handed her the new doll I bought for her. She used to be such a joyful little thing, all sunshine and curls. Something tickles the back of my nose, and I have to set my jaw against it.

I kiss her forehead again and leave, closing the door behind me.

"How is she?" Dickey asks, his voice a whisper.

I shake my head. "I feel like she's fading away."

"What are you gonna do?" His tone is almost accusing. Am I going to risk her life for the sake of my own stupid pride? Or am I going to do what needs to be done?

Sighing, I steel myself. "I need to go to the club tonight," I say, retrieving my borrowed suit coat from the couch. "Dutch says he wants to introduce me to some of his crew."

"What did your ma say about that?"

I frown. "I didn't tell her. I want to keep her out of it as much as possible. But I gotta do something. Aggie needs to see that specialist in Albany."

He slaps me on the back. "Well, if your ma finds out what you're doing, you'll be praying for someone to pump you fulla lead again."

I almost tell him I don't care. That it doesn't matter. Both of those things are true. I'd sign a deal with the devil himself to help that little girl. And besides, it's not as if I had much of a choice. Something tells me that Dutch Schultz is not a man used to being told no.

But I don't say any of that. I just nod solemnly. "And don't I know it."

MASIE
EIGHT

MY DRESSING ROOM IS UNUSUALLY COLD TONIGHT, I REALIZE, lighting the French lavender candles on my vanity. The room has electric lights as well, but I prefer the dim, dancing glow of firelight. The pulse of the music beyond my door creates soft ripples in the mirror. I retrieve my pink satin and lace chemise, wrapping myself in a robe before sitting to apply my makeup. Rubbing lotion into my hands to help warm them, I examine my face closely. The recent weeks of not sleeping are taking their toll, and deep bags rest beneath my eyes. I struggle to remember the last time I slept deeply, the last time I woke feeling rested.

If I'm honest with myself, it had been the first night after I returned home, and even that was more likely caused by sheer emotional and physical exhaustion.

With a deep sigh, I open the drawer. Pulling out my compact powder, I begin meticulously applying it layer after layer, grateful for the semester of theater classes I'd taken and everything I learned about applying stage makeup. Over the past months, I've concealed more bruises, dark circles, and red, post-crying eyes than I ever imagined possible.

A gentle tap at my door makes me pause.

"Masie? It's me."

Without waiting for an invitation, my father steps in. He's in his evening suit, hair carefully combed back so it lays tight against his scalp.

"Hello, Daddy. Is everything alright?"

He takes a seat in the empty chair behind me, and I have to turn to face him.

"Masie, have you seen Vincent recently?"

A lump forms in my throat. I was never good at lying, especially to him. But evasion, that's quite another thing. "Not in a few days, at least. Not since you brought him to the house. Why?"

He stands, drawing one hand down his face as he paces the small room. "I got word from one of my boys. He's got a warrant out on him. They're saying…" He hesitates, locking his eyes on mine after a tense moment. "They're saying he murdered a kid."

"A kid?" I ask, sure I'd misheard. Vinnie was many things, but a child killer? "There's got to be a mistake."

Daddy leans against the door. "He was just supposed to take the kid for a few days. Shake up his father a bit so he'd be more reasonable. Something musta went south."

I'm so appalled I can hardly speak. When I finally do, my voice wavers for only a few words before my mouth runs away with me. "Wait, you knew about this? Kidnapping children? What's next? You gonna start drowning babies in the river like a sack of unwanted kittens? Is there no line you won't cross? Nothing and no one you won't sacrifice in pursuit of your all-mighty buck?"

He takes two long strides my way, closing the gap between us so quickly I almost don't see it. I pop to my feet, standing toe to toe with him, knowing I've said too much, gone too far. But I can't help it, can't stop the words from spilling out of my mouth, filled with bitterness and disgust. "What kind of coward tortures children for their own benefit?"

I see the hand coming, but I don't move. Don't flinch. He smacks me across the face so hard my knees nearly buckle. It's not the first time I've taken a blow, and I've learned that the best thing to do is to crumple to the floor, let the tears flow freely to stop the beating. But I don't. I hold myself upright, and though my face stings so badly tears roll down my cheeks, I straighten, looking him in the eye.

"I'm your father and you *will* show me respect."

"Respect is earned," I bite back.

This time, the hand shoots out, taking me by the throat and squeezing. "How dare you?" he screams in my face. "Everything I do is for you, for this family."

Fighting to draw breath, I gasp, dark spheres forming in my vision. "If you break my neck, I won't be able to sing." I force the words out, a hoarse whisper.

He drops me almost instantly, and I fall back into my chair.

"Why do you do that? Why do you make me hurt you like that?" He mutters something. Although my heart is pounding in my ears, I think I hear him whisper my mother's name like a curse.

I glare at him, but I say nothing.

He strides back to my door, glancing at me over his shoulder to deliver one final warning. "Vincent's gone too far this time. If you see him, stay clear. He's become ruthless, dangerous."

I don't bother to remind him that it'd been different before—that Vinnie is only the monster he is because that's what my father made him. If he is ruthless and violent, it's because my father needed him to be. Vinnie's moniker, *Mad Dog*, is all too appropriate. My father is plenty willing to let him loose on others—no matter the consequences—but he lives in terror of the day when that dog turns on its master. And from the sound of it, that day is fast approaching.

We always create the thing we fear the most.

The door slams shut. Alone once more, I begin my makeup routine again. This time, I have to cover the handprint slowly bruising across my face and angry red fingerprints dotting my collar bone in a nearly perfect string. I can't help but wonder about the poor child, and a swell of pity fills me. His parents must be devastated. I can't imagine something like that. Accident or not, Vinnie needs to be punished for this. If it's true. He's been out of control for too long now, each act he commits taking him further and further from the boy he'd been. Each drop of blood he spills staining his soul a little more.

We have that in common.

And for what? My father? Our family? The business? It doesn't feel worth it anymore.

Normally, I might consider bowing out on my set after an event like this, but I don't. Benjamin is going to be in the crowd tonight, his first night working as my father's new security guard. The idea is laughable. Benjamin is a buck sixty if he's lucky, and lean as they come. Besides, he has no training of any kind. Hell, I doubt he's thrown a punch in his whole life. He's not the sort of person to make a guard. He is, however, kind, selfless, and genuinely…good. This place—these people—will eat him alive.

I can't help but wonder if that's Daddy's intent. Benjamin, clever and honest as he seems to be, might be more useful in other places. Places like running rackets or even hosting clubs. Any of which will put him directly in JD's line of fire. Or worse…what if he's looking to replace Vinnie? Looking to create a new dog to do his bidding?

I blow out a slow breath as my mind settles around the idea.

Standing so quickly I nearly topple my chair, I grab my bag from the dressing table. I can't let that happen. Not again. I ran away, hid in school while my father corrupted Vinnie. I won't run again. Grabbing my coat, I sneak out the back door, spilling onto the street to where I flag down my waiting driver. Knowing I'll have to hurry so I don't miss my first set, I bark the address and we speed off into the night.

THE HALLWAY REEKS OF SWEAT AND SIN, THE ODORS WAFTING
up from the brothel below. With one gloved hand, I rap
on the wooden door, a hollow, dead sound. I hear footsteps
beyond, hushed whispers, and finally, Loretta pulls it open,
one hand clutching the front of her sky-blue kimono.

"Whaddya want, sugar?" she asks, her voice gravely.
"I'm all booked up for the night. You could come back
tomorrow—"

I don't bother to explain myself to her. She's nothing
special, one of a dozen of Vincent's girls. He has them
scattered about the city in cheap apartments. This seems
to be his favorite though, the place where I can always
leave a message for him and know he'll get it quickly. But
tonight, I know he's here. His cologne sticks to her skin,
the scent a mixture of bourbon and spice unique to him.
Looking past her disheveled brown hair, I call over her
shoulder.

"Vinnie, it's Masie. I need to talk to you."

Loretta frowns, tilting her head to block my view.
"Look, honey, ain't nobody here—"

Before she can say more, a hand clutches her arm,
dragging her out of the doorway. Vinnie pokes his head
around the jamb, glancing down the hall behind me. "You
alone?"

I sigh. "Of course."

He waves me in with one hand, closing the door behind me. Loretta flops down onto the sofa, her kimono
falling open to reveal a lacy cornflower-blue negligee. She
lays her back flat against the seat cushions, draping her
long legs over one upholstered arm and rolling her feet at
the ankles.

"Shouldn't you be at the club?" he asks, lighting up a
Lucky and blowing the smoke toward the ceiling.

"I've got some time, and I want to talk business."

He takes another drag. "So not a social call then? I'm
disappointed."

"Do we need to speak privately?" I ask, motioning to
Loretta as I slide off one glove and tuck it into my purse.

Loretta opens her mouth to protest, but Vincent waves her away. Reluctantly, she gathers herself and glides out of the room with a glare, leaving me to take her seat.

"What's the matter, Mas?"

I slide off my other glove, clutching it in my lap, "That's what I'm here to ask you, Vinnie."

He frowns, his deep-set brown eyes casting a gaze at the wooden floor before he flicks the cigarette to the ground and stomps it with the toe of his boot. "You heard about the kid."

It isn't a question, but I respond anyway. "Of course I did. The whole city heard about the kid—and they're out for blood. *Your* blood. Which you already know or you wouldn't be hiding out here."

He shakes his head, taking a seat beside me. "It was an accident, Masie. I swear I never meant to hurt the brat. Things just got out of control."

I rest one hand on his knee. "I believe you. But this has to end. Surely you see that?"

His chin snaps up, his expression stern. "Tell it to the old man. I just do what I'm told."

Releasing his knee, I turn to face him more fully. "Daddy...he's gone too far. Vinnie, you don't have to do this anymore. You don't have to be his executioner. You can help me talk some sense into him, help me bring him back from the edge before he goes too far."

For a moment, his expression softens. He's the boy I remember, the one with skinned knees and a missing front tooth. In another second, that boy vanishes.

"Maybe he hasn't gone far enough. If he'd stop playing these petty games, we could actually do something to end this war before it begins."

His voice is tense, his eyes wild, as he continues. "Masie, it's two guys, three tops. We take them out, and we rule the city. We wouldn't need Rothschild and his money; we could have it all. I could do all three in one night. By the time the sun comes up, every family on the island would answer to us."

I shake my head. He sounds less like a businessman, less like my friend, and more like a zealot. "It doesn't end there, Vinnie. You know that. The families don't just fall in line behind whoever kills the heads. We go after them, then they come after us. It's war. It's blood in the streets. It's retribution without end. You know that. I know you do."

He blinks, one corner of his mouth turning up into something that should be a grin but feels far too menacing for that. "I can protect you."

"And Daddy? JD? You can't protect us all."

He shrugs. "Maybe what this family needs is new leadership. Someone who isn't afraid to do what needs to be done."

For the briefest moment, I think he's talking about JD, but that illusion fades quickly. JD can be brutal, but even he has the good sense to negotiate rather than attack outright. No, he's talking about himself, about a coup. A chill crawls up the back of my neck at the malice in his words. "You don't mean that."

"You should go, Masie. You should go far away from here. Go to Paris. You've always wanted to go to Paris. Go now, before things get any worse. Because maybe you're right. Maybe I can't protect you. But change is coming, and there's nothing you can do about that."

He stands, and so do I. I follow him across the room to the door, taking him by the arm and turning him to face me.

"Vinnie, please. I don't want to see you get hurt."

He stares down at my hand on his arm, a strange look crossing his face before he raises his gaze to me, his chin still tucked into his chest. "And why is that, Masie?"

His words hit me like a bucket of cold water.

"Because I love you," I say weakly. We've been over this so many times it's difficult to force the words out again. And I know that every time I say them, honest as they are, they cut him more deeply than a knife, mostly because it doesn't matter. It doesn't change anything. He chose the business over anything we might have had a long time ago. "I love the boy who used to sneak cookies out of the kitchen with me in the middle of the night, who taught me to drink whiskey and play poker. I know you're not that boy anymore, but you will always be that boy to me. You're family."

Even as I speak, I feel the tears welling up in my eyes, but I refuse to let them spill. I refuse to use that last, most desperate weapon in my arsenal against him.

He pulls me to him. Wrapping his big arms around me, he squeezes gently, whispering into my hair. I let myself melt against him, basking in the warmth and comfort he's offering. Because deep down, I know it's the last time. He's right about one thing at least. Things *are* changing. We're on a roller coaster, and neither of us can get off. Not now. Maybe we never could.

"I fell for you as a boy, Mas, and truth be told, I never quite grew out of it. But I haven't been that boy in a very long time. I'm a bad man who does bad things, and I don't deserve you. Maybe I never did. Either way, it doesn't change anything. Neither of us can be who the other one wants; we can only be who we are."

"I won't run away," I say, still clutching him to me. "I don't have it in me."

He lays a gentle kiss on the top of my head. "You're a fighter—always have been. But this isn't a fight you can win, Mas. Dutch is gonna take care of the charges against me; he always does. But things are already in motion, things neither of us can control. You should get out while you can."

"I'm not leaving my family," I say, pulling free of the embrace. "And like it or not, that includes you."

He shakes his head. "Can't save us, Mas. Me, Dutch, JD, we're already ghosts. Dead and buried. Save yourself if you can."

"It doesn't have to be that way, you stubborn jackass," I protest.

"There's my girl." He grins, opening the door, "You

66

take care of yourself, Masie."

There's nothing else I can say. No plea, no reason, no warning is going to get him to see the light. He's as tangled in this life as Daddy. Both thinking they have to play the game, both determined to win. Maybe he's right and they are all lost causes. Maybe I am too, and I just don't know it yet.

BENNY

NINE

THE STREETS OF TIN PAN ALLEY OVERFLOW WITH BLEATING horns and ivory-keyed notes as Dickey and I make our way to The Green Door Club. Swanky cinema patrons empty onto crammed sidewalks where stage-door Johnnies wait, blowing their cigarette smoke into the night air. Flappers and high hats drunk on their bootleg gin bandy from one club to the next, the thrill of their decadence glowing in their rosy cheeks.

"Hey, spot me some kale," Dickey whispers as we stop just outside the most famous green door in the city. Dutch's club, marked by the familiar color, stands unique against all the other speakeasies in Manhattan. His club boasts the biggest players in the city, the highest-quality booze, and, of course, the most beautiful club canary in recent memory.

"What happened to yours?" I ask, rifling through my wallet for a buck and handing it over.

A slit in the door opens, a set of eyes looking us over. "Can I help you?"

"I'm looking for a place to water my horse," Dickey whispers. It's the correct secret phrase, and the door opens.

He taps me on the chest, not looking at me but at two brunettes nearing the club. The taller of them offers a flirtatious wink over one bare shoulder.

"If you'll excuse me, I need to go buy that dame a drink."

He jogs to catch up with the girls, drapes an arm across each of their shoulders, and escorts them inside.

I follow a few steps behind. As soon as I step inside, I feel the familiar tug of the club. Only now, it's nearly overwhelming. The stage is full, the band beating away as a handful of dancers wiggle across the floor to the unyielding *Charleston*. Couples sit, sipping from mismatched tea china as sprays of golden tinsel and martini glasses overflowing with confetti and pearls decorate the tables. The lamps flicker a warm, golden glow, laughter ringing from every corner as the masses throw caution to the wind, their fancy shoes and shimmering dresses reflecting their exuberance. Speakeasies are supposed to be quiet, secret places, but this is bold, daring. They are challenging anyone to walk through that door and spoil their good time. Dickey beats it to the bar, sharing a drink with the two dolls, his smile easy, his posture confident. He jerks his head, silently inviting me to join them.

The club has cast her net, and I know it would be very easy to get caught up in it. But that's not why I'm here. Forcing myself to focus, I scan the room.

Quickly comparing myself to the other patrons, I tug self-consciously at the hem of my borrowed jacket—my only real suit is full of holes, soaked in blood, and probably rotting in a trash bin somewhere. It hadn't been cheap, nearly twenty-five dollars plus the tailoring, and now I'm going to need a new one. But if this gig pays as well as Dutch insinuated, my money problems will quickly become a thing of the past. I'll have enough to get Agnes to that specialist in Albany and to replace what Ma lost after Dad died.

It's more than enough motivation to agree to whatever he asks of me.

I scan the room for him. He must see me first because by the time I spot him, I can feel the weight of his gaze on me, his eyes narrow and cautious, as if he's been watching me for some time.

I recognize most of the men at his table from the day before, but JD is nowhere to be seen. Dutch waves me over, and I dutifully obey.

When I arrive, he stands, shaking my hand.

"Glad you could join us, my boy," he says, a hint of a German accent in his words.

"Yes, glad to see you recovered so quickly," another man says, offering me his hand as well. He's tall and yellow haired. Quite a bit younger than Dutch, in his mid-twenties maybe. He's got his coat hanging on the back of his chair, wearing a blue-checkered vest with a fancy paisley ascot wrapped around his neck and tucked into it. "Alistair Rothchild."

"Benny—um, Benjamin Fleischer," I stammer. "Pleased to meet you."

"Fleischer?" the portly man across the table asks with a chuckle. He's in a tuxedo, though it appears at least a few sizes too small. The white vest struggles to hold in his girth, the fabric bunching beneath the jacket. He doesn't stand or offer his hand, so I simply nod. "Another Red at the table?" I open my mouth to protest—I'm no communist—but he waves me off. "No, of course not. Just a gas, my boy, just a gas."

"Please, have a seat." Dutch snaps his fingers, and a steward waiting in the wings hurriedly pulls up an empty chair. "These are my associates. Alistair is my business partner—"

"Financier," he corrects with a sly grin. "It's much nicer than being called a pocketbook."

"Quite so, and this fella is Simon Dunn, or as you may know him, Councilman Dunn." Dutch winks and takes a long drink from his teacup.

Looking up, Dutch waves again. I follow his line of sight to a grey-haired man making his way across the dance floor toward us. When he arrives, I stand, offering my hand as Dutch makes the introductions.

70

"Benny, this is my friend Jack Berman. Jack, this is my newest associate, Benjamin Fleischer."

His name strikes something inside me like a tuning fork. Everyone knows the Bermans are the left hand of the Luciano crime family—cousins or something along that line. They have their fingers in everything from booze to dope to running books. It's all I can do to meet his sharp blue eyes and not look away.

"Sir," I say.

"Benny, yes. He's the young man who took a bullet for you, is that right?" He stares at me as if I were a bug in a jar, examining me, all while continuing to shake my hand. The pain of the motion zings up my arm and into my still-raw wound, stealing my breath. "Amazing, just amazing. Dutch was lucky to have you there."

"We should all be so lucky," Alistair mutters, taking a drink. "But now that we're all here, we should take this to the private room."

Leaning back in his chair, Dutch slaps the table. The steward shows up within a minute with another round of drinks for everyone, including me.

"What's the matter, boy? You don't partake?" Simon asks, his chubby face in a sort of pout.

"Better not while I'm supposed to be working." I turn to Dutch. "I am working tonight, correct, sir?"

Dutch grins and slaps me on the back. "Quite so. But I don't imagine one belt will impair you all that much."

Seeing I don't really have a choice, I lift the cup to my mouth. It's Irish whisky in coffee, and it slides down my throat easily.

"What do you think?" Dutch asks eagerly.

"It's so smooth I think I've already got an edge," I respond with a grin.

"Not like that swill they're slinging down at the Hub," Jack chimes in. "This is superior quality, as promised."

Dutch slaps me on the back, and I wince as pain shoots through my shoulder.

"I expected nothing less," he says, swirling his own

drink before gulping it down in one swallow. "Neither of those things are the concern."

Alistair picks a bit of lint from his white trousers, crossing his legs. "It's an investment not without risks," he says, glancing across the table to Jack.

The music stops, the crowd breaking into riotous applause. A slender fella in a white suit approaches the microphone, hushing the clubgoers. "And now, the doll you've all been waitin' for...The Golden Canary herself, Miss Masie."

I feel my chest tighten as Masie steps out from behind a beaded curtain and raises her satin-gloved arms into the air, cheers and whistles filling the room. She's in a sea foam-green getup, her long legs made seemingly longer by her high-heeled shoes and fishnet stockings. Her dress is so short her garters are nearly showing, the silver beads dangling and catching light as she sashays onto the stage. Her golden blonde hair is perfectly waved to her chin, a silver beaded band across her head and multiple strings of pearls falling from her long neck. Taking the microphone in her hands like she's about to kiss it, she tilts her chin, sweeping a sultry glance around the room from beneath her dark lashes.

"Hello, floorflushers," she begins, her voice low and smooth. "Are we ready to have some fun?"

The crowd cheers again, the walls shaking with the sound.

The corner of her mouth curls into a seductive grin. "Well fellas, grab your best dame. We're going to start with something for the lovebirds."

The double bass starts up first, plucking each note as her hips sway to the sound. It's a slow melody. Across the room, couples take hands and make their way to the floor. The atmosphere changes as the first lonely, aching bleat of the saxophone wafts through the air. The trombone joins in next, layering its deep buzzing into the music, and finally, my heart now pounding in my chest, Masie begins to sing.

I don't know the song, but she's singing of yellow diamonds and the night sky, of shadows and water and love. Unlike so many club canaries with their high, nasal voices, hers is a low tone, thick as molasses on a winter's day. Something about it draws the breath from my lungs. I force myself to look away, to take stock of the room around me. There is no sound. Even the barmen are frozen, staring at her in rapture. Dutch has his eyes closed, his head swaying gently with each note, but the other men just stare. Beside me, Alistair is particularly caught up. He leans forward on his arm, his cheeks flushed as he watches her with greedy eyes.

There's something about it that rubs me wrong. Not just the tiny bubble of jealousy rising inside me, but the look of desperation on his face. Obviously a man of means, no doubt Alistair Rothchild is very used to getting whatever he wants. And there's no doubt in my mind that, at least in this moment, he would do anything to possess her.

I smirk, wondering what he might think if I told him that only a few short hours ago, she'd been nursing me back to health—while I was naked as the day I was born.

It's a ridiculous thought, but it brings me a perverse sort of pleasure.

I catch sight of Dickey on the dance floor with one of the flappers he'd come in with. She's staring at him, clearly smitten, but he looks past her, his eyes glued to the stage.

In fact, the whole crowd is enraptured with Masie. She's pretty enough—stunning to be honest—but I doubt her looks, or even her voice, is what holds these people hostage. No, it's something about her. Her confidence, her *charisma*, perhaps. Something about her makes you feel grateful to simply be in her *presence*.

Finally, the song ends, and the crowd applauds again.

"Your daughter is a marvel," Alistair says, seeming to regain himself.

"She takes after her mother," Dutch says, his voice wilting. "Bless her soul."

"A tragic loss. You have my deepest sympathy, of

course," Councilman Dunn adds.

Dutch nods graciously. "Thank you for that. It's been over a year now. It's hard to believe." He pauses, catching Masie's eye and raising his hands so she can see him clapping for her. She doesn't acknowledge the gesture. The music begins again, drums picking up a much-quicker tempo, and the room erupts into a frantic, foot-stomping swing.

Dutch leans forward. "I do think it's time to retire to a more private setting." Then he turns to me. "My boy, you keep watch here. Should anything get out of hand, or the flatties come knockin', there's a light switch by the door. Just push it, and we'll take the back way out. You got it?"

I nod once. "Yes, sir."

The men stand, taking their drinks with them as they retire behind a panel of wood that looks like a full mirror in a frame. To the left of it is a single lamp, the switch just below. It's not until it closes behind them that I take up my post, back to the mirror, watching the club. The song changes again.

There's something wild,
about you, child...

It's all I can do to keep my gaze continually scanning the room and not falling back to her face. The pull is magnetic.

That's so contagious,
let's be outrageous...

Even as her voice reverberates from wall to wall, from parquet floor to tin-tiled ceiling, as it flows around me, through me, it's impossible not to imagine her standing in front of that window, light spilling around her.

Let's misbehave.

I'm almost lost in the memory when the green door opens and JD steps in, a petite brunette all draped in furs hanging on his arm. Behind him, two more men stride in. Their faces are familiar, but it takes me a moment to realize where I know them from. Cops. I'd seen them during my processing. They look different tonight, their faces flushed

74

and smiling, their blue uniforms traded in for grey suits and fedoras. JD waves to the barmen, then catches sight of me. I offer him a polite nod, which he returns, releasing his doll and the two flatties to a table. He works the crowd, shaking hands and offering warm, friendly smiles as he makes his way across the floor to me.

"I take it Dutch is in his meeting?" he whispers, barely loud enough for me to hear over the music.

I nod, jerking toward his table with my chin. "Those two fellas are cops; I recognize them from my time in the joint."

Slipping one hand into his packet and the other onto my shoulder, he lets out a barking laugh. "Half our guests are law of some flavor. We cater to judges, senators, sergeants, and even the occasional flattie. Less they come blazing through that door in unies, guns drawn, they ain't no worries of ours."

I nod.

"But good lookin' out. Pop was right to bring you in. You're a sharp tack." A young woman in a slinky pink fringe dress wanders over, silver tray of teacups in hand. JD snaps his fingers and she pauses, grinning. "What's the flavor?" he asks.

"Gin Rickies," she answers in a bubbly voice. He gently adjusts the pink feather in her wavy red hair before taking a cup. She bats her dark eyelashes and flushes, her freckles almost disappearing. He has an effect similar to Masie, I realize. Charisma must be an inherited trait.

He takes a long drink. "We've only got a few rules here, Benny. Show up by dark and stay till the evening's take has been put in the vault. Be sure to always be dressed to the nines. Don't fraternize with the giggle girls, if you can help it." He winks at the redhead as she passes by again. "And do whatever you're told."

"Sounds easy enough," I say.

"And, this should go without saying, nothing you see or hear ever gets repeated. Dutch rewards loyalty—as you've seen. But he punishes treachery in equal measure."

"Of course." As I speak, the song ends and my words are eaten by the frenzied crowd.

With a farewell pat on the back, JD makes his way to his table and takes a seat. I turn, adding my applause to the masses. Masie dips, raising one arm in a playful wave, then blows the audience a kiss and steps off stage. The bassist begins plucking again, and the band strikes up. The sax man takes the mic, crooning into it.

It don't mean a thing if it ain't got that swing.

Masie makes her way through the throng of dancers, practically throwing herself forward across the bar. Whatever she whispers to the barman makes him smile. He mixes her a pale purple concoction and pours it into a cup, handing it to her. Leaning across the bar, she plants a playful kiss on his chubby cheek, earning her a grin as he slings a towel over his shoulder and waves her away. Turning her back to him, she leans against the bar, watching the room over the edge of her cup as she takes a sip. Her eyes fall on me, one delicate eyebrow raising. She walks my way, her yellow curls bouncing slightly with each step.

"You look like a man who needs a drink," she says, holding her cup out to me.

I should refuse. Some faraway thought in my head whispers *no*, even as my lips form what I'm sure is a stupid grin. "Thank you." I accept her cup. Taking a small sip, I frown as the herb flavor rolls around my tongue.

"Lavender gin, they make it special for me," she continues.

"It's…disgusting," I admit, handing the bitter liquid back to her.

That earns me a radiant smile. "An acquired taste, I suppose." She takes another sip. "How are you enjoying your first night?"

"Well, this is one of the nicest juice joints I've ever been to. Though I think that has more to do with the entertainment than the hooch."

She touches her chin to her shoulder, the dangling beads from her headband tickling her neck. "Don't feed me a line, Benjamin. I'm not a fish you can reel in."

"I wouldn't dream of it," I say honestly.

She grins. "In that case, I'm absolutely flattered."

Just then, the dark-haired dame JD brought in rushes Masie, throwing her arms around her neck and embracing her tightly.

"Oh Mas, that was just the bee's knees," she says merrily, stepping back but keeping a hold of her hands.

"Benjamin, this is my dear friend June," Masie says.

June releases her friend, stepping forward to place one satin-gloved finger on my chest.

"Well, a new face. I think all new faces should be this handsome to look at, don't you agree, Mas?"

Her flattery is kind, but she's close enough I get a whiff of her rose-scented perfume mixed with the gin on her breath. It makes me momentarily nauseous.

"Thank you," I manage. "It's nice to meet you, Miss."

She steps back, holding out one gloved hand, palm down. "June West. Like Mae West. She's a distant cousin of mine," she explains.

I have to admit, once she says it, I can see a small resemblance. Though June has coal black locks in a chin-length bob, she has the same long, wide nose and half-moon eyes as her famous cousin. She's a real knockout, in fact. But somehow, standing next to Masie is like standing next to an eclipse. June is completely overshadowed.

"Miss West," I say, taking her hand and grazing a polite kiss along her knuckles as I've seen gentlemen do.

"Oh, please. June is fine. So, have you been working for the family long, Benny?"

"It's his first day," Masie answers for me, taking her friend by the arm. "And we best let him get back to it."

But June seems disinclined to leave. Instead, she makes a snapping gesture with her fingers. "Wait! Are you the fella who got shot?"

When I don't answer immediately, she flails. "That's dreadfully exciting. I mean, you're a real-life hero, saving a man's life like that. Do you think you'll have a scar? I think scars on men are so sexy."

I glance up at Masie, looking for help because I have no idea what to say, but she just offers me an apologetic shrug. It's not until June steps forward, running her hands across my chest, that she intercedes.

"Where is it?" June asks, her voice high. "Oh, there it is," she declares, her fingers finding the edge of my bandaged shoulder. I wince.

"June, JD is looking for you. Better go see what he needs," Masie says, gently tugging her off me.

"Oh, poo. I'd better go." She turns back toward her table, pausing to shoot me a glance over one shoulder. "See you around, Benny."

I wave, pressing my lips into a tight line. It's only when she's out of earshot that I sag in relief. "Thanks for the save."

Masie's mouth twitches, and she rolls a strand of pearls between her fingers. "June's a sweet girl. Really. She's just...enthusiastic."

Probably not the term I'd use, but I say nothing.

"How is it, your shoulder?" she asks after a moment of silence.

"Better," I say. "Sore, but healing. The doc did a great job. Say, are you singing again tonight?"

"I am. I always close the night out with a song."

"Well, I'm glad I'll be around to hear it."

She sets her cup on the bar and chews her bottom lip, turning back to me. "Oh, I'm sure you'll get tired of having to listen to me every night."

"I doubt it."

"In that case, I'll sing something special tonight, just for you. But, if you'll excuse me, I need to retire to my dressing room for a moment and freshen up."

"I look forward to it," I say, straightening. My words are easy, but something clenches inside at the statement. There's something about this girl, a feeling she evokes, and the anticipation I have to figure it out is almost tangible—smart idea or not.

MASIE
TEN

AS SOON AS I OPEN THE DOOR TO MY DRESSING ROOM, I SMELL the roses. A dozen long-stem crimson cadenzas sit in a crystal vase in the middle of my dressing table. My heart leaps into my throat at the sight. A giddiness I haven't felt in a very long time seizes me as I imagine my admirer, Benjamin, sneaking in, nervous and flustered in his sweet way, to leave a gift for me. I can see it so clearly it's as if I'm watching it happen in my mind.

Smiling, I close the door, humming softly to myself as I cross the room. Taking my seat with a flourish, I tug the white envelope free of the bunch and hold it to my lips. Though I know it's silly to be so excited, part of me can't help myself. It's been so long since I met someone like Benjamin, someone I felt so at ease with. I feel the flush creep into my cheeks as I open the envelope. I don't know what I'm hoping for. Poetry maybe—he seems the poetic sort—or even just a simple, awkward expression of his affection.

Inside, I find two first-class steamer tickets to France.

"You should take June," a familiar voice whispers from behind, making me spin so abruptly toward the shadows at my back that I knock over my vial of perfume. The scent of gardenia suddenly overpowers the rose as I quickly dab at it with the edge of the doily.

"What are you doing here, Vincent?"

"It's Vincent now, is it? I suppose that's fair." He sighs deeply, stepping forward. "I wanted to hear you sing."

Turning my back to him, I slide the vase aside, staring at him in the mirror as I toss the envelope on the table and re-apply my pressed powder.

"You should go."

Stepping forward, he reaches out, taking hold of the red boa hanging on my dressing curtain. Letting the feathers slide though his fingers before catching hold of it, he walks to me, draping it over my shoulders.

"I had another thought after you left today. A way we might both get what we want," he says, pulling my hair free from the boa and stepping to my side before kneeling. "If you won't run away—if you're determined to stay—then marry me, Masie."

The idea is so absurd that it takes a full minute before I can form words. "Have you lost your mind?"

He grins. "Not the reaction I was hoping for, I admit. But it makes sense, if you think about it."

My mind is moving so slowly I can't understand what he's trying to say. Had he really just proposed to me? Or was the alcohol from the spilled perfume making me loopy? Everything feels like a bad dream, surreal and achingly distant.

"Think about it, Masie. The only way for me to take over the business is if I were to eliminate Dutch and JD. Neither of us wants that." His words are so callous, so matter of fact, that I shudder. He doesn't seem to notice as he continues. "But if you and I were married, your father could hand the reins over to me as his son-in-law. He could make me his second, then quietly retire somewhere far from the city. He'd be safe. JD would be safe. And you and me, we could run this racket together."

The look on his face is so familiar that it makes my chest hurt. It's the excited puppy face he'd worn so often as a boy. Only now, instead of making me excited, it makes me want to vomit.

"What makes you think Daddy would hand the business over to you and not JD?"

He snorts. "Because—to be frank, Mas—I know where the bodies are buried. Literally."

The ache in my chest turns to something else, bile rising in the back of my throat. I physically have to swallow it back. He doesn't want to marry me because he loves me. If he did, he'd have run away with me when I asked so many months ago. No, this is him looking for leverage, looking to use me, to exploit me.

Just like everyone else.

Vincent is a monster. Maybe it's because my father made him one, or maybe he always was and I simply never saw it before now—either way, the truth is undeniable.

He continues, obviously mistaking my revulsion for hesitation. "Masie, you can be my canary. I'll take charge of the families—all the territories—and you'll be at my side. You can keep your family safe and help me at the same time. I'd be a good husband, Mas. I would keep you safe, and I'd get rid of my other gals..." Taking the damp doily from my table, he wipes it down the side of my face, exposing the bruise beneath. "I'd never hurt you, Mas. You'd never have to be afraid again."

"I'm already afraid," I admit. "You terrify me, Vincent. The things you've done, the people you've..." I can't even bring myself to say the word. I've always known what he was capable of, but there had always been that flicker of hope that I could bring him back. That he wasn't too far gone to save.

Stupid me.

"It's just business, Mas. You know that."

"I know. I do. But there has to be a line, Vincent. There must be a point where you say, *no, this isn't right*. Do you have that? Are there any lines you won't cross?"

I stare at him, hoping for the answer I know I'm not going to get.

"No," he says finally. "I've done it all, and I'd do it all again. Not just because Dutch told me to, but because it's

81

who I am. I'm not asking you to forgive me here, Mas. I'm just asking you to marry me. You're a smart girl—much smarter than your old man or anyone else gives you credit for. You gotta know that this is your best option. Besides, you loved me once, or you almost did. Would it really be so bad?"

I stand, tossing the boa aside. "No, Vincent, I won't marry you. I don't love you in that way, and even if I did, I still wouldn't marry you. Because everything I hate about this life, everything that scares me, everything that makes me want to run away, that's what I see when I look at you. The boy you were, the boy I cared about, he's gone. You killed him."

My accusation is stark. For the second time in one day, I've let my mouth run away with me. I steel myself for the same blow I'd received earlier. But it doesn't come. Something else happens, though. A chasm opens between us, a gap neither of us can bridge. I can feel it in the air, a shift so real I can nearly touch it.

Vincent stands, disappointment filling his eyes as he points a single finger in my direction. "Use the tickets, Masie."

With that, he disappears out my door, slamming it closed behind him.

Falling back into my seat, I grab the vase of flowers and hurl them into the shadows. They slam against the wall, the vase shattering into a thousand crystal splinters. Rose petals litter the floor in the dim light.

Vincent, my Vinnie, is dead. Dead and buried, as he'd said. The man wearing his face is a stranger to me. No, worse. He's my enemy. He will come for my father and brother. Maybe not today, but soon. I will warn them, tell them what's transpired tonight, although it will be a death sentence for him.

He is right about one thing.

I can't save him.

But I can keep him from hurting my family. Hopefully, I can keep my family from hurting anyone else, too.

BENNY
ELEVEN

The music rolls into the night, with Masie singing two more sets before the first lights of dawn threaten to creep in and kill the party.

"Last call," the barman calls, earning him a chorus of groans. The crowd has thinned. Only the die-hards remain, though most are languidly sitting about at tables or the singular long booth stretched out along the far wall. It's then that Dutch and Alistair emerge from behind the secret door. I glance in behind them. The room is empty, save for the two red velvet couches and two high-backed paisley chairs surrounding a round marble table and a dormant brick fireplace. His other guests must have made their way out the back exit. If I had to guess, I'd say it's probably hidden behind the gilded-frame portrait of a woman in a blue dress holding an infant that runs all the way to the floor. There's also a free-standing globe, cracked open to reveal a bottle of champagne on ice inside.

I let the door close and follow Dutch as he makes his way through the room to the bar.

Dutch slaps Alistair on the back. "It's going to be wonderful, just you wait and see."

Alistair nods, but he doesn't smile. "I hope you're right."

"Have I ever let you down?" Dutch asks indignantly.

The men exchange a few more words, and Alistair buttons his suit coat. I hang back, close enough to be only two steps away, but far enough not to overhear.

Masie takes the mic again, the music falling into a slow, gentle melody.

There's a saying old, says that love is blind...
Still, we're often told, "seek and ye shall find"...
So I'm going to seek a certain lad I've had in mind.

My heart hitches in my chest and I turn to her, her eyes locking onto mine.

Around me, time slows until each beat of my heart echoes in my chest. She smiles, releasing me from her gaze long enough to sweep a glance around the room. I have just enough presence of mind to turn my chin toward Dutch. He and Alistair have frozen, also unable to refuse her siren call. Dutch wears an expression of pride, the sort a man wears while driving a new Rolls Royce down the square. Alistair, by contrast, has a tic working in his jaw, his expression giving nothing away.

There's a somebody I'm longin' to see...
I hope that he turns out to be...
Someone who'll watch over me.

It's impossible not to grin as I turn back to her. No one else in the room recognizes my serenade, our shared secret.

Yes, I will watch over Masie, along with JD and Dutch. I will watch over them all.

THE CLUB CLEARS OUT SLOWLY, AND I WIND UP HELPING JD and another man load some of the more intoxicated patrons into cabs. He's a brute of a fella, with a cracked front tooth and thin moustache, named Donnie Brewster. Donnie sweeps up the last of the confetti while I sit with JD at the bar, watching the barmen counting the night's take.

JD peels off two fresh hundred dollar bills.

"Here you go, Benny. I'm giving you this week's pay and an advance on next week's too. You need to go down and get yourself some new glad rags. Can't have you in the same borrowed suit every night, now can we?"

Taking the dough feels surreal, like a dream I've had a hundred times finally coming true.

Dutch slides through the beaded curtain, Masie on his arm. She's traded her dress for flowing grey pants and a long white blouse. She's still wearing the pearls, but her hair is covered by a tan cloche hat with a little yellow bird embroidered on the side.

"Ah, I'm afraid I need to ask you a favor, Benny," Dutch says, releasing Masie. She rounds the bar and helps herself to s shot of whiskey. "I'm going to have to head out of town for a few days. JD, I'm leaving you in charge of the club, but I've decided to take Tony with me."

Masie sets her glass on the bar. "Tony? Why on earth would you need to take *my* guard?"

"I'm meeting with the DelVecchio family. Tony used to work for them before the war. Plus, he knows his way around Chicago. But don't worry, I'm not gonna leave you unprotected. Not when someone just tried to put a hit on me."

That's when he turns to me. "Benny, you can look after Masie for a few days, right? Just while she's out and about. We have security at the penthouse. She just needs someone to stick close when she's outta the nest."

"Of course, sir. I need to get some new suits tomorrow. What time will you need me, Miss Masie?" I ask.

She throws back another shot. "As it happens, I have some shopping to do tomorrow as well. Why don't you come pick me up around two? That way, we can go together?"

"I can certainly do that," I say, still a bit unsteady with the entire situation.

"Good man." Dutch pulls me away, walking me across the now-empty floor toward the back room as the barmen follow us, cash bags in hand. He slips me five hundred dollars. "This should cover any," he waves his hand, "extraneous expenses you might incur while minding my daughter. I don't need to tell you that I'm trusting you with my most prized possession, do I?"

The inflection in his voice makes his meaning crystal clear. If I let him down in this, if anything happens to his daughter on my watch, I won't have to be worried about getting shot again. I have no doubt he'd kill me with his own hands, so I nod as we turn into his private office. It's a formal desk with a stack of ledgers and a candlestick phone on one side, a newspaper in the middle, and a cigar box on the other corner.

"Though I should mention, she *can* be a bit of a handful. I brought Tony in because he was Special Ops back in the war. He's the only guard she's never given the slip or tricked into doing…well, whatever."

"I'll watch her like she was my own sister, sir."

Seemingly pleased by my response, he smiles. "Glad to hear it. I doubt there will be any trouble, though. Everyone loves Masie, you see." Releasing me, he crosses the office to a tall metal filing cabinet. I think he's going to open it, but he pushes it aside, revealing a safe built into the wall. I deliberately turn my back as he spins the dial and cracks it open. I turn back around to see the barmen hand him the bags and the night's receipts, which he slips inside and closes with a click.

I follow the three of them out. That's when I see Tony for the first time. He's tall and sturdy with short grey hair and a well-groomed beard. He glances me over in a way that makes a shiver roll up my spine before opening the car door for Masie and Dutch to slip into. Once they're inside, I take the moment to offer him a handshake.

"I'm Benny, the new security guy," I say, offering him a hand. He looks at it distastefully and turns his back on me, sliding into the front passenger seat. As soon as his door closes, the car rolls away into the dawn.

"Don't worry about Tony," JD says, patting me on the back once. June stands beside him on wobbly legs, one arm draped across his. "It's been his life's dream to take lead for Dutch, but he never had the chance. He used to work for one of the Chicago families, you see. Until one of them took a bullet to the head on his watch, that is. That's why he came out here. He wanted to be Dutch's guard, but with something like that on your record, it's hard to be trusted. For a fella like that, being stuck babysitting the boss's daughter is quite a demotion."

"Watching after Masie can't possibly be that bad," I say, earning me a sympathetic grin.

"Never underestimate the fairer sex's ability to cause a ruckus, Benny."

His own car rolls up to the curb, and he helps June into it before sliding in himself. "You need a ride?" he asks out the window.

I'm about to say yes when I see Dickey sitting on the curb across the street, sucking on a Lucky. "Nah, I'm jake. Thanks anyway. See you tomorrow."

I cross the road to my friend who, despite the pained grin on his face, turns his chin toward the sun. "If I didn't know better, I'd call you the luckiest bastard on the planet, Benny."

I offer him a hand up, which he accepts. "Yeah, all I had to do was get shot and almost die."

He shrugs, tossing the butt on the ground and stomping it with the toe of his shoe. "You just remember who made the introductions there, Mr. Big Shot."

"I doubt you'll let me forget," I joke, slapping him on the back. "What happened to the dames you were with earlier? I expected to find you necking in a back booth."

Now he grins. "What, those baby vamps? Nah, chunks of lead compared to that canary I saw you beating your gums at."

"She's Dutch's daughter," I say, shaking my head as we walk toward the trolley stop. "Might as well have *hands off* tattooed across her forehead."

"Man might risk it for a dame like that," Dickey says, shooting me a warning scowl. "Don't go getting crushed now. Them fellas, they may walk like us and talk like us, but make no mistake, Benny, we ain't nothin' like them."

"What do ya take me for, a sap?" I mutter, grabbing a seat on the trolley home. Dickey stands next to me, though the car's nearly empty. I don't mention the wad of cash in my pocket, or the cush job I'm gonna be working for the next few days.

"Course not, Benny. Just want you to watch your back, that's all. You're swimming with the sharks now."

When I finally walk in the door, I'm greeted by Ma. She's sitting on the sofa knitting. Seeing me, she drops her sticks in her lap and sighs.

"Hey, Ma."

"Don't you *hey Ma* me! You stay out all night with not a word, not even a note to tell me where you'd gone? Let me guess, you and Dickey decided to go throw your money at the clubs by the river?"

"I was working," I say, slipping out of my suit coat and hanging it by the door.

"What kind of respectable job keeps you out till dawn? Only thing open after midnight are bars, legs, and morgues."

I swing back to her so fast I feel the muscles in my neck tense. Ma's never spoken to any of us in such a crude way before, and I can't hide my surprise at her words. "Ma, come on."

Biting her thumb, she looks away, out the window. "I'm sorry," she says, chewing her nail. "I know you're a good boy. I just got so worried."

Retrieving the wad of cash from my jacket, I make my way to her. "I know, Ma. And I'm sorry I worried you. But I took on some extra work so we can take Agnes to the doctor."

Blinking, she drops her hands into her lap and looks at me, her expression hopeful but wary. "R-really?"

I nod, handing over the money. She takes it, staring at it for a few moments before standing and adding it to the tin.

"Call the specialist and make an appointment for Agnes. I have enough to cover the train, the visit, and any medicine she might need."

Her back still to me, she shakes her head. "If this money came from some caper—"

"Ma, it didn't. My boss gave me an advance, enough to get some new clothes and take care of Agnes to boot. But I'm gonna be working a lot for the next few days. I'm looking after his daughter during the day and working security at night. I know it's a lot, but I can make some real dough here, enough to get new clothes for you and the twins, to keep food on the table, and maybe even pick up a nicer place eventually." She turns to me, leaning against the windowpane. "Ma, I can make back everything we lost when Pa died, and then some. You just gotta back off and give me some breathing room, here. Okay?"

"I just want you to be safe, Benjamin." Her voice is soft now, and I know I've got her on the ropes.

"And I will be. I promise."

She takes a breath, raising her chin. "Then you'll get no more lectures from me." She brushes past me, grazing my shoulder with her open hand as she moves toward her room. "I'm gonna go get some shuteye. I have a shift at ten. But I'll make the appointment before I leave. You'll get the twins up and fed?"

"Of course. I have to be at work at two."

Without another word, she walks to her room and gently closes the door. As soon as I hear it latch, I release a deep sigh. It's still early, just after six in the morning according to the old wooden clock on the wall. I don't want to get the twins up just yet, so I turn on the radio. Making the volume real low, I stretch out across the lumpy old sofa. Before I realize what's happening, I drift off, the rhythmic lilt of the *Lindy Hop* dancing through my head.

The next time I open my eyes, it's to see Thomas standing over me. I jump, startled, and he springs back.

"Geez, Thomas. You nearly put me in an early grave."

He chuckles the way only mischievous little boys can,

waving his wooden sword. "I'm pretending to be a pirate."

"Oh, and what do you know about pirates?" I ask, sitting up.

"I've read all the pirate stories, Benny. I'm going to be a real pirate someday."

I open my mouth to ask if there are pirates anymore, but promptly shut it again. Of course there are. Only now, rather than sailing the seven seas plundering merchant ships, they hold backroom poker games and sneak booze past the Coast Guard in unmarked crates. They just wear suits and ties instead of patches and peg legs.

I glance past him to the clock. "Aw, applesauce," I swear, making Thomas freeze mid-swing.

"What is it?" he asks.

"I gotta be at work soon," I say, standing and doing my best to pat out the wrinkles in my shirt. "I gotta shower. I gotta get cleaned up. Have you and Agnes eaten yet?"

He nods. "I fixed us some oats while you were sleeping. Ma left a bit ago, said to let you rest." I rustle his hair as I walk past, retrieving my coat and heading for the bathroom. There's a note on the counter, and I snatch it up as I walk past.

Dr. Moyer
872 Gable Street, Albany
3:15 Thursday

Good, Ma was able to get the appointment. Hastily, I add the address of the club and the penthouse for good measure. I call out to Thomas, "I'm leaving the address I'll be at today and tonight. I'll be gone most of the day and back late tonight. But if you need anything, you can get me at one of these two places. Okay?"

He nods absently, so I peek in on Agnes. She's sitting upright in bed reading *Huck Finn*.

"Hey, Aggie, we got your doctor's appointment all set up," I say, forcing a cheerful tone. "You'll be crossing swords with Thomas again before you know it."

Lowering the book, she offers me a slip of a smile. "Mother told me. I've been praying all morning that it'll go well. I hate to be such a bother for everyone."

Pushing the door full open, I walk to her side, sitting on the bed beside her. "Don't be silly, how could someone as tiny as you ever be a bother? Besides, I have a special surprise for you once you're feeling better. We're going to go to the store and get you as many new dresses, ribbons, and books as we can carry."

Dropping the book entirely, she lunges forward, pulling me into a long hug. I rub her back, mentally taking note of every rib, every backbone I can feel under my fingers.

MASIE

TWELVE

*DADDY AND JD HOLD ME HOSTAGE IN THE DEN WHILE I RE-*count my meeting with Vincent and his impromptu proposal. Daddy's face turns three shades of red before I'm done, but JD seems unsurprised.

"It's not like we didn't expect something like this," JD says, downing a glass of Scotch.

Daddy paces the floor, his hands clasped behind his back. "Shame I already had the charges dropped. A few years behind bars mighta done him some good. I'm going to have to speak to Alistair, see what he thinks should be done. In the meantime, you keep your distance," he says, stopping long enough to point at me.

I raise one hand. "I promise."

"This meeting in Chicago is too important to let anything throw a wrench in the works now. JD, keep the boy placated until I get back. Tell him I wanna meet with him when I return. Maybe tell him I might be looking to bring him on as a partner."

JD pales. "Is that really your solution?"

Daddy waves his hand. "Course not. But it should keep him from doing anything too stupid while I'm gone."

Daddy crosses the floor, kissing me lightly on the cheek he'd slapped not twelve hours earlier. I wince, but he pretends not to notice. "Keep safe, baby girl. I'll see you in a few days."

Once he's gone, JD pours himself another glass. "I'm taking him to the train tomorrow morning. I'll swing by and talk to Mad Dog after."

Once upon a time, I would have protested my brother using that nickname for Vincent, but now, it feels right somehow. He's not really Vincent anymore, after all.

"Thank you, JD." I stand, bone weary and ready to fall into my bed. "Oh, and one other thing. I know Daddy has plans for Benjamin, plans to bring him more into the business."

JD nods. "He's a good egg, that one. Can't decide if that's a good or a bad thing in this line of work."

"That's my point exactly. He's a good guy. Can we try not to...?" I fumble for the right words.

"You don't want me to throw the kid to the wolves, I get it. But I gotta say, if you're going sweet on this fella, you might want to rethink that."

Closing the space between us, I steal the glass from his hand and take a deep, long drink, handing it back empty. "And why is that, brother?"

"Because this kid, he's just breaking in. He's so green I could plant him in a jar on the patio, but he's got the goods. I just think you're moving in different directions is all," he adds, setting the empty glass on the cabinet. "Plus, there's the simple matter that Dutch would have him skinned alive if he even suspected anything between you two."

I laugh. "That's fair enough. But maybe Benjamin just needs some looking after. Maybe he needs someone to pull back the curtain and show him what's hiding in the shadows. Someone who can make sure he doesn't go down the wrong path. A friend."

Now JD makes a face, wrinkling his nose. "Don't go all pious on me, Mas. Your hands are as dirty as anyone's. Besides, he's supposed to be lookin' after you, remember?"

I shrug. "I suppose we'll have to look after each other then. There are worse things than having a friend like me."

JD barks a laugh. "Name three."

Turing my back on him, I look over my shoulder and stick my tongue out at him.

He laughs again. "My point exactly, Masie. You're gonna eat that poor fella alive."

As I creep down the hall to my room, I can't help but wonder if JD has a point.

BENNY

THIRTEEN

WHEN I ARRIVE AT THE PENTHOUSE, MASIE IS STILL IN BED, OR so the butler informs me. I'm heartily tempted to go stand at her bedroom window, watch her sleep as she'd done to me, but the inclination fades quickly. She may have seen me as a patient to be watched over, but I doubt I could muster the same detachment.

Instead, I take a seat on the terrace. The maid brings me a cup of tea and some biscuits with peach marmalade. My groaning stomach quickly reminds me I haven't eaten all day, and I devour the entire tray in minutes. A rustle behind me draws my attention, and I fully expect to see Masie. Instead, I'm faced with June. Her short auburn bob is disheveled, a pink satin sleep mask pushed hastily up the side of her head. She's petite, but well curved, her smeared lipstick and eye kohl betraying just how much she drank last evening. She sidles onto the balcony, wincing against the midday sun, and pouring herself a cup of joe from the cart near the door. At first, I'm not even sure she sees me, but then she turns, her floor-length green silk robe slit open to expose matching satin lingerie beneath. I jerk my head in the opposite direction almost before I can make sense of her attire.

She laughs, a bubbly, cheerful sound, even as I blush.

Sure, I've seen those sorta things in magazine ads, even, on occasion, on the giggle girls down at the club on the wharf, but never like this. And certainly not on JD's dame.

"Sorry, Benny. I thought it was just us girls in the house. JD took his pop to the station this morning and never came back." She wilts into the chair beside me, raising her cup into the air. "So I took the opportunity to catch up on my beauty sleep."

She stares at me expectantly and I fumble, wondering what I am supposed to say to that.

"That, my dear, is called fishing for a compliment," she says with an exaggerated sigh. "How can I possibly be expected to flirt with you if you can't even keep up your part?"

I set my cup down on the table, plucking a yellow daisy from the centerpiece. "My apologies, Miss June. Please accept this humble consolation."

With a flirtatious grin, she takes the flower from my finger and tucks it behind one ear. "It's a start, I suppose. Though ladies prefer roses."

"I'll take note of that," I say, tugging at my suit coat. "It certainly is warm today; don't you think?"

She waves her hand. "If you're overly warm, I'd be glad to help you out of your jacket."

I feel the heat hit my face and turn away before she can mock me for it. "Perhaps I just need some water."

"Why, Benjamin, you look positively flushed." The voice comes from behind me, and I glance over my shoulder only to confirm its origin. Truthfully, I'd know that sound anywhere.

"Miss Masie," I say, pushing my chair back to stand. She's leaning against the French door on one arm, the other hand on her hip. Her dress is red velvet, with a drop waist and a string of black pearls so long she could probably skip rope with them if she were so inclined.

"It's just Masie," she corrects. "No formality between friends. Isn't that right, June?"

June makes a chirping noise, but I don't look at her. I can't pry my eyes off Masie. Her golden hair flows in waves to just past her chin, her lips the color of burnt cinnamon. Between the crimson dress and her alabaster skin, her steel grey eyes are startling.

"You look lovely today, Masie," I stammer, mentally cursing myself for not being able to come up with anything better to say.

"Don't sound so surprised," she says with a warm, throaty laugh.

"Where are you off to?" June asks, her tone more longing than curious.

"Well, we have some shopping to do. Isn't that right, Benjamin?"

I straighten, pulling my shoulders tight. This isn't social hour, I remind myself sternly. It's my job. "If you say so, Mi—Masie."

"Well, best get a move on then," she says, spinning on one toe like a ballerina. "Fifth Avenue waits for no one."

<hr />

AS SOON AS WE ENTER THE ELEVATOR, SHE TUCKS HER HANDBAG under one arm. "Sorry about June. She's a bit…flirtatious."

I shrug. "Doesn't bother me."

"I'm sure it doesn't," she muses.

Knowing there's no way to respond and not sound like a mook, I shake off the comment. "What's on the agenda today?"

"Well, we have a bit of shopping to do first. I know just the place."

The elevator releases us onto the ground floor of her building. The foyer is brass and marble with vases of flowers on ivory pedestals. Her heels clack along until we step past the doorman and outside, her town car already waiting at the curb. Brushing past her, I pull the car door open and she slips inside. I close the door, meaning to sit up front, when she pokes her chin out the window.

"What are you doing?"

I pause, fingers still on the handle. "I was going to sit

up here."

"And how do you plan to protect me from over the seat?" she asks, clicking her tongue. "No, sit back here and keep me company."

I obey, catching a glance from the driver.

She slides over, and I take my spot at her side. Leaning forward, she addresses the driver in a loud voice, "Albert, we're going to Bergdorf, please." Sitting back, she leans her head toward me and whispers, "Albert is my chauffer. He's been with the family since before I was born. Deaf in one ear, the poor darling. But his eyes are sharp as a tack."

As we pull away from the curb with a jerk, I can't help but wonder if she's overestimating his acuteness. He's clearly an older man, his white hair thin and poking from beneath his black cap, his skin pruned and spotted with age.

We crawl toward Fifth Avenue with the windows down, sweltering in the lack of breeze. The traffic is slow in the city, roads so crowded with pedestrians that we have to stop every block to let them swarm across. People bustle across thin streets in clumps. Dock workers heading toward their afternoon shifts in worn trousers, wrinkled shirts, and old suspenders, bankers and stock jockeys returning from long lunches to crunch numbers at their tiny paper-covered desks. Tourists with maps in hand struggle to navigate the heart of the city, wanting to see all the sights she has to offer. Children, hot with the summer air, play stick ball on corner lots or dance in hydrants that spill their fountains of water under the close eyes of firemen. Shop owners adjust signs and baskets of wares on the sidewalks while women, arms full of shopping bags, idle past.

I take a deep breath, inhaling all of it. My city. My home. It's as much a part of me as the blood in my veins. I've walked each of these streets. I know the sound the concrete makes under the soles of my shoes. Know what the park smells like in spring and how the river swells in the fall. I've experienced it more times than I care to count. But today, seeing it all from my seat beside Masie, the smell of her perfume heavy in my nostrils, it somehow seems like the first time. Everything feels new, feels possible. As if the city itself is opening itself up to me.

Sky's the limit, it whispers. *Anything can happen. Anything is possible.*

It's that contagious, alluring hope that draws people to this tiny island.

And for the first time in my life, I allow myself to embrace the possibility of actually having everything.

"Penny for your thoughts," Masie says, drawing my attention to her.

I scratch the side of my head, embarrassed to admit my childish contemplation. "My friends call me Bad Luck Benny. Did you know that?" She smiles and shakes her head. No, of course not. How could she? "I have a bit of a knack for being in the wrong place at the wrong time. But I was just thinking that maybe my luck's changing. Do you think that's possible, Masie?"

She leans back, sprawling in her seat, her back pressing against her door. "I don't believe in luck. Or rather, I think perhaps we make our own luck, if such a thing even exists."

"How so?" I ask curiously.

"Well, my father is a self-made man, you see. He started with nothing. His own father died when he was just a child, forcing him to leave school to support his mother and sister." She pauses, rolling her pearls in one hand and gazing out the window before continuing. Inside me, something tugs. At first, a pang of sympathy—I know all too well the burden her father faced. But then something more, a desire to comfort her as she speaks. But she seems distant so I remain still, watching her with careful measure.

"He worked odd jobs where he could, then he fell in with a minor mobster in Harlem. He rigged craps games for him. That's when he met my mother; her father worked for the organization too. They got married later that year. He got in some trouble after that, did a nickel in Blackwell Island prison. Once he got out, he used what he'd managed to stash to start up the trucking company. JD came along soon after, then me a year later. By the time prohibition hit, he'd already opened his first club, and his trucking company became one of the biggest liquor-smuggling operations in the state. Mother hated it, the business. Always talked about the day he'd be able to retire, to go live on a farm upstate. But that was her dream; I doubt it was ever his."

"Where is your mother now?" I ask.

Her eyes flicker to me, something passing across her face that hardens her. She straightens, smoothing her dress across her legs.

"She's no longer with us."

Mentally kicking myself, I apologize. "Oh, Masie. I'm so sorry. I didn't mean to dredge up the past."

She shrugs it off, looking away again.

"I lost my father just last year," I continue. "I know how painful it can be."

"It feels like a long time ago," she responds, her voice thin and strained.

The car swerves against the curb before I can apologize again.

"We're here, Miss," Tony announces.

When she faces me again, her smile has returned. "Well, Benjamin, are you ready?"

I step out of the car, scanning the street before offering her a hand. The building is massive, easily five stories. The first floor is divided into several smaller shops—a perfume shop, a hat maker, even a watchmaker.

As soon as we stroll in, the salesman greets us like old friends. He's slender, with a wire thin moustache and a thick French accent.

"Mademoiselle Schultz, so lovely to see you," he says, reaching out to her. She offers him her hand, and he lays a chaste kiss across her knuckles. "What can I do for you today?"

She slides her arm through mine. "I think we are in need of some clothes for my friend Benjamin."

He claps. "Of course, Monsieur. This way."

"Masie, what are you doing?" I ask as she half drags me through the store.

"I told you, we're shopping. Father said you need new suits, so who better to help you pick them out than me? I have a keen eye for size and style, you know. I help JD pick his all the time," she says cheerfully. Releasing me, she finds a rack of jackets and runs her hand along the fabric. "Besides, it's not just suits. You'll need socks, shirts, and hats. If you're going to be part of the organization, you need to look the part."

Even as the wisdom of her words sink in, I struggle to reject them.

"Masie, I know your father gave me a wad of dough, but I had to use most of it already," I admit, my voice low.

She spins on her heel, her skirt fluttering with the movement. Narrowing her eyes, she strides toward me. "Please tell me you didn't blow it all on cards and women."

I shake my head. "No, it's my little sister. She's been real sick. We need the money to pay for this specialist she's seeing this week."

Her doe eyes widen as she steps back. "Truly?"

I nod once, sharply. "I was going to use what's left to get a few things, but I can't afford all this," I say, waving to the racks of expensive shirts.

When she steps close—so close I can feel the warmth radiating from her skin—I freeze, reduced to feeling like prey waiting to be devoured. She lifts the lapels of my coat and slides it off my back. Then, her delicate fingers work the buttons of my collar, then my sleeves. I know I should stop her, but there's something far too intimate about her closeness, her undressing me, that prevents me from forming a clear thought.

"Masie…" I manage to say her name in a breath. It's a plea, though whether I'm asking her to stop or not, I can't decide.

She looks up, her silver eyes locking on mine. "Benjamin, you're a good man with a good heart. I knew it the first time I saw you, half unconscious and bleeding on my kitchen table. Let me do this for you. Let me help."

Her words are soft, and they float through my head. I can only nod in response. Smiling, she takes a step back.

"Marcel, let's begin with the trousers. And everything is to be put on my account."

I open my mouth to protest, but she raises a single finger to silence me. "And that's that."

We spend the better part of the afternoon trying on clothes. Most fit right off the rack—Masie really does have a gifted eye for size and pattern—only a few items need tailoring at all. She drinks a never-empty glass of champagne and has me walk this way and that like a living doll while she decides on colors, patterns, and cuts. All in all, I wind up with three new pairs of shoes, three suits, and countless shirts, vests, slacks, ties, pocket squares, suspenders, and several pairs of socks. She even sneaks in a few pairs of undershorts in light blue silk when she thinks I'm not looking.

"Now, we should look at the back-lot items," she says pointedly to Marcel. He nods once and motions us to follow. We move through the store and are escorted through a set of double doors leading into a mirrored sitting room. It's brightly lit, every surface shining silver or pure, milky white. There are two walls with waist-high cabinets and one with a long, creamy white chaise lounge stretched out along it. Once we step inside, Marcel locks the doors behind us. Not quite sure if this is part of the typical shopping experience, I step protectively between him and Masie, my body tensing to fight my way past the little Frenchman if I have to. But he simply walks to the first cabinet and opens the drawers in descending order, revealing velvet-lined cases of knives and brass knuckles.

As I watch, he moves to the next cabinet and does the same. Only, that case holds small guns, revolvers, and such. Some hardly the size of a palm, some larger and much more dangerous. Masie moves past me, waving him away. Obediently, he crosses the room and stands, hands folded, in the corner near the doors.

I whistle. "What's all this?"

She picks up a pearl-grip pistol and points it at the mirror experimentally. "If I need to explain these items to you, I fear you might not be cut out for the security business, Benjamin."

I sigh and stand beside her. "I know what they are; I just didn't think fancy joints like this sold these sorta goods."

Returning the gun to its place, she brings her chin to her shoulder and wags her eyebrows. "Well, they don't carry the big stuff. But a fella in your line of work should have at least a little something."

I shake my head. "I've never needed a gun before."

"Well, you've never been a mobster before, now have you? These boys, they don't play nice and they don't play fair. And if possible, I'd rather not have to help stitch you up again," she says pointedly. Retrieving a slick silver revolver, she holds it out to me. "What about this?"

I hold up my hands. "I'm just a bodyguard. I'm no mobster."

"I swear you're so green I feel like I need to water you twice a day," she says absently, more to herself than me.

"Are you making fun of me?" I ask, pretending to be insulted. "Not that I mind, I just thought I outta know."

For a moment, she grins, but then her smile slips. "Well, I hate to be the one to destroy your illusion, Benjamin, but you are the company you keep."

I realize from her tone that I've somehow managed to insult her without meaning to. Sliding up so we're shoulder to shoulder, I offer her a grin. "I keep your company. You're no mobster."

She rolls to the side, now pressing her back against the cabinet. "Of course I am, Benjamin. I was born to the life. I've got gun smoke and Quick Lyme in my blood."

"A mob moll with the voice of an angel," I joke.

With one hand, she draws up the hem of her dress, her nails grazing the stockings until her red garter is revealed, along with the tiny gun it holds at her thigh. "I'm no angel, Benjamin. I never start a fight, but I can damn sure end one, and that's the honest truth. I'm just a girl, doing the best she can. Which begs the question—what are you?"

It's in that moment I realize what she's really doing... trying to prepare me for the harsh reality of what I've signed up for. She must think I can't handle it, that I'm too inexperienced to protect her. What makes me the angriest is that she's not wrong.

Determined to prove my worth, I pick up the revolver she discarded. "I suppose we'll find out together."

MASIE
FOURTEEN

AS SOON AS HE PICKS UP THE REVOLVER, I STEP BACK. HE'S probably never held a gun in his life, but there's no way I'm going to have him running around completely unarmed, especially not with Vin—Mad Dog out looking to start trouble.

"My family, we have dangerous enemies, and sometimes, even more dangerous friends. I just want you to be able to defend yourself, Benjamin," I say, clenching my hands into fists at my sides.

He turns to me, an expression of concern forming across his features. Discarding the gun, he reaches out, taking me by the arms. "Are you alright, Masie? You look shaken."

I hesitate, partly because the gesture is oddly comforting, partly because I'm not sure how to respond. Curse this boy, something about him... Before I know it, the truth is spilling from my lips.

"A fella I grew up with—he was like part of the family really—he's...he's become someone I don't know anymore. Someone dangerous. Last night at the club, he told me to leave town."

"If you're afraid he's going to hurt you—" Benjamin begins, but I don't let him finish.

"I don't think he'd hurt me, not deliberately at least. But he's gunning for the boys. He as much as said so." I shrug. "Which is nothing new really. In this business, there's always someone who wants to take you down. But he was such a good kid. This life, it did things to him. Changed him. And I suppose I'm partly to blame."

Benjamin raises a hand, motioning me to have a seat on the long bench in the center of the room. I do, and he follows.

"Masie, I am truly sorry about your friend. But I don't think you can take the blame for what happened. He made his choices, just like the rest of us. And every choice we make, it leads us down a road. Maybe it wasn't the road you would have chosen for him, but it was never your path to choose."

He presses his lips together solemnly.

I look away, my gaze falling on my shoes where I hold it, fighting to block out the memory of our last encounter. "You're right, of course. It's still hard. It's an awful thing, watching people you care about get turned upside down and inside out. But that's what this life does to you."

Beside me, Benjamin goes very still, taking a deep breath before speaking. "And you're afraid I'll go down the same road as him, aren't you?"

I chew at my bottom lip, debating how much to admit. "Would you blame me if I were? I've seen this life, this business, take good men and chew them up until there was nothing recognizable left. I watched it happen to my father, my brother, then my dearest friend. I don't think I could stand it if that happened to you as well."

With a thumb, he lifts my chin so I'm facing him once more. "Then I give you my solemn promise that it won't. No matter what. And if you see me headed down a wrong road, feel free to shoot me yourself."

I raise one eyebrow. "And I absolutely will, too."

He nods, grinning. "I have no doubt. But aim for something I won't mind losing, okay?"

I shrug, the tension slipping from my shoulders. "No

promises."

He nudges me playfully. "And in the meantime, I will arm myself, if only to better defend those I hold dear."

He moves to stand, but I tug him back to his seat. "Promise me, Benjamin, promise me if my father ever asks you to cross a line, to do something truly awful, that you'll say no. Promise me."

The weight of my request hangs between us. It's a terrible thing to make him swear to disobey my father, a man who could, and easily would, kill someone for such an offence. But I won't accept any less. I'd rather him be on the run far from here than to become the person Vincent did.

Would I rather he be killed? a small voice in my mind asks.

But I don't have an answer for myself.

He holds my gaze, his eyes locking onto mine. "I promise."

BENNY

FIFTEEN

I DROP MASIE BACK AT HER PLACE, AND ALBERT DRIVES ME home. He offers to help me carry the boxes up, but I wave him off. The poor old fella'd just as likely take a tumble down the stairs, and I'd hate to cost him his gig. The way Thomas and Aggie go through the boxes, you'd think it was Christmas. They ball up the wrappings and toss it aside before carefully hanging each jacket in the closet, then folding each shirt and making room for it in the dresser. I don't have time to help. Masie requested I pick her up early so she might have dinner at the club before she has to perform, so I need to shower and change quickly. I fix the twins some chicken and potatoes while still in just my towel, then settle them down to eat before dressing. I'm nearly ready when I realize what I'm missing. Making my way to Ma's room, I open the top drawer of her bureau and remove a tan box. Cracking it open, I take a moment to run my thumb over the gold and pearl cufflinks before pouring them into my palm and threading them into my sleeves.

Pa's cufflinks. The only valuable belonging Ma had been unable to part with. The pocket watch, well, that was supposed to be mine someday. Even with its loss, these are meant to go to little Thomas. As soon as I can, I'll get

108

a set of my own and return these to their box to wait for that day. But for tonight, they'll have to do.

After grabbing a trolley to Park Avenue, I am quickly ushered into the building by the night doorman and ride the gilded elevator to the penthouse. The butler sees me inside and takes my jacket and hat before leading me to the library to wait for Masie.

The room is impressive, floor-to-ceiling mahogany shelves cradling row after row of novels. Stepping forward, I run my hand along the spines, reading what titles I can. Several volumes are in German, others Latin or French. A few I recognize, others I can only guess upon. Curious, I slide one particularly worn spine from its space.

"The Magician," a light voice calls from across the room. "Are you a fan of Maugham?"

Looking up, I see Masie leaning against the door in her singularly relaxed manner, her chin high, one shoulder drawn forward, a bemused smirk settled across her full lips.

"No, I've never read it. But I saw a street magician in Harlem once. He made a monkey disappear."

"How terrible for the monkey."

I feel myself flush at her words. Her tone, friendly but mocking, reminds me I am not her equal, despite our earlier closeness. Not in any imaginable way. Quickly sliding the tome back on the shelf, I turn to face her fully.

"Are you ready, Miss?"

She clicks her tongue and pushes off the door, slinking toward me. "I told you, it's just Masie."

"And do you let your regular guard address you so informally?"

Each step she takes in my direction resonates inside me, an unfamiliar ache punctuated by each inch separating us, until she finally stops. Reaching up, she adjusts my tie, her eyes not meeting my own. I take a breath, trying to ignore the strange, magnetic pull I feel toward her, but only manage to inhale the heady scent of gardenia riding on the undercurrent of gin—the unique and undeniable scent of Masie. Closing my eyes, I hold the breath until my lungs threaten to burst before releasing it. When I open my eyes again, her storm-grey gaze is fixed on mine.

"Admittedly no, but then…" She hesitates, and my heart pounds in anticipation of her words. Lowering her chin, she sighs. "I suppose I am a fickle creature, like most women. We always want what we cannot have."

My chest swells even as she turns away. It's shallow consolation that she might feel the same about me as I do about her. Is it only the impossibility of it that pulls us toward each other? I shake my head, wondering if she's right.

"Forbidden fruit?" I ask, watching her walk away, committing to memory each sway of her hips, each clap of her t-strap shoes across the marble floor, each glimmer of light shining off her sunshine curls. I pull to mind the feel of her arms in my hands, the touch of my thumb on the tip of her chin. Somehow, virtually alone in that little room, we'd made a connection. Only now, back in the harsh reality of our positions, it seems more like a dream than a memory, so much so that I begin to wonder if it had actually happened at all.

She spins in the doorway, sending the long, golden beads of her red dress whipping across her. "Precisely."

Seeming to have shed herself from the momentary melancholy, she grins radiantly. "Let's be on our way now, Benjamin. I am meeting a dear friend for supper, and I don't want to keep her waiting."

It's barely dusk when we arrive at the club, too early for the flappers and daddys to be out just yet, but even so, the night crowd is beginning to spill out onto the streets. Ushered inside through the private entrance, we head downstairs, past the dressing rooms and into the heart of the club. The band isn't on stage yet, so a gramophone is playing slow melodies from the corner of the room. A handful of diners sit at the candlelit tables. They're dressed to the nines, chatting, laughing, drinking giggle water from tall, bell-shaped glasses. Masie shrugs out of her fur drape and hands it to the waiter. I pull out her chair, and she relaxes into it gracefully. When I move to stand in a nearby corner, she holds up one bangled hand, crooking her finger in my direction.

"Yes, Masie?" I ask, stepping toward her.

She points to one of the four empty seats. "You're not going to make me sit here all alone, are you?"

I stammer my reply. "I, uh, assumed your friend would be along shortly."

"Even so, have a drink with me." She waves to the waiter, making a two-finger gesture with her hand.

"I shouldn't," I say, reminding her I'm not her guest, but her employee. Her frown at my words makes me instantly regret them. "That is, I'm not much of a drinker."

"Don't tell me you're in favor of the eighteenth amendment?" she offers with a light, twinkling laugh.

"No, it's not that," I say quickly.

"Then what is it?"

I clear my throat, picking absently at the linen tucked beside the plate in front of me. "My pa, he was a drinker."

Her smile falls. Stretching an arm across the table, she covers my hand with her own. "I take it he wasn't pleasant when he imbibed?"

I shake my head, sliding my hand out from under hers. "You could say that."

The waiter hurries over with a bottle, showing it to her before popping the cork and filling two tall glasses with the bubbly.

She raises a glass to me. "Well, Benjamin, here's to not being like our parents."

Reluctantly, I raise my glass, toasting with her.

As soon as I take a sip, flavor explodes across my tongue. "This is really good," I say, forcing myself not to drain the entire glass.

She sits back in her chair. "It better be; that's a hundred-dollar bottle of champagne."

Lurching forward, I nearly spit the frothy liquid out of my mouth, forcing myself to swallow so I can cough some air back into my lungs.

"A hundred clams?" I stare at the glass. It's good, but I don't know if anything could ever be *that* good.

She opens her mouth to say something, but the sound is drowned out by the woman who just entered the club. Her voice is high, nasal, and full of near-forced giddiness.

"My darling Masie." She claps her hands. "What a dreadful time I've had today."

Stripping off her gloves and hat and half-tossing them at the doorman, she strides into the room, gesturing wildly with her hands. "New York is far too crowded these days."

Masie stands, crossing the distance between them, and offers her friend a kiss on each cheek, motioning her to the table. I get up, sliding my chair back and pulling out a seat for the dramatic brunette. Her face is heavily rouged, but beneath that is a true beauty. Her brown eyes are wide and fawn-like, her nose a perfect slope. Even her long, olive-green and silver beaded gown, which might seem gaudy on someone else, seems perfectly complementary to her. Folding herself into her seat, she reaches up, her hands smoothing out her straight, chin-length hair.

"It took nearly forty-five minutes to take a cab from the hotel; the streets are absolutely crawling with people. How do you tolerate the crowding? It's simply suffocating."

Unsure what to do, I remain standing long after both ladies have taken their seats. Noticing me for the first time, she turns her chin my direction. "And who is this handsome gentleman?"

Masie waves in my direction. "Zelda, this is my friend Benjamin. Benjamin, this is my dear friend Zelda Fitzgerald."

She holds out her hand and I take it, grazing a chaste kiss across the back of her hand.

"Pleased to meet you," I offer, realizing who she is the moment Masie says her name.

"Le sentiment est réciproque," she responds, the words

rolling off her tongue.

"Zelda is visiting from Paris," Masie explains. "Won't you join us for dinner, Benjamin?"

"Yes, please," Zelda chimes in. "I insist."

Unable to refuse, I take my seat. The waiter brings over and pours another glass, which Zelda drains immediately before lighting up a cigarette. She offers one to Masie, then to me, but we politely refuse.

"I'm singing tonight," Masie jokes. "Gotta keep the pipes clear."

"Music is such a foreign art to me. Of all my endeavors, it's the one I've never quite been able to master," Zelda retorts, offering a playfully humble glance in my direction.

I can't help but grin. Her voice, shrill as it is, would no doubt bring every stray cat in the city to her doorstep. Even as the thought appears, I remember June's words about fishing for a compliment.

"I'm sure an accomplished woman such as yourself can achieve any endeavor you choose."

That earns me a genuine smile. "True, of course. I've decided to take up ballet again in Paris. I studied it during my formative years, and I was always told what an exceptional talent I had, so I thought, why not? Scott's always so lost in his own work, so what's holding me back?"

Her husband, the wildly famous F. Scott Fitzgerald, is the author of one of my very favorite novels. *This Side of Paradise* had been one of the few books donated to the prison library that caught my eye, and it had stuck with me long after finishing it.

"I must say," I began, "your husband is an incredibly talented writer."

She frowns, scoffing. "You'd think so, wouldn't you?"

Not sure how to take her words, I sit back until the waiter returns with the first course, small round crackers and an unfamiliar lumpy spread. Letting the ladies eat first, I mimic their actions, holding the round just so and using the small flat knife to apply the spread before taking my first bite. It's salty, though not overly so, yet the texture bothers me so much I have to take a long drink of champagne to wash it down.

"Tell me, Benny, how old are you? You look fresh as a baby," Zelda asks between bites.

"Nearly eighteen, ma'am."

She smirks knowingly. "And how long have you been in the life?"

I don't have a chance to answer before she continues, "I mean, Masie told me of your recent heroics. I just wonder how long you've had your eye on all this." She motions around the room with one hand, taking a long draw off her Lucky with the other.

I shake my head. "I'm no social climber." I try to keep from sounding offended at the suggestion but fail. "I fully mean to make my own way in the world. This is just..."

I hesitate because the full weight of Masie's gaze falls upon me.

Admittedly, I was going to say temporary, but with Masie's grey eyes drilling into me, I can't seem to manage it.

"This is just a stepping stone," I finish finally. "A way to earn enough dough for college, to take care of my family in the meantime."

Now Zelda is absolutely sparkling with delight. "A college man, how spiffy. Princeton, perhaps?"

I flush at her words. Light as they are, they cut like a razor. She must know full well a place like that is beyond me.

"Or something smaller," I say flatly, taking another drink.

She leans back, fanning herself with a row of feathers she's produced from somewhere in the folds of her gown. "Don't sell yourself short. Masie's father has many connections. One good word from him, and the sky's the limit. As a matter of fact... Masie, aren't you planning on the Ivy League? Vasser, perhaps?"

Now it's Masie's turn to frown. "That was the plan, though since Mother..." She trips on the word. "Since she passed, Daddy has decided I'm better off close to home."

Zelda's mood sours as she downs another glass of bubbly. "And that is the greatest tragedy of our generation, my darling, that women must always be under the thumb of a man. First her father, then her husband. One wonders why we were given brains at all when we are denied the ability to think for ourselves."

Just then, Dickey walks in the door, JD only a few steps behind. JD jerks his head in a *come here* gesture.

Scooting out of my chair, I lay my linen napkin across my empty plate. "If you ladies will excuse me for a moment."

I join the boys at the bar where JD takes a shot of whisky before speaking.

"Listen, Benny. We got word one of our competitors is looking to take a run at us while Dutch's gone. I want Masie taken home right after her set tonight. Me and the boys are gonna be watching the door here, and we've got a few guys posted around town at the warehouses."

I can't help but wonder if this is the friend Masie had spoken about, but I bite back the question. "Sure thing, JD. Is there anything I can do?"

He wipes his hand down his chin. "Just keep an eye on my sister. These mooks like to hit us where we're soft."

"Will do."

"You packing heat, just in case things get hairy?" Dickey asks as I turn back to the table.

I nod.

"Never thought I'd see the day," he quips, slapping a hand on the back of my neck. "My little Benny is becoming a man."

I brush him off. "Very funny. Where are you in all this?"

He shakes his shoulders, tugging his jacket. "I'm headed up the street to watch the back entrance."

I nod once, then head back to the table. I'm still a few tables away when I begin to pick up pieces of their conversation.

"Oh, I know, dear. I had an affair with my own guard once. He was delightful—for a time. Though I at least had the decency to get married first."

"Zelda, this truly isn't—"

Masie is cut off by her friend. "All I'm saying, my darling, is to marry the money—not the help. A man should make something of himself before you consider him."

"I'm not marrying anyone, Zelda. For heaven's sake, I'm barely seventeen," she scoffs.

"Better now, while you have the good looks and perky bosom to snag a fella, than to wait till the fruit's gotten overripe," Zelda says with a laugh. "Though your dowry is probably large enough to make any man overlook such things."

"Ladies," I say, taking my seat.

"Is everything alright?" Masie asks. "We took the liberty of ordering for you. I assume duck confit is alright?"

Truthfully, I've never eaten duck in my entire life. "Sounds jake, thank you. And it's nothing, just business."

"What he means is it's nothing for you to worry your pretty little head over. Isn't that right?"

Zelda's tone is scathing. Squaring my shoulders, I stare her down. I've had just about enough of Masie's friend. "On the contrary, I fully plan to discuss the issue with Masie, but we are not in the habit of talking business in polite company."

She takes another long drag off her cigarette, pointing a finger at me as she exhales, "Darling, I'm neither polite nor company."

As our dishes arrive, the girls continue chatting, pausing only occasionally to ask my opinion on this or that. I try to listen politely while also keeping distant. Rather, I focus on the room around me, making note of every face that rolls in the door, watching the waiters, bartenders, and staff for any sign of issues. I barely taste the duck except to notice how succulent it is as the juice from my first bite dribbles down my chin, managing to catch it with my napkin before anyone notices.

116

Zelda, for her part, alternates flirting with me and cutting me down. Her mood fluctuates like the seasons. One moment, she's warm. The next, frigid. As the night rolls on, the club fills. It seems the legendary Fitzgerald has let word slip about her visit. Soon, all manner of hangers-on arrive. They fawn over her as if she were the queen of Sheba, hanging on every—often nonsensical—word. The liquor flows more freely than the night before, much of it consumed by Zelda herself, and the entire crowd is riotously bent.

Masie heads to her dressing room to change for the show. After a quick sweep of her room, I opt for a post near the stage, where I can get a full view of the assembly. When Masie comes out, the cheers are deafening. She and the band strike up a quick tune, *The Charleston*. She doesn't slow down for a moment. Five songs later, the rhythm of the club is trance educing. It's all I can do to keep my eyes moving, Masie at my back, as I watch for any sign of danger.

A handful of cops sit at one table, each with a giggle girl on their lap as they drink and smoke sweet-smelling cigars. At the bar behind them, a judge I remember from my own farce of a trial sits, neck deep in bourbon. Beside him is a bald, bespectacled man I'm fairly sure is a senator. And not least of all, Alistair Rothchild has arrived and is sitting at a bench, whispering to Zelda. He keeps one hand on her leg, and she giggles at whatever he's saying.

The presence of these men should make me feel safer, but it only adds to my tension. Which of Dutch's enemies would be crazy enough to risk a move with so many influential people in attendance?

Masie finishes her final song to thunderous cheers and steps off the stage, leaving the band to continue without her. I gently take her arm, drawing her into the corner so she can hear me better.

I quickly relate JD's warning and his instructions to take her home immediately.

She frowns, but nods once. "Fine. Let me say goodbye to Zelda and change."

Releasing her, I watch as she is drawn once last time into the lavish web of Zelda Fitzgerald, who immediately tugs her by the arm until she falls across Rothchild's lap. Though he doesn't take terrible advantage, I watch as he clutches Masie by the waist with one hand, offering her a glass of gin with the other. Masie takes it, offering him a flirtatious smile that makes me grind my teeth. The trio dissolve into a puddle of gin and laughter, and—possibly for the first time since I'd met Masie—I feel the differences between us like an impassible chasm.

When she finally makes her escape, she slinks behind the curtain and down the hall to her dressing room. Once she's inside, I take a moment to scan the crowd again. The handful of guards are ever vigilant. JD, however, has joined the group hovering around Zelda, who is flirting mercilessly with everyone orbiting her. Behind them, near the secret entrance to Dutch's private room, a waiter lingers. He's in the standard black slacks and white short jacket, his hands in white gloves. In one hand, he's balancing a tray. In the other, he's retrieving a folded napkin from his pants pocket. It's the bulk of the napkin combined with his look of general disdain that prompts me to move.

If it's a gun he's hiding under that linen, there's no way I'll reach him in time. I know it even as I push my way through the crowd. His black hair is parted in the center and slicked back on either side, a wire-thin moustache riding across his upper lip. I'm maybe five steps from him when our eyes connect. He sees me coming and immediately hits the switch that opens the door to the private room. I'm hot on his heels though, and he doesn't make it far.

Barreling into him, I take us both to the ground. He's on his face, the tray skittering across the wood floor, exposing the linen napkin and its contents. JD is three beats behind me. As soon as I hear him call my name, I turn, a firm grip on the waiter's wrists as I wedge them behind his back.

"Benny?"

"I thought he had a gun," I say, nodding toward the tray and the stack of cash lying half-wrapped in the linen. "He was acting shady, and when he saw me, he ran in here."

Reaching down, JD helps me hoist the waiter to his feet.

"Tommy, isn't it?" JD asks, pointing to the money. "Where'd you get the dough?"

In our combined custody, Tommy stutters, "Sir, I…I was…"

In a surprising move, JD pounds the guy in the stomach, making him double over.

"You trying to steal from me? From my family?"

Tommy is in tears now, gasping for breath. "No…no, sir…I just…"

With a shove, JD pushes Tommy to the floor, then turns to me. "I'll take care of this. You get Masie home."

I nod, leaving Tommy to JD's tender care, closing the door behind me. Making my way through the crowd once more, I head down the hall outside Masie's dressing room. A loud thud draws me to her door.

"Masie, you alright in there?" I put one hand on the knob, twisting.

Locked.

I tap on the door. "Masie?"

A strangled scream comes in response and I take a step back, kicking the door once, twice, until it finally gives way.

The room is in shambles. The vanity is overturned, its mirror shattered, the chair toppled, and the rack of clothes in a broken heap on the floor. Masie is on the ground, a man I've never seen before standing over her, a knife clutched in his meaty fist.

MASIE
SIXTEEN

I DON'T SEE THE MAN, WHO MUST HAVE BEEN HIDING BEHIND my dressing screen, until he's already on me. Both of his meaty hands wrap around my throat, lifting me from my feet and into the air. I can't scream—I can scarcely draw breath into my lungs. Black spots erupt in the corners of my vision. In one desperate move, I kick wildly, knocking my tray of perfumes and powders to the floor with a crash. My attacker is thrown off balance. As he struggles to regain himself, I wrench myself free, falling to the ground with a thud. Gasping, I crawl toward the door, but before I can get anywhere, he catches hold of my ankle, dragging me back toward him. I kick out again, this time catching him up high and sending him backward into the vanity. It falls over, the mirror shattering on the floor.

Swearing, he draws a long dagger from the side of his boot. As I catch the gleam of the blade in the dim lamp light, I scream, the sound cutting its way out of my wounded throat.

BENNY

SEVENTEEN

I'M MOVING BEFORE I CAN THINK ABOUT MOVING, AND I'M ON him before he sees me coming. I get in one solid punch before he slices wildly, clipping me in the arm. Hissing, I lower my head and ram him into the wall. The knife falls from his hand and clatters to the floor. I punch him in the gut. Backing up to put a little space between us, I jab him in the throat, the jaw, then the gut again. He crumples to the floor, and I follow him down. Grabbing his collar, I raise his head up, punching him over and over until my arm is numb, my knuckles surely broken, and his face a ruined, bloody mess.

It's Masie's voice that stops me, hoarse and broken.

"Benjamin," she whispers.

Releasing the attacker, I crawl to her. She's on the ground, the side of her face red and quickly swelling. I cup her face as gently as I can, inadvertently smearing it with blood. "Are you hurt? What did he do to you?"

With shaking hands, I begin examining her, running my hands down each arm, leg, then holding her neck. It's only then I remember the small pistol holstered at my side. The weight of it is suddenly a terrible burden, but even as the thought nauseates me, I know with a chilling certainty I'm about to have to use it.

121

Behind us, the man struggles to his feet, retrieves his knife, and makes a break for it. I move to draw my weapon, but Masie holds me firm. "No, let him go. Just take me home." She cups my face in her cool hands. "Benjamin, take me home."

She's right. I have to get her out of here. Scooping her into my arms, I carry her up the rear stairs. We spill out into the chilly night air, the music from the club wafting out the door and along the boulevard as I motion to her driver to open her door. He obeys surprisingly quickly for a man his age and I slide her in, taking a seat beside her and drawing her onto my lap as I close the door.

"Get us out of here," I order. As we peel off, I glance back out the rear window, looking for any sign of her attacker, or—maybe more importantly—my friend who was supposed to be keeping watch on that back door.

I see neither.

Masie is quiet on the way home. My heart slows to a steady beat, and I wonder if she can hear it as I cradle her head against my chest. The car swerves against the curb, the engine stuttering to a stop. Albert circles the car and pulls the back door open. Leaning her upright as gently as I can, I step out, turning to help her.

One eye swollen, she slaps my hand away. "I can walk, you know. You don't need to carry me like some helpless child."

Her tone surprises me enough that I take a step back, watching as she clutches the door frame for support and steps out. I hold out my hand as she falters just a bit, but she ignores it, brushing past me into the building.

The butler opens the penthouse door before we've even left the elevator. She strides in, tossing her fur to the ground and making a straight line to the cart of crystal decanters on a tray in the front room. Her hands shake as she pours a glass of whisky and shoots it back before filling the glass again.

Spinning on her heel, she glares at me.

"Why are you still here?" She waves her empty hand.

122

"Just scoot on home. Your job here is done."

"Was he the one you told me about? Your friend?" I nearly choke on the word, but she shakes her head.

"No, it wasn't. I thought at first that it might be, but it was someone else."

My stomach lurches. I was supposed to protect her, and she'd been attacked on my watch. This is all my fault, and I have no idea how to even begin to apologize for failing her.

"I'm not going anywhere. I'm not leaving you alone here, not after this."

She takes another long drink. "I'm not alone. Butler is here. Probably the maid as well."

I fold my arms across my chest.

She rolls her eyes, wandering to the fireplace, drink in hand. Pausing in front of a photo of a woman, she sighs deeply.

"I need to call the club and talk to JD. Maybe he can go after the guy. He should know what happened," I say, moving toward the candlestick phone.

"Don't you dare," she says, grabbing the frame and slapping the photo down so it's out of sight. "We aren't telling anyone what happened. Not ever."

I hesitate, wondering if I've misheard her, but her expression is unrelenting.

"Of course we need to tell JD. He has to know what happened. He has to find the person who attacked you…"

She huffs. "Oh, you really *are* new, aren't you?"

"What's that supposed to mean?"

"I mean, this is how things work in this world, Benjamin. Why do you think they came at me instead of JD or hell, even one of the trucks? Because that's how these people *operate*. It's how they send messages. You want to hurt a powerful man, an untouchable man, you do it through the women he cares about. See, they go after JD and it's a declaration of war. They go after me, they hurt my father, they hurt the club, but no real harm done. I'm *expendable* to them. It's not the first time."

"You've been attacked like this before?" I can't hold back my rising anger.

Her expression sobers, "Not me." Her voice is small, wounded. I want to press but she continues. "We're nothing to these people."

"No, that's not true."

"Of course it is." She begins pacing the room in a long circle, hugging the walls. "When Richie Cuzano decided he'd had enough of Legs Diamond running beer through his territory, he sent a man to cut up his girl's face. Message received. It's a dangerous life, but it's even worse for us. Because we're arm candy. We're disposable. Replaceable."

I shake my head, because the idea of what she's saying is so...reprehensible.

"No, your father loves you. He'd do anything for you," I say, stepping in front of her to stop her in midstride.

"Exactly," she says quickly. Motioning to her face, she continues. "This wasn't meant to be a shot fired. Just a warning from a very powerful man. But my father, he'd hunt the person who did this down and kill him. You don't think I know that?"

"Then why?"

"Because he would start a war for this. A war we can't fight, much less win. All it would do is get people, some of whom are innocents, killed in the crossfire. Because that's what war does. It never destroys the people who need to be destroyed; it just punishes the people who get in the way."

The side of her face is already a brilliant shade of purple, a nearly perfect handprint slowly becoming visible. I reach out to touch her cheek, but she backs away.

"You can't hide this," I offer softly despite the sting her action brings.

She drains the glass. "Of course I can. God knows I've done it before. And I'm sure I'll have to do it again."

"Who hurt you before?" I demand, a red-hot rage boiling inside me.

Spinning on one foot, Masie hurls the empty glass against the mantle, sending shards of broken crystal flying as I duck reflexively.

"What the hell was that for?" I demand. "I'm trying to help here."

"I don't need your help. I don't want your help. You think you can walk into my life with your puppy-dog eyes and slick words and take away all my problems? I've got problems you can't even imagine, problems that would keep you up at night. I handle them just fine on my own. I don't need you or anyone else to swoop in and save me." She strides to the table in the corner, lifts a vase of roses, and hurls it across the room at the wall, smashing it to bits, white porcelain and pink petals falling to the ground like rain. The rage rolls off her in waves. For a minute, I'm completely off balance.

I hold up my hands. "I'm sorry." I take a step toward her, and she flinches. "I'm sorry for what you've gone through, and I'm sorry you've had to live like this. More than anything, I'm sorry I wasn't there when you needed me tonight. I'm sorry I couldn't protect you. But I'm not sorry for trying to help you. I'm not sorry for worrying about you, and I'm certainly not sorry for caring."

She takes a step back and wobbles just a bit. "Just doing your job, right?"

Letting my hands fall to my side, I close the space between us in four long strides. I'm close enough I could reach out and curl my fingers in her hair, but I don't.

"We both know it's not just that," I admit. "I want you to be safe. Just like you want me to be."

"Well, I'm sorry to disappoint you, but *safe* is the one luxury I can't afford," she mutters, stepping forward and pressing herself against me. "If you were smart, you'd run as far and as fast as you can." Then her voice changes, barely a desperate whisper. "Please don't, though. Please don't leave me."

Wrapping my arms around her, I allow myself to relax, to breathe in the smell of her as I bury my face into her

125

hair. Soon, the full weight of her body collapses against me and her head lolls to the side. Dipping, I scoop her into my arms once more.

A noise behind me draws my attention. Butler is sweeping up the glass from the floor. He pauses, a look of concern crossing his wizened face. He's not an old fella, but he's probably Dutch's age, stout with dark hair, glasses, and a thick brown moustache.

I motion to her. "Passed out cold. Can you show me where her room is so I can lay her down?"

He looks from me to her, then nods. "This way, sir."

He leads me down the long hallway to the room at the very end and pushes the door open. Stepping inside is like stepping onto a cloud. Everything is pristine white, from the thick fur rug at my feet to the lace valances to the white lilies in a white vase beside her bed. After laying her carefully across the fluffy white pillows, I take a step back. She rolls onto her side, murmuring something I can't make out.

Turning to the butler, who is carefully turning down the lamps, I gesture to the white chair beside the window. "Mind if I stay here, keep an eye on her till JD gets home?"

His stern mouth twitches, but he shrugs. "I suppose so. But keep the door open."

"Will do, pal. Ah, say, what's your name?"

"Rudolpho, sir."

"That's a mouthful. Mind if I call you Rudy?"

He looks as if I've slipped a plate of rotten eggs under his nose, but simply says, "As you will, sir," before leaving.

The room is dark, but my eyes adjust quickly to the sliver of pale moonlight slithering in from the window behind me. I stare at Masie, counting each rise and fall of her chest until my eyelids grow heavy. Can I really let her keep the truth about her attack a secret? And if I do come forward, what does that mean for my position here? I still need this job to take care of Ma and the twins. Clearly, Masie isn't just a pretty, spoiled rich girl. Maybe her life is more terrible and complicated than I gave her credit for.

But what can I do about it? Her regular guard will be back soon and I'll be off doing whatever job Dutch throws at me next. My life will go back to normal then, right?

The real question, the one doing laps inside my skull, is much harder to answer.

How can I protect someone who won't let me?

*A HAND ON MY SHOULDER JERKS ME FROM MY SLUMBER. BLINK-*ing, I lean forward in the chair.

"What is it, Rudy?" I ask, my body waking quickly as adrenaline floods my veins.

"Someone to see you, sir."

"Me?"

He nods.

I follow him out into the hall, one hand twitching, ready to draw my weapon at a moment's notice. A familiar mop of blond hair greets me.

"Tommy?" I say, relaxing just a bit. "What are you doing here?"

He rushes into my arms. It's only then that I notice his face, red and tearstained. "It's Agnes," he says, the words rushing from him so fast I can barely catch them. "She got real sick last night. I couldn't wake her up, and she was moaning. Ma called an ambulance. She's in the hospital now. She needs you."

"Where is she?" I ask, retrieving my jacket and hat from the rack beside the door.

He sniffles, wiping his nose with his sleeve. "Booth Memorial."

I'm about to step out the door when Masie calls out. "Give me a minute to dress. I'm coming with you."

Looking at her over my shoulder, I wave her off. "No. You stay here. I don't have time to wait."

She shifts her hands to her hips. "You're supposed to be guarding me, remember? Besides, we'll take my car. It'll save more than the time it would take you to get a trolley or a cab. Two minutes." Turning to Rudy, she orders, "Call down for the car. Have it out front in two minutes."

And with that, she heads back down the hall.

I practically growl. "Two minutes."

Rudy makes a quick call downstairs, then disappears into the kitchen. Just when I think he's vanished entirely, he returns with a basket of muffins, cheese, and some apples. Bowing, he hands the basket to Tommy. "Ran all the way here, did you? You must be famished. Why don't you take this for you and your mother?"

"Thanks, mister," Tommy says, accepting the food like it's made of gold.

Just as I'm about to shout my intention to leave without her, Masie glides back into the room. She's changed into a snappy white pantsuit and matching cloche hat. By some miracle, the bruise riding the side of her face is all but invisible—no doubt hidden by copious amounts of powder and rouge. She grabs her hand bag and strides to the door, which Rudy hastily opens.

I have to admit her sudden change of attire surprises me. Gone is the flirty ingénue show she puts on for the club crowd. Replacing her is a sophisticated, well-bred lady to match any deb or socialite. It's Tommy who draws me from my momentary stupor as he takes my hand, pulling me through the door and into the elevator.

We pile into the back of the town car and race off to the hospital. Along the way, Tommy recounts being woken from his sleep by Agnes gasping for air, how Ma had panicked and called an ambulance, and how, by the time they arrived, Agnes' eyes had rolled back in her head and her lips had gone blue.

We arrive at the hospital in good time, thanks to the extremely early hour giving us mostly clear streets. The sun is just rising over the towering skyscrapers as we head inside and Tommy leads us to her room.

As soon as she sees me, Ma rushes forward, pulling me into her arms. She smells of oysters and stale cigarettes, telling me the stress had made her pick up the habit again.

"What did the doc say?" I ask, peering through the white curtain at Aggie, who looks impossibly small and pale in the bed, a tall tank with various tubes and hoses feeding into a large tent with a clear window that covers her head and shoulders.

"The infection is in her lungs. They are trying everything, but the specialist can't make it in until tomorrow." Her voice breaks, fat tears rolling down her cheeks as she clutches me. "They don't expect her to make it through the night."

Behind me, I hear Masie's footsteps wander off—no doubt giving us some privacy. Tommy takes a seat across the hall and digs into one of the muffins from the basket.

I hold Ma, rubbing her back and soothing her as best I can before she lurches away, her hands running down my sides and finding the lump of metal strapped there.

"Benjamin Elias Fleischer, are you carrying..." She leans forward, dropping her voice but with her blue eyes still drilling into me. "A *gun*?"

I sigh, taking her hands in mine. "Yes, Ma. Just something small, for protection."

"Protection from what?" she fumes. "What have you gotten yourself into?"

"It's my fault, I'm afraid," Masie offers sweetly. I hadn't heard her return, but she was barely a foot from me. Ma cocks her head, squinting her eyes at the response. "My father is out of town, and he hired Benjamin to look after me while he's away. The gun is for my protection."

Ma sniffles, straightening herself and wiping the tears from her face. "And you are?"

Masie steps forward, holding out one gloved hand. "Masie, ma'am. Masie Schultz."

Hesitantly, Ma accepts her greeting. "My Benjamin is a good boy. He doesn't need any trouble," she says sternly.

Masie smiles, and the first cracks appear in Ma's rigid expression. "Of course not, we certainly aren't expecting any. But my father has a better-safe-than-sorry policy. He only hired Benjamin because of his quick thinking and trustworthiness." Dropping her shoulder, she opens her purse and withdraws a small silver flask. "I don't normally approve of this sort of thing, but you certainly look like you might need a little something to calm your nerves. And my butler sent some food as well. You must be starving."

With a deep sigh, Ma offers her a light shrug. "Perhaps just a little something—for my nerves. And a bit of food sounds wonderful."

Masie discreetly passes her the flask. Ma heads over to where Thomas is sitting, plucking an apple from the basket.

Once she's out of earshot, I mutter, "Is there anyone you *can't* charm the wool off?"

Masie smirks. "If there is, I have yet to meet them. And that includes the kind orderly who is about to personally drive to Albany and retrieve the specialist. He should be back with him by about two o'clock this afternoon."

I blink, processing her words. "How did you—?"

She waves me off. "Benjamin, with the right amount of dough, anything is possible."

I shake my head. "I can't..."

"Of course you can, and you will. In the meantime, I'm going to sneak down to the shop and grab a few magazines to keep me occupied. Should I bring you some coffee?"

"I don't know how I'm ever going to be able to repay you for this, but I will. I swear I will."

Touching my arm gently, Masie drops her voice even further. "I'm sorry about last night. I was badly shaken and edged to boot."

"It's fine," I assure her. "We can talk about it later."

Glancing over her shoulder at Ma and Thomas, she smiles, pats me once on the chest, and struts off, saying nothing more.

The ward is lined with beds on the left, with chairs and a large nurse's station on the right. Each bed is separated by hanging curtains. A few are closed, but most are open, the beds empty. I slip into Aggie's room and take a seat on the stool next to her bed. The machine whirrs as it pumps oxygen into her tent. She struggles to take it in, wheezing from deep within her chest loudly enough that I hear it despite the other noise. There's an IV poking out of her tiny little arm and I take her hand, careful not to graze the tube.

"Sweet Aggie, I need you to be strong. Be strong for just a little longer," I whisper, winding my fingers through hers.

I sit with her for some time, watching the rise and fall of her chest, listening to the dull droning of the machine. I'm not sure how much time passes, but I start to nod off, jerking awake each time my head begins to fall. A hand on my shoulder makes me jump.

"Benjamin," Ma whispers, rubbing my back. "Why don't you go home and get some rest?"

Stretching, I shake my head. "No, I want to be here."

"You're no good to anyone if you can't even keep your eyes open. Go rest. I'll stay here. Take Tommy home too. He could use a nap."

She jerks her head to where Tommy has fallen asleep, stretched across two chairs with his head in Masie's lap. Masie absently runs her fingers through his hair with one hand and holds an open magazine with the other.

"Go," Ma urges again.

Capturing her hand, I kiss it gently. "Alright. Just for an hour. And if anything happens…"

She nods. "I'll telephone."

Rolling my head to the sides, I crack my neck, then puff out my chest to do the same to my stiff back before rising and making my way to Tommy and Masie. She closes the magazine with a flick and looks up at me.

"I'm gonna take you and Tommy home. JD's probably back by now, so you won't be alone."

She nods, so I scoop Tommy off the chairs and into my arms.

131

"Drop me at home, then Albert will take the two of you home with the car," she says. By now, I know better than to argue.

"Thank you."

When we arrive back at the penthouse, I leave Tommy snoozing in the car with Albert and walk Masie upstairs. As I'd hoped, JD is home having an early lunch with June on the terrace. I peek outside, my hat in my hands.

"JD, do you have a minute?"

He nods and waves me over. June is busy spreading butter across a slice of nearly burnt toast, taking only a moment to look up and acknowledge me with a smile.

"Morning, Benny," she chirps though it's nearly noon. "I hear you had a wild night."

For a moment, my heart leaps into my throat. Had someone found out about Masie's attack?

JD laughs. "Yes, Benny managed to take down a waiter who was stealing from the club. Dutch will be quite pleased when he gets back."

I sigh, relief flooding me. "Glad to help. But, um, I have a family emergency. I have to go today."

JD sets down his fork and leans back in his chair. Masie floats onto the terrace and takes a seat next to him. "His little sister is in the hospital, poor thing. Very ill. I told Benjamin to take the day to be with his family. I'll spend the day with you, dear brother, if that's alright?"

JD frowns, raking his hand through his slicked-back hair. "Yes, of course you should go, Benny." He jerks his head toward Masie. "I will keep the monster on a leash today."

Grinning, he turns toward her. She sticks her tongue out at him, then announces, "And I will be an absolute brat."

"So, like every other day, then?" JD digs, tossing a bit of cheese at her.

They share a laugh. For a moment, I imagine Tommy and Agnes, grown and teasing each other across the breakfast table. It draws an ache from deep within my chest.

"Do let me know how it goes today," Masie requests, the smile dissolving from her face.

"I will," I say, turning on my heel and heading for the front door. I wave to Rudy. He offers me a slight nod as I make my way back to the car.

Albert takes us to our tenement building, and Tommy wakes just as we hit the curb. Both of us groggy, we walk up the four flights of stairs into the house. Stripping of his shoes, socks, and jacket as he walks, Tommy heads to the bedroom. Knowing I must be a bit more careful, I slide out of my holster, hang my coat to cover it, pull my suspenders down off my shoulders, and strip off my shirt, hanging it as well. Only then do I flop onto the couch, stretch out, and close my eyes.

The sound of fists beating against the front door stirs me from my sleep. A glance at the clock tells me it's nearly three o'clock. Mentally cursing myself, I throw on my shirt and amble toward the door.

They beat again.

"Hold your horses, I'm coming," I grumble, fully expecting it to be the landlord looking for rent.

I throw the door open. Two men I've never seen before stand across from me. One in black slacks, a white shirt, and a black-and-white striped tie, the other in a long trench coat and grey suit with matching hat.

"Are you Benjamin Fleischer?" the one in the striped tie asks, drawing his black jacket back to reveal the gun holstered at his side.

"I am," I say, drawing in a deep breath. Both men are clean shaven, the man in black obviously the younger of the two, and something about them makes me clench my jaw.

"I'm Detective Dewey," the trench-coat fella says, introducing himself. He holds out a friendly hand, which I shake cautiously. The other offers no such formality.

"And I'm William O'Hara from the office of the special prosecutor. We'd like to speak with you for a moment."

MASIE
EIGHTEEN

"SO, BENJAMIN BUSTED YOUR WAITER SKIMMING?" I ASK, TAKING a sip of badly needed coffee.

Beside me, JD bristles. "Don't know what you're implying…"

"Oh, please," I say, saucer in hand. "I'm not implying anything. You've been skimming off the club for months. Did you think I wouldn't notice?"

JD folds the day's paper and lays it in his lap. "Have you said anything to Dutch?"

I blow gently across the top of my cup before taking another sip. "Of course not."

"So, this is extortion, then? What do you need, Mas?"

I lower my cup, setting it aside with a clank. "I want to keep Benjamin on as my guard."

JD glares at me. "You are playing with fire, sister."

"I don't know what you mean," I say, feigning offense.

"Why can't you just neck in the back of cars with college boys like the other dames do?"

"This isn't a romantic request."

He rolls his eyes. Sometimes, when he looks at me like that, I see so much of Daddy in him that my chest aches with it. "Of course it is. You've got a soft spot for Benny, and you want to keep him close. I've seen the way you look at him—and the way he looks at you."

"And I suppose you're going to tell me not to bed the help? Don't worry, Zelda already covered that lesson."

Reaching over, he pats my hand. "Dear sister, I honestly couldn't care less. I'm perfectly happy to let you be perfectly happy. Dutch, on the other hand, well, I doubt he'd take it that well. I'm just saying to be careful."

I grin. "So you'll help me?"

"If you'll keep your mouth shut about my extra income, then yes. But be aware that Dutch has big plans for you, and living happily ever after with some boy from the wrong side of town is not a part of that picture."

I sigh. It's nothing I don't already know, of course, but it's frustrating all the same. "You know, there's something deeply unsettling about not having a say in your own life."

JD clicks his tongue, returning to his paper reading. "Tell me about it."

"If you could do anything, go anywhere, what would you do, JD?"

Folding the corner down to look at me, he smiles. "I'd like to head west, to Nevada. There are some people making plans for that dust bowl. I'd take June and settle out that way, maybe start up a racket of my own. What about you? Hollywood bound?"

"College first, but then maybe acting. I do love being on stage, though I think it might be better if I didn't come home every night wet with a drink some schmuck spilled on me, smelling like booze and cigarettes. Or maybe just something quiet, a little house on the ocean, a couple of kids. Honestly, I haven't thought about it in a really long time."

"Well, that's probably for the best. Because I don't need some nickel fortune teller to know where we're gonna end up. We're here till we die, Mas. No sense dreaming otherwise."

BENNY

NINETEEN

WITHOUT WAITING FOR AN INVITATION, O'HARA PUSHES HIS WAY into the living room, his beady eyes scanning the apartment. Beneath his black fedora, hair a startling shade of red pokes out around the edges, matching freckles riding across his nose and beneath his eyes.

Detective Dewey follows, removing his own fedora as he steps inside. His face is stern, his mouth thin and wide, his hair dark, bone straight, and parted down the center.

As soon as I close the door, O'Hara turns, strutting toward the window and drawing the curtain back with one hooked finger. "We'd like to talk with you about your employer, Dutch Schultz."

The muscles in my back tighten into knots as I wave for Dewey to have a seat, then settle into the chair across from him. "Of course." I manage to keep my voice emotionless. "Though my employer is his son, John David."

At the window, O'Hara snorts.

Dewey shoots him an impatient glance before turning back to me.

"And what is it that you do for John David?"

"I unload and load trucks."

"What sort of trucks?"

I shrug. "Regular trucks, sir."

Now O'Hara turns to me, glaring. "And what is on those *regular trucks*?"

"Crates, sometimes barrels. I don't know what's inside, sir. Only that some are marked fragile, so I assumed some sort of glassware or dishes. But I never asked what was inside. I would just load and unload."

"And where would you deliver this cargo?" Dewey asks, taking a pad of paper and pencil from his coat pocket.

"Everywhere, sir. Restaurants, private clubs, warehouses, even folk's houses. It was different every time."

"And on one occasion did you deliver goods to the Schultz's own club?"

I nod.

O'Hara cuts in. "We know you took a bullet for Dutch Schultz. We have a witness. Still want to tell us you're just a moving boy?"

"No, sir, that's true in a manner. I was outside the club when someone drove by and fired at a group of us standing around, including Mr. Schultz and some other fellas. I didn't take the bullet for him on purpose, sir. I was just standing in the way."

"Well, isn't that lucky for you?" O'Hara gripes.

"I think the hole in my shoulder would disagree with you. But when I woke up after being shot, I was in their house. He'd taken me there and brought a doctor in to stitch me up."

O'Hara continues to glare, but he clamps his jaw shut. I can see the rage beginning to boil in his expression. It's Dewey who continues.

"This doctor's name?"

I shrug. "I don't actually know. He'd come and gone before I came to."

"And Schultz did all that for some nobody he never met before?"

I can only nod. "He was very grateful." I hesitate, trying to choose my next words carefully. I'm sure they've already done their homework on me, so I have to assume they know about Aggie as well. "As a matter of fact, when he heard my sister was taken ill, he offered to pay her medical bills, even send her to a specialist. He's been very kind."

It's stretching the truth a bit, but it's close enough to make my point.

"And how do you reciprocate that kindness?" Dewey presses, scribbling notes in his little pad of paper.

"He asked me to accompany his daughter shopping while he is out of town. Her regular chaperone is ill." Okay, the last bit is a lie, but I'm hoping they assume it's what I was told.

"Not a bad gig for some nobody from the wrong side of town, is it?" Dewey asks.

I shake my head. "Not at all. The whole family has been very kind, sir."

"Have you ever heard any mentions of Dutch's business or his associates?"

I shake my head. *This is it*, the little voice nags in the back of my mind. *The other shoe dropping, my typical bad luck rearing its head once more. I should have expected it.*

"Do you have regular access to the Schultz home?"

I shake my head again. "No, sir. Other than when I saw the doc, I've never made it past the front door."

"Have you ever been asked to do anything illegal?"

"No, sir."

"Have you ever witnessed the illegal sale or transportation of alcohol on their premises?"

"No, sir," I lie, keeping my expression neutral.

Closing his notebook, Dewey looks at O'Hara and shrugs. Apparently not ready to let the matter drop, O'Hara takes a seat beside Dewey and pulls a large envelope from the inside of his jacket. Opening it, he takes out small photographs, one by one, tossing them on the table between us. I pick up the first photograph. Even in its monotone stillness, it's nearly enough to make me sick to my stomach.

The bloated, beaten face of a man with half his head

138

missing stares at me with one eyeless socket.

"You seem to be under the impression that these are good people, Benjamin. But you need to ask yourself, would good people do this?" O'Hara continues tossing photo after photo until they are strewn across the table in a grotesque collage.

"Benny?" Thomas' small voice calls from the hallway where he stands, clearly afraid.

Leaping to my feet, I go to him, putting my body between him and the horror show in the living room as I usher him back to his room.

"Hey, Tommy. Why don't you get cleaned up and put on some fresh clothes? We're heading back to the hospital soon, okay?"

Leaning over, he looks past me down the hall. "Benny, who are those fellas? Are you in trouble?"

"Nah, of course not. It's alright. Just let me take care of this. Then we'll go, okay?"

Reluctantly, he nods and heads toward the bathroom. Hurrying back to the living room, I gather up the photos, trying not to look at them and failing. I heave involuntarily.

"It's good that these images bother you, Benny," Dewey offers, taking them from me and passing them to his partner. "It tells me that you're a good kid. But you're in bed with some very bad people."

I shake my head. "No, I can't believe JD would do that. Or Dutch for that matter."

"These were all done by one Vincent Coll. You know him?"

I shake my head.

"He's Dutch's enforcer and personal assassin. Goes by the name Mad Dog."

"I've never met him or heard the name, sir."

Leaning forward, Dewey taps the table with his knuckles. "And I hope for your sake that you never do. But if you should overhear anything or come across anything you'd like to talk about, here's my card." Producing a plain white business card from his pocket, he hands it to me. I take it, stuffing it in my pants. I know all too well what will happen if I appear anything less than totally cooperative. I've seen the broken knuckles and the half-caved in faces of men who'd thought to speak out, or worse, outright challenge the cops in this town.

"Yes, sir."

The men stand to leave. On the way out the door, O'Hara slaps me on the back and whispers, "Be seeing you real soon, kid."

By the time I shut the door, my heart is racing. How can I possibly reconcile the people who took me in and treated me like family with the ones responsible for those photos? The only thing I know with any certainty is I'll be seeing those faces again the next time I close my eyes.

THE SPECIALIST ARRIVES AT THE HOSPITAL BEFORE US—THANKS to city traffic—and I barely have a minute to give the still-unconscious Agatha a kiss on the forehead before they rush her to surgery. Thomas curls up in Ma's lap, clutching her while she rocks him gently. Stealing a cup of joe from the nurse's station, I take a seat beside them. None of us speak. There's nothing to say now. Finally, Ma closes her eyes. Probably for the first time since Pa died, she murmurs a prayer without being asked.

If the worst should happen, I wonder how any of us will survive it. Being twins, Thomas and Agnes share more than a special bond. Since before they could talk, they developed their own language—complicated hand gestures that seemed to change just when I thought I might have it figured out. They are the counter balance to each other. Where Thomas can be mischievous and brooding, Agnes is light, bubbly, and full of wonder.

There's an emptiness in my chest at the thought of losing that light. It aches so deeply it's as if someone has their fingers around my heart, squeezing it.

The waiting is the worst.

Not knowing what's happening on the other side of the off-white double doors. Watching helplessly as every possible worst-case scenario plays in my mind like a moving picture. Holding my head in my hands as guilt eats away at me.

If only I hadn't taken the fall for Dickey, I'd have been there for her. Maybe she wouldn't have gotten sick. I should have let him do his own time—though it would have been much worse than what I got with him being a third-time crook. I should do what Ma wants and get a job sweeping up at the cannery. Leave the dangerous business of mobsters and gin joints behind. Yes, the money's been nice, but is it worth putting my family at risk?

No.

I know the answer before I even ask the question. And if my dangerous new life blows back on them, I won't be able to live with myself.

Sighing deeply, I run a hand down my face. I'll tell Masie tomorrow. Once Dutch and her guard get back, I'll have to back out. I'll gather the stuff Masie bought me—I haven't worn most of it anyway—and she can return it. The rest I'll have to pay back slowly, over time. Surely Dutch will understand. He's a family man; he knows what it means to put loved ones in danger.

By the time the doctor comes out, the coffee in my hand has long since grown cold. Ma is snoozing in her chair, and Tommy is drawing a card for his twin on a piece of paper one of the nurses had given him.

Shaking Ma gently, I stand. She quickly does the same. We are braced against the other, searching his face for any hint of the news he's about to deliver, but finding it frustratingly neutral.

BENNY

TWENTY

"*THE GOOD NEWS IS WE'VE RELIEVED THE FLUID AROUND HER* lungs and heart," he begins with no preamble. "The bad news is there has been some scarring from the infection. But, with proper care, I'm confident she will make a full recovery."

Ma sags against me, and I struggle to hold her upright.

"She'll stay a few nights to recover, and so we can keep an eye on her vitals. We've given her the medicine that will fight off the last of the infection. It will probably keep her asleep for a bit yet, though that's the best thing for her right now, to just rest."

"Can I see her?" Tommy asks, squeezing between Ma and me.

The doctor frowns. "I'm afraid not just yet. We need to keep her room sterile for now. We don't want to risk a secondary infection."

I nod.

Ma clutches my shirt. "Can't I stay with her? She'll be so afraid if she wakes up alone."

"I'll tell you what…one of you can stay with her tonight, but keep your hands washed and keep your distance."

"Thank you so much."

Ma hugs Tommy, and I wrap my arms around them both.

Wiping the freshly fallen tears from her eyes, Ma smiles. "Alright, you take Tommy home and I'll stay here—"

I cut her off. "Ma, why don't you go home and rest? I'll stay here tonight."

She opens her mouth to protest, but I continue. "I mean it. You're so tired you can barely stand. She'll probably sleep all night anyway, and if anything changes, I'll telephone you right away."

I watch as indecision plays across her face.

"Will you give her the picture I made her?" Tommy asks, thrusting his drawing at me.

"Of course I will."

With his now-free hand, he takes Ma's, twining his fingers through hers. Finally, she nods.

"Alright," she says, her voice heavy, but resigned.

Scooping Tommy into her arms even though his legs are so long they dangle nearly to the ground, she grabs her coat and hat and heads down the hall. Jogging to catch up with her, I hand her a few bucks.

"Here, take a taxi home. It'll be safer this time of night."

With a frown, she accepts the money and pockets it.

The nurse leads me toward a large washbasin and shows me how to scrub myself clean.

"Wash any exposed skin," she demands. "And use this scrub brush to get under your fingernails, too."

I obey, washing and scraping until every piece of my arms, neck, and face are red and raw. Only then does she lead me into the private room where little Aggie sleeps.

She drags in a hard-back wooden chair and places it in the room, as far from my sister as the space will allow.

"You stay here. If you, or she, need anything, just pop your head out and ask for me, Margot. I'm on duty till seven am."

"I will, thank you."

With a sympathetic smile, she turns, drawing the door closed behind her. The oxygen tank and tent is gone, leaving little Aggie, her yellow hair splayed wildly across the stark white pillow, looking very small in the large, iron-framed bed.

I sit with her for hours. Dawn breaks, and though I can't see it from where I sit, I feel the energy of the hospital shift with the new day. Every so often, a nurse comes in to take a look at Aggie, one even brings me a cup of joe, which I accept with a groggy thanks.

Finally, Aggie stirs. Opening her bright blue eyes as if for the first time, she yawns, takes a deep breath, then coughs.

"Hey there, Aggie," I say, standing and moving to the foot of her bed. "Take it easy. You don't want the surgeon to have to come back."

Opening and closing her mouth with a frown, she whispers hoarsely, "Can I have a drink, Benny?"

"Let me see," I offer, poking my head out the door and motioning to a nearby nurse. "She's awake and asking for a drink."

"I'll be right there," she says curtly before heading down the hall.

I sigh and pop back inside. "She says she'll bring you something in a minute. How are you feeling?"

She blinks a few times, then wiggles experimentally. "Better. I feel better, Benny."

"Not too much pain?"

She shakes her head. "No, just sleepy. But I can breathe. Look." She takes another deep breath, forcing a tender smile. "Is Ma here?" she asks finally.

I shake my head. "She wanted to stay, but I sent her home to get some rest. I'll call her to come back if you want."

She nods. Behind me, the door swings open, the doctor and a nurse squeezing into the room. "Okay. I'll be right back, Aggie."

144

Stepping outside, I head for the nurses' station and grab the telephone. Waiting for the operator, I request a connection to our tenement's hall line. When a man answers—I'm not even sure who it is—I give our apartment number and ask if he can get Ma on the phone. There's a clatter as the phone is set down, and I wait with only the clicking of the party line to break the silence until I hear loud, sharp raps, which must be the man knocking on our door.

I can tell she just woke up when she finally says, "Hello?" in a voice scratchy from sleep.

"Hey, Ma. Aggie's awake and asking for you."

I hear her shout down the hall to Thomas before returning to me. "Of course. We'll be right there. How is she?"

I smile. "She looks really good, Ma. She said she feels good too. The doc just went in to check on her."

"Okay, we are on our way," she says and hangs up.

I catch the doc just as he's leaving the room. "How's she doing?" I ask.

"She's doing better than expected. The incision was small, but it looks good—no sign of infection. Her fever's down and her color is good. I want to make sure she's eating well and walking before we release her. I sent the nurse down to get her a tray of food. But I think she's going to recover just fine."

His words lift a weight from my shoulders that I hadn't even realized I was carrying, "Thanks, Doc."

BY THE TIME MA AND THOMAS ARRIVE, AGNES IS SITTING propped up by two thick pillows, poking experimentally at a tray of runny eggs and burnt toast. When Thomas bursts in, her face lights up with delight.

"Tommy," she shouts. "Mama."

"Aggie, you look so much better," he says, crawling onto the foot of her bed.

I watch Ma cross the room and lay a long kiss on her forehead, then brush her hair back over her head.

I relate the doctor's orders about her eating and walking, then pull Ma to the side and whisper, "I need to go to work. You gonna be alright here?"

She nods, patting my chest. I expect her to protest or at least make a snide comment, but she doesn't. Between her relief at Aggie's recovery and the charm Masie laid on her yesterday, I'm sure she's far too content to rock the boat now.

I give Aggie and Thomas a quick peck on the cheek and head to Masie's before I lose my nerve.

Deciding to walk—it's still early and I know how they love to lie in—I make my way uptown, practicing my speech in my mind. I'll stay with Masie until Dutch gets back, then I'm out. But no matter how much I replay it in my head, it never sounds quite right. I'm a well-spoken fella, thanks in no small part to my pa's dedication to our schooling and his determination I not sound like the son of a poor immigrant, but even so, I can't seem to say what I really want to. At least not without sounding ungrateful at best, like a bumbling palooka at worst.

By the time my wing-tip shoes hit the pavement below the penthouse, I've exhausted every possible scenario and decided I'll just have to play it by ear. The doorman greets me with a nod and opens the door for me. The elevator ride feels longer than usual, probably my nerves getting the better of me.

Slipping off my fedora, I hold it in one hand and knock with the other.

Rudy pulls the door open and gestures me inside, taking my hat and coat.

"Miss Masie is on the terrace," he says, waving me in that direction.

She's dining alone, to my surprise, and when I step outside, she flutters her hands. "Benjamin, how is your sister?"

I rub the back of my neck. "She's swell, thank you.

The doc thinks she'll make a full recovery."

She claps. "That's wonderful. I'm so glad. Won't you join me?"

I pull out the chair opposite her. Despite my desire to get this over with, my stomach growls, reminding me I haven't eaten in a day and a half. "Thank you."

She takes a long gulp of her champagne and orange juice. "You really must stop thanking me. That's what friends are for, after all."

I don't look up at her as I assemble a plate of food. "And is that what we are—friends?"

She cocks her head to the side. "I thought so. Do you disagree?"

I shrug, once again trying to form coherent sentences in my mind but failing miserably. "It's just that I overheard your friend Zelda... I believe she referred to me as *the help*?"

Laughing, Masie sits back in her chair, fussing with her hair. "Oh, Benjamin, you can't listen to a thing Zelda says. She's miserably unhappy in her own life, you know—despite what it might look like from the outside. I mean, she hasn't been dry for five years. Her husband is either locked away writing or philandering with his Hollywood starlet. So she amuses herself in whatever way she can, including offering unsolicited advice."

"If she's so unhappy, why doesn't she just divorce him?"

The grin slips from Masie's face. When she answers, her tone is flat. "Because sometimes—for some women—that simply isn't an option."

I take a bite of sausage, and it melts in my mouth like butter.

"Besides, it's the name she wants. The prestige and affluence it affords her."

I simply grunt, filling my mouth with a bite of hardboiled egg.

"In any case, I thought perhaps we'd have lunch at the club today," she offers, resting her elbows on the table and clasping her hands beneath her chin. "It's supposed to be lovely outside and…"

Swallowing quickly, I cut her off. "Actually, there's something I need to speak with you about first."

"Oh?"

Wiping my face with a napkin, I decide to just dive in. "The thing is that it's my fault Aggie got sick. After my pa died, Ma was working double and triple shifts to make ends meet because I got locked up."

She waits for a moment, but I'm still choosing words in my head, so she fills the silence. "Benjamin, I fail to see how it's your fault she got sick."

"Because I wasn't there to take care of her, of any of them. If I hadn't gone to jail, Ma would have been home with the twins and Aggie never would have gotten sick. So it's my fault."

"I disagree, though somehow I doubt it matters." She looks at me, then down at her empty plate. "What are you getting at, Benjamin?"

Taking a deep breath, I force the words out. "You and your family have been wonderful to me, to my family. But I can't risk leaving them again, or worse, having one of them get caught in the crossfire with Dutch's business."

Now her eyes dart back to me, stern as iron. "What happened?"

I shake my head. "Nothing. I've just been thinking about it…"

"No," she says, her expression stoic. "No, something happened and it scared you. Please, trust me enough to tell me."

My thoughts go back to O'Hara's rage-filled eyes, to the photographs he showed me. How can I tell her about any of that without making myself her enemy?

"I can't. I have to protect my family. I just can't risk going to jail again, or worse."

"And yet, the last time we spoke, you were determined to stay." She looks down, scooping up her glass and downing the last of her drink. When she sets it back down, she glares across the table. "You don't trust me."

"I want to," I say softly, hoping she'll hear the truth in my words. "But we're from two different worlds, Masie."

Her mouth twitches. "We aren't as different as you seem to think, Benjamin."

"You know I'm right," I say flatly. "You told me as much yourself. This life is dangerous, even more so to the people we care about."

Scooting her chair back, she rises. I move to stand, but she waves me back into my chair. For the first time, I realize she's still in her nightclothes, a thin, sky-blue satin gown with a matching robe over the top, the front drawn open. Beneath the fabric, I can see every curve of her. I have to force myself to look away. Walking to the edge of the terrace, she turns her back to me. The wall around the edge is taller than waist high, but even so, watching her lean against it to peer at the city below make me grind my teeth nervously.

After a few minutes, she turns back to me. "I want you to stay, Benjamin."

Before I can respond, she holds up one hand, silencing me. "I want to show you something. After you've seen it, if you still want to leave, I won't stop you."

"What is it?" I ask curiously.

She shakes her head. "I can't tell you. I can only show you."

I swallow, unsure exactly what she's saying. All I know is I won't deny her. I doubt I could if I were inclined to.

"Alright," I promise.

Licking her lips, she nods once. "Then you finish up breakfast; I'll go get ready and ring for the car."

She sashays back inside and down the hall. I tear off another bite of sausage, momentarily wondering what I've gotten myself into.

BENNY

TWENTY-ONE

WE HARDLY SPEAK DURING THE LONG DRIVE. MASIE, IN A bright floral dress and pink cloche hat, spends most of the time staring out the window, watching the trees fly past as we make our way upstate into the fresh, country air.

Every so often, I catch a glimpse of her reflection in the glass. Her expression is pensive, her shoulders tight, hands fidgeting with the purse clutched in her fingers. Finally, the road turns and we pause in front of a tall iron gate, a large letter R fixed to the center with a flourish. I can barely make out the rooftop of a building beyond, hidden away behind rows of tall, thick pine trees. Albert steps out of the car, leaving his door open, then retrieves a telephone from a box mounted to one of the stone columns holding the gate. I hear him say Masie's name, then something else I can't quite make out, before setting the earpiece back on the cradle and returning to his seat.

A few moments later, a young man dressed in all white unlocks the gate, throwing either side wide so the town car can pull through.

"What is this place?" I ask, staring out at the building slowly coming into view. It's tall, with three-story high wings flanking a cathedral-like main building with a massive clock face beneath the peak. Ivy crawls up the stone exterior, and ornate concrete planters display mounds of bright crimson tulips. We round a stone fountain and pull into a circular drive, the car stopping at the wide staircase leading to the main doors.

"It's the Rockfort Mental Asylum," Masie answers, her voice trembling.

"Asylum?" I ask, tearing my gaze from the building to look at her. Her face has gone a pale gray shade, the crimson lipstick has been chewed from her mouth, and dark circles sit beneath each eye. "Masie?"

She blinks and swings her gaze to me, holding up one hand. I open the door and slide out, taking her by the hand as she slides across the seat and steps into the light. Though she retracts her hand quickly, I don't miss the coldness of her fingers or the light shaking she seems determined to hide.

Taking a deep breath, she leads us up the stairs and inside. The sound of her shoes hitting the beige tile floor echoes down each hall as we approach the glass window where the nurse sits, staring at us with wary eyes.

"Masie Schultz, here to see Laura Lynn Schultz."

The nurse, in her starched white hat, looks around Masie to me, her mouth set in a permanent frown, her skin wrinkled and pale. "Family only," she barks, sliding a thin ledger across the desk.

Masie takes a pen, hastily scribbling our names.

"This is my personal guard. He will accompany me during this visit. Unless you'd like me to report to my father that you refused to allow security during my visit?"

Masie slides the ledger back, slapping the pen down in the spine with more force than was probably necessary. The nurse looks from me to her and then back once more before hitting a buzzer on the other side of the wall. To the left, a door swings open and an orderly steps through, waving us in. He's shorter than me. I can't help but notice the difference as I walk past, but he's stout and as thick necked as any boxer I've ever seen. I want to pull Masie aside, ask her why we're here, ask her who Laura

Lynn Schultz is. A sister? Aunt? But despite the barrage of questions coursing through my mind, I bite my tongue. It's only when she falters, a slight stumble that has her grasping the wall for support, that I step up, taking her arm and wrapping it gently over mine.

The hallway is wide and tall, vaulted ceilings overhead supported by massive wooden beams. On the left, there's a row of arched windows letting the daylight stream in. On the right, matching arched windows open to a large common room. There are a handful of people, most sitting in high-back chairs or laying across settees. There's an old Victrola in the middle of the room playing a soft tune. An orderly dressed like the one escorting us dances with a pretty young woman in a gauzy silver dress while she laughs.

It seems peaceful, for a moment. But as soon as I think it, a scream echoes down the hallway in front of us, the sound bouncing off the walls like sunlight, only sharp and jagged. Beside me, Masie stumbles again, leaning all her weight against me until she regains her footing. She's shaking in earnest now, and the small hairs on the back of my neck rise, tension flooding me with each step. At the end of the hall, we turn the corner, another hallway stretching out in front of us. Unlike the last, this one is darker. No windows, no soft music, and no laughing. Just stone wall to the left and wooden doors, each bolted shut with tiny, caged windows carved in the center. At first, it's quiet, then the unmistakable sound of sobbing escapes one. When we reach the last door, a nurse and orderly step out, the nurse carrying a tray of bloodied metal tools half covered in stained cotton bandage cloths. Behind the door, a second scream erupts. I have to fight back the urge to burst inside, to help whomever is making that awful sound.

"They do special surgeries here," Masie whispers, her voice shaking nearly as badly as the rest of her. "Experimental procedures. A damaged mind is much more difficult to repair than a broken bone, or even a bullet wound."

I'm not sure if she means to comfort me or herself, but either way, it's only her arm on mine that prevents me from rushing into that room.

We turn down another hall, then through a door into a sort of atrium. The walls are made completely of windows, some with arched panes of glass, others with metal bars separating the inside from the outside. Potted flowers blossom from stands in the corners of the room, a long row of wooden benches in the middle for people to sit and take in the view of the lush gardens in the back of the building. Masie releases my arm, walking forward slowly, hesitantly, her hands in the air in a gesture of calm.

Hidden behind a row of tall, purple irises is a rocking chair with a woman sitting quietly, gazing out the barred window.

Her hair is a dirty yellow, long, stringy, and badly in need of a wash. Her skin is sallow, her head lulled to the side so I can't make out her face.

As she approaches the woman, Masie begins humming gently. Reaching out, she strokes the side of her cheek.

The woman turns her head, a moment of confusion followed by a slowly spreading smile. She says nothing. She doesn't have to. The resemblance is enough.

Not a sister.

Not an aunt.

This woman is clearly Masie's mother.

MASIE
TWENTY-TWO

MY HAND TREMBLES AS I REACH OUT TO TOUCH THE SIDE OF her face. When she turns to me, I hold my breath.

Will she remember me today?

I haven't been here in so long. Not because I didn't want to see her, but because the last time I'd come, she'd lashed out, spitting and hissing like a wild animal.

"Benjamin, this is my mother. Mother, this is my friend, Benjamin," I say softly, kneeling at her side.

Her eyes follow my face, never even acknowledging Benjamin behind me.

"It's lovely to meet you, Mrs. Schultz," he says, laying a hand on my shoulder.

"I don't think she can understand us, not really," I admit. "I think she recognizes my face sometimes, but she can't speak anymore."

"I'm so sorry," he whispers, releasing me. "Not to be rude, but I thought she was…"

He trails off, but I know what he means.

"It's the lie my father tells—makes us tell. She was unwell for some time. Even when I was little, I could see it. She was always so sad and tired. Sometimes, she wouldn't leave her bed for days at a time. I thought she was ill. For a long time, I believed that. But as I got older, I came to understand the truth." I pause, humming a few more bars before continuing. "She hated the business. When she married Daddy, I think he promised that he'd get out. But he didn't. The more successful he became, the more she sort of faded away. Until one day—and I don't know what happened, I only heard bits and pieces—they had a terrible fight. Daddy stormed out of the house in the middle of the night. That was the first time she…" My voice breaks. The memory floods across my skin. I'd found her in the bed, unconscious and hardly breathing, an empty bottle of bichloride pills next to her pillow.

"She recovered, slowly. But by then, Daddy had taken a mistress. It was quite a scandal at first. But it seemed to me that people took his side almost immediately. Here he was, this big-time fella, and his wife wouldn't even put on a dress and go out to dinner with him. They felt sorry for him, I suppose. No one really understood. That's when she sent me off to boarding school. Didn't want me drawn into the drama. Didn't want me to have to watch my father be unfaithful."

Opening my purse, I take out a delicate golden bracelet with black pearls dangling from the clasp. It was a wedding present, a gift from her father to her the day she said her vows. I never knew him myself—he passed before I was born—but my mother had entrusted it to me the day I left for school. Lifting her palm, I slide it on her hand. It's so thin I don't even have to open the clasp.

I reveal the paper-thin white scar running just on the underside of her wrist. "And this was the second time."

I don't tell him I'd been the one who found her again, unconscious on the powder room floor, a pool of blood soaking through the white cotton bath carpet. She'd done it just after I returned home for Christmas, just after Daddy announced he'd be spending the holiday working, which was his code for staying at the lavish apartment he furnished for his mistress.

"The hospital committed her to a state facility that night. But Daddy couldn't have that—the scandal of having a crazy, suicidal wife made him look weak, put us all in danger, or at least that was his take on it. So he brought her here and dropped a fortune to keep the whole thing quiet. JD and I were ordered to tell everyone she died." I swallow the hard lump in my throat, the one threatening to choke me to death even as I confess my greatest sin. "So we did. The story was that she'd fallen in the bath and hit her head. We were never allowed to speak of it again. He didn't even let me visit until I agreed to come home permanently."

I'd had my own small revenge by meeting with his young ingénue in secret. Using a combination of paying her off and threatening her, I got her leave to town and never return. It was all I could do not to strangle the girl with my bare hands. Had she not accepted my offer, I might have done it, too.

"Why did you go along with it?" he asks quietly, no judgment in his tone.

It's a fair question, one I've asked myself often. "I think it was fear as much as anything. I was in shock, not to mention scared out of my mind. He made it seem reasonable. She could be here, out of harm's way, get the help she needed—the best help money could buy. It didn't even occur to me at the time that even if the treatments worked, even if she got better, that she could never come home again. And even once I put the pieces together, I wondered if it was what she would have wanted. She got out of the life the only way someone really can—by dying. She was free. That thought is the only thing that lets me sleep at night." I laugh dryly, remembering the unopened bottle of laudanum on my nightstand. "When I can sleep, that is."

"And what about you? Do you want out of the life?" he asks. I tear my gaze away from Mother long enough to meet his eye.

"More than anything," I admit. His gaze is so intense I have to look away again. "I thought I could do it, Benjamin. I really did. I thought I could step into the business and keep my family safe. But I can't. I thought I could be, if not happy then at least content. The idea of getting out now is like a daydream, something you hold onto just to keep the reality from driving you crazy. But that's not in the cards for me, Benjamin. And even if I could leave it all behind, I wouldn't. I wouldn't abandon Daddy and JD—no matter what they've done."

"There must be some way…" he begins.

Mother looks out the gated window and toward a hummingbird sipping nectar from a honeysuckle bush nearby. I stand, dusting off my skirt. "The only out is through, Benjamin."

Crossing the floor, I take a seat on the bench beside him.

"The doctors think she suffers from some form of schizophrenia. Her first treatment was sterilization. After that, they began other things, removing teeth and pieces of her intestine and liver. They even tried fever and water therapies. Nothing had any effect. Eventually, she became catatonic. Now she is just this…most of the time at least. Sometimes she has to be strapped down for days at a time when she has an episode."

Benjamin's hand slithers across the bench and onto mine, squeezing it tightly.

"Masie, I'm so sorry."

I feel a tear slide free, and I hurriedly wipe it away. It upsets Mother when I cry. Though she doesn't speak, I can see it on her face.

"I think that's part of the reason Daddy wants to keep me close. He'd never say it out loud, but I think he's afraid I'll turn out like her. That I'm sick and don't even know it."

I don't see him move, but I can feel it like the wind changing direction. His arms wind around my shoulders, pulling me into his chest. I turn to face him, resting my head in the crook of his neck.

When he finally speaks, his voice is strong, confident. "Masie, I don't know how things are going to turn out for either of us, but I do know you're the strongest person I've ever known. And no matter what happens, I'm not leaving you. I'm not going to let you end up like this. I swear it."

I let him hold me like that for a long time, the sunlight warming our backs. It's so selfish of me. He'd been so close to making his escape—to getting out. But the thought of having to do this alone, to be here without him, it's suddenly too much. Every dark fear I've ever had coming back to haunt me. I'm just like my father. Poison to everyone around me.

Somehow, in the blink of an eye, Benjamin has become my rock, the touchstone that keeps me sane in all this madness.

Eventually, a soft sound draws me out of his embrace. Mother is rocking slowly in her chair, her head tilted toward us, a ghost of a smile playing on her lips as she hums a familiar tune, the lullaby she'd sung to me as a child. Then I realize her eyes are unfocused, her pupils wide.

Part of me doubts she is even aware we're here, but part of me, the unyieldingly hopeful part, wonders if she sees us and can somehow feel the comfort Benjamin brings me. Maybe, in her own way, she's offering us her blessing.

BENNY
TWENTY-THREE

THE DRIVE BACK TO MANHATTAN IS LONG. MASIE SPENDS THE bulk of it leaning against me as I hold her, wrapping my arms around her like a blanket. She tells me stories about her mother—tales of happier times, when she was young and before her father took over the business. She describes their humble home, the way her mother used to play the piano at night while Masie sang for her father and brother. I hang on each word, on each memory, and her words are so achingly vivid it almost feels like I was there. When we hit the bridge, she sits upright.

"I'm absolutely famished; should we stop for lunch?" she asks.

I point out the window. "I know a great place not far from here, but I don't think it's your sorta crowd."

She narrows her eyes. "Oh? And what *is* my sorta crowd?"

I grin. My challenge had been deliberate, and I'd known even before I spoke that she'd take the bait. "Oh, you know. No fancy waiters or bottles of champagne. It's a working fella's sort of place."

"So it's a dump?" she bites back, smirking. "Sounds perfect."

I rattle off the directions to Albert, who frowns but

says nothing. When we reach the place, he pulls the car to the curb. I help Masie from the car and into the shop.

"B/G Sandwich Shop? Is this one of those cafeteria places?" she asks, taking a spot in the long line of folks waiting to order.

"It is, in fact. A meal in a minute, that's their slogan."

The line moves quickly. Soon, we are standing in front of a row of mailbox-type windows. Walking up to one, I dig a quarter out of my pocket and put it in the slot. The box springs open to reveal a sandwich wrapped in white paper, a bag of French fries, a bottle of soda, and half a dill pickle—all on a small grey plate. She slides it out hesitantly while I repeat the process at another window, retrieving my own food.

There are a handful of tables, but each is occupied so we spill back out the door. I lean against the hood of the car. Masie pokes her head in the window where Albert sits reading the paper.

"Albert, would you care for a sandwich?" she asks loudly.

He lowers the paper, then looks at the sandwich as if it might bite him instead. "No, but thank you, Miss. I'll wait."

"You're missing out, Al," I say, unwrapping half my pastrami sandwich and taking a huge bite.

Masie circles me, handing her plate to me before sliding onto the bulbous car hood and crossing her legs daintily. Once in place, she holds her hands out, taking the plate and setting it neatly in her lap. Taking a bite of her sandwich, she chews slowly, her eyes scanning the people hustling past as we eat.

"What do you think?" I ask, taking another bite.

She swallows. "It's not bad at all." Lifting her bottle, she hands it to me. "Can you open this, please?"

Taking it along with mine, I walk back to the door and the bottle opener affixed to the brick exterior. I pry them open, the fizz rising and spilling just over the tops as I return to the car. I hand one to her, and she takes a long drink. The bubbles rise and she coughs, half spitting the liquid all over herself. I can't help but laugh as she struggles.

Finally recovered, she wrinkles her nose. "Not the kind of bubbles I'm used to."

"It's an acquired taste," I say, handing her a napkin. "Kind of like that grey goop you fed me at dinner with Zelda."

"The caviar?"

"It was disgusting," I say, taking a drink of my own.

She shrugs. "What do you expect from fermented fish roe?"

I cough, the bubbly liquid shooting out my nose when I close my mouth against the eruption. She grins devilishly, tossing the napkin back to me.

I have to put my plate on the car to wipe off my face and the lapel of my suit. Finally, I just strip the jacket off, rolling up the sleeves of my white shirt against the heat.

"Feeling warm?" she asks, taking a bite of pickle.

"Yes, as a matter of fact. Aren't you?"

She lifts her plate with one hand and kicks her feet playfully. "The only advantage to women's clothing. We at least get a breeze every so often."

"Lucky you," I say, laying my jacket in the backseat before returning to her.

"We should go to the shore, Benjamin. We could take a swim, maybe sit under an umbrella, sip cocktails and pretend we're in the South of France."

"Alcohol, heat, and partial nudity—that absolutely sounds like something your father would approve of," I tease. When her smile falters, I realize I've said something very wrong. "But sure, if you wanna go, I'll take you. It sounds fun."

It's then I see it. Something catches her eye and her chin snaps up, her entire body going rigid at the sight. I turn quickly, trying to follow her line of sight, but all I see is a crowd of people bustling down the sidewalk. Instinctively, I step in front of her.

"What is it? What did you see?"

She slides off the car, thrusting her plate at me. "Nothing, just..." She hesitates. "We should go."

I open the door and usher her safely into the car before dumping the plates and food into the return bin and sliding in beside her.

Albert doesn't need any encouragement. As soon as the door closes, he revs the engine to life and peels out into traffic, to a chorus of blaring horns. We speed down the road and Masie stares out my window, scanning the faces as we pass.

"What did you see, Masie?" I ask again.

She shakes her head. "I swear I saw..."

Her voice trails off, her mouth slamming closed in a hard line as she locks onto someone in the crowd. Turning, I see a familiar face. Though I've never met him personally, I've seen him hanging around Dutch—and of course, his face is regularly splashed across all the papers seeing as until very recently, he was wanted for murder.

"Vincent," she whispers. Albert turns the corner and he's gone, a ghost in the street.

Once we are clear, Masie sits back, visibly shaken. "Albert, take us home."

Albert obeys with a nod and Masie folds her arms across her chest, staring out her window.

"Why don't you tell me about this fella," I suggest. "I should probably know what to look out for."

She turns to me, frowning, but nods once. "Vincent—Mad Dog, that is—is Daddy's enforcer. Only recently, he's gotten..." She lifts her hands, as if struggling to locate the right term. "Greedy," she decides finally. "He wants to take over the business. He got it in his head that the way to do that—and keep everyone loyal to my family still on his side—would be to marry me."

Sitting back from the verbal blow, I whistle.

She continues. "I refused, of course. As if Daddy would ever allow such a thing in any case. But, well, let's say I know him well enough to know how he thinks. He's not great with subtly, or patience for that matter. I expect he'll make his move as soon as Daddy gets back from Chicago."

"Does Dutch know?"

She nods once, folding her hands and interlacing her fingers. "Yes, and I suspect he's got some measures in place to deal with it."

Her face pales, the rose blush bleeding from her cheeks.

"So why do you look so nervous?" I have to ask, the feeling in my gut warning me that she's holding something back.

Her eyes flicker back up to mine. "To be frank, I'm not sure which of them will win this battle, but either way, I lose."

"You still care about him?" I press, leaning forward.

She clears her throat before answering. "I keep telling myself I shouldn't. Keep reminding myself he's my enemy now. I suppose it's hard to reconcile how much he's changed. And the worst part is I'm not even sure if I'd save him now, even if I could. I honestly just want it all to be over."

I chew the inside of my cheek, processing her words before I speak. "People aren't all good or all bad. And caring for people—even people who do bad things—it doesn't make you a bad person. Just the opposite, Masie."

"The problem with caring about people is that they always let you down, you know?"

All I can think about in that moment is Dickey, how I'd taken the rap for him. How, even after what it cost me, I'd probably do it again, too. For better or worse, he's like a brother to me. And deep down, we are all capable of doing terrible things for the people we care about.

"Not everyone will let you down, Masie."

She snorts. "I'll believe that when I see it."

I open my mouth to say more, but the car jerks to the side of the curb and comes to an abrupt stop, nearly flinging me forward in my seat. I step out, holding my hand

163

for Masie behind me.

She slides out of the car, purse tucked under one arm.

"Are you alright here for a bit?" I ask. "I need to go check on Aggie. She's coming home from the hospital tomorrow."

She smiles. "Of course. Give her a kiss from me."

Then, without warning, she leans forward. Resting one hand flat against my chest, she kisses my cheek. In that moment, everything slows down, the space between heartbeats aches deep in my chest. She pulls away, just a bit, her black lashes grazing her cheek as she blinks, then she exhales, looking back up at me. I close the space between us before the next beat of my heart, one hand wrapping around to cup the back of her neck, the other at her waist, drawing her closer.

I shouldn't. People can see. Someone will notice, and tell her father. I could lose my job—or worse. Even as part of me demands to pull away, another, much louder part, refuses to care.

Her lips part beneath mine and I taste her for the first time, cherry soda still dancing on her tongue. For a moment, I'm afraid I've made a mistake. A small voice in the back of my mind screams for me to release her, but my fingers refuse to obey. Then I feel it, her smile against my mouth, the line of her body relaxing against mine as she takes the side of my face in one cool, open hand. When she draws back, her lips swollen and flushed with color, she grazes her hand across my jaw, her thumb catching my bottom lip and chin as she pulls away.

Without a word, she takes two steps back, spinning on one foot and waving to the doorman. He opens the entrance for her. Before I know it, she's gone, vanished inside, and I'm standing there, grinning like an idiot.

Behind me, Albert clears his throat loudly. "Would you like a ride to the hospital?"

I shake my head, retrieving my jacket and hat from the front passenger seat. "I think I could use the fresh air, but thanks."

He smirks and disappears inside as well, leaving me to slide the fedora onto my head and step off down the sidewalk. I haven't gotten far before a voice calls me from the shadows.

"Well, Benjamin, I think you and I need to have a little chat," O'Hara announces, stepping from the space between two buildings.

MASIE
TWENTY-FOUR

I PRACTICALLY DANCE INTO THE APARTMENT. TOSSING MY purse aside, I kick off my shoes and twirl on my tiptoes all the way to the French doors.

"Can I get you something, Miss?" Butler asks, but I wave him away.

"No, not right now, thank you." I snap my fingers, thinking better of it. "Wait. Music. Bring out the Miki-phone, will you? I want to listen to some jazz."

He vanishes and I toss myself into one of the lounge chairs near the edge of the patio, tucking a pillow under my head so I can stare at the clouds passing overhead. Butler returns with the silver pocket phonograph Daddy had gotten me when I went away to school and a stack of discs.

He selects one, my favorite of late, and gently releases the needle. There's a moment of scratch, then the first clarinet cries out, followed by the deep bassoon. The trumpets and French horns join, the sounds weaving together in a playful dance as *Rhapsody in Blue* wafts its way into the air, the melody wrapping around me like a velvet cloak.

Each long draw of the violin, each delicate note of piano, mingles in a bluesy chorus, spilling the soulful emotion of the piece over me like rain. Each crash of the cymbal is like a strike of lightning, each thump of the bass drum like a roll of thunder—a perfect storm of sound.

As the music ebbs and flows, I close my eyes, soaking in the sound and sun. When I open them again at the end of the song, Butler has left a dry martini on the table beside me. Sitting up, I take a sip just as June floats onto the terrace.

"Masie, where on earth have you been? I've been looking for you all day."

I slide my feet to the ground, and she falls into one of the high-back chairs around the dining table.

"Why? What's happened?" I ask, a swell of fear rising inside me.

She shrugs off the delicate embroidered shawl covering her shoulders and lifts the hem of her skirt, plucking a miniature flask form her garter and helping herself to a long sip before answering.

"JD's gone to meet your father at the train station. He's coming home early. Supposedly, there's some sort of big news."

I raise my glass, my nervousness evaporating quickly. "He must have made the deal for the new club. Good, that should keep him occupied for a while."

Staring at me sharply, June narrows her eyes. Pointing my direction, flask still in hand, she says, "You look different. Radiant, in fact. Did you finally take that handsome piece of man into your bed?"

I flush at her words. June, never one to pull punches, has had at least a dozen lovers—that I know about. It amuses her endlessly to casually toss such suggestions my way. I'm far from a prude, but I'm not a vixen like her, either. Trying to sound casual, I wave her off. "Don't be silly. I haven't the time or the inclination to complicate that particular relationship."

I'm lying; it might as well be written across a billboard on Fifth Avenue. Just our short kiss had set my heart racing in a way I've never felt before, like gunfire at the Brighton Beach Race track, the one that sends the thoroughbreds sprinting across the track. Even now, just the memory of it is enough to bring a warm blush to my face.

June raises one pencil-thin eyebrow. "Whatever you say, doll. I know that look."

I bring my shoulder forward, lightly touching it to my chin. "Well, I never said it wasn't a lovely idea."

"Aren't they always?" She chuckles and takes one more drink before returning the flask to her garter.

"Do you have any idea when they'll be back?" I ask, standing and lifting the needle of the Mikiphone, plunging us into near silence.

She shrugs. "No tellin. JD said they're doing a business dinner with Alistair and Lucky first. I don't expect them till late. What about you—no show tonight?"

I shake my head. "There's a dame in from Jersey tonight, a special feature. I have the evening to myself."

The news makes her sit forward and clap merrily. "Oh Masie, we should go out on the town. We could see a show or hit up one of the speakeasies on Ocean Parkway. Maybe we could wander over to that place that does feather fan dances. We'll get right up on stage and join in, just like old times."

I take a deep breath through my nose, exhaling it slowly. Truthfully, none of that sounds like where I want to be tonight. Licking my lips, I thrust the thought of Benjamin from my mind.

"How about dinner in Tribeca, then a show? And if we still have our feet after that, we can surely find some sort of trouble to get into."

"Dinner at Delancey's in SoHo? Then we can go see *The Jazz Singer*. I know you like that one."

I pause. Truthfully, it is one I've seen a few times and have quite a soft spot for. Something about the way they actually include the music into the reel makes for a stunning theater experience.

"Oh." I snap my fingers. "I forgot, I gave Benjamin the night off. I have no guard to accompany us."

She gives me a withering look. "Since when has that stopped us? You used to try to lose your guard as a matter of principal."

I chew my bottom lip, debating how much truth to reveal. "With everything going on..."

June's expression doesn't change. "Mas, there's always something going on. Always some reason for Daddy to keep his precious Canary locked up in her gilded cage. Besides, I'll be with you the entire time. There's strength in numbers, you know."

I tap my fingers on the table. She's right; the danger today is no worse that it normally is. I doubt very much that Vincent would do anything to put me directly in danger, and I'll be far from Daddy and his crew in any case. June and I have snuck out dozens of times over the years. The worst thing that happened was a one-night stint in jail after being rounded up in the raid of a local speakeasy.

As if sensing victory, June presses forward. "Masie, let's go have fun. Take your mind off your father and Benjamin and whatever else has that scowl set in your face. You need it. Lord knows I need it. It's practically medicinal."

She has a point. I've been burning the candle at both ends for as long as I can remember. A night out actually sounds like just what the doctor ordered. "Oh, alright. Let's change into something fabulous."

She grins wickedly. "This town won't know what hit it."

THE MELT-IN-MY-MOUTH STEAK DINNER SOMEHOW DOESN'T taste as good as my humble sandwich earlier in the day, and I can't help but wonder if it's the company that makes the difference. I push the last bite of potato around my plate, half listening as June recounts her latest melodrama.

"And so I told her... darling, it's nineteen-twenty-seven, not the dark ages. Flappers are brazen by nature. Are you even listening, Mas?"

"Of course," I say, looking up from my bone china. "You were traumatizing a saleswoman."

June rolls her eyes. "Well, you could be a bit more enthusiastic. It's bad for my ego when you sound so desperately bored of me."

I release my fork and wipe the sides of my mouth with the linen napkin. "Not bored, never that. Just distracted."

"You've got it bad, don't you?" she asks, raising a glass of champagne to her lips. "Not that I can blame you. He's absolutely delicious."

"It's not that, it's the new club," I say, which is only partially true. "It may be a feather in JD's cap if Daddy hands the reins over to him, but it's just a ball and chain for me. One more thing shackling me to this town."

She perks up. "And what's wrong with this town?"

She waves her hand toward the room around us, a room filled to the brim with boozy debs and their slick-talking daddies, with bearcats and bohunks, everyone dressed to the nines for an evening of decadent food and hot music. The city practically pulsates with the energy of the night, a living, breathing thing, mesmerizing and enchanting.

Once, what feels like a lifetime ago, I, too, had been under its thrall. But now when I look around, I feel outside of it, as if separated by a pane of glass. I can see it, but it no longer touches me the way it once had.

"It's the city that never sleeps," she continues, raising a toast, which I take part in, not because I feel inclined to do so, but more out of a sense of obligation.

The problem with never sleeping, as I've come to discover, is that the weariness eventually takes its toll. That's what's happening now. I'm weary of all of it.

"Come on," I say, pushing my seat back from the table. "We'll miss the show."

We bramble arm in arm toward Broadway, stopping every so often to admire the latest offering in the shop window or to bum a cig from a passing Joe. When we finally get our tickets and wander into the theater, the lights are already down, the room dark as we fumble to find our seats.

The opening title card flickers to the screen.

In every living soul, a spirit cries for expression—perhaps this plaintive, wailing song of jazz is, after all, the misunderstood utterance of a prayer.

The film rolls on, telling the tale of a young fella eschewing the path his father laid out for him. After a severe beating, he runs away for the bright lights of California to fulfill his dream of being a jazz singer. He finds himself and makes a life he's happy in until tragedy and longing bring him back to the streets of Harlem—and the father who disowned him. They make peace, of course, and while it's not a happy ending, it's at least one of hope.

It's a shame the real world doesn't offer the same opportunities for redemption and forgiveness. Normally the final frame brings me a kind of peace, as the young fella takes up the mantle his father had always wanted for him—leaving his own dreams in shreds for the sake of his family.

But tonight, my stomach rolls, a familiar desire rising inside me. The desire to burn it all to the ground—the business, the club, all of it. If I can't escape the life, I can at least live it on my terms.

The film ends and June discards her ticket stub as we exit the theater, stepping back into the night air. Sliding her arm through mine, she grins wildly.

"Whaddya say, Mas? Night's young and the whole world is our oyster. You up for getting into a little trouble?"

"I think trouble is just what I need tonight," I admit, leading her down the street, through the crowds, and toward a certain burlesque club.

Despite having been here before, neither of us know the ever-changing password to gain entrance, but June manages to flirt with a couple of fellas who do and they lead us in. Once inside, we quickly ditch the boys and make our way backstage where a middle-age woman with grey curls stands with a signup sheet on a clipboard.

"We'd like to dance," I say boldly. June is at my side, giggling nervously.

She looks us over once, nodding in approval. "Your names?"

I glance to June before responding, "Lady Lola and Duchess."

The woman raises one eyebrow, but scribbles our phony names on her sheet. With a wave, she leads us back into the dressing room. It's obscenely hot inside, the odor of sweat and perfume mingling in a wet, sticky fog. Rows of mirrored walls reflect the bright lamp light, and a long table down the center of the room with chairs at each spot is covered with various bits of costumes, props, and makeup.

The woman points to the far wall and a set of trunks. "There are some costumes in there. You can use whatever you like. The fans are in the closet. You'll each dance for one song—Lady Lola will go first. Dougie, the stage manager, he'll tap on the far door three times before announcing the next girl. There's only three ahead of you, so better get ready quick. If the crowd likes you, the door pays thirty-five cents. If not, you get nada. Got it?"

We nod in unison.

She folds her arm across her chest. "You gals ever danced before?"

June snorts. "Of course."

The woman grunts her disbelief but releases us to the dressing room. There are a handful of other girls in various states of undress wandering the room. Three taps on the door sends one of the girls in a tall, black-feathered hat and long fur coat toward the door at the back of the room. Taking a deep breath, she throws it open and steps out onto the stage.

The crowd goes wild, cheering and whistling. In another moment, the music begins.

"Well, let's find something to wear," I say, releasing

June and heading for one of the empty seats. I quickly deposit my hat and jacket, stripping down to my pink lace bra and panties. June heads straight for the costume trunks and pulls out a handful of long, beaded necklaces and a pair of white fishnet stockings and matching garter.

"For you," she says, dropping them on the table in front of me. One of the other dancers slides a box across the table toward me as well.

"Don't forget these, sugar."

I quickly pluck out a pair of beaded, flower-shaped pasties and the small bottle of gum arabic with which to attach them before sliding the box to June.

"I can't believe you agreed to this," she muses, taking out a set of her own. "Considering the last time."

I smirk. How could I forget? It'd only been a few months ago. On JD's eighteenth birthday, she'd dressed up like a cabaret girl and popped out of a giant cake. I'd had to help her dress and apply the pasties, something I'd sworn I'd never subject myself to after having to help her remove said pasties later.

"Well, it sounds like a gas," I admit. "Besides, I've gotten used to being on stage, commanding an audience, as of late. This is going to be old hat, really."

"Just the same." June hands me a delicate white feather mask, the sort that covers just the eye area. "Best wear this so your daddy don't find out you've been parading around with the Follies. He'd tan you good, and probably Benny too, for not keeping a better eye on you."

It's only her last words that convince me to accept the mask from her fingers. Part of me hopes Daddy finds out—the careless, rebel part of me—but the other part—the part that wins the argument—only wants to keep my actions from reflecting on Benjamin, especially when I'm about to ask to keep him as my full-time guard. Yes, better that Daddy never knows. After all, I will know, and really, that's all that matters.

June and I dress quickly. She opts for a slinky chain-mail type of costume, a vaguely Egyptian-looking brazier and long skirt with slits all the way up both sides. She draws long cat eyes and piles on the rouge before choosing a set of peacock feather fans. When her knock comes, we are all but alone in the dressing room, the other girls having either performed and left, or have gone out to mingle with the clubgoers to make a few extra nickels.

I hear the stage manager announce June to the crowd, and a cheer rises. She offers me a flirty wink before opening the door and stepping out on stage. I can't see what's happening, but judging by the roaring crowd, she's well earned her thirty-five cents for the evening.

I clench my fists. It's not that I'm nervous, not really. It's the same warmth spreading through me now that does every time I step on stage. When I stand under the bright house lights, singing, I'm baring much more than my body—and I feel just as naked then as I do now. Truthfully, the first time I'd sang in the club, I'd been so nervous I'd nearly gotten sick afterward. Then, it became more like a thrill, seeing how I could sway the crowd, how I could bring them to tears or to the very edge of ecstasy with only my voice.

The novelty of it all had faded fairly quickly, though. As good as I am on stage, performing isn't my true love. I find I'm much happier alone in my room reading philosophy or poetry than standing in the spotlight with all eyes on me.

Even as I think it, the song ends and the crowd roars. The stage manager knocks, then announces me, the mysterious Duchess, to a round of applause. Tying the mask across my face, I straighten myself and open the door, taking my place behind the red curtain.

When the lights dim, I step out, covering myself completely with the creamy white ostrich feathers, then the house lights come back up, red and white and fixed so brightly on me that at first I can't even see the audience. The first slow beats of music fill the air and I let myself move to the rhythm, swaying and flicking the fans in turn, revealing just a bit, just a tease, of my body beneath.

Finally, as I move, the crowd becomes clear, and in that moment, I know I've captured them. There's no cheering, no whistles, just face after face of abject awe. Wide eyes, open mouths, person after person, both male and female faces leaning forward in their seats, straining to get a better look. I spin gently, waving the fans to expose my mostly bare backside, then step forward, sauntering with each footstep accentuating the strike of the piano, each hip punctuating the beat of the drum. Their energy fuels me, and each sway becomes more confident until I melt away, leaving behind a living flame, all my inhibitions burned away in a blaze of desire—mine, theirs—the energy of life.

I haven't felt this alive in a very long time.

I wave and spin, each motion giving them a little more, and a little more, building to a crescendo of raw need. Finally, as the last notes soar through the air, I reveal myself, but only for a moment, smiling suggestively before covering myself once more.

The audience goes crazy, leaping to their feet, shaking the walls with their enthusiastic cries.

Another sound cuts through the madness. Before I can make sense of what's happening, June and a fella I recognize as Benjamin's friend Dickey, rush the stage, dragging me back through the curtain.

"It's a raid," he yells over the chaos, taking my arm. June pushes us toward the fire exit.

"Wait, our clothes," I say, struggling against them. "We can't go out in the street looking like this."

Dickey curses under his breath. "You two go, I'll get your stuff and meet you."

"You don't know what's ours," I say, planting my feet indignantly. "I'll go."

June cuts in, taking my other arm. "Are you blotto? You want your daddy to have to come bail you out of the clink looking like that?"

I sigh. She's right, obviously. "Fine."

They release me and I follow June out the exit, spilling

onto the street with nothing but my feather fans to cover me. She drags me down the street into the dark shadow between two buildings. Shivering against the night air, I watch the door, silently praying that Dickey can escape with our clothes before the Johnnies bust him. As soon as I see him spill out the door, I sag in relief. June steps into the street, waving him toward our location.

He stuffs a pile of clothes at us. "Here. I wasn't sure what was yours so I just grabbed everything I could carry."

"Great," June says, taking the clothes and waving her fingers at him. "Well? A little privacy?"

He snorts. "Not to be uncouth, but I just saw both of you in nothing but your birthday suits. I think the time for modesty has passed."

She narrows her eyes, and he turns his back to us with a sigh.

Unfortunately, none of the clothing was, in fact, ours. Still, we slide into two dresses that must have belonged to the other dancers and quickly discard the fans and beads down the alley.

Once we're fully covered, June sighs deeply. We both dissolve into a fit of nervous giggles.

"I'm glad you find this amusing," Dickey says, turning back to us. "What on earth were you doing in a place like that, anyway?"

"Probably the same as you, just looking to have a little fun," I say, adjusting my hair. Then another thought seizes me. "And if you breathe a word of this to anyone…"

I don't have to complete my threat. He raises his hands in surrender. "Don't worry. No one would believe me anyway."

I poke him in the chest. "I mean it. Not a word to anyone."

Now he grins. "Oh, I get it. You don't want me to tell Benny. Well, that's gonna cost ya."

June cuts between us, batting her eyelashes. "What'dya have in mind?"

He looks past her to me. "Well, I was thinking, how

about a promotion?"

I sigh. With men, it almost always came down to one of two things, ambition or sex. I can't help but be glad he'd chosen the former. "Done."

He grins, holding his arm out to June. "In that case, how about I escort you fine ladies home?"

BENNY

TWENTY-FIVE

THE NEXT DAY, I REPLAY O'HARA'S THREATS OVER AND OVER IN my head as I make my way toward the penthouse to pick up Masie.

"*Seems like you undersold your position in the Schultz organization,*" *he hisses.*

I shake my head, frantically trying to think up an excuse for what he'd just witnessed. "No, sir. I'm still just a bodyguard, as I said."

"*Miss Schultz seems to have taken quite a shine to you.*"

I frown. "Oh, no, she's just…" *I wrack my brain for some way out of this conversation.* "Flirtatious."

"*Even so, this is a great opportunity for you, son.*"

"How so?" *I ask, not really wanting the answer.*

"*You have unprecedented access to the family. You're bound to hear things… If you should decide to share those things with me, well, I'd be very grateful.*"

I stop walking, turning to face him fully. "As I've told you, I'm not privy to any information that might help you. I don't know anything about their business dealings. I'm sorry."

He grabs my arm, pulling me in close. "Maybe not yet. But you will get me the information I need. If you don't… well, let's just say a fella with a record like yours is likely to reoffend. And it'd be a damn shame if something were to happen to your family while you were behind bars again."

Something inside me snaps at his words. "Are you threatening me? My family? What kinda cop are you?"

When he answers, his eyes are dead, void of emotion, his voice matter of fact. "The kind of cop who will go to any lengths to get scum like Dutch Schultz and his ilk off the streets. And you'd do well to remember that, Benny."

Releasing me, he steps back, a sour grin spreading across his face. "Now, you just keep yourself close to that ripe tomato, and I'll be in touch to hear what you can ferret out. Oh, and just so you know, Schultz keeps a ledger of his business dealings. Anyone who might come into possession of that ledger could be in for a big-time reward. You keep that under your hat, though."

I clench my jaw against the memory as I hop the trolley uptown. The real question is should I come forward with what happened? Would Dutch see it as a betrayal, see me as a potential rat? Would my honesty earn me a reward, or a one-way ticket back to the loading docks, far from Masie and any secrets I might learn? And even worse, if I don't give O'Hara something to use against Dutch, would he make good on his threat to have me thrown back in the clink?

My head aches with questions. By the time I reach the penthouse door, the only thing I'm certain of is that no matter what I choose, someone I love could be hurt. There must be a way out of this pickle, but it's going to take time to figure it all out, so until I do, I resign to say nothing.

I fully expect Rudy to open the door, so when it's Dickey's face I see, it takes me a minute to recover myself.

"Dickey, what are you doing here?" I ask, looking him over. His trousers are wrinkled, his shirt askew, half untucked, one suspender up, the other dangling haphazardly at his waist. His hair is a mess, his eyes rimmed in red.

Basically, all the signs he'd gotten blotto, then fell into bed and passed out. Only, why had he done so here?

"Oh, Benny, what time is it?" June calls from across

the room.

I follow the sound of her voice and find she's lying across the sofa, Masie half sprawled in her lap. Their faces are flushed, eyes drooping, still in the clothes they must have worn last night and looking all the worse for the wear.

My gaze swings back to Dickey, who is looking at the girls and smiling slyly. I slug him in the arm.

"Mind telling me what you got up to last night?" I demand.

Dickey shrugs, fixing his other suspender and running a hand through his hair before answering. "Not much really."

I lower my voice. "You know I'm supposed to be looking after Masie. If anything happened that I should know about..."

He blinks, widening his eyes innocently. "I ran into the girls after dinner." He hesitates, and I immediately recognize the telltale tone he uses when he's lying. "We had a few drinks and then came back here. That's all I swear."

Taking him by the arm, I mutter an excuse and drag him into the kitchen. Rudy is bustling around, setting up a tray of coffee.

"I know when you're lying, Dickey," I accuse.

He just shrugs, and I know I'm not going to get any more out of him. Say what you will about the fella, but he can keep his mouth shut when it matters. Which reminds me of something else.

"Fine, but I've been meaning to ask you—the other night at the club, when you were supposed to be watching the street, did you see anyone come in the back entrance to the club?"

He frowns, shaking his head. "Nah, why?"

I frown. It doesn't make a huge difference now, but part of me still wants to know who attacked Masie, so I can make him pay. An irrational thought, but there it is.

"We just came out the back way after her show, and I

didn't see you."

"I mighta gotten distracted by a choice piece of calico," he jokes, tapping me in the chest with the back of his hand.

I slap it away. "It's not a joke, Dickey. When you're on watch, I need to know that you're actually looking out. Anyone coulda gotten in that back door. Someone coulda gotten hurt."

"I knew it, you're sweet on that dame. Can't blame you, really…"

He doesn't have a chance to finish the thought because I pop him in the side of the face, not a hard slap, but a sharp one nonetheless. "I mean it, Dickey. I need to know you've got my back here."

He steps back, looking genuinely offended. "You know I do, Benny. Always."

I nod. "Good."

"And for what it's worth, I think she's sweet on you too."

It's all I have not to press the issue, not to dig for a reason behind his words. Had she said something to him about me? Instead, I opt to try to play it off. Mostly because he's not wrong, not about me anyway. I'm over the moon for that girl. And I'm pretty sure that nothing good will come of it. The idea that she might feel the same, well, I can't decide if it makes it better or worse.

"Yeah, well, keep your opinions to yourself about it."

"Don't you worry about that. I know all too well what a dame like that can do to a fella's heart."

Brushing him off, I return to the now-vacant living room, then follow the sounds of people chatting out onto the terrace. Rudy is fixing a cup of coffee for June, who is draped over one of the lounge chairs, her eyes hidden in the crook of her elbow.

"Long night?" I ask, helping myself to a handful of grapes from a bowl on the table.

She half lifts her arm, looking at me with one eye. "You can say that again."

"Where's Masie?" I ask, scanning the terrace but finding no trace of her.

"She's gone to wash the gin off," June says with a dry laugh. "And where were you last night? You missed an absolute riot."

Behind me, Dickey helps himself to the coffee Rudy has left behind. A maid bustles in with a tray of muffins and he winks at her, taking one and popping it into his mouth before returning to stirring the cream.

"I was visiting my sister in the hospital," I lie smoothly. I'd stopped in only briefly on Ma and Aggie, too shaken from my earlier encounter to be any real company. Then I'd spent the rest of the evening cleaning and washing the blankets on Aggie's bed in anticipation of her return home. The mindless work had been enough to keep me busy—distracted.

And the girls had taken advantage of my absence to go out on the town to get into who knows what kind of trouble. My instinct is to chastise them, to remind Masie how dangerous it is to wander out alone, but I bite my tongue. She doesn't need a lecture from me, and apparently Dickey had tagged along, so they weren't completely unchaperoned at least. But I make a mental note not to let the matter repeat.

Rudy interrupts, holding a silver tray out to me. "A message for you from Mister Schultz."

I take the folded letter, reading over it quickly.

"Dutch wants us to meet him for supper," I announce. "Masie, June, JD, and me."

"What time?" Dickey asks, reading over my shoulder.

"Five. But I don't recognize the address."

"Oh, that's the new place he just bought. It's on Fifty-Eighth Street," Dickey offers. "I helped a crew clear out some old timbers and furniture last week."

"He's opening a new club for Masie," June interjects, her arm still draped across her face. "His trip to Chicago musta gone well."

I read over the note once more, then hand it back to

182

Rudy, who bustles out of the room. "Can you let JD know, June?"

"Oh, I suppose. If he's not here, he's probably holed up in his little apartment downtown. It's closer to the club, so he crashes there on late nights. He bought it for me, in fact, but I prefer it here. So much more elbow room." With a deep sigh, she sits up, swinging her feet to the ground. "Let me get changed and I'll head over there. I haven't seen him in a few days, and I'm sure he's missed me terribly."

"I'm sure you're right," I add quickly, remembering her remark about fishing for compliments.

She grins at my words, then steps into my arms, offering me a warm, if unexpected, hug. Kissing me once on the cheek, she whispers in my ear. "I expect you to join us next time."

"Count on it," I say, releasing her to Dickey, who quickly drains his cup and holds an arm out to her.

"I'm about to make my way home, too. Can I walk you down?"

She takes his arm and the two slink out the French doors, leaving me alone on the terrace with the chirping birds mingled with the sounds of the congested city below. Fixing myself a cup of joe, I walk to the edge of the building, leaning against the stone wall.

The breeze blows in from the east, and the scent of the river is thick and mossy in the warm air. I let it sweep over me, mussing my hair, as I tilt my face up to the sunlight. I can't help but wish Dickey had remained behind. I was hoping to confide in him about my predicament—hoping he might have some idea what I could do to wiggle out of the spot I found myself stuck in. Betraying Dutch was as good as a death sentence—not to mention I'd lose Masie forever. But on the flip side, how could I justify putting my family in danger yet again? With Aggie only just beginning her recovery, who's to say she doesn't backslide, maybe irreparably this time, if Ma has to go back to scrounging extra shifts at the cannery. And that's best-case scenario. I may not know much about Agent O'Hara, but one thing is abundantly clear—he's a man willing to go to any lengths to get what he wants, and I very seriously doubt he'd stop at hurting innocent people.

I'm so lost in my own thoughts I don't hear Masie creep up behind me. It's not until the wind changes, carrying the fresh floral scent of her to my nose, that I glance over my shoulder. She is already so close she leans against my back, wrapping her arms around my midsection and resting her head between the blades of my shoulders. Closing my eyes, I allow myself to revel in the feel of her. I slide my hands down her arms, twining her fingers in mine.

"I should be upset with you for going out without a guard last night," I say finally, unable to hold my tongue any longer.

"And are you? Upset with me, that is?"

Her voice is soft, a whisper, but also firm. There's no shame in it, no regret.

Turning in her embrace, I face her, tipping her chin up with my thumb. "No, I know you're very capable of taking care of yourself, despite what your father might think. But I just wish you didn't have to. I wish I could be there for you every moment, so you never had to be alone again."

"Benjamin," she begins. But hearing my name on her lips unravels my resolve, and I quickly seize her mouth with mine.

In that moment, there's no distance between us—no reason there should be. I'm just a boy and she's just a girl, and everything feels right in the world.

As usual, it's not long before reality crashes in and she pulls back, dragging her thumb across my bottom lip before releasing me completely.

"Daddy's home from Chicago early. He left a few hours ago, but before he did, I spoke to him about keeping you on as my guard. He's promised to think about it. I want you, every minute. I may not need you to protect me,

184

but I want you to. I feel safe when you're with me. And that's something I haven't felt in a really long time."

I want to kiss her again. The desire spreads through my veins like wildfire, but I stand firm, settling for reaching out and brushing a still-damp tendril of yellow hair off her face, tucking it behind one ear.

"I got a note from him when I arrived. He wants to see us, all of us, at the new club for supper."

The smile falls from her lips, quickly replaced, but it's enough to give me pause.

"What's wrong?"

She shakes her head. "Nothing at all. He's been working on this deal for some time. I knew it was coming..." Turning her back to me, she heads to the coffee cart. "I guess I didn't really expect it to happen so soon. There were issues with the labor unions." She waves her hand in the air. "You know, things had to be negotiated before the renovations could begin."

"Well, it sounds like he got it all worked out," I offer, crossing to the table and pulling out a chair for her.

She fixes a cup and takes the seat. "Yes, it does."

I sit across from her, putting enough distance between us that I'm not tempted to touch her, even though everything inside me demands to do just that.

"You don't seem too pleased about it."

She lifts the cup, looking at me over the rim before taking a sip. "It's not that. It's just...I suppose I'm a little nervous about starting this new endeavor."

She's tiptoeing around something, I can tell that much, but I'm unsure how much to press so I settle for offering my support. "Well, is there anything I can do? Any way I can help?"

She smiles, and it's real. Genuine and relaxed. It's not like the smile she normally uses, not the one I see her offer from the stage or to her friends. It's somehow smaller and bigger at the same time. "Just being here helps, thank you."

I nod, taking another handful of grapes from the bowl and popping one into my mouth. "So, is there anything else you'd like to do today? Because I had a thought, if you're up for it."

Sitting back, she crosses her legs, the slit in her silk robe falling open to expose her bare knee. "What did you have in mind?"

I swallow the grape whole, nearly choking on it as I drag my gaze up to her face. "I was thinking I'd like to take you to Coney Island for the day, if you're interested."

Her face lights up, and my chest swells. "That sounds delightful. Let me go and get ready. We should pack a lunch, so we can picnic at the beach. Will you let Butler know?"

I stand, checking the pocket watch at my side. "Swell. We can be back in plenty of time to get changed for supper with Dutch. Oh, and I've been meaning to ask, how come you call Rudy *Butler?*"

She laughs. "Rudy? Is that what you call him? I suppose he loves that. Um, well, I suppose it's what Mother always called him, so it just sort of stuck. Do you imagine he's terribly offended by it?"

I consider her words. "Honestly, I doubt it matters much to him either way."

She makes a face. "I will speak to him on the matter. Later. My hair isn't going to do itself."

"I think you look perfect as you are," I say honestly. Her hair, naturally wavy as it is, is drying into soft, bouncy curls. The bruise along the side of her face has mostly faded, leaving behind a greenish tint.

She points at me. "June has been a terrible influence on you, you know? Thirty minutes, that's all I need."

Rudy and I pack a basket of food. By the time we're done, Masie steps into the kitchen, perfectly done up. Her hair is bone straight, bobbed to just above her shoulders, a simple lace ribbon tying all but her fringe bangs back. She's changed into a short-sleeved blouse with a gauzy grey scarf and matching wide-leg slacks.

"Are we ready?" she asks, leaning across the marble countertop.

I hold up the basket. "We are now."

MASIE
TWENTY-SIX

"*I HAVEN'T BEEN TO CONEY ISLAND SINCE I WAS A CHILD,*" I admit as we make our way toward Brooklyn in the new subway line. It's crowded with people—mostly businessmen on their way to lunch. There are only a few children, grasping tightly to the rail, making their way toward the amusement park with parents in tow. It's impossible to squelch my excitement. The best part of the crowds, there will be no one watching, no prying eyes who might go whisper back to my father. Today, I can just be a girl, out at the beach with a boy she adores.

"Oh?" Benjamin says. "I took Aggie and Thomas a few summers ago. We rode the roller coasters until we were all so sick we couldn't even look at food for two days."

I grin at the thought of him, green and ill, stumbling across the beach with the little ones nipping at his heels.

"Daddy let me ride the carousel. JD wanted to ride the horse, of course, but I was determined to ride the camel. I seem to remember that I actually raced to it as soon as it was our turn in line, and I knocked some poor child out of the way to get to it first. I'd say I'm not proud of that, but it'd be a lie." I grin.

"Typical Masie," he says, his tone joking. "Always getting what she wants."

187

I have to look away before my expression can betray me. *If only that were true.*

When we finally arrive, the place is bigger than I remember. As we spill out onto the street, I squint against the sun, hurriedly crossing the bridge leading toward the dreamland tower and lagoon. Ribbons, banners, and flags flap in the breeze where they hang from every spire and rooftop along the boardwalk. The entire place is teeming with people, nearly shoulder to shoulder. Reaching out, I take Benjamin's hand so we don't get separated in the chaos. We stop just long enough to drop off the basket in one of the penny lockers and purchase a fistful of ride tickets.

"They've just opened a new rollercoaster," Benjamin says, pointing toward a towering wooden beast of a ride down the boardwalk. "The Cyclone."

"Well, what are we waiting for?" I demand, dragging him toward the entrance.

WE RIDE THE COASTER TWICE BEFORE I NEARLY LOSE MY VOICE from screaming in delight and decide we'd best let it recover if I'm to have any hope of performing at the club later. Stopping at one of the many game tents, Benjamin hands over a quarter in exchange for three softballs, which he lobs at empty milk jugs one at a time. Finally, the last toss hits them just right and they fall. The mustachioed game operator claps and pulls a large stuffed bear from the pile behind his booth.

Benjamin stops him. "Actually, can we get the camel instead?"

The man shrugs and makes the exchange. Benjamin quickly thanks him and hands the plush animal over to me.

Something swells inside me, an uncontainable joy, and I throw myself into his arms. He stiffens for only a moment before returning the embrace.

"It's wonderful, thank you."

He nuzzles the side of his face into my hair and kisses the tender skin behind my ear, a quick peck, but more than enough to reignite the passion I'd managed to hold at bay since our first kiss.

Forcing myself to release him, I blush furiously, turning away before he can see.

He takes my hand again and we wander further down the pier, stopping every so often for a game or small ride. When we finally stop, I realize where he's been leading me. To the crown jewel of the park—the giant Ferris wheel.

Handing our tickets to the operator, we slide into a car, strapping ourselves in. The wheel spins just a bit, letting the next load on, until we reach the tip top, the entire city skyline to one side, the vast ocean to the other. In the distance, the Statue of Liberty peeks through the clouds, torch in hand, welcoming ships as they pull into the harbor. It's then that Benjamin drapes one arm across my shoulders, leaning in.

"Isn't it beautiful?" he whispers.

I can only nod in agreement…until I turn to see that he's not staring at the view at all, but rather at me. This time, when our lips meet, the fire is instant and all consuming. His free hand moves to my hair, and I press myself into him, as close as I can manage in the confines of the chair. I'm not sure how long we neck, but it's long enough that I lose track of everything—time, space. I can't even tell whose air I'm breathing.

I know we shouldn't; I know it's dangerous. Daddy would never let me keep him as a guard if he found out— if he didn't lose his temper and beat him half to death. Still, I can't stop myself. And here, in this place, it feels safe. Alone in a crowd.

I'm lost in the moment. Lost in Benjamin's embrace.

The wheel begins moving in earnest, and in that moment, he pulls away, practically growling in frustration as we slice through the air, up and down. He leans one arm over the rail, discreetly taking my hand with the other.

"I'm sorry, Masie," he says, shaking his head. "I know I

shouldn't—we shouldn't—but I can't seem to control myself."

I tighten my grasp on his hand. "Please don't apologize."

"But I should. I should be sorry. I know we can't..." He leaves the thought unfinished.

"I'm not sorry," I say, jutting my chin into the air defiantly. "Not even a little."

He sighs deeply, like a great weight has settled onto him. "What do you want from me, Masie?"

Everything. The thought comes without hesitation, the voice in my mind strong and determined. I want him in every way one person can want another. I want everything he can give me and everything he can't. But that's not fair of me to ask. Not when I've already taken so much.

"I want whatever you're able to offer," I decide. "And I'll take it, with no regrets."

He looks down at our entwined hands, rubbing my knuckle with the pad of his thumb.

We don't speak for the rest of the ride. He just holds my hand in silence. Occasionally, his eyes flicker up to catch mine, emotions rolling across his expression like the tide. When we step off, my legs are weak and wobbly, and not from the ride.

"I need to sit down," I admit, clutching his arm.

He leads us down the remaining boardwalk toward the beach, depositing me on a bench near the umbrella rental stand.

"Why don't you sit here a minute? I'll go get lunch, and we can have a picnic in the sand."

I smile half-heartedly and he marches off, leaving me to stare at him until he vanishes into the crowd.

The beach is packed—as always this time of year. Some people simply stand in the sand, chatting, making castles, or staring out at the blue beyond. Others frolic in the surf, splashing and laughing. A nearby beach patrol cop pulls a group of bathing suit-clad ladies aside, whipping out his tape measure to make sure their shorts are long enough to adhere to the public decency laws.

When a person plops down next to me, I'm sure that it's Benjamin and I turn to remark on his speed. Only, it's not him at all.

I nearly leap from my seat in surprise.

"Oh, Vincent, you startled me."

He grins wickedly.

"What are you doing here?" I demand, trying to sound normal, as if the proximity to him isn't making my skin crawl. "Following me again?"

He shrugs, stretching out and crossing his legs at the ankles. "Just keeping an eye out. Oh, and I brought you something."

He hands me a brown bag and I open it, revealing my clothes from the night before, the ones I'd abandoned at the follies during the raid.

In that instant, my mouth goes dry, my chest constricting painfully.

"You were a vision," he says, his words practically dripping with lust. "I'd always wondered what you looked like, if your skin was as white as I imagined."

It's all I can do to withhold the bile rising like acid in my throat. How had we come to this? Once upon a time I'd run to him, the sound of his voice filling me with joy. How had we come so far?

"What do you want?" I demand again, determined not to let him see how his words are sickening me.

"Who's the new boy toy?"

"He's my guard," I say flatly, dropping the bag in the sand beside me. There's no way any of those clothes will touch my skin again, not now that Vincent's had his hands on them.

He laughs, a sour dry sound. "Is that what they're calling it nowadays?"

"Yes, he is my guard, and unless you want him to report to my father that you're harassing me again, I suggest you go before he gets back." My voice trembles on the last word, betraying me.

"Are you afraid of what your daddy will do to me, or are you afraid of what I'll do to this bum for putting his hands on ya?"

Taking a deep breath, I straighten my shoulders. "Stay away from us."

He grins again. "I'm meeting with Dutch tonight. Should I mention the little display I saw today? Or would you rather take odds on what dirty errand he's going to have me run this time?"

"He knows you're moving against him," I say, the words coming out in a hiss. "He'll never trust you again."

He seems completely undaunted by my threat. "Maybe. But he still needs me. Even if he doesn't know it yet."

With that, he stands, brushing off his one-piece bathing suit. "If you'll excuse me, I'm going to go take a dip before I head back to the city. Be seeing you, Mas."

As soon as he's gone, I break out in goose bumps, crossing my arms over my chest and rubbing my arms to stave off the sudden chill. I only have a few moments to compose myself before Benjamin returns.

"Everything okay?" he asks, holding the basket out to me.

I open my mouth, not entirely sure how to answer.

BENNY

TWENTY-SEVEN

MASIE IS UNUSUALLY QUIET ALL THROUGH LUNCH, HER EYES continually scanning the crowds of beachgoers. When we finish, she gathers her scraps and a brown bag I don't remember seeing before, depositing it all in a nearby waste bin.

"We have a few tickets left," I say, trying to gauge just how upset she is with me.

She shrugs. "Save them. You can bring Aggie when she's feeling better."

I've clearly upset her, and I silently curse myself. It wasn't my intention to hurt her feelings, but I clearly have as she's barely speaking to me, much less meeting my eye. I reach out to take her hand to lead her back to the subway, but she flinches at my touch. Everything in me wants to pull her close, to drive away her doubts by kissing her until we're both senseless. But I don't. My inability to keep my hands to myself is what got me in this situation in the first place, and I don't think she'd want me to besides.

She's gone cold, and it's entirely my fault.

Even worse, I have no idea how to make it better.

We step onto the subway car, squeezing into the cramped space at the very back. There's no seats open, so

193

we clutch the bar, our fingers just barely touching. It's only then that she looks up at me again, her expression unreadable.

The train starts with a jerk. She pitches forward into my chest, and I catch hold of her with my free arm. I fully expect her to pull away, but she doesn't. Instead, she remains there, unmoving, her head on my chest and my arm around her waist, all the way to our stop.

My arms are reluctant to release her, even to pick up the now-empty basket and make our way back to the penthouse. The whole way, I'm mentally cursing myself for not being able to come up with something clever, witty, or reassuring to say.

When we reach the elevator, she turns to me.

"Thank you for today; it was lovely."

I laugh dryly. "Yeah, right up until I ruined it all."

She blinks, then takes my arm. "You didn't ruin anything. You only asked what I wanted from you, and all things considered, it was a more than fair question."

"I know we can't..." I struggle for the right way to say it. "Be together, not really. But sometimes when I'm with you, I forget. It doesn't feel impossible when you're beside me."

Dropping my arm, she looks away from me before responding. "I know. I feel it too. And I don't mean to lead you on, truly. I'm just being selfish, I suppose. I don't mean to put you in a difficult position."

Her matter-of-fact tone is so dry that it makes me instantly regret saying anything all. When the door opens, we see JD and June having a drink in the living room. June's got her glad rags on, and she sparkles from head to toe in caramel-colored beads, a stark contrast to the condition in which I'd found her this morning. The record player is spinning a slow, jazzy tune, and JD, ever classy in his formal suit, swirls a glass of brown alcohol before downing it in one swallow.

"Benny, glad you're here," he says, ushering me in and offering me a drink, which I politely accept.

194

I take a long drink, hoping it will at least help calm my frayed nerves. Instantly, it warms me, offering a temporary respite from the chilly conversation I'd just endured.

"My father has brought back some interesting news."

"Oh?" I ask, taking another drink.

Masie pokes her head between us. "I'm going to change. You boys stem the gossip until I get back."

JD rolls his eyes. "As if you won't hear soon enough as it is." Then, once she's skipped from the room, he lowers his chin, whispering, "We had a meeting with Alistair last night. He's brokered a deal that will link our organization with the Luciano family business. It's a huge feather in our cap. Not only do we now control all the trucks in and out of the city, but we also get access to their local brew houses and distilleries. Plus, the combined forces guarantee that no one else in the city is strong enough to move against us."

"Wow, that's great. What do they get in the deal?"

JD grins into his glass, which is full once more. "Mostly properties, a handful of trucks, and a few other minor perks."

The way he says the last bit makes me instantly curious, but I don't press. The less I know about the business, the less I can be forced to hand over to O'Hara.

He slaps me on the back. "And I know Masie wanted to keep you on as her new guard, so I took the chance to put in a good word for you last night."

"Thanks, I appreciate it."

He shrugs, as if it's nothing. "Things are going to be in flux with the transition. Some of ours will go to work for them, and vice versa. Plus, the new club and a new numbers racket we're going to be operating jointly in Harlem. Plenty of new positions to go around. You sure you wanna settle for babysitting my sister?"

I finish my drink quickly, setting down the empty glass. "I'm sure."

Turning from me to June, who is swaying to the music, he sets his glass beside mine and crosses the room to her, taking her by the hand and dancing with her.

He whispers something and she giggles, spinning in his arms.

I hear something, barely audible over the spinning record. A soft, melodic humming. I remember the tune from our visit to the asylum. Unable to stop myself, I follow the sound down the hall, stopping just outside Masie's closed door.

The humming turns to full-blown singing and I lean back against the wall, folding my arms as I take in the sound.

When the door flies open, I lurch upright against her surprised gaze. Her hair is fully waved, a silver sequined band holding a bundle of white and silver feathers to the side of her head. Her neck is wrapped in string after string of diamonds, dripping down the front of her like armor. Her dress, shorter than anything I've ever seen her in, exposes the top of her black stockings beneath a layer of fringe. Honestly, it's more like something I'd expect to see June in, but that's not a complaint. Quite the opposite, actually, as she looks stunning. Alluring.

Those poor suckers at the club tonight won't know what hit them.

"Did you need something?" she asks, tossing a mink stole over one shoulder.

I shake my head. "No, I just heard you singing. What is that song?"

She looks away, tucking a purse under her arm. "It's a German lullaby my mother used to sing to me. Der Mond ist aufgegangen. It means *the moon has risen*."

"It's beautiful."

When she looks back up at me, her expression is so sad I don't even try to resist the urge to console her. Stepping forward, I open my arms and she walks into them, letting me hold her.

"I don't know what the future will bring for us, Benjamin. Let's get through tonight, then we can deal with the rest tomorrow. Is that alright?"

"Of course," I whisper, kissing the top of her head lightly, hoping I can make good on all the promises I've made her.

WE ARRIVE AT THE NEW CLUB SITE JUST BEFORE EIGHT. THE last fragments of daylight are bleeding orange at the horizon, the first streetlamps flickering to light.

Watching the city move from day into night is like watching a butterfly emerge from a cocoon. Something which during the day is plain, dirty, and grey becomes bright and alive with colors and sounds. It's as if the city itself is born again at dusk, only to die each dawn before repeating the cycle.

I step out of the car first, holding the door for JD, then the girls. Masie follows her brother into the boarded-up door. There's not a single light visible from the sidewalk, all the windows are covered with boards and canvas tarps. Once inside, however, a string of bright work lights hang from the half-demolished ceiling. In the very center of the room, a long table has been set with a white linen cloth and two tall candelabras. There are a half dozen chairs. At each seat, there's a perfect setting of fine china. Chilling at each end of the table are bottles of champagne in silver ice buckets. Dutch is already there, leaning against the bar in deep conversation with Alistair Rothschild and another couple I don't recognize.

Dutch breaks off the conversation and approaches us, waving his arms in the air. "Isn't it incredible?"

JD chuckles. "Sure, if you like condemned buildings."

Dutch waves him off, turning to me instead. His enthusiasm and boisterous tone make my stomach flip flop, and he drapes on arm across my shoulder. "You can see it, can't you, my boy? We'll raise the ceiling and create balcony seating there." He points around the ceiling. "And over there will be the stage. There'll be poker in the back, of course, and roulette. The kitchen will stretch back that direction. We'll bring in the finest chefs in the country."

I have to admit, as he speaks, I can picture it in my mind. Pointing to the far wall, I add my two cents.

"And if you took out that wall, it would open up a nice dance floor. How far back does the building go?" I ask.

He smiles, patting me on the chest. "All the way to the next block. And we have all three stories. For opening night, I want circus girls, the kind they have at the follies, the ones who hang from the ceiling in hoops and cages. I'll dress them all in yellow feathers." He glances to Masie, who is taking everything in. "What do you think, darling?"

When she smiles at him, I realize it's not her real smile, not the secret smile she rarely shows anyone but me. It's her fake smile, her let's-make-the-crowd-happy smile.

"It'll be wonderful, Daddy. Just perfect."

"It'll put the other clubs out of business, that's what it'll do," Alistair chimes in, handing her a glass of bubbly. "And with you on the stage five nights a week, we'll pack them in."

She returns the toast he offers, but quickly turns her back to him, making her way around the piles of boards and buckets of paint.

"You have to admit, it needs more than a little work," JD says, clearing his throat. "That's all I meant."

"The crew arrives tomorrow to start demolition. Lucky thinks with his team in here, we could open in as little as a month. Whaddya say to that?"

Again, Dutch's question is directed more to me than to JD, and it puts me ill at ease.

I force myself to nod. "I think that's doable. It's the details that will make it great, though. The little things. Like the chairs at the other club, they're a little stiff. You might do more benches here, and perhaps even an area with couches where people can just sit and drink. Things like that."

When Dutch turns to the other couple, it's with an I-told-you-so expression. Holding one arm out toward them, he walks me over. "Let me introduce you to Charles

'Lucky' Luciano and his lovely gal Genevieve Dupre. Lucky, this is the kid I was telling you about, Benny."

I hold out my hand to shake. "Pleased to make your acquaintance."

"Likewise. Dutch told us you were the young fella who took lead for him first day on the job."

"Well, that's a bit of an exaggeration. It was my second week."

The bosses share a laugh. Genevieve joins in a heartbeat too late, her voice stunningly high and phony. It's June who saves the poor dame, rushing over and taking her by the arm.

"I'm June West. You simply must sit by me. I'm dying to hear all about how you came to meet Lucky." She swiftly ushers the girl toward the other side of the room, taking seats at the table.

Three waiters appear, each of them in white suit and tails, each with a silver tray in one hand, a white towel draped over one arm. The one in the center lifts a small bell from the tray and rings it once, loudly announcing, "Dinner is served."

We take our seats. Without deliberate thought, I end up elbow to elbow with Masie on one side and Dutch on the other.

Standing, he pulls the bottle nearest him free from the ice and clears his throat, passing it off to the nearest waiter, who opens and pours the drinks with the grace and speed of a practiced man.

"This club has been a dream of mine for some years now, since my darling wife passed away." He pauses, as if offering a moment of silence. Beside me, I can feel Masie tense. "And now, thanks to my dear friend and partner Alistair Rothschild, and his financial backing, I'm able to finally make this dream a reality. And, of course, none of it would have been possible without my new friend and ally, Lucky. So I'd like to offer this toast to old friends and new, and to the beginning of a new era for the Lucky-Dutch Organization."

We all raise our glasses. "Cheers."

When he sits back down, the waiters begin delivering the first course of food, some sort of white fish in a fruity glaze. The evening continues, Masie with her show smile engaging Lucky in pleasant conversation. If he weren't easily twenty years her senior, I might worry about the way his eyes follow her, the way he measures her every word, as if sizing her up somehow. It's still enough to set me on alert, my muscles constantly tense, my senses hyper-vigilant.

It's only as we are finishing up that I allow myself to relax.

"Oh, I do hope you'll come hear me sing tonight. You simply must," Masie says, taking a bite of whipped chocolate mousse.

Lucky sits back, tossing his napkin over his plate. "I'd love to, dear. But I'm afraid I have other engagements tonight. Nothing I wouldn't much rather set aside to see you, but its business. You understand."

She lifts her glass. "Another time then."

He nods once.

"Before we go our separate ways, I have one more announcement," Dutch says, standing again. "After giving the matter some thought, I've decided to task Benny with managing the Canary Club."

My head snaps up, my gaze settling on JD before I can stop myself. His face flushes, his mouth setting in a hard, thin line. But he says nothing.

"JD will help train you on the bookkeeping and such. But I want someone who I can trust, someone devoted to my family, to run my newest endeavor. And you get along so well with my daughter, who I'm sure will want to be involved in every piece of the renovation—after all, it's her club as much as ours."

I'm simply too stunned to speak. "Sir, surely there is someone with more experience?"

He waves me off. "And modest too. No, you, my boy, are exactly who I want at the helm of the Canary Club. I'll

200

be busy tending to some other new enterprises." He tilts his head toward Lucky, who returns the gesture.

Now it's JD's turn to speak. I'll give him credit—his voice is calm, his demeanor stoic. No trace of the rage that I'm sure must be boiling just under the surface.

"And what about me, your son?"

Dutch lowers his chin, his eyes narrowing. "Don't be petulant, boy. I have an important job for you as well." He uprights himself, his jovial smile returning. "And it's settled. The grand opening will be four weeks from tonight."

As everyone filters out of the room, I stay behind, shooting a glance at Masie as she heads toward the car. Her expression, like her brother's, gives nothing away.

"Sir," I call after Dutch. He's talking with the wait staff. "Do you have a minute?"

He pats the waiter on the shoulder and waves me toward the rundown bar. "I know this must have come as a bit of a shock," he says, lighting a cigarette. "But JD told me about how you caught the bartender who'd been skimming from the club receipts. Between that and the way they both raved about you, I knew it was the right call."

"I've never done anything like this before. I'm afraid I'll let you down," I admit, not adding my desire to continue as Masie's guard.

"Nonsense." He blows a cloud of smoke into the air. "You're honest, hardworking, and clever. And more than that, you see what this place can be. I have no doubt that between you and my daughter, you'll have this place ship shape in no time. And don't worry about the budget. The sky's the limit."

"To be frank, sir, JD should rightfully have this position. He's been running the other club for a while, and he knows his potatoes." I pause. "Plus, he just might kill me for taking it out from under him."

Dutch chuckles. "See, that's why I like you, my boy. Managing a club is about two things, the first to show people a good time. JD's got that down pat. But the second is responsibility. It's counting the receipts every night and making the deposits; it's making sure the schedule is made and the staff are on time and presentable. It's about organizing and promoting various shows and acts. JD treats the other club like his personal playpen, and he'll continue to do so. Besides, he's going to be working more with Lucky's people, dealing with the Indian Hop we're going to bring in from out west."

I rest one arm on the broken bar top. "Well, if you're sure this is where you want me, of course I'll do my best, sir."

He nods. "It is." He stubs out his Lucky and taps the bar with the palm of his hand. "Now, I'm off to a meeting with Lucky's people to make a similar announcement. You take Masie to the club tonight and keep an eye on her. I'll probably treat myself to a night at one of Lucky's creep joints to celebrate the deal."

He winks at me, and it makes me physically ill. "Of course I'll look after her, sir."

"Good, you scat now, the car's waiting."

BENNY

TWENTY-EIGHT

JD IS NOWHERE TO BE FOUND WHEN I REACH THE CAR. MASIE suggests he opted to walk, citing his need for some fresh air, though I'm sure there's more to it than just that.

"So much for my staying on as your guard," I say, attempting to break the silence building between us.

She sighs heavily. "I suppose we talked you up too much—not that you don't deserve the position, of course."

"At least it still sounds like we'll be seeing quite a lot of each other," I offer, earning myself a sad smile.

"We should talk about it tonight after my show," she says, her tone hesitant.

I chew the inside of my cheek, unable to stop the small rumble of disappointment at her words.

HER PERFORMANCE THAT NIGHT IS INSPIRED. SHE BELTS ONE jazzy tune after another, opting for one long set rather than two with a break between. Maybe it's the energy of the crowd that spurs her on, or the desire to lose herself to the stage, just for a while. She barely glances my way all evening, her eyes gliding over the audience instead.

It's late when JD stumbles in, June hanging on his

arm. He's already blotto, judging by the sway in his step and the slight slur in his words as he approaches where I stand, leaning against the bar.

He points a finger at me, closing one eye. "We need to have a talk."

I motion for him to join me in the back, hoping to at least keep whatever beating he's about to deliver from the prying eyes of the patrons.

Following him through the curtain, I tense, expecting the first blow to come fast and without explanation. But when he turns, I make no move to defend myself. I won't raise a hand to him, my friend, Masie's brother. That much I've already decided. I'll take my licks if it will somehow soothe his rage.

To my surprise, there's no punch, no angry words. He smoothes his hair with one hand and leans against the wall, as if the room has begun to spin and he needs the support.

"I want you to know I'm not angry with you, Benny," he says calmly.

I lean against the opposite wall, crossing my arms and ankles. "I wouldn't blame you if you were. I never meant for this to happen."

He nods, then, closing his eyes, takes a deep breath. "I know. Dutch has been trying to whip me into shape since long before you came into the picture." He grins, opening one eye. "And without much success."

When I say nothing, he continues. I'm not sure if it's the booze talking or if he's just in need of a friendly ear, but either way, I listen patiently.

"Dutch has this idea about what we should be, Mas and me. And no matter what we do or how hard we try, we never quite live up to his expectations. Ah, it doesn't bother me so much anymore; I'm used to being the family screw-up. I worry about Mas, though. She never wanted any of this, and I know she's not happy here. This new club, it's not about business—it's only about keeping her here, making sure she can never leave." He snorts. "The

Canary Club, more like The Canary *Cage*."

"I know she's unhappy; I can see that. I just want to help," I say, pushing off the wall and peeking out the curtain as she begins a new song. Her eyes flicker to me, a moment of concern crossing her face. I wave, just to let her know everything's alright, and she looks away, returning to her performance.

"You're a good fella, Benny. And I know you genuinely care about her." He steps forward, shoving his hands into his trouser pickets, wobbling just a bit. "The best thing you can do for her is to stay close. Help her make the club into something she can at least live with, if not love. She's been through enough."

"What about you? Is there anything I can do for you?" I reach out, drawing back the curtain for him to pass through.

On his way by, he pats me on the shoulder. "Oh, I doubt it, but thanks for the offer."

Masie finishes her song, making a beeline off stage toward her brother. They exchange a few words—I can't hear over the noise but it ends in Masie giving him a hug, so it can't be too bad—and she charms her way through the audience back toward me.

"Everything alright?" she asks, brushing past me toward her dressing room.

"Surprisingly enough, yeah. We're all right."

She glances over her shoulder at me, her hand on the doorknob. "I expected him to beat the berries outta you."

"You and me both," I admit, waiting outside as she steps into her dressing room, closing the door.

"Well, I'm glad you're alright," she calls. "I'd hate to have to put you in a hospital bed beside Aggie."

"Oh, Ma never woulda let me hear the end of it either."

"Which reminds me, when does she come home?"

I lean against the door. "Today, in fact. She's recovering so quickly, it's like a miracle. Ma was bringing her home today."

"Well then, why on earth did you waste the day with

205

me?" she asks. "Coney Island could have waited."

I pick at the peeling paint of the door with my thumbnail, scraping flake after flake free before answering. There are a million things I want to say, but it doesn't seem like the right time for any of them.

"You should come over tomorrow. I know she'd love to meet you."

The door opens, and I step back. Masie, still in her same dress, only with the addition of a long brocade jacket, steps out.

"I just may do that."

Taking the back stairs, we spill out onto the street. There's still a line of folks trying to get into the packed club, but we ignore them, turning the other way down the street to her car. Albert, who'd been leaning against it, pulls her door open and she slides in.

"Thanks, Albert," I mutter, taking my seat at her side.

"It was a great show tonight," I say as we pull away from the curb. "As always."

She waves one gloved hand. "They come to escape their problems, at least for a while. I'm happy to help them do just that."

"Are you? Happy, I mean?"

She turns in her seat, her knees toward mine, almost touching. "Sometimes. For moments, here and there. I suppose it's all any of us can hope for, in the end. What about you, Benjamin? Are you happy?"

My gaze sweeps over her and I realize, maybe for the first time, that my time with her has been some of the happiest in my life.

Rather than answer, I graze the side of her face with the back of my hand, trying to commit to memory the feel of it, the smooth warmth, the way her breath catches in her chest when I touch her, how her eyes soften, her lids closing just a touch, her lips parting. Whatever happens next, I want to keep the memory of it—of her—preserved forever like a fly in amber.

She catches my hand in hers, turning it over and leaving a chaste kiss in my palm, her scarlet lipstick stain the only proof that it ever really happened.

It's all I can do to keep my distance as we arrive, leaving behind the car and heading up the elevator to the penthouse. The lights are low when we make our way inside. Rudy, still puttering around in the kitchen, greets us in his robe.

"Miss, do you need anything before I retire for the evening?"

I could laugh. Evening? It's a few scant hours from dawn.

"No, thank you, Butler—I mean, Rudolpho."

Nodding once, he scuttles down the west wing to his room, abandoning us to the dim lamplight.

Masie takes my hand, weaving her fingers through mine, and pulls me down the hall to her room, pausing outside her door for only a moment before opening it and tugging me inside.

Her room is dark, and for a few heartbeats, that darkness constricts around me, making my heart pound furiously in my chest. I reach out for Masie, unable to see beyond my own nose, and I find her, her back pressed against the now-closed door.

A deep need seizes me, and I know that if left unchecked, it will run a riot over us both. Leaning against her, I run my hand down the wall, searching until I find the button, and press it. The electric lights flare to life, blinding us.

Once I can see again, I find her expression a mixture of longing and disappointment. Brushing past me, she steps further into the room. The distance between us is painful at first, the ache of blood behind a bruise, but it's better. I can breathe again in the absence of her.

"Masie," I begin, though I have no idea what I want to say. Part of me wants to lay myself bare to her, to beg her on my knees to be my girl. But I know that's impossible. I know that doing so would only break me—and that it might break her to do it.

"I'm only going to ask you this once, so I need you to be completely honest," she says, stripping off her gloves and draping them over the back of her vanity chair. "Do you want to be with me?"

I lick my lips. If she were looking at me, I'm sure the answer is written all over my face, but she's not. Her back is to me, her shoulders straight, her head high.

"We can't. Your father would never allow it."

Her tone is like dark glass, sharp and dangerous. "That's not what I asked," she snaps, spinning to face me.

I set my jaw, clenching my fists at my sides. "Yes. Of course I do. You know I do."

She turns away from me again, this time sitting in the chair as she begins stripping off her jewelry, piece by piece.

"My father trusts you. He's given you a great deal of responsibility in running the new club. Which makes me wonder, if, in time, he might be open to the possibility..." Slipping ropes of pearls off her head, she curls them into a wooden box.

"You think he might give us his blessing?" I ask, stuck somewhere between disbelief and hope.

She turns in her chair. "I think, if the club is a success, and if you continue to gain his trust, then it might be possible."

My mind reels at the thought. She may be right. As a simple errand boy, I'd been nobody, certainly nobody worthy of his daughter. But if I can prove myself to him, if I can become a real part of the organization, then he just might consider it.

There's just one flaw in that idea.

Agent O'Hara expects me to help him bring Dutch down. How can I justify putting my family at risk?

When Masie speaks again, her voice is as fragile as I've ever heard it. That alone draws me from my thoughts. "It will take some time, I realize. So I suppose, what I'm really asking is this—do you care for me enough to wait for me? Do you care enough to try?"

Before I can even think of moving, I'm on one knee

at her side.

"I can, and I will. I'll do whatever it takes," I say, and as soon as I speak the words, I'm overwhelmed with the truth of them. Whatever I have to do to earn my place at her side, whatever I have to do to keep O'Hara off my back and away from my family, I'll do it. For the first time in weeks, I truly believe I can.

Leaning over, she captures my face in her hands and kisses me deeply. It's not desperate or wild, as our last encounter had been. This is slow and calm. It's a promise being sealed.

When she draws back, it takes all my willpower to let her go rather than hold her to me. "In the meantime, we'll spend every moment together, working to make the Canary Club the best gin mill this side of the Mississippi."

"We'll do it together, and when it's done, I'll talk to Dutch about us," I pledge. By then, I'll be able to tell Dutch about O'Hara putting the screws to me. He'll know how to handle it. In the meantime, I just have to keep the detective at bay long enough to make myself indispensable.

Somehow.

MASIE

TWENTY-NINE

THE DAYS SEEM TO FLY PAST AS WE PREPARE FOR THE GRAND opening. Benjamin and I spend nearly every day, sunup to sunset, in the new building. He busies himself ordering tile for the floors and new brass rail for the bars, asking my opinion on every light fixture and chair covering. Somehow, he manages to make the process feel less like a chore and more like an exciting new adventure.

He even brings the twins in for lunch a few times a week. I spread blankets on the floor and we pretend to be sitting on a beach in the south of France while I nibble cucumber sandwiches and Thomas devours his weight in hot dogs from the cart outside. Agnes, it turns out, has a gifted ear, and I wile away my spare time teaching her to play the new grand piano as Benjamin watches us from across the room. I even teach her the lullaby my mother had sang to me as a child. Every time she sees me, she runs into my arms, burying her face into the crook of my neck when I lift her off her feet. I hum a few bars, and she hums the next. We sing the last line in unison, then I usher her off to sneak truffles from the kitchen as a reward.

Even his mother comes to see. The pride in Benny's eyes is unmistakable as he shows her his plans for the new kitchen, and she seems impressed despite herself.

It takes a few days to find a new band, and while Benjamin gives me complete autonomy to choose my new players, I do force him to sit with me through each audition.

We are always very careful of how we interact. The place is constantly crawling with workmen—both my father and Lucky's—and we are all too aware of their watchful eyes upon us, not to mention my once-again guard-come-chaperone Tony. Though, he quickly tires of sitting around, and it doesn't take much for me to convince him to leave me in Benjamin's care during the day. He'd been my guard once too, after all. Tony quickly agrees to meet me at the penthouse at night and escort me to the club. Though before I leave, Benjamin and I sneak into the back office in the guise of settling the day's accounts to spend a few stolen moments in each other's embrace.

It's a sweet torture, made bearable only by the hope of things to come.

Each night I sing, it's with a lightness I haven't felt in as long as I can remember. For the first time, I let myself relax in the promise of the future. Not the perfect future, not the future I'd imagined, but a future where I can carve out some measure of happiness for myself.

It's something I never dared dream possible.

Even Daddy notices the elevation in my spirits, commenting on it over breakfast one morning as I race to eat and make my way to the club.

"It might be time to ease off on the coffee," he teases as I bound onto the terrace where he and JD sit, both with their noses in the morning paper.

"The new stage is finally finished," I say, popping a grape in my mouth and squishing it with my tongue to release the sweet syrup. "Which means today we're going to hang the lights. I want to be there to make sure it's all set up properly."

Daddy folds the paper down, smiling. "I was thinking of taking you across the river today, maybe rack up some time in Atlantic City. We could go wander the boardwalk."

I feel myself freeze, my mind spinning with a way to reject his offer. Before I say anything, he leans forward, pressing the issue.

"Surely Benny can supervise without you for one day?"

I shrug, looking away. "Well, yes, but what does he know about stage lighting? I'd hate for him to get it all wrong and me just spend twice the time tomorrow fixing it."

For a moment, I think he's going to argue, but he just sits back. "I can't tell you how glad I am to see you enjoying this so much. I know you had your doubts about it."

Forcing a smile onto my face, I cross the room, throwing my arms around his neck. "It's going to be perfect, Daddy. You'll see. The absolute bee's knees. Everyone in town will be raving."

He pats my arm and I peck him on the cheek, winking at JD, who glances up at me for only a second before retuning his attention to the paper. "You should tell her," he says with an exaggerated sigh.

I glance from him to Daddy and wait. Daddy clears his throat, taking me by the hand. "Yes. You should know. Mad Dog came to see me last night."

I swallow a dry lump forming in my throat. I'd read in the paper that he was wanted for another murder, and part of me had been glad because it meant he'd be forced to go underground. I was hoping that meant he'd leave me and my family alone. I suppose I should have known better.

"He made some demands, a few outrageous accusations, and finally, leveled a very serious threat against us all."

That's it then, he's playing his cards. I feel my knees quiver under me, and I let myself lean against Daddy's chair for support. He squeezes my hand.

"I don't want you to worry, sweetheart. I spoke to the other bosses, and we've decided to deal with him once and for all. I know he was your friend, but he's got to be stopped."

I feel the air rush from my lungs, then I'm paralyzed from drawing another breath. Yes, I'd wanted him gone. But not dead. Never that. The room spins around me.

Daddy pats my hand. "Don't worry. The whole business will be over soon. I'm not going to let him hurt you, I promise."

A wave of sickness washes over me in a tide. Vincent will die, and Daddy will justify it as doing it to protect me. When in reality, I'm probably the only person in the world Vincent wouldn't hurt.

The whole matter makes me queasy.

"I should go," I say, standing and slipping my hand from his.

I spend the whole ride to the club wondering if there's something I can do, something I should have done that might have prevented this.

When I burst through the back door, Benjamin is already there. His gaze swings from a set of blueprints up to my face, his expression elated, until he sees me. I duck into the office and he's only a minute behind me, closing the door to the sounds of hammers and saws beyond.

"Masie, what is it?"

He doesn't hesitate, just takes me in his arms, his body instantly going rigid against me, as if tensing to defend me from some unseen foe.

I just let him hold me, forcing myself to draw in one long, slow breath after another before I can finally speak and not burst into tears.

"Daddy had a contract put out on Vincent." I hesitate, because there's no way to convey the weight of guilt that's threatening to crush me. "I never wanted this, Benjamin. I never wanted him dead. And now there's nothing I can do..."

He strokes my hair. "There never was, Masie. He chose his own path. Just like Dutch, just like all the others. He was never yours to save."

He's right, of course. I doubt anything I could have said or done would have made any difference. He wasn't a good person who did bad things. The capacity was always within him. You can't change someone's base nature, after all. The world might not be black and white, but I have to believe that there are those who fight their inner darkness, and those who embrace it. Vincent had always been the latter.

"I guess I just wish the world could be different," I say finally, forcing myself free of his comforting arms and wiping my face.

Grabbing me by the hip, he pulls me back to him, cradling my cheek in his other hand. "That's because you see the good in people. In all this darkness, you're the light, Masie. You're what brings me home."

His face dips, and I close my eyes in anticipation of his kiss. A knock at the door forces us apart, moments before JD bursts in.

"Dutch has decided to come by to check on the progress today, just thought you might need a head's-up," he says, glancing between us. "And I think he's bringing some of the other investors with him, so you need to be ready to show some real progress."

Benjamin nods. "Thanks."

"Ah, one other thing before I scram," he says, stepping into the office fully. He rounds the new mahogany desk and lifts his brown leather briefcase, popping it open with his thumbs.

"Here, this is for you." He slides a tall green-and-brown ledger across the desktop toward Benjamin. "For the books."

Benjamin takes it, running his fingers over the words emblazoned across the cover in gold lettering. *The Canary Club*.

"Thank you," he mutters, holding it as if it were made of gold rather than paper, leather, and glue.

"Sure thing," JD says, closing his briefcase back up and dragging it off the desk. He offers me a quick peck on the cheek before heading out the door, leaving us standing there in silence.

"We should get ready for Daddy," I say finally.

Benjamin frowns, but nods, tapping the ledger against the edge of the desk. "Right, of course."

BY THE TIME DADDY ARRIVES, WE'VE GOT THE PLACE AS PICKED up as we can in the organized chaos. The bulk of the renovations are finished, and the minor tidy-up work has begun. Teams of men finish hanging the chandeliers and affixing the embossed copper tiles along the ceiling. The walls, recently plastered, are getting fresh coats of paint. A team of craftsmen finish the scrolling in the wood beams that support the now-raised balcony seats. The granite bar top is polished to a shine, the new tables and chairs being unpacked in the back.

"Ah, she's looking beautiful, Benny," Daddy says, walking in with his arms raised over his head. "Just stunning."

Benjamin shakes hands with Alistair and Lucky, as well as a fourth man I've met but whose name I can't quite place until Daddy calls me over from where I'm supervising the hanging of the gold framed mirrors at the back of the stage.

"Masie, this is Artie Berman, Lucky's nephew."

Ah, of course. He's Jack Berman's son. I've seen his father around Daddy enough; it's the family resemblance that makes him seem so familiar. I hold out my hand and he accepts it, grazing a kiss across my knuckles. "I believe we've met, though I can't quite place where," I admit.

He smiles, his shaggy blond hair falling into one eye. "I'm certain I would never forget an encounter with such a lovely creature," he says finally.

Benjamin shifts his weight, then holds out one arm. "Can I give you gentlemen the tour?"

"That'd be wonderful, my boy," Daddy says, snapping his fingers at his guard. The man promptly pulls a cigar out of his vest pocket, clips it, and hands it and a brass lighter to him.

As Benjamin begins the tour, Artie holds his arm out for me and I take it gently. We follow the main group, hanging back a few feet. Occasionally, he whispers a question about a shelf or door and I murmur my answer in return. He seems genuinely curious about every detail, from the type of wood in the flooring to the crystal in the lamps. I watch him as he makes observations about this or that. He is obviously well educated and well traveled, which he makes known not too subtly by regaling me of a tale of a quarry he visited in Italy that boasts the most perfect blue-veined marble. The more he speaks, the more it's evident that he's trying to impress me.

I know my part in this game, and I play it well. I laugh at his jokes, and I listen intently to his stories. Though he's fair to look at, with a long, sloping nose, icy blue eyes, and a thin, graceful mouth, the more he speaks, the less attractive he becomes.

"Of course, I've never managed a club myself. Though I've had plenty of experience keeping the masses entertained at a few of my uncle's more lucrative tea pads."

I swallow, forcing myself to look away before he can see the disgust fill my eyes. The Luciano's are well known for their import of drugs into the city. The tea pads are nothing more than fancy opium dens with whores to keep the junkies amused. They are, in my opinion, the worst of both worlds.

The tour ends back in the main room, the area we've designated as the ballroom. The bar stretches in an L shape around us, and Benjamin waves everyone over to it.

"Would you care for a drink?" He whistles and one of the new bartenders steps out from the kitchen, wiping his hands on his white apron. "We don't have everything in yet, but there's a twenty-year-old bottle of whiskey that's just waiting for an occasion."

Alistair slides onto a stool, patting the bar in a here-here gesture. Daddy slaps him on the back.

"Well, it's a good thing that I have an occasion, then." Pulling the cigar from between his teeth, he curls one fin-

216

ger around it, using it to point to me.

"Masie, I was going to tell you tonight at dinner, but I never was much for being patient," he begins, drawing a laugh from the men around him.

"Lucky and I've discussed it, and he's proposed a more binding union between our families. I'm happy to say that young Artie here has asked for your hand in matrimony, and I've accepted on your behalf."

His words hit me like a brick, and my hand slides free of Artie's arm. I blink, trying to remember how to form words. Everything rushes at me at once. Had I heard him correctly? Surely not. It had to be a joke. I watch him, waiting for a crack of a smile to announce his foolery. But there's nothing. And the longer I stare at him, the more he flushes, his expression going from mild amusement to barely contained rage.

I don't look to Benjamin. I can't. The emotions battling for control of me won't allow it.

Shock moves through first, then confusion. Followed by the familiar spark of rage as it begins its slow burn. I clamp my mouth shut because I know if I speak my mind now, if I embarrass him in front of these men, he might actually kill me. Or worse.

Is there a worse? a rebellious thought demands. How could this possibly get any worse?

If he hits me here, in front of Benjamin, that would be worse. Because Benjamin would stop him, would take him on to save me. It would be as good as a death sentence.

It's only that realization that keeps my feet planted, my mouth closed against the fury.

"Well, we should go," Alistair says, laughing nervously. He, too, must sense what's about to happen. The powder keg inside me is barely restrained—threatening to blow.

"We will see you later, dear," he says, slipping from the bar and offering me a peck on the cheek.

"Of course, I'm so glad to welcome you into the family," Lucky says, doing the same. As he releases me, I fight to hold myself still.

It's Artie who approaches me next, and though he's careful not to touch me, he steps in very close, close enough I can feel his breath on my face as he speaks, his voice barely above a whisper. "I know it's a lot to take in. But I'm sure as we get to know each other better, you'll come to accept this is the right choice for everyone." When he kisses me on the cheek, my palm itches to slap him. He draws back, no mercy, no regret in his eyes.

And why should he care? He'll be free to see whomever he wants, to do whatever he wants, even after he's married. That's the way with these men. A marriage will unite the families in name, but that's all it is, another contract.

"I'll make the formal announcement tonight," Daddy declares, offering me a cautionary scowl. "Meet us at the club at nine?"

I lick my lips. Truthfully, I'd planned to spend my night off here, having a quiet evening with Benjamin. Now other options flow through my mind—like jumping off the Brooklyn Bridge.

It's not until I hear the door close that I scream, pushing past Benjamin, who reaches out to catch me, but I'm moving too fast. I race up the back stairs, spilling out onto the street and the harsh glare of afternoon sun. I don't stop, though. Racing through the crowds of people bustling along, I run, my feet hitting the pavement in perfect time with the pounding of my heartbeat in my ears. My lungs burn, my muscles ache, but I don't stop. Not even the sound of Benjamin's voice calling out can reach me now.

I race, full out, down Fifty-Seventh Street, all the way to the pier. My feet thunder across the concrete until finally, gasping for air, I reach the end, flinging myself against the steel cable barrier separating me from the Hudson River.

I scream.

Around me, dock workers stare, but I can't seem to make myself care.

Maybe someone will call the police, thinking I'm a lunatic. Maybe I am. Maybe they'll put me in a room next to mother.

How could I have thought there was a chance for me?

This isn't some fairy tale in a book. It's the real world and in the real world, happiness is a commodity that's sold off to the highest bidder.

I'd been so stupid. Of course Daddy would sell me off to secure his own business. It wasn't enough to chain me to his side with the new club. No, he'd have to use me as a bargaining chip as well.

"Masie," Benny calls, gasping my name. I turn to him, the wind taking my hair and brushing it off my face.

"It's no good, Benjamin. Don't you see that?"

He walks forward, holding his hands out the way a zookeeper might approach an angry tiger. "Please, Masie. We can figure this out."

Turning my back on him, I recite the poem to myself, truly understanding it for the first time.

Nature's first green is gold,
Her hardest hue to hold.

"Masie," he calls again, his desperation growing.

Her early leafs a flower;
But only so an hour.

"Masie, please. Come back to me. We will figure this out."

Then leaf subsides to leaf.
So Eden sank to grief.

"Don't you leave me, Masie."

So dawn goes down to day.
Nothing gold can stay.

"I love you."

I blink, the first tears spilling free from my eyes, rolling down my cheeks in a race against the wind, which dries them away. I feel his arms wrap around me, his lips on my ear, my neck, in my hair.

"I love you," he whispers again, his voice on the cusp of anguish.

BENNY
THIRTY

SHE TURNS IN MY ARMS, TEAR STAINS CUTTING THEIR WAY through her makeup.

"I love you," she whispers despondently, shattering me into a million pieces.

Leaning over I kiss the tears from her cheeks. "We will figure this out, Masie. I promise we will. Whatever it takes."

She laughs dryly. "Maybe it's just not in the cards for me, Benjamin. Maybe I'm not meant to be happy. It's my punishment for being such a terrible, spoiled, selfish person. Life hands me everything I've ever wanted just to take it all away."

I shake my head, unwilling to believe that God could be so cruel as to bring her into my life just to snatch her away again. She lets me lead her back down Fifty-Seventh Street, hand in hand as we walk, taking our time. There's no rush now. I'm sure she's engaged in the same mental battle as me, trying to think of a way out of this new situation.

"I deserve it. I do," she mutters. "I've done bad things, Benjamin. So many terrible things."

I shake my head, unable to believe her words. "You're not a bad person, Masie. You don't deserve to be in pain."

My first instinct is to take her by the hand and run away, to get on a train tonight and vanish entirely from this place. But it's a fool's thought. There are too many others to consider.

My family, for one, who would become a target not only of her very wrathful father, but the overzealous detectives to boot. Plus, there's JD and June, and I doubt she'd ever willingly leave either of them behind.

By the time we arrive back at the club, the first bands of sunset orange streak across the sky. I dismiss the workers and the cooks, leaving only her driver Albert, and he, in his quiet way, leaves to wait in the car outside.

Once we are alone, I drag her back into my arms, brushing the tousled golden hair from her face. "I'll speak to your father tonight, before he can make the formal announcement."

Pulling away, she sighs. "You won't change his mind," she says, retrieving our blanket from behind the bar and spreading it in the middle of the room as we have so many times. She sits, curling her legs under her, and pats the lace at her side for me to join her.

Once I do, she leans into me and I envelope her in my arms again, tucking her head under my chin. Her arms slide around my middle. Warmth pulses through me where our bodies touch, but I keep my mind focused on the problem at hand. The prospect of losing Masie is almost too much for me to bear.

"I have to try," I say, though I know the odds are stacked against me.

"No." She shakes her head, her cheek against my chest. "Let me try to talk to him."

Her words should make me feel better, but her tone is already sounding defeated, resigned.

"I won't lose you, Masie. Whatever happens, I won't let them take you from me," I say, instinctively tightening my arms around her.

"You won't lose me." Wriggling out of my grasp, she crawls onto my lap, straddling me.

Her dress rides up, baring her thighs, and I take a deep breath, trying to concentrate on finding a way out of this mess. But when she slides her hands up my chest to my shoulders and presses into me, her legs locking around my waist, I lose my battle with sanity.

Something erupts from deep within me, a primal, possessive need. As I kiss her, inhale her, marvel at the feel of her flesh under my fingertips, I know she belongs to me, and me to her. It spreads like wildfire, consuming me with each breath. When she finally pulls back, tearing her mouth from mine, I see the same desire reflected in her steel-grey eyes. Slowly, deliberately, she unties my tie, tossing the scrap of silk aside before turning her attentions to my buttons, her eyes never leaving mine. Pressing herself against me, she strips the shirt off my shoulders, then the suspenders, and finally, the white undershirt, leaving me bare chested and panting.

Reaching around her, I find the top of her zipper at the base of her neck. I peel it away slowly, the fabric of her blue dress separating under my fingers. She moans against my touch and I rise, kissing her bare shoulder as I draw the top of her dress free, exposing her white lace brazier.

I pause for a moment, unable to move, unable to breathe. Drinking in her beauty, I marvel at the complete ridiculousness that this goddess is mine. The hot pulse of need that has been slowly building in my abdomen quickens at that thought. *Mine.* I want to make Masie mine in every sense of the word.

I take my time then, exploring every inch of her, kissing the milky skin as I expose it. In one motion, I lift her and turn, laying her beneath me. When I finally come to rest beside her, I can barely speak. Pressure is built up inside me, a pleasure bordering on pain. Even so, I will go no farther until I'm sure.

"Masie..." Her name escapes my throat in a sort of growl. There are so many things I want to say, but my mind is too crowded to form a full thought. Instead, I slide my gaze down the length of her, marveling at each curve.

She props herself on one elbow, running her hand down my bare chest, her fingernails grazing my stomach, down into the top of my trousers.

This time I moan, unable to make anything other than the most basic, guttural sound as she unfastens my pants, tugging them down with one hand as I frantically try to assist.

"Are you sure?" I manage finally, my palm flat against the smooth skin of her stomach.

Her eyes shine in the soft yellow light, her lips parting as she licks them. "I don't want to be anyone else's, Benjamin. Make me yours."

And with that, I cast the final, frayed strands of my inhibitions aside and do as she demands.

AFTERWARD, SHE LAYS HALF DRAPED ACROSS MY CHEST, OUR legs entwined. Her hair, short as it is, is splayed across my torso. I roll a few strands between my fingers.

"You should probably go," I say, though it's the last thing I want.

She turns her head, dragging her chin along my skin. "I'd never move again if I could manage it. I'd just stay here, like this, with you."

She rubs herself against me and a familiar pressure grows, tugging at places below my waist.

"I don't want you to go," I admit. "But, nice as it sounds, we can't stay here forever."

She sighs. "I know."

"What are you gonna tell Dutch?" I ask, already planning my own plea for her hand.

"The truth," she says, sitting up. "That I'm wildly in love with you. That I don't know how to be happy without you."

In the absence of her touch, my skin cools instantly, a shiver working its way through me.

"Hopefully, I can convince him that my happiness is more important than his merger," she adds, frowning.

"I'm coming to the club tonight; I'll talk to him too. Maybe between the two of us..." I can't count on Dutch to bow to either of our wishes, that much I already know. I keep wondering if there's something else I can offer him, something I can do to win him to our side. The problem is that I have nothing he wants. He's holding all the cards.

We dress slowly, neither of us quite ready to let go of our time together. I try to console myself in the knowledge that despite the situation, it's not goodbye—not really. Even if Dutch won't budge, we still have weeks, maybe months, before any wedding might become a reality.

Wedding.

The thought of it turns my stomach.

No, I'll have to figure something else out. There's time. Maybe I can cut some kind of deal with Detective Dewey; he seems more reasonable than his counterpart at least.

We dress slowly, putting ourselves back together as much as we're able to before closing up the club and heading for the car. The thoughts continue to tumble through my head as Albert drives me home, dropping me off outside my door.

Throwing caution to the wind, I pull Masie across the seat into a long, slow kiss before I finally release her and exit the car. She presses a hand to the window, and the car speeds off. I barely have time to turn toward my door when O'Hara steps around the corner.

"A little birdie tells me you've climbed up the ranks with the Schultz gang," he begins, a toothpick gnashed between his teeth. "I gotta admit, I never took you for a mountaineer."

I wipe one hand down my face, pulling the door open and beginning the ascent up the stairs to our apartment.

He follows me, never more than a step behind.

"So, you've had a few weeks, what've you got for me, Benny? Because I've got something for you."

Stopping midstep, I turn. "Whatever you have, I don't

want it."

He pulls the toothpick from his mouth, looking affronted. "Is that any way to show your gratitude? Why don't you invite me in and we'll chat about it?"

He follows me up the last flight of stairs and I stop at my front door, pulling out my key.

"Just keep it down; the twins are sleeping," I say, stepping inside and holding the door for him to follow. It's not like I have a choice, clearly.

"And yer ma's on shift. I know," he says, pushing past me and helping himself to a seat at the kitchen table. "I know."

I suck in a breath, gritting my teeth. "You're watching them now too?"

He leans forward, resting his elbows on the table, then kicks the chair opposite him out for me to take a seat in. "I find it helpful, when dealing with informants, to know exactly where to apply the pressure. Then it hit me." He snaps his fingers. "You might not be afraid of going back to the big house, but you'd probably do anything to keep your sweet ma outta the clink."

I sit, turning the chair backward so my chest is resting against the back. "What are you flapping your gums about? Ma ain't done nothing wrong."

He clicks his teeth together twice, then leans back in his chair. "Not exactly true. Seems she never paid her taxes last year. It'd be a shame if someone brought that to the attention of the special prosecutor. Oh wait, that's me."

"You're bluffing," I say, trying to sound more confident than I am.

After Pa passed she tried to keep up with the finances on her own, but it's completely possible it'd slipped her grief-ridden mind.

He raises his hands as if to say, *am I though?* "If she ended up behind bars, your little brother and sister would probably be hauled off to the city orphanage—seeing as you aren't legally old enough to care for them." He wrinkles his nose. "Unpleasant place, that. I doubt little Agatha would get the medical attention she needs from the state doctor."

"What do you want?" I manage finally. Whether the accusation is true or not, I realize it doesn't really matter. He'd just make up whatever he needs to make me pay if I refuse him.

"What can you offer?" he asks finally, folding his arms across his chest.

I shake my head. "I haven't seen the ledger." Then, I realize that's not entirely true. "But I have seen a new one, the one for the Canary Club. There's nothing in it that will help you."

He makes a face, wagging his head back and forth. "Not yet, maybe. What else ya got, kid?"

My mind races. What can I say that won't endanger Masie and JD? What is the most and least I can offer? And moreover, is there a way to use anything I might know to my advantage?

"I know that Dutch just inked a deal with the Luciano family. Rothchild brought them together to edge the other families out of their territories."

He licks his lips, but says nothing.

"I know that the Lucianos are going to be using Schultz trucks to bring Indian hop into the city from the west to fill their tea pads."

He raps his knuckles on the table. "I need something else, something actionable."

"Like what?" I demand, raking my fingers through my hair.

"How about this—where are they storing the booze for the new club?"

I swallow. I could lie and say I don't know, but it's such a small thing, a drop in the bucket compared to anything else I could say. And at worst, it puts us behind a day as we shift to take our opening-night supply from one of the other stashes Dutch has all over the city. "It's not in the club yet. They're keeping it warehoused down by the 92nd pier, in the old textile plant."

He nods once. "Good enough, for now. But what I want is the ledger, so here's the deal. You make sure it's in the club on opening night. We'll set up a raid, and you and your family will be off the hook—so long as I get what I want."

Not giving me a chance to respond before standing and rounding the table, he pats me once on the shoulder before he leaves.

"You made a smart choice, kid. Can't trust the likes of Dutch Schultz."

I snort at the remark. Mostly because I can't trust anybody—not even the law.

"You, ah, you got some lipstick on your collar there," he says, flicking me behind the ear as he heads for the door. "See you opening night, Benny."

MASIE

THIRTY-ONE

I SHOULD HAVE EXPECTED HIM TO BE WAITING FOR ME IN THE dark of the living room, but perhaps I was simply too drained, too tired to care. The warmth I'd been able to steal from Benjamin, the pleasure I'd taken from him, had long since faded away, leaving me cold and alone. When Dutch flicks on the lamp beside the chair, I freeze, a deer caught in the headlights of my father's angry stare.

"I thought you'd be at the club by now," I say, dropping my purse on the table near the door.

He says nothing for a moment, a shiver crawling its way up my back. My guard, who is supposed to be here, is nowhere in sight. No doubt he's been dismissed for the evening by my father, a fact which makes my heart sink into my stomach. He only dismisses the guards when he doesn't want any witnesses to his tantrums.

"Where were you?" he demands finally.

"The docks. I needed some air." It's only partly untrue.

A bitter comment on his surprise announcement flitters through my mind, but I don't give voice to it. I know better, I know all too well what it is to be walking on Faberge eggshells.

He stands, pulling himself to his full height, his jaw set in an angry line. "Get changed. We're going to the club tonight to make the announcement publicly."

"Daddy," I begin, hesitating as I carefully choose my next words.

As it turns out, I don't have a chance to speak. His hand shoots out so fast there's no way to absorb the blow. His knuckles connect with the side of my face in an earth-shattering collision, sending me sprawling to the floor.

"You ungrateful little bitch. How dare you embarrass me like that today?" He spits the words, and though he's gone blurry in my vision, I'm sure he's shaking with rage. I've seen him this angry only once before, right before my mother tried to take her own life.

A strange mixture of terror and rage flood through me, the emotions competing as I speak.

"You sold me off like I was nothing. You didn't even think to ask how I might feel about it. You just offered me up like a cheap watch to a man I'd never even met." I fight to constrain my tone, to keep the anger from seeping into the words.

"Everything I've done is for you, for this family. This marriage will keep us all safe. I know what's best for you, I always have." He shakes his fist in my direction. "And you will be a good girl and do as you're told."

I crawl to my feet, using the armchair beside me to pull myself up. Once I'm standing, I meet his eye, the ache in my face throbbing painfully. "I won't marry him, Daddy. I'm in love with someone else. If you care about me at all, you won't make me."

Now he waves me off. "You're a child. What could you possibly know about love? Not that it matters, the deal is made and you will marry who I say. I've made up my mind."

"I won't," I say, finally releasing my full defiance. "I'd rather die."

Something flares across his face, an emotion I haven't seen in some time. My retort is the same one my mother had once uttered, and he hadn't believed her then. I can only hope he believes me now.

He takes two giant steps, closing the gap between us before I can move, and seizes me by the throat. He squeezes and I feel the tips of my fingers begin to tingle. Lifting me off my feet, he pulls me in so close we are nose to nose.

"You think you can defy me?" He laughs in my face. "I doubt your new husband cares what condition he receives you in. He'd probably be just as happy to have you catatonic in a chair like your damn mother!"

Just as I begin to lose consciousness, he tosses me, like swatting a fly, and I career back into the door, rattling the knob. I gasp, rolling onto my knees and struggling to draw air in through a neck that feels like it might be broken.

I don't see him approach again. I only feel the swift kick, the tip of his shoe connecting with my ribs, sending me flying again, this time across the parquet floor. Pain explodes through my middle. Each cough is like hot coals in my lungs and throat.

Still, he continues to rage, grasping the table and flipping it, the vase of flowers it'd held shattering to the floor with a crash.

I want to beg him to stop, but I can't speak, can't force sounds through my injured throat. Desperately, I hold up a hand in surrender. Finally, he stands over me, his face red, panting with effort.

"Why do you make me hurt you like this? Just like your mother. Why can't you just do what I tell you? I am your father, and you will respect me."

I shake my head; it's all I can do. My final act of defiance. Respect is earned, not given. If I could shout the words, I would. But I can't. Not now, maybe not ever again.

He waves his hand through the air. "Look at all this. People would kill to live so well. Do you have any idea how lucky you are? How much you owe me?" He pauses, his eyes settling on my face. I'm not sure what he sees, but whatever it is, it's enough to stem the flow of his rage.

"Whoever this boy is you're so infatuated with, forget him. You have a job to do for this family…and you *will* do it," he says finally, straightening his tie. "Family is all that matters, Masie. We're all you have and all you can count on."

"Sir," Butler interrupts from the kitchen door. "Your car has arrived."

Daddy nods, looking back down at me. "Well, you can't go anywhere looking like that. You stay here, get yourself cleaned up. I'll make the announcement without you. If anyone asks, I'll tell them you wanted to come but fell ill. Do not leave this apartment. So help me, if you try anything stupid, I'll lock you in your room until the wedding."

With those final words, he disappears out the front door. As soon as he's gone, Butler rushes to my aid, lifting me into his lap. "Miss, do I need to fetch a doctor?"

I shake my head, wincing at the pain the gesture brings. "Get Benjamin," I whisper hoarsely.

BENNY

THIRTY-TWO

I'VE BARELY BEEN HOME AN HOUR WHEN A KNOCK AT THE DOOR draws me from the bathroom where I'm shaving my face. I wipe my hands on the white towel, then sling it over one shoulder as I make my way to answer it, silently praying it's not O'Hara or his partner.

To my surprise, it's Albert, Masie's driver, standing in my hallway, his hat in his hands.

"Sir," he says formally. I wave him in.

"What is it, Albert?"

Once inside, he hands me a folded letter. I open it and scan it quickly.

Dear Sir,

Miss Masie requests your presence at her home, as soon as possible. Please use the staff entrance in the rear of the building. Albert will show you the way.

Sincerely,

Rudy

"What's this all about?" I ask, earning me a frown.

Nothing good, that's what his expression says.

Wiping the last of the soap off my chin, I throw on a shirt and jacket and we're out the door. I can't help but notice that Albert is driving unusually fast, weaving in and out of traffic so quickly it makes my stomach flip.

When we arrive, he pulls the car into a lot beneath the next building over rather than parking on the street. He leads me up a back staircase and into an elevator not nearly as nice as the one that accesses the front door. As soon as we hit the top floor, he pulls the rusty cage upward, and we come face to face with Rudy, who's holding the rear door open. Stepping through, I realize I'm in the servant's wing of the house, on the other side of the kitchen.

"What's happening?" I demand, obeying when Rudy waves for me to follow. Albert vanishes back down the other direction.

"There's been an incident," he says flatly. "I'm afraid Miss Masie is badly injured."

I brush past him, running flat out until I reach her room. Throwing her door open, I find her, curled on her side on the fluffy white rug. The side of her face is swollen, her lip cut and bleeding.

"Masie," I say, dropping to my knees beside her. She lets out a small, pained sound as I lift her into my lap.

"What happened?"

She blinks up at me, tears shining in her eyes, then nods toward Rudy in the doorway.

"I'm afraid she can't speak. She got into a rather nasty altercation with her father."

My heart pounds painfully in my chest. "Dutch did this?" I don't mean to say it out loud, but she closes her eyes and nods.

The guilt that washes over me is like the Hudson in winter, chilling me down to the marrow of my bones. *This is my fault*, I realize. I never should have left her to talk to him alone. I should have done it myself, somewhere public where he couldn't lash out.

I should have kept her safe.

Then another feeling takes hold, this one slowly warming me, first thawing the blood in my veins, then heating it until it feels as if it's boiling beneath my skin.

I'll kill him.

For this, for what he's done, I will rip him apart with my bare hands.

Masie makes another small, strangled sound, cupping the side of my face in her hand. The only thing keeping me from going after the old man right now is the feel of her in my hands, fragile and broken.

"Call the doctor," I say over my shoulder to Rudy, who nods.

Masie draws me back to her, shaking her head and wincing.

"You need a doctor," I urge, but she shakes her head again. Stubborn little thing.

"Fine," I relent, for the time being at least. "Rudy, can you have the maid run her a hot bath with some salts?"

"Of course, sir."

"And fetch whatever you have that might help with the pain," I add. "And some warm tea for her throat."

I don't have to look back to know he's gone. Carefully, I examine her. Besides the damage to her face, there's a red and blue bruise in the perfect shape of a hand forming around her throat, which is also swollen. She's got a nasty lump on the side of her head, and her shoulder is bruising as well.

"I'm so sorry," I whisper, brushing her hair back with gentle fingers. "I should have talked to him myself."

She clutches the front of my shirt, shaking her head forcefully.

"Okay, okay, be still. I've got you now."

The maid scuttles in. "The bath will be ready shortly. Should I help her undress?"

"Run along, Patsy," Rudy says in his no-nonsense tone. "Her guard and I will help her."

She shoots a look between us, as if she's debating commenting on the impropriety of it all, but he silences her before she can utter a word.

"I've been with this family since before she was born. I've rocked her to sleep and changed her diapers. I assure you, she's in capable hands."

Patsy curtsies and disappears.

Once she's gone, he steps into the room, holding out a brown bottle and a scrap of cloth. "I found this in the kitchen. It should help with the pain."

I take the bottle of Laudanum and the spoon with one hand. Masie sees it and shakes her head.

"Just a little," I say, "so I can get you to the bath without hurting you."

She shakes her head again, and I catch her chin, "It's this or the doctor."

Finally, reluctantly, she nods. I sprinkle several drops onto the spoon and gently part her lips, letting it slide down her swollen throat. She swallows, coughing at first, then I feel her muscles relax as she slumps against me. I quickly hand the spoon and bottle back to Rudy, who watches over my shoulder.

"Hey, you doing alright there, Masie?"

Blinking slowly, she nods once.

Scooping her up, I follow Rudy down the hall to the bathroom, where the large copper tub is nearly filled with steaming water.

Slowly, and with forced detachment, I strip her down—under Rudy's watchful gaze—taking stock of every welt, every bruise, every single evidence of Dutch's abuse. Then, as gently as possible, I lower her into the steaming bath, soaking my shirt sleeves as I struggle to hold her from slipping in too far. The laudanum must be taking hold because her muscles are completely relaxed, and she can't seem to hold herself up.

"Rudy, can you grab her a sheet?" I ask, turning so I'm cupping her under the arms from behind.

He returns, folded linen sheet in hand.

"Here," I say, motioning to the front of her. "Just put it in the water over her."

He obeys, flicking it open, then soaking it in the water, adjusting it to offer some modesty, at least. Then, lifting her forward, I kick off my shoes and step into the tub behind her, water lapping over the sides of the tall tub as

I wriggle in, laying her back against my chest.

"You'll ruin your suit," she manages to whisper, her voice raw and wavering.

Cupping my hand and filling it with water, I pour it over the back of her hair, repeating the movement over and over. After a few moments, the maid returns, a tray of tea in hand. Rudy, who has taken a seat at the vanity table, accepts the tray, motioning her away. He quickly fixes a cup and leans over, handing it to me.

"It's honey and lemon. It will help her throat," he says as I accept the cup by its tiny handle.

"Here," I say, holding it to her lips. She takes a reluctant sip, then another, wincing with each swallow.

After a few drinks, I hand it back and Rudy sets it on the tray, fixing a cup for himself. As I watch, he pulls a small silver flask from his vest pocket, pouring it into the cup, then drinking it in two long gulps.

"This isn't the first time, is it?" I ask quietly.

He doesn't answer, but the guilty look that settles across his face is answer enough.

I grind my teeth, forcing myself to look away. Finally, after a few long moments, he speaks, his German accent heavier than usual.

"Mister Schultz isn't a bad man; he just has a very short temper—especially with his children."

I bite my tongue against the accusation trying to claw its way out my mouth. He knows—he's seen Dutch do this before, and probably worse too, and yet he does nothing. While the rational part of my mind understands that to step in at her defense would mean dismissal from his position here, at best, I can't help the righteous indignation boiling inside me. How can he watch and do nothing?

"He could have killed her," I manage through gritted teeth. "And you would have stood there and let him."

"It isn't my place to…"

I cut him off with a sharp glare. "You aren't a slave, Rudy. You had a choice."

236

"Spoken as a man who has never truly served another," he retorts. "As it is, I have risked everything bringing you here tonight. What do you think would happen if he were to return now? To find us like this?"

My mouth twitches because the answer is simple. He'd kill me, probably with his bare hands. And Rudy, well, who knows.

"I care for Miss Masie as my own child. But I'm as unable to stem his temper as the late Missus Schultz was." He looks away, taking a long, deep breath. "We can only do what we are able."

A silence passes between us then. What a trip we make, each chained to a life that is little more than a prison of our own making. Desperate to break free, but shackled to the person who makes freedom impossible.

"I have to take her away," I whisper finally, as much to myself as to Rudy.

I can't let this forced marriage continue. I can't let Masie continue to live in Dutch's cage. I can't keep risking my family and my freedom and playing both sides.

Rudy shakes his head. "I didn't hear that. Because if I had, I'd be duty bound to tell Dutch, and I won't."

He stands then, lifting the silver tea tray and exiting the room.

The water is no longer steaming, the once heat-pink skin of Masie's shoulders fading back to its normal alabaster. She turns just a bit, looking up at me over her shoulder.

"I can't leave JD, and I can't leave my father to be devoured by his demons," she says finally. "He wasn't always this way. It's poison, this life. It destroys everyone and everything it touches. It will destroy us all, if we let it. You have to let me go, Benjamin. You can still walk away from all this."

Even as she says it, I know she's trying to do right by me. But I also know that there's always a way—it's usually just a matter of being courageous enough to seize it.

"I think there might be a way," I say finally, the vague

edges of a plan congealing in my mind. "If you trust me, I think we can do it. Can you trust me?"

For a moment, I expect some sassy retort, but instead, an expression of pure, blissful acceptance settles across her face. "Of course."

I MENTALLY MAP OUT MY PLAN AS THE WATER COOLS AROUND US, both of us shaking and frigid when I finally lift her from the tub, free her of the wet sheet, and hand her a soft hemstitched damask towel to dry herself with. I drip onto the white tile floor, assisting her first, then releasing her to the seat Rudy recently vacated while trying ineffectually to pat my trousers dry.

Finally, Rudy reappears with a pair of pants, undershirt, and jacket that must belong to JD.

"Here, I'll help Miss to her room while you change," he orders. "If you leave your wet things here, I'll see that they are laundered and returned to you."

"Thanks, Rudy."

I change swiftly, abandoning my own clothes as instructed. While the pants are a little big and the shirt a little tight, I don't squabble about the fit. As he pointed out, Rudy risked a great deal bringing me here, and I'm not about to be ungrateful about it. Once I'm done, I make my way to her room, taking a seat on the bed beside her.

"Masie, I'll need some time to get things into motion," I say, shaking my head. "But in the meantime, I need to know that you're safe. I don't want Dutch to have any reason to lay hands on you—not ever again."

She blinks. "What are you saying?"

I take a deep breath, expelling it with gusto before answering, as if hoping to lessen the bitter taste of what I'm about to say. "Tell him you agree to the wedding. Go forward as if it's going to happen. Do...whatever he wants. Just for now."

She looks down, her chin tucked into her chest. "It

will mean engagement parties and announcements—a full social discourse. Are you certain you can handle that?"

I nod once, firm in my decision. "Yes. If it keeps his hands off you, then yes. We'll still have our days at the club, finalizing the plans. And then, once everything is in place, we'll leave this place and never look back. Once the people we love are safe, we'll go."

"It sounds like a miracle, Benjamin. I don't know if I believe in miracles."

I take her hand, kissing her knuckles gently before releasing it back to her snow-white bed cover. "For you, I will be a miracle worker. I just need some time."

"How much time?"

I chew at my bottom lip, running over my plan in my head. "A week, two at most."

"Alright then," she manages, her voice still dry and cracking. "But you have to promise me one thing."

"What's that?"

"You have to swear to me that if you can't do it, if you can't make this miracle, that you will take your family and leave this city. Because if you can't, then I'll be forced to go through with the wedding, and I couldn't bear for you to see that. I'd rather know that you're free of this life, safe, far away from my father and his sins. Promise me."

I stand, and although I have no intention of leaving her behind, I utter my oath.

"I swear."

Nodding once, she nestles into her pile of pillows and lets her eyes drift shut. I mutter a thanks to Rudy on my way back out the rear entrance. Albert is at the bottom of the elevator, hat in hand, but I wave him off.

"I'm gonna walk," I say, sliding on my borrowed jacket. "The air will do me good."

MASIE
THIRTY-THREE

I DON'T REMEMBER BENJAMIN LEAVING, ONLY THE ABSENCE OF him, only waking to the cold sheets pulled tight around me, alone in my darkened room. The clock on my mantle suggests it's nearly noon, but I have a hard time believing that. It feels like weeks have past, though as I sit up and the impact of yesterday's brawl hits me once more, I know it to be true. The pain in my shoulder is the worst, as if I've torn every muscle and ligament holding my arm to my body. It sears through me like molten steel.

The other pains are less, though still aching. The side of my face, my neck, my tender ribs. I ring for the maid to help me dress, something I haven't done since I was a child. She bobs into the room, eyes cast downward, asking no questions about my current condition. Once I'm dressed, she holds out a silk brocade scarf, and as I'm about to refuse, she speaks for the first time.

"A sling for your arm, Miss? It might help with the pain."

When her eyes finally meet mine, they are meek and silently hopeful. I nod once, my own voice still raw, and she gently ties it across my body to take the weight off my injured shoulder.

"Would you like me to help you with your makeup as

well?" she asks, emboldened by her success with the sling. I pause, leaning forward to catch a glance of myself in the vanity mirror.

The dark circles under my eyes are normal, but the wide bruise across my face is startlingly blue and red, the same shade as the handprint perfectly cradling my neck like a string of macabre pearls. My hair is stringy and wild from having been slept on wet, adding to the overall look of someone who has just lost a boxing match with a bear. Or, more accurately, making me look startlingly similar to my mother.

"No," I say finally. "Let him see me." Perhaps his guilt will be enough to earn a reprieve from any further outbursts—at least for the time being. Benjamin is right about one thing, in order to survive, I must pretend to accept Daddy's decree of marriage. And I will have to play my part perfectly to please him.

I only hope I don't have to go through with it.

Benjamin didn't tell me the details of his scheme, but I hope against hope it will work. The alternative is nearly unthinkable.

I hobble my way to the terrace for breakfast. As usual, JD and Daddy are seated at the bistro table near the glass doors. June is there this morning as well, and she sees me first, her eyes flickering over me, a sour grimace on her face.

"Masie, darling, good of you to join us," she says, knowing better than to mention my wounds. "Shall I get us some coffee?"

It's a code we worked out some time ago. If I refuse, it means I'm not alright and it's her cue to make an excuse to get us both out of there. If I accept, it means I'm alright and she shouldn't try to excuse us.

"That would be lovely," I croak. "Thank you."

She hops out of her chair, bounding to the silver tray service where the coffee sits in a warming pot, and pours us both a cup.

JD's eyes drift off the newspaper in his hand and

across me, silently assessing the damage. He stands, pulling out the only remaining seat, between him and Daddy.

"Good morning, sister," he says, taking his seat once more. "I hear congratulations are in order."

At his casual mention, Daddy drops his own paper into his lap. "Everyone was disappointed you couldn't be there for the announcement," he says, folding his hands across his lap. "I told them that you fell ill."

"Thank you, Daddy," I manage, taking a drink of coffee when June sits it in front of me, the heat soothing the dry, swollen insides of my throat.

"Give us a minute," Daddy demands, jerking his head at JD.

JD stands, taking June by the hand. He offers me a single pat on the shoulder, the only show of support he dares express, then leads her from the terrace.

"Stubborn, just like your mother," he chastises. "I don't enjoy hurting you, Masie. I'm trying to do what's best for you."

"I know," I say, unable to meet his eyes. With a deep breath, I force the practiced lie from my lips. "And I'm sorry. I shouldn't have behaved as I did. Of course you know what's best. Of course I will marry Artie, if you think I should."

He takes a long breath, puffing out his chest. "Of course you will. I'm glad you finally saw the error of your ways." He hesitates, finishing off his own cup of coffee. "I realize I've spoiled you, Masie. Given you freedoms most other girls would never be allowed. All this free thinking, I bear the responsibility for that. But you're about to be a wife. It's important you behave like a proper lady, that you know your place."

The idea is so laughable I nearly break my meek façade. "I will, Daddy."

He seems at least placated by my act of contrition. When he stands, sliding his chair from behind him with a scraping sound, I tense. Adrenaline and pain flood through me in anticipation of his touch.

He pauses, kissing me gently on the top of the head as if all were forgiven.

"I'll find a replacement act for the club for the rest of the week. You need to recover before the grand opening."

"Thank you," I manage.

"Do you need anything else?"

"No, I think I'll be alright. I just need some rest."

"You have a lunch date with Artie tomorrow. He wants to go over some thoughts he had about the wedding. You should hire someone to help you with the planning," he says. "Sky's the limit. We want to show the entire world just how strong our untied families are."

I nod. Of course he does. Even my own wedding wouldn't be about me. It'd be a display, a warning to our enemies and a show to our supporters that we are lousy rich and untouchable. Still, it presents me with an opportunity to smuggle some funds, under the guise of wedding spending, into my secret account—something we will badly need if Benjamin makes good on his promise.

*I MAKE IT TO THE CANARY CLUB LATER THAT DAY, HAVING FI-*nally let my maid curl and press my hair and apply enough makeup to keep passersby on the street from staring. If Benjamin is surprised to see me, it doesn't show. I continue hoping he'll let me in on his plan, but he keeps frustratingly silent. He does, however, settle me into one of the newly finished private booths, the heavy damask curtains pulled open with braided tassels. The kitchen works me up a nice tomato soup and soft bread, and I watch as Benjamin bounces from place to place, adding final touches and last details.

The hand-carved spindles arrived for the staircase to the second-floor balcony seats and he rolls up his sleeves, helping the workers glue and hammer them in place. There's something equally glorious and sad about seeing it nearly complete. On one hand, it's been my refuge these past weeks, the place I've felt most at home. And on the other, it isn't meant to be my haven, it's meant to be my cage.

A pretty cage for a pretty bird.

I'm not altogether surprised when my guard Thomas arrives, taking up a seat at the bar. Father and his newly imposed desire to prevent me from running free—what a laugh—clearly means to keep me from going back on my word, from doing anything reckless.

JD comes by soon after, under the guise of bringing a truck of frozen meat for the kitchen, but while it's being unloaded, he joins me in the booth.

"You doing alright, sissy?"

I smile at the nickname I haven't heard since we were children.

"I'm as good as I can be, considering," I admit. Truthfully, other than the shoulder, I'm feeling better. "I doubt I'll be singing any tunes in the next few days, but it no longer feels like I'm swallowing glass whenever I speak, so that's an improvement."

He fiddles with his fedora on the table between us. "Might not be so bad, being married to Artie. He's a decent-enough fella."

I raise one eyebrow. "Then maybe you should marry him."

He frowns. "You know what I mean."

"I do," I say, sliding my tray of food away. "You tell me, what would you do if Daddy ordered you to marry someone? Because, much as I love June, you gotta know you aren't far behind me on this train. Once he decided he can marry us off to cement alliances, it's only a matter of time before he finds you a nice broodmare and puts a saddle on you."

He visibly flinches.

"Oh, has he already?" I ask, leaning forward across the table.

"He introduced me to Caroline Tate yesterday. She's an heiress from England. Family's in the lumber racket or something. Made it a point to tell me she's worth a cool mil in dowry alone—not to mention what she stands to inherit when her old man passes."

"Oh, I'm sure June just loved that." A guilty look creeps across his face and I reach across the table, slugging him in the arm. "You cad. You didn't tell her."

He shrugs. "Nothing to tell, not yet anyway. But it's different for me. I could marry the dumb Dora and still keep June on the side."

I fold my arms across my chest. We both know June would never agree to that, no matter how much she might be smitten with him. "Balderdash."

He holds up his hands in mock surrender. "You're right. I have no intention of walking down the aisle with anyone but June. But I'm not sure we have a choice, Mas."

I bite my lip, debating mentioning Benjamin's plan, but force myself to stay quiet. Because if it fails, then once Benny's gone, once he's safe, I've already decided I'm not going to be anyone else's property, not ever again.

"The town's buzzing about opening night next week," he says, turning the conversation away from my impending nuptials. "The mayor himself will be attending, not to mention a who's who of Hollywood bigshots, city bosses, senators, and judges."

"Hey, you two, come check this out," Benjamin says, interrupting us.

We slide from the table, and he leads us toward the bar.

"I designed it myself," he says, motioning to a glass display of various colorful booze bottles. "JD, there's a switch by the front door. Will you go flip it?"

He nods and crosses the room, poking his head around the corner so he can still see us, then he hits the switch. In an instant, the whole case falls into the back of the bar, hiding all the bottles under what suddenly looks just like a long serving bar. He pulls a piece of wood forward, covering the case completely, as if it never existed.

"Well, that's swell," JD offers with a whistle. "How do

you bring it back up?"

Benjamin points to a rope hanging near the exit. It looks like something to open and close the curtain affixed above it, but when he crosses to it and gives it a tug, the case swings back up and into place.

"Well done," I offer with a clap. "What other secret goodies have you added?"

He waves his hand around the room. "Every booth has a secret exit, via a trap door in the floor, that leads to the basement and a rear tunnel. Not to mention the alarm at the door that can be sounded at the first sight of cops outside, giving us a decent head start on ditching the booze. You have to know the password to get the secret drink menu, and even then, at a glance, it will all appear very on the level."

JD, who has met up with us back at the bar, slaps him on the back. "Well done, truly. Dutch made a good choice, putting you in charge."

Benjamin nods once, turning to me formally. "Masie, it's been lovely to have you here today to supervise. I hope to see you again tomorrow?"

I almost balk at his formality, then I remember my guard is on the seat not three feet away, listening intently whilst pretending not to.

"I have a lunch appointment, but I'm sure I can come by after," I say, offering him my hand, which he kisses chastely.

"I look forward to it. JD, I have a few questions about the ledger you gave me. Do you have a few moments to show me how to enter some things properly?"

JD nods. "Of course. See you at dinner, sissy?"

I put a hand to my forehead dramatically. "Actually, I'm feeling a bit faint with all the excitement. Think I'll call it a night. Do extend my apologies?"

"I will."

With that, I walk over and tap Thomas once on the shoulder. "I'm ready to go."

"Home?" he asks as we spill out into early evening,

pulling my car door open for me.

"I need to make a stop first," I say, sliding in and closing the door myself.

BENNY
THIRTY-FOUR

*I CLOSE THE HEAVY OFFICE DOOR. IT'S HIDDEN BEHIND A BOOK-*shelf, so once shut, it's completely invisible to the club.

"Oh, check this out," I say, motioning JD to the far wall where a painting of a log cabin in a winter meadow hangs in a silver-and-white frame.

With one hand, I pull it away from the wall, exposing a hinge and slit that when opened, allows us to look out over the stage.

"Impressive," he offers. "But that's not really what you brought me in here for, is it?"

Taking a deep breath, I replace the painting, rounding the antique mahogany desk and taking a seat in the high-back chair. Pulling open the top drawer, I retrieve the ledger and toss it on the desk.

"I want to help Masie," I say flatly. "I'm afraid that if I don't…I'm afraid she'll end up like your mother. Or worse."

At the mention of his mother, JD flinches. "What do you know about it?"

Okay, time to lay my cards on the table. None of this works unless I can get JD on board. I need to make my pitch, and I need him to swing at it.

"Masie took me to Rockford," I admit. "She's afraid

she's going to end up the same way. And if she's forced into this marriage, I believe that she will."

Narrowing his eyes, JD takes the seat across the desk, crosses his legs, and draws a hand down his long face. "What do you want to do about it?"

"She won't leave, not so long as you and Dutch are here. She's afraid for you, and for what Dutch will become if she does."

He nods, pursing his lips. "Dutch would never let her go. He'd hunt her to the ends of the earth and drag her back. And he'd eliminate anything or anyone who tries to take her from him."

I rake a hand through my hair. "I know. But I think I know a way that we can get you both out, and get Dutch out of the business, too."

"I'm not killing my old man," he says, raising his chin defiantly.

I hold up both hands. "No, I wouldn't let anything like that happen. But what I need to know is, if I can manage it, if I can oust Dutch from the business, will you go? Or will you stay here and fight for him?"

Leaning on one arm, he rubs his chin, contemplating his words carefully. "If something happened and Dutch wasn't the boss anymore—if he were out of the game— then Masie and I would have to leave, for our own safety. He'd understand that. If, say, Lucky took over, we'd be viewed as a possible threat to his leadership. We'd have no choice but to go."

"And how would you feel about that?" I press.

"I'm not gonna say I'd be heartbroken. Dutch will never trust me to run the show, that much is abundantly clear. And I've always wanted to go my own way—find my own niche. And besides, he's already made it very clear he's not gonna let me and June live our own lives. Getting outta this racket might be the best thing for both of us." He pauses, pointing at me. "Though if you tell him I said so, I'll deny it. But I won't move against him either. He's still family. He's still blood."

"And I wouldn't ask you to. Just to be clear." I stand, pressing my palms into the warm, dark wood. "But I have to get her out of here. I have to get us all out of here. I can do it. I can get you and June somewhere safe, get Masie and my family clear of this, if you'll help me. So can you be ready to move by opening night?"

He snorts. "I can't believe I'm saying this, but yeah, I can be ready. What do I have to do?"

"I need help with one small thing, then you just be ready to go on my signal."

"What signal?" he asks.

I sigh, righting myself. "Oh, you'll know it when it happens."

WE GO OVER THE PLAN FOR THE BETTER PART OF AN HOUR BEfore I hitch a ride with JD to the other club, where the evening's festivities are in full swing. We sneak in through the rear entrance, passing the dressing rooms and spilling out onto the dance floor.

Dutch is there, as expected, sitting at a table with Jack and Artie Berman as well as Alistair Rothchild. I cross the room at JD's heels, and once at their table, Dutch stands.

"If you gentleman will excuse me, I need to speak to Benny for a moment. JD, you join me as well."

Artie snickers, and a chill drives its way into my veins. I follow Dutch toward the back meeting room. Once inside, he waves me to the leather chairs nestled by the fireplace.

"I received a disturbing report today, Benny. Seems Artie saw you cozying up to one of New York's finest last night. You care to tell me what all that's about?" I open my mouth, and he holds up a hand. "And you should know that if you lie to me, the punishment will be extremely severe."

"It's a fella named O'Hara," I say quickly. "The special prosecutor. He's been on me since the day I got shot. They were following you, I guess. He and his partner came at me hoping to get the goods on you."

Dutch wrinkles his nose, helping himself to a glass of champagne from the ice chest hidden inside the antique globe beside his chair.

"How many times have you met with him?"

"He's tracked me down three times. The first time at my place, the second a few weeks ago after I dropped Masie off, while you were in Chicago, then last night. He just showed up at my place."

"And what did he want?"

I can't help feeling he already knows all the answers to each question he's asking—this is just some kind of test to see if I'll lie. So I make up my mind that I won't. No matter what.

"You. Specifically, any information about you and your dealings. He inquired about a ledger. I told him I didn't know anything, and he backed off, for a while at least."

He waves a hand at me. "Continue."

"Last night, he came with some bogus charge, said he'd throw my ma in jail and take the twins away unless I gave him something. And he'd do it; I know he would."

Dutch stares at me for a long moment, as if gauging my words before he speaks again. "And what did you do?"

"I gave him the location of one of your warehouses. The smallest one, near the river, by the horse stalls. I had to give him something, but I knew it had nothing he could trace back to you, not really." I pause, taking a deep breath. "I'm sorry. I know I betrayed your trust. But I had to do something. He threatened my family."

"And the next time he threatened them? What would you do then?" He leans forward in his seat. "What piece of my business would you give away to save your own skin?"

I shake my head. "I came here tonight to tell you, sir. I knew I was in over my head. But I didn't want to come last night. I knew you'd be celebrating with your partners, so I came today as soon as I was finished at the club." It's a lie. I'd never intended to tell him, but I know I have to say something, have to convince him I'm still on his side for this plan to work.

When JD speaks, drawing my attention to him for the first time during this interrogation, his lie is smooth and convincing. "I came by the club today. He had just told me what was happening. I told him to bring it to you directly, so here we are."

"Is that so?" Dutch says, sitting back. "Why don't you give us a minute?" he says curtly.

JD rises from his chair, grabs the bottle of champagne by the neck, and heads out the door. Once he's gone, Dutch stands, rounding his chair and leaning against the back of it.

"Benny, Benny. What am I going to do with you?"

"I understand that I did wrong," I say, trying to sound sufficiently humbled as I let my head hang. "I'm still adjusting to this life, sir. I've never been threatened by the cops before. But, of course, I'll accept whatever punishment you see fit."

He groans. "Ah, applesauce, kid, why you gotta be sucha damn saint?"

Now I'm sure I've misheard him. "I'm sorry, what?"

"My daughter's crazy about you, did you know that? She thinks she's in love." His words are like a bucket of cold water dousing me. Before I can protest, he continues. "I've seen it. I'm not blind—and I'm not stupid either. I've seen how she looks at you, and how you look at her. It's a fool's errand, love. Does nothing but awful things to a man. I let it go till now, figured it was harmless and that she'd get tired of you soon enough, but it seems I was mistaken."

"I wouldn't know, sir. But I know Miss Masie is engaged to Artie. I know my boundaries, sir." Another lie, another silver-tongue deception. I only hope he buys it.

"Do you, now?" He snorts. "She loves you because she thinks you're better than me—better than us. She knows your hands are still clean. But I think it's time to change that."

If I weren't scared stiff at his words, I'd scratch my head. "What do you mean?"

"Well, I've just gotten the go ahead from my business partners to eliminate a problem I've been having. You see, my former associate, Vincent Coll, recently came to me, demanding to be made an equal partner in the organization, or he'd go to the feds about certain work he's done for me."

He doesn't have to explain. It's common knowledge that Coll is—or was—Dutch's enforcer. He'd done more dirty work than half the trash men in New York, and he was, apparently, Masie's childhood friend.

"Needless to say, I'm not about to let this dumb mick take me down. The partners agree, he's gotta be dealt with."

"Then why not just let the cops arrest him?"

"Because, my boy, he'd flip on me in a hot minute. Can't have that. So, instead, I want you to deal with him."

I hear his words, but it takes a moment for his order to really register. "Are you telling me to take him out?"

He nods, splaying his hands. "You do this favor for me, and I'll forget about your little rat session, and about the eye you've got on my daughter. You do this, and your hands are just as dirty as mine—no more risk of you turning on me, because I'd have the goods on you as well."

The air rushes from my lungs, the room growing uncomfortably hot.

He continues. "And not to press the matter, but you gotta know that the first place he'll hit me is through the people I care about."

"You mean Masie."

He nods again. I feel my eyebrows knit together in a deep frown. Hadn't she said he wouldn't hurt her? Is there a chance she could be wrong?

"He's already threatened her once. And now, with the engagement, she's even more of a target."

The horror of what he's saying hits me like a truck. Of course he'd have to move on Masie now, to prevent the families from joining forces, to dismantle their union

253

and keep Dutch weak. If it goes through, then Dutch becomes practically untouchable—no matter what evidence he might have.

As my mind works through all this, another thing hits me. He knew this would happen. He knew that by announcing the engagement, he'd be making Masie a target. He'd done it knowing—and not caring—about the danger it'd put her in. His own daughter.

It's everything I have not to lunge forward and deck him right in the face.

Still, intentions aside, Masie is in danger, and I need to keep his trust for my plan to work. Finally, slowly, I stand.

"Then I should get to it. Any idea where I might start looking for him?"

Dutch grins, a hard, bitter smile that changes every feature on his face, twisting it into something cruel and barely human looking. "Try the penthouse. I'm sure he'll show up there soon enough. And take your buddy Dickey. Trust me when I tell you not to underestimate Coll. He's as devious as he is strong. You find him, you take him to Saint Raymonds, to the shed behind the cemetery. That's where we do our work. I pay off a gravedigger who will add him into one of tomorrow's burials."

Nodding once, I make my way out of the office, unable to stop myself from shooting Artie Berman a nasty glare as I pass by. Luckily, Dickey is at the bar chatting up a couple of shebas in fringed dresses.

"Hey," I say, approaching. "Dutch has a job for me, and I need your help."

The girls murmur their disappointment, and he bows gracefully. "Duty calls, girls."

BENNY
THIRTY-FIVE

WE SIT ACROSS THE STREET FROM THE PENTHOUSE FOR AN hour as I explain my plan to Dickey. He whistles, shaking his head.

"You are one crazy mook. You know that, Benny?"

"I know," I agree. "But I got no other play here."

Silence between us stretches across the dimly lit sidewalk. We stand in the alley, each of us with a back against one side of a building, watching down each end of the street. I'd already warned Rudy to keep the back entrance locked up tight, and Albert is in the garage keeping his own eyes peeled.

Masie is already asleep, Rudy informed me, and I'd told him to let her rest. No need to worry her for maybe nothing.

"You know, it means you'll want to leave town too," I say finally.

He chortles. "Nah, you know me, Benny. This city's in my blood."

"What will you do, then?"

He curls his fingers like claws and swipes them through the air. "I'm like a cat. Nine lives and all." Dropping his hands, he shrugs. "I'll make nice with the Luciano's, take a spot with them. They'll protect me. It's you I'm worried about."

Now it's my turn to shrug. "I'll be fine. Miss you though."

He groans. "Benny, don't go all sappy on me." Then, after a chuckle, he adds, "I will miss mooching off ya, though."

I grin, knowing that's as close to a teary farewell as I'm going to get.

Two cars pass by, then a third, which swerves to a stop right in front of us, across the street from Masie's door.

"Listen," he begins. "I know I ain't said it before, well it kinda goes without saying. But what you did for me before, taking the wrap on that heist—" He doesn't get to continue.

I raise a finger, gesturing for Dickey to quiet, and we draw back further into the shadows. A man steps out of the car in a long trench coat and brown fedora. He slams his door, then stares up at the top floor of the building. A breeze blows past, ruffling his open jacket, exposing the telltale glint of a gun in his hand.

Dickey lifts the Louisville Slugger he's brought with him, and I raise my own gun as we slowly approach the man from behind. I whistle, and he jerks my direction, giving Dickey a clear shot at him.

He makes the most of it, the wooden bat colliding with Coll's skull with a sickening crunch, followed quickly by the sound of his body crumpling to the ground.

"Quick," I say, holstering my gun. "Help me get him in the car."

Dickey abandons the bat next to a trash pile and grabs the gun at his feet, sticking it in his belt before taking Coll's legs in each hand. I open the back door of the car, then grab his arms. We barely manage to get him across the backseat he's so bulky and awkward. I have to climb back over him to get out, holding my hand in front of his face to see if he's still breathing. There's a lot of blood pretty much everywhere, soaking my suit jacket, shirt, and the leather seats.

To my relief, he's still alive.

Not that it matters, because he won't be for long.

Dickey slides in the driver's seat, and I give him directions to our destination. We drive slowly, careful not to draw any unnecessary attention to ourselves as we make our way to the outskirts of the Bronx.

"I'm just sayin' thanks is all," he finally finishes.

Nodding I look back down at the unconscious man. "Oh, I think we're about even."

MASIE
THIRTY-SIX

I'M JOLTED AWAKE BY A STERN KNOCK AT MY BEDROOM DOOR. Sitting upright, I flick on my bedside lamp and swing my legs out of bed.

"Who is it?" I call, the breath hitching in my lungs as I wait for the sound of Benjamin's voice.

"It's me," JD responds, and I exhale a disappointed breath.

Quickly grabbing a robe, I cover myself and open the door.

"What is it?" I demand, suddenly very awake. He never comes to my door in the middle of the night, which means something must be very, very wrong.

"It's Benny. Dutch found out he's been talking to the cops."

I take a step back, waving him into the room. "What? That can't be right."

There aren't many things I know with every fiber of my being, but one of those things is that Benjamin is no rat.

"He says they threatened his family."

For a moment, the room around me launches into a tailspin and I have to sit on the edge of my bed to steady myself.

"Did you know anything about it?" he asks, watching me intently.

I shake my head.

No, he never told me. Why didn't he tell me? Unless he planned to sell us out all along. Is that all this is? Is our entire relationship just so he could get the goods on Dutch?

As soon as I think it, I dismiss the notion.

"I don't believe it."

JD sits beside me, patting me on my uninjured shoulder. "Believe it. Artie saw him. He's the one who told Dutch."

I blow a raspberry. "Well, now I really don't believe it."

"He admitted it to Dutch when he was confronted tonight. And that's not the worst of it," he continues. "Dutch has sent him to take out Mad Dog Coll."

I sit, stunned into silence. Either Benjamin will go up against Vincent and be killed, or he'll be exactly what Vincent was—my father's personal assassin. The thought sickens me and I lean forward, cradling my stomach.

It makes sense, in the twisted way only my father can.

"You can't let him do this," I beg, grabbing the lapel of his jacket. "JD, please. You can't let Benjamin do this."

He takes my hand, pulling it free gently. "It's too late, him and his friend Dickey are already on the job."

I lick my lips, the world no longer spinning. Instead, it focuses onto a singular, pinpoint truth.

I'll have to stop him.

"Where will they take him?" I ask. I'd never wanted to know the details before, but I've overheard enough over the years to know there's a place they take people to face their maker. JD looks at me, clamping his mouth shut stubbornly.

"I mean it, JD, you tell me right now or so help me, I'll spill every nasty secret you've ever told me, I'll tell June about the heiress, I'll tell Daddy about the secret accounts, all of it."

When he still doesn't speak, I change my tactic.

"Please, JD, I couldn't live with myself if I don't at least try."

"Try to what? If you save Mad Dog, then Benjamin is as good as dead. Dutch won't let him live if he refuses. And you know it."

"Where?" I demand again. He is right, of course, but I can't force myself to care about the consequences right now. I promised him I wouldn't let him become my father's monster, and whatever it takes, I'm going to keep that promise.

JD rubs his hand down his face. "Saint Raymonds."

Throwing my arms around him, I squeeze him tightly, ignoring the pain shooting though my still-injured arm. "Get dressed and we'll go together," he says when I draw back. "My car is parked out front.

I dress quickly in a black chiffon pantsuit I purchased for Mother's phony funeral. Slinking down the hall and into the kitchen, I quietly unlock the service entrance and slip down the rear elevator. As good as his word, his car is parked at the curb and—typical of JD—he's left the key in the ignition.

I crank it quickly, speeding off before anyone can stop me.

It was kind of him to try to come, but an altogether terrible idea. If he's involved, there'd be no limit to Daddy's rage. At least if it's just me, then no one can blame him for any of it.

I speed down the roads, zigzagging my way across town into the Bronx.

The cemetery is dark when I pull in, quickly dousing the headlights as I roll through the rows of headstones toward a car parked in the distance. It's Vincent's. Even in the moonlight, the automobile is unmistakable—a deep navy-blue Studebaker with whitewall tires and mint-green leather seats, the only one in the entire city.

Pulling up alongside, I cut the engine and carefully open my door. A few feet away, there's a tall equipment shed with a flickering light visible from beneath the closed doors.

Slinking around the cars, I head for it, pressing my ear to the door and struggling to hear.

"Make sure the rope is tight," Benjamin orders.

"I don't see why we're wasting time with this. Let's just plug him and be done with it," Dickey's voice answers.

A knot in my chest loosens. They're all alive. It's not too late. My hand is on the door handle when another voice freezes me in place.

Vinnie spits, then offers a wet, choking laugh. "You ain't got it in ya, kid. I can see it in your eyes. You aren't like me and Dutch—hell, Masie has more ice in her veins than you. You really think you can pull that trigger? Nah. I don't think so." He hesitates and I lean closer, straining to hear the soft voice that follows.

"You don't know me," Benjamin whispers. "You have no idea what I'm capable of doing to keep the people I love safe."

More laughter. "Sure I do, kid. I was just like you once. Young and green and willing to go as far as I had to, to get the job done. Willing to do anything to keep my family safe. To give them what they needed. I made myself a monster for them. You think you're different? Better? You ain't. You just don't know it yet."

"Shut your trap," Dickey snaps, his feet scuffling across the dirt floor, passing so close to me that I jerk my hand from the door. "Let me do it, Benny. I got no problem making swiss cheese outta this jerk."

"If you want to live, give me an option, Vincent." Benjamin's tone is calm, too calm. The kind of calm my father gets right before he lashes out. It's enough to send a shiver through me. 'I know you care about Masie. She considers you family. I don't want to hurt you, for her sake. But I will keep her safe, no matter what it costs me. So give me another option. Tell me you'll leave town tonight and never come back. Start over again somewhere far from New York. Tell me you'll do that, and I'll put you on a train myself."

Relief floods through me, making my knees weak

and my stomach roll. Benjamin, my Benjamin. How could I ever compare him to my father? How could I ever doubt the goodness in his heart? When everything else is stripped away, he's still there, my light. My path through the darkness.

"I will break her. I'll break her in every way a person can be broken, then I'll lay her bloody body at Dutch's feet so that he will understand what he's done to me, so he will hurt like I've hurt. I will take every good thing away from him and leave only ruin in return, then, when he's at his lowest, I'll put a slug in the back of his skull." Vinnie's words flow from his lips like gasoline on water, igniting something deep within me. I hear the cock of a hammer being pulled back on a gun and I'm moving, rage burning inside me.

There's only one person in that shed worth saving.

Grabbing the handle, I slide the door open. Benjamin spins, leveling his pistol at me, then, the instant he realizes it's me, he lowers the barrel to the ground.

"Masie, what are you doing here?" he demands, circling behind me and closing the door. "Did you come alone?"

"Yes, I'm alone, and I told you I wouldn't let you do this—become this—and I mean to keep my promises, even if you don't."

"How'd you know where to find us?" Dickey asks, and I shoot him a sour look.

"Wait, whadda you mean even if I don't?" Benjamin cuts in.

I glance over his shoulder to where Vinnie hangs from a rafter, his hands tied together over his head. "JD told me you've been talking to the cops. So I gotta know... was any of this real? Or was it always just about informing on my father?"

Holstering his gun, he takes me by the arms. "How can you ask me that? How can you still not trust me, after everything?"

"I don't want this. I never wanted this. You know that,"

I snap, pulling free of his grasp.

"He was outside your place, Masie. He was coming for you, and he would have killed you—or worse. I wasn't going to let him hurt you. I'm still not."

"You hurt me," I bite back, feeling the sting of my words as they strike him. "You told me you loved me."

"This is insane, of course I love you. Can't you see I'm doing this for you? To keep you safe?"

I step back again, the blood turning to ice in my veins. "That's what my father says, too, to justify doing terrible things."

At Benjamin's back, Vinnie wriggles furiously, tugging on his restraints. "You can't save him, Mas. Can't save any of us. It's too late for that."

I slide past Benjamin, who has been rendered mute by my accusation.

"I heard you talking about what you were going to do to me, Vincent. To my family. I didn't realize you hated me so much," I offer softly, holding his gaze until he stops struggling.

He hangs mute, then spits a mouthful of blood onto the dirt floor. "I can't let you marry that kid, Mas. It gives them too much power. Do you have any idea how dangerous this alliance makes him? Makes them all?"

I step around him, forcing him to swing around to look at me, walking until I can hardly see Benjamin in the corner of my eye.

"He came to Dutch demanding to be a full partner. When they refused, he threatened you. That's why Dutch sent me to whack him," Benjamin says, stepping a bit closer to me. "That and...Dutch knows...how we feel about each other. He thinks if I get my hands dirty, you won't want me anymore, that you'll marry Artie without complaint." He pauses. "And I'm beginning to think he's right. He knows you hate him, Masie. And he wants to make me like him, so you'll hate me too."

I shake my head. "And yet, you agreed?"

His mouth hardens into a firm line before he finally

answers. "Yes, to keep you safe, I would do anything. Don't you get that? I love you enough to lose you if I have to."

"Don't you dare, Benjamin. Don't you dare lay this on me. You'd lose me to protect me? What a crock. I don't need it. And I don't think I could live with myself if you did," I say, grabbing the small pearl-grip pistol hidden in my garter. "Besides, I'd rather do this myself."

Before I can think twice, I point the gun at Vincent. I'd rather shoulder this burden, scar my own soul, than lose Benjamin to the darkness.

Just as I fire, Benjamin hits me full force, driving us to the ground with a thud and a puff of dirt. The gun flies from my hand and I cry out as my wounded shoulder gives, a fresh fire licking its way through my arm and chest.

"Masie, oh God, Masie, are you alright?" he asks, crawling off me.

It takes me a full minute to remember how to breathe through the searing pain.

Several things happen at once now. Vincent falls free of his ropes. I must have shot the rope accidentally when Benjamin hit me. He scrambles, his hands still tied together in front of him, to grab my pistol from the dirt. Standing, he levels it at me and I hold his dead, remorseless gaze. Benjamin rushes him, raising the gun over his head and firing a shot that hits the single light bulb—plunging the shed into darkness.

I squint, unable to force myself to stand through the pain and unable to force my eyes to adjust to the darkness.

Then a flash of muzzle fire, followed almost immediately by a second flash.

The sound of multiple bodies hitting the floor.

A scream rips its way out my throat.

BENNY

THIRTY-SEVEN

I DON'T MOVE UNTIL MASIE SCREAMS. THE WEIGHT ATOP ME IS too great, the desire to lie there in the dirt equally strong.

Her voice cuts through the darkness and I heave, rolling Coll's limp body off mine. I feel for a pulse on his neck, but there's nothing. Just a wet, sticky stillness.

"Benjamin," Masie calls again.

I crawl toward the sound. Has she been hit? I'd distinctly heard two shots. When my hand finally clasps onto her leg, she squeaks.

"It's me. I'm alright," I assure her, feeling my way up her body until I can cup her cheek in my hand. "I'm alright," I repeat over and over as I feel the first damp drops roll down her cheek and into my palm.

"Dickey, you alright?" I call into the darkness.

No response.

"Dickey? This isn't a gas; you better answer me."

Silence.

Releasing Masie, I pull myself to my feet, stumbling toward the doors. When I slide them open with a groan, the moonlight pours in, offering me at least some vision. Masie lays to my left, Coll not far away toward the center of the floor, and to the far right, Dickey lies in a crumpled heap. I rush to his side, one leg slow and aching at the knee from Coll landing on top of me at an odd angle.

When I reach him, I pull him to his back. His eyes, glassy and lifeless, reflect the blue moonlight. Rocking back on my heels, I fall to the ground, an inhuman cry escaping my throat.

Soon, I feel Masie at my back, her arms wrapping around me, her head resting at the base of my neck while she softly hums her familiar lullaby.

We sit like that for what feels like hours, until the first tendrils of morning crawl into the sky, the moonlight vanishing in the early yellow glow.

"We have to go," Masie says, releasing me finally.

"I know," I say, wiping the last tears from my cheeks. There's nothing else we can do now, nothing but run. We'll run so fast and so far we might be able to outrun the devil himself. "You need to take your car and go, before someone notices you missing and comes looking."

I can feel that she's about to protest, so I turn, stopping her with a kiss.

When I pull back, I notice there's dry blood smeared across her cheek, and I look down at my hands, which are caked with dry blood and dirt.

"What will you do?" she asks quietly.

"The gravedigger will be expecting a body," I say quietly. "So I'll give him one. As far as your father will know, I did as he ordered. Everything is in place for us to get out the night of the grand opening."

For a moment, she says nothing, then she pulls herself to standing, offering me a hand.

"I'll be ready," she says, her voice strong.

"It's only a few days," I reassure her. "We can do this."

"We can do this," she agrees.

Once she's gone, I clean up as best I can. Carefully, I drag Dickey's body to the corner of the shed and drape a canvas tarp over him. As soon as I do, the first crimson spot appears, spreading like a blossoming flower over the hole in his chest.

The sickness hits me too fast to swallow back, and I rush to a corner, heaving up the contents of my stomach onto the dirt floor.

It hurts in ways I don't expect, deep down into my bones.

What will I tell his family? They've been estranged for years, but even so, they deserve to know what happened to their son.

When I finally stop the rolling in my stomach, I kick some dirt over the pile of vomit, more to hide it from myself than from the gravedigger likely to stumble upon it tomorrow.

Turning my attention to Mad Dog, I roll him onto his side, tugging the billfold free from his jacket pocket. I leave the cash. Pulling O'Hara's card from my own pocket, I slip it inside before returning the wallet to its original place.

It takes me a long time to get his body into the car, slumping it across the backseats again. Only this time, my hands are slick with blood.

Blood of my friend. Blood of my enemy.

Blood I'm quite sure no amount of soap will ever truly wash away.

I may not have killed Dickey, but I brought him here—got him entangled in this mess. It's my fault he's gone as much as if I'd pulled the trigger myself.

Masie should have let me kill him, a bitter voice echoes inside my head as I stare down at the dead body in the backseat. *If she had, there'd still be blood on my hands, but at least Dickey would still be here.*

As soon as the small voice makes itself heard, I shake it away.

Masie had only been trying to save me, to keep me from becoming like Mad Dog—a killer. She'd been willing to do the deed herself to spare me that. And I'd only been trying to save her by bringing him here, set on letting myself become a monster to keep her safe.

God, how many more people are going to die in our

desperate quest to save each other?

None. I swear. Whatever happens next, however we have to get free, we will do it, and no one else will die because of us—not if I can help it.

I slide into the driver's seat, cursing myself for never learning how to drive. Sure, I'd seen it done enough that maybe I can at least fake it. There won't be too many people on the road at this ungodly hour. If I take it slow and stick to backroads, I should be all right.

Cranking the engine to life, I wrack my brain for where to head. I need a place where the body won't be found for a few days, not before Masie and I can make our break. I chew at the inside of my cheek, my hands clutching the wheel like a man clutches a lifesaver in the ocean, hands shaking, knuckles white.

There's an empty beer warehouse down by the wharf. One of Dutch's places that's sitting empty until the next shipment arrives in two weeks.

Grabbing the shifter in one hand, I pull it back, gears grinding, then press the pedal.

I manage to make it to the warehouse without hitting anything, which is a minor miracle, though I practically crawl the entire way. Once I open the massive double barn doors, I opt to push the car inside rather than try to drive it.

Struggling once again with the body, I finally wrestle it into the driver's seat, just as it's beginning to stiffen up.

My shirt is ruined, and the sun is finally crawling up the sky. Slipping out of my dark jacket, I take off the shirt. Digging through the dead man's pocket once more to find a box of matches, I take it around the corner and light it on fire, watching it burn to the last ember, then stomping on it and scattering the ashes.

Slipping my jacket back on over my white undershirt and suspenders, I pull the heavy doors closed behind me and walk out into the sun.

Slinking back down the wharf, I grab a trolley uptown, back to the penthouse where by now Masie has safely snuck back inside—hopefully no one the wiser.

It's a long trip, Dickey's absence hitting me in ways I don't expect. We've been friends so long I can't help but lament the fact that he'd never again tell me a dirty joke, never talk me into attending a poker game in a sketchy back room in China Town, never come over for dinner and teach Thomas inappropriate slang.

Each realization hits me like a bullet to the chest, filling me with holes no one can see, but that I can feel all the same.

He deserved better than this. Better than being unceremoniously dumped in a grave that doesn't even bear his name. A specter rises inside me, demanding justice. Demanding revenge.

No, my revenge will have to be my escape, the careful dismantling of the empire that sacrificed him, and my determination to live my own life the best way I can.

That is how I will honor him.

Not with vengeance, but with life.

By the time I arrive at the penthouse and make my way up, the entire family is already eating brunch, gathered around the table as if nothing happened. Masie is nursing a cup of coffee, her arm in a sling. I wince at the sight of her, badly bruised but freshly washed, her still damp hair held back by a colorful scarf. JD is showing off an article about the grand opening that made the front page of the paper, and Dutch sits, his back to the doors as I arrive, a puff of cigar smoke in the air above him like a thunder cloud.

"Sir," I say, making my entrance. "Do you have a minute?"

Glancing over his shoulder, he nods, waving me in. "Of course. Do come in, my boy."

"I did as you asked," I say boldly, hiding my shaking hands in my pockets. "Vincent Coll will no longer be an issue."

Now he turns in his seat. I pull my hands from my pockets. They're still covered in dry blood and dirt. My hands, I say without speaking, are as dirty as yours.

He glances from me to Masie, who, playing her part perfectly, slides her chair back and storms off into the house without a word.

"Well done, my boy. Well done."

"Yes, sir. Am I to finish the preparation for the opening now?"

He flicks his hand. "Yes, yes."

With that, I turn and leave, hoping with everything in me that I'll never have to step foot in that place again.

MASIE
THIRTY-EIGHT

I HEAR THE FRONT DOOR SLAM, AND I KNOW BENJAMIN IS GONE. I feel the absence of him the way one feels the sun moving behind a cloud, as if warmth is being drained from my skin. Sitting at my vanity, I stare at myself in the mirror, taking careful stock of each of my injuries.

I hate that I'd had to leave him to deal with the bodies alone. I hate that he'd even ended up in that shed, and I hate what he'd been about to do—to keep me safe. Hearing those words—my father's words—spill from his mouth had been the worst blow of all. With my free hand, I slide open the small drawer, moving aside my lacy scarves and shimmering headpieces, searching until my fingertips touch the cool leather billfold. Pulling it free of the mess, I crack it open, looking carefully at the numbers tucked away in my personal ledger.

Daddy is unaware of the account. I'd taken it out under Mother's maiden name when I first came home. It was meant to be my secret rebellion, my stash of dough that was beyond his ability to monitor—or cut off. But, over the past few months, I've been able to funnel away more and more—selling the expensive jewelry he gave me whenever his conscience got the better of him for one of his tantrums or from asking for funds for trips I never

271

actually took, for clothes I purchased and then returned.

I actually have a nice little egg sitting in the savings and loan, untouchable and untraceable to anyone but me.

But it won't be enough.

To get away, to start over. Sure, it might last a bit, but I know myself well enough to know I'll blow through it in no time, even being as frugal as I'm able.

I fold it up and tuck it away, my mind drifting to the safe in Daddy's bedroom. In it, there's some cash, some bonds, and all Mother's expensive baubles.

It will be enough, I decide, any guilt at the idea of theft instantly assuaged by the knowledge that whatever it is, I'm owed at least that much. It's mine, the only inheritance I want from this life.

I close the drawer just as a single knock bounces off my door, a hand sliding it open before I can respond.

Daddy steps into my room, and I turn just a bit in my seat to face him.

"Yes?" I ask, allowing my voice to warble but keeping my expression carefully neutral.

"You alright, Masie?" he begins, his tone one of concern, but with something else beneath, an undercurrent of haughtiness. "I know Mad Dog was your friend."

I turn away, shielding my face from him. "He hasn't been my friend in a very long time. You saw to that."

"I was just trying to keep you safe—to keep us all safe. Why can't you get that through your stupid little head?" I glance back at him. The thick vein in his forehead pulses beneath the skin, a telltale sign of his barely withheld anger.

"Of course, Daddy."

He rakes a hand down his face. "You think you're so much better than me? Just like your mother."

I shake my head. "Not at all. I'm not better than you or anyone else. I'm your daughter, through and through. I know that—I know that better than anyone. The difference between us is that I *want* to be better. I can be, if you'd let me."

He just stares at me for a long moment. In that time, I'm not sure if he's going to rage again or just fling back some verbal abuse. To my surprise, he does neither. He simply turns quietly and leaves, pulling the door closed behind him with a click.

BENNY
THIRTY-NINE

OPENING NIGHT ARRIVES AS SCHEDULED. MASIE, FOR HER PART, has been casually aloof, no longer spending days with me at the club. If not for the note JD delivered only yesterday, even I might have bought the act.

> *Dearest Benjamin,*
>
> *I have had to keep my distance these past few days, so as not to arouse Daddy's suspicion. I've been very carefully planning, and I believe I have everything I need in place.*
>
> *Know that whatever happens now, I love you—and I will go to my grave loving you—nothing can ever change that.*
>
> *When I sing tonight, it will be for you alone, and if it's God's will, then I look forward to singing for only you, for the rest of my days.*
>
> *All my affection,*
> *Masie.*

I've read it so many times the paper is thinning and wearing in the creases. Even now, I have it tucked inside my breast pocket, close to my heart. Dutch and his cronies sit at one of the private booths on the main floor, already sampling the new drink menu as well as several trays of fresh oysters, caviar, and pickled herring—Dutch's favorite dishes. The door opens and the first line of patrons, those with VIP tickets, enter. I immediately recognize two actresses, a baseball player of some note, the governor, and Mayor Jimmy Walker. The band strikes up, a smooth jazz number, the horns and double bass greeting each person as they enter.

I, too, make my way around the floor, floating from group to group as Dutch makes introductions. Finally, knowing I need to prepare for the real show, I make my way to Masie's dressing room. When I turn the corner, I see Artie, two dozen yellow roses in hand, standing outside, straightening his tie before knocking. She pulls the door open, smiling her stage smile, and greeting him with a peck on the cheek.

She accepts the flowers, then, catching sight of me, waves. I step forward, trying not to look as jealous as I feel.

"Thirty minutes to show time," I say. "Artie, good to see you." I hold my hand out, and he shakes it hesitantly.

"Benny, you've done wonders with this place," he says. I take the opportunity to lead him away from Masie.

"Thank you so much. Say, I happened to notice Mayor Walker out there with Dutch. Have you met him yet?"

Artie shakes his head, a strip of yellow hair falling free of his coif. He quickly smoothes it back.

"Well, let's rectify that, shall we?" I pat him on the back.

He mutters a farewell to Masie. She blows a flirtatious kiss, and while it makes him grin, I'm secretly sure it was meant for me.

By the time Dutch stands at the microphone, silencing the crowd, the place is packed to the gills. Every seat is taken, each table full. Resplendent in their glad rags and tuxedos, the patrons sip their expensive cocktails and munch on the hors d'oeuvres circulating on trays carried by waiters in top hats and scantily clad giggle girls.

The main room, circular in design, is Grecian in style, with stone columns supporting the upper-level seats. Tall palm trees rise from each corner, their green leaves seeming to create a lush canopy above. The stage is set back from the dance floor. On the far side, a handful of open tables sit in the middle of the room. Beneath the balconies, a half-circle of booths line the lower level, each with a privacy curtain thick enough to drown out the roar of the crowd when drawn. The upper level is the real wonder. Each table is at the very edge of the balcony, held back by a long, black iron gate reminiscent of an Italian villa, each chair with a green velvet cushion and the backs the same iron, only with spindles of ivy inlaid in the pattern.

Pulling my pocket watch from my vest, I check the time. Nearly ten.

Nearly time.

Stepping behind the long bar, I quickly flip the small switch below the first wall sconce, the one that disables the alarms. Then, after helping myself to a shot of whiskey, I wait.

Dutch finishes his speech to a round of wild applause and announces Masie to the stage.

I must admit, she looks more beautiful than I've ever seen her. Her golden hair is in perfect waves along the sides of her face, her feathered headpiece like the plumage of an exotic bird. Half a dozen long strands of pearls hang from her neck, and her dress, a sparkling white beaded number, looks like a snowflake under a microscope, iridescent and fragile.

She offers the crowd a flirtatious grin. "What are all you people doing in my club?" She laughs, and it twinkles like church bells. "Alright, you troublemakers, where are my rebels?" The crowd cheers. "Where are my rabble rousers? My flappers and dandies?"

They cheer again, and she cups her hand over her ear, encouraging them to shout even louder. "Well, I have something to tell you. This ain't no speakeasy. We're going to shout it into the night, so even the flatties across the river know we're having a good time. Ain't we got fun?"

The cheers go up once more as the band kicks off. Couples take to the dance floor like fish to water, stomping until the walls vibrate with each footstep.

It's about this time that JD enters the bar, offering

276

me a subtle nod. He's actually been in the office the whole night, adjusting the ledger as I'd asked him. Now, he heads toward Lucky Luciano, who is sitting at the bar with one of his girls hanging off his arm. Leaning in, JD whispers something. Lucky nods once, taking his date by the elbow, then follows JD behind the beaded curtain toward Masie's dressing room and one of the secret exits.

The third song in, the door swings open and uniformed officers swarm in like angry wasps. I have only a minute to hit the lever that hides away the liquor and the till at the bar. People scatter, screaming, for the exits. Taking advantage of the chaos, I grab Masie off the stage, ushering her back to her dressing room and the rear exit.

"Time to go," I whisper. "See you soon."

I release her, but she clings to my arm a moment longer, her expression fierce.

"You'd better not stand me up, Benjamin."

"Wouldn't dream of it," I say, pushing her into the room and pulling the door closed behind her.

Bursting back into the main room, I slide a glance to Dutch, who closes his booth curtain, blocking himself and his party from view. Mayor Walker swaggers toward O'Hara, who has his gun drawn. All around us, cops are gathering up whoever they can get a hold of, mostly club employees and a handful of notable faces, each demanding their release.

"What's the meaning of this?" he demands loudly.

"I think you know, Mister Mayor. And you should be ashamed, cavorting with criminals."

Detective Dewey walks up behind his partner, his trench coat brushed back at the hips where his hands are stuffed into his pockets.

"Cuff him," O'Hara demands of a beat cop so green he literally fumbles with the cuffs at his belt.

"Don't you dare," Mayor Walker challenges. "I'll have your badge for this, O'Hara."

The two of them go at it for a minute, shouting at each other while the poor Johnny, still too scared to move, looks on.

I move toward the office door, jerk my head toward Dewey, who abandons the hotheads to their screaming match and heads my direction. I push the bookshelf open and lead him into the office.

Tugging the ledger free of its place in the top drawer, I hand it over. "I think you need to have a good look at that before your partner shows up," I say, taking a seat in the chair.

"Oh, and why is that?"

I lean forward, resting my elbows on the desk. "Well, your partner threw around some pretty heavy threats when you weren't around. He threatened to have me thrown back in the clink on whatever charges he could trump up, and when that didn't work, he threatened my mother and the twins. He seemed determined—desperate even—to get his hands on that ledger. I was curious as to why, so I took a hard look at it. Turns out that Dutch has been paying off several cops to look the other way at his interstate shipments. One of those cops, incidentally, is O'Hara."

I let that hang in the air between us for a few minutes, letting him thumb through the ledger and find the payoffs listed before I continue. "That's his badge number, isn't it?"

He mutters something I can't quite make out, but it sounds a bit like, *well, I'll be damned.*

I expel a breath of relief. I'm sure JD's careful forgery, written in what appears to be Dutch's own hand, will be more than enough evidence to see both Dutch and O'Hara behind bars. It's the only way to get Dutch out of the business without having him wind up on a slab, and to keep my family safe from whatever O'Hara has up his sleeve.

I stand. "All I can figure is he wanted to get a hold of the only evidence that implicated him and destroy it before anyone else could take a look."

"We found Coll's body this morning—got an anonymous tip to the station. They found one of his cards in

Coll's wallet. You wouldn't know anything about that, would you?"

I shrug, lying through my teeth. "I only know that Dutch said the problem had been taken care of."

Just then, O'Hara bursts through the door, pointing a finger first at me, then at the ledger.

"That's mine, Dewey. This is my bust and that's my evidence."

"Officer Van Pelt," Dewey hollers, holding the ledger back from O'Hara when he tries to snatch it from his hand. Once the portly officer enters the room, Dewey nods to his partner. "Arrest this man."

O'Hara takes a stumbling step backward, his mouth hanging open, his cheeks flushing as Van Pelt slaps the cuffs on him. "What are you doing? How dare you? I'm the special prosecutor on this arrest. You can't do this."

Van Pelt leads him out, kicking and screaming the entire way. Once he's out the door and loaded into the paddy wagon with the rest, Dewey holds up the ledger. "This was good work, son. The city owes you a debt of gratitude."

"Just keep my name out of it." I snort. "There's more than enough in that ledger to put Dutch away for a very, very long time, and I expect you to do it, too. And I expect you to keep O'Hara behind bars as well."

"I think I can manage that. Especially if Mayor Walker has anything to say about it."

"And if anyone asks, I got out of here before the bust went down, escaped into a secret passage, right?"

He nods. "Will do. And you'd best hightail it out of the city tonight. We've got people outside waiting to arrest Dutch and his crew when they try to leave the basement, but he's probably gonna figure out it was you who set him up at some point."

"Don't worry, my family and me, we're already gone. We square?"

"Five by five."

"Good. If you'll excuse me then." Taking my hat and

jacket off the rack in the office, I grab my leather satchel and make my way to the exit in Masie's dressing room, the one that leads out to the west side of the street where my cab is waiting.

We circle the block for the better part of an hour before I double back and re-enter the club through the back-access door. The club is empty. Broken glasses litter the floor, reflecting the minimal light like stars in the night sky. Making my way to the hidden bar, I hit the lever, grabbing the cash out of the till and stuffing it inside a small leather satchel.

Once I'm finished, I hit the lever again, then take one last glance around the club I'd poured so much of my time and energy into. I can see, like ghosts, all the hours Masie and I wiled away here. I can hear the twins laughing as they ran around the busy feet of the workers painting the ceiling. This place, once so full of light and hope, is now nothing but another corpse, the remains of another thing Dutch and his people destroyed.

As I turn to leave, a shadow crosses in front of me and I drop my sack, pulling the gun free of my holster with an awkward jerk.

"Benny, Benny. You didn't really think you were gonna get off that easy, did you?" Artie stands between the door and me, his hands stuffed casually in his pants pockets as he approaches.

"Just let me pass, Artie," I say, forcing my hand not to tremble on the handle of my weapon.

"Why? So you can run off with my money and my fiancée?" He snorts. "That ain't gonna happen."

I take a deep breath, my confidence waning. "I don't think you're in any position to stop me, seeing as I'm the one holding the piece."

Artie shrugs, leaning casually against the bar, only two steps from me. "If you had the juice to pull the trigger, you'd have done it by now. Besides, you kill me and the whole Luciano family comes crashing down on you. And my uncle isn't a man you want on your heels, trust me on that."

"So whaddya want then?" I demand, lowering the gun. "You're a businessman. What are you angling for here?"

He shakes his dirty yellow hair off his forehead, grinning. "I want this. And thanks to you, I'm going to have it. Not just part of it, but the whole shebang. With Dutch behind bars, Rothchild is going to be looking to us to run his operation. And since I was practically family, I'm the logical choice." He runs a single finger over the marble bar top. "Needs a new name, though. I was never overly fond of canaries."

"So why are you here?" I ask, an uneasiness building inside me.

"Well..." He pulls a short black knife from his pocket, exposing the blade with a flick of his thumb. "I mean, I can't just let you off the hook that easily. Someone has to be punished for this mess. An example must be made. Gotta say, though, I didn't think it'd be you. I figured JD was behind this."

My breath catches in my chest, and I tighten my hand around my gun.

"Plus, you did sleep with my future wife," he adds, lunging so quickly I barely have time to dodge the blow.

His advance continues. He swings and swipes the knife through the air as he advances on me. All the while, I'm backing away.

"Calm down, Benny. It'll be over quick." He grins, "Or maybe not. I ain't decided yet."

He lunges again and I trip over a fallen chair, flailing backward as the gun flies from my hand and skids across the floor. Before I can draw a surprised breath, Artie lands on top of me. It's all I can do to keep the blade from my throat as we wrestle across the dirty floor. I feel the cold steel slice my cheek, and the warm blood seeping from the wound.

"Don't worry, I'll find Masie and take good care of her. Maybe find a nice plot next to her mother."

Something inside me breaks at his threat and I roll,

managing to reverse our positions. With the added leverage, I turn the knife, twisting it in his hand until he cries out in pain, then driving it forward until it sinks hilt deep into his shoulder.

He screams and I push myself off him, taking the knife with me, though my hands are soaked in his blood. Rushing to the bar, I toss the knife in the sink and grab a white towel, balling it up before I return to Artie where he writhes on the ground.

"Here," I say, pressing the towel to the wound.

He laughs dryly. "What are you doing?"

"I'm saving your life. Now stay still. I'll call an ambulance."

Standing, I retrieve my gun. I balance it in my hand for a moment before finally emptying the bullets onto the floor and tossing it away. "I just want out."

Artie sputters. "You want out? There is no out. There's only a pine box and six feet of dirt."

Ignoring him, I move toward the phone, curtly ordering the operator to send an ambulance to the club before hanging up.

"It's not over," he screams from the floor. "It's never over. There is no out!"

MASIE
FORTY

JD AND I MAKE IT BACK TO THE PENTHOUSE BEFORE THE RAID is even over. We're both already packed, but I take the time to sneak into Daddy's room and stand over the safe.

"Do you know the combination?" he asks, making me jump.

"Don't scare me like that. I thought you were Daddy."

He snorts. "By now, Dutch is in the back of a paddy wagon on his way to the tombs, then, probably to Blackwell Island to do a nice long stretch."

"This isn't how I wanted this to go down," I admit, shaking my head.

JD wraps me into a tight hug, something he hasn't done in so long that the smell of him is foreign for a moment and my body tenses. "Benny is right, Mas. This is the best thing—the best possible way this could have ended. Otherwise, it ends with one or all of us dead. You know that. Besides, it's time Dutch paid for his sins."

"And he should," I offer, pulling away. "So why do I feel like such a louse?"

He smirks. "Because you, dear sister, are a good soul and whatever else Dutch may be, he's our father. Like it or not, family means something."

I sigh. "Thank you for helping, for doing all this for

us."

Crossing the room, he takes a seat on the edge of Daddy's bed. "Oh, I didn't do it for you. Or not just you, at least. June and I need a fresh start." He hesitates, licking his bottom lip before continuing. "I know about what happened to her, what Lepke did."

I swallow before speaking. "She told you?"

"Didn't have to. I could see it in her eyes, the hurt, and then, when I touched her for the first time, after, well, I knew." He shakes his head, "You took care of her. I'm grateful for that, but it should have been me. I should have been able to protect her, but I was so wrapped up in trying to be the man Dutch wanted me to be that I let her get hurt. And I'm not going to let that happen again."

"You really love her, don't you?" I ask, seeing for the first time the genuine tenderness in his expression.

"I really do. But I'm not good for her, not here, not like this. We need to get out just as much as you and Benny."

I nod once. "So do you know the combination?"

He bites his bottom lip. "It's your birthday."

The revelation hits me like a shot, adding to my already profound guilt. My fingers moving swiftly, I open the safe and pull out the contents.

"You want half? It's as much yours as it is mine," I offer.

JD shakes his head and stands. "Nah. I've been skimming off the club for years. I've got more than enough dough to get us started. Consider that your dowry, because I fully expect Benny to make an honest woman of you."

I laugh. "It's gonna take more than a ring to make an honest woman of me."

He chuckles as well. "Fair enough. But what happens now? I mean, do you know where you're headed?"

Nodding, I close the safe back up. "I've got a pretty good idea. And you?"

He tilts his chin up, looking off into the distance. "Going out west. Benny and me, we talked about it already.

284

He knows where to find me when you're ready."

"I'll miss you," I manage to say without my voice cracking. The realization of what we've set in motion— the distance we'll need to keep—settles in fully.

His face turns back to me. "I'll miss you too, Mas. Try not to get into too much trouble without me."

I shrug. "No promises."

He holds out a hand, and I take it in mine. Together, we walk out of the room and down the hall to where our bags sit, already packed, in the foyer. I stuff the cash and bonds into my smallest leather suitcase and strap it shut.

"Sir, your car is waiting," Butler says, stepping into the room.

JD nods, gathering his things. "So long, Butler," he says, saluting with a finger to his forehead. "Keep an eye on the place while we're gone."

Butler nods once, then adjusts his glasses, which have slipped down the narrow bridge of his nose.

"Rudolpho," I say, holding my arms open. He does the same, and I step into them for a long, warm hug. "I'll miss you." I say, and though I've carefully practiced the speech in my head, how JD and I are fleeing town to escape the heat from the cops—and our enemies—for some reason, I can't bring myself to say any of it. Can't bring myself to lie to him.

Finally growing uncomfortable, he steps back, his shoulders squaring. "Miss, if I may say something?" I nod, and he continues. "You should go say goodbye to your father."

My face immediately falls into a frown. I've betrayed Daddy, in the worst way I could, and now he'll spend years behind bars—just to buy my own happiness. The guilt is nearly suffocating.

"I can't." I say finally. "He'll understand."

Even as I say it, I know it's both true and a horrible lie. Yes, he'll know why we fled. He might even hate us for it for a while. But he won't understand why, not really. And I don't have the courage to tell him.

"He is your father, whatever else he may be, and you should say goodbye. Not for his sake, but for your own."

I sigh, knowing he's right, but feeling like the worst coward who ever lived.

"Goodbye," I say again.

"Goodbye, Miss. I shall miss you dearly."

His words are enough to start my eyes filling with tears, which I blink back swiftly. Hefting my bags, I make my way down to JD's waiting car.

"JD, take my bags. I'll meet you at the station. I have something I need to do first." Pulling a pen from my purse, I scribble an address across it and hand it to him. "Here's the pickup spot."

He presses his lips together in a thin line. "Alright. Just don't be late."

Hugging him quickly, I launch myself into the side street and flag down a taxi.

"To the Tombs, please."

As I sit in the small room, the metal chair digging into my back, I can't help but retrace my steps in my mind. How had we gotten this far off course? I replay, rethink every choice, every action that's brought me to this place. And I can't help but wonder if there's something I could have done, some way I could have avoided this.

The door opens and Daddy shuffles in, the shackles still attached to his wrists. The cop, one of the handful of regulars I recognize from the club, sits him in a chair across from me.

"You have ten minutes," he says to me, nodding.

"Thank you."

Once he's gone, Daddy huffs. "How much did this little visit cost ya?"

I shrug. "Does it matter? I needed to see you. Make sure you were okay."

He slumps back in his seat, raising his hands. "Do I

look okay?"

I lick my bottom lip. "Considering the alternative, yeah. You do."

He huffs again, avoiding my gaze.

"JD and I are leaving town today," I begin. I'm not sure what kind of reaction I expected, but he just sits in silence, staring at the door, so I continue. "Your partners are taking over the club in your absence. As soon as they can get the property released back to them, that is."

He opens his mouth, running his tongue along his teeth, but still says nothing.

"Is that it? You don't have anything to say to me?" I demand, my voice rising.

He finally swings his gaze to my face, his expression slightly amused. "You know, I always figured JD would take over for me one day. Even though I knew he really didn't have the stomach for it. He could never do what it took to survive in the business. But for some reason, it never even occurred to me to take a closer look at you." He sighs. "I suppose I saw too much of your mother in you. I never realized just how like me you really are, not until it was too late."

My mouth goes dry. I didn't expect him to put it together so quickly, but I'm sure now. I'm sure he knows, or at least suspects, the part I played in his downfall.

"You can always trust a dishonest man to be dishonest. It's the honest ones you have to look out for," he adds, turning away again.

"I would have stayed," I admit. "I would have done anything you asked, if only you'd loved me enough to let me make my own choices."

He shrugs, scratching his chin with both hands. "Doesn't matter now, does it? Can't change the past."

"It matters to me," I admit, leaning forward, my elbows on my knees. "Would you really have sacrificed my happiness—my life—for the sake of your own?"

When his eyes swing back to me, his gaze is ice cold. "I would. I suppose we have that in common."

I swear, rising to my feet. "You stubborn ass. I'm about to walk out that door and out of your life forever...and that's all you have to say to me?" He says nothing. "Fine."

Crossing the room, I grab the doorknob, but before I can open it, he stands. "Wait. There is something I want to say to you."

I spin on my heel, folding my arms across my chest to deflect what I'm sure will be another one of his cruel barbs.

"I want to say I love you. Always have. And if I were in your shoes, I probably would have done the same thing. So," he hesitates, "take that how you will."

"I love you too, Daddy," I say, tucking my chin into my chest, my eyes on the floor. I don't tell him that I never wanted it to be this way, because he's right. I'm too much like him for my own good. That's why I want to be with Benjamin so badly. He makes me want to be better, makes me try harder to keep the dark parts of me at bay. Vinny had once told me that I was the light, but he was wrong. Benjamin is the light, and I never want to live without that light ever again.

Maybe, if Daddy had embraced the light instead of choosing the dark, our lives would have turned out differently. But he had no use for the light, or for those who brought it. I see that now. And my heart aches for him.

"Be safe," he whispers after I turn my back to him.

I don't look back at him when I leave. Part of me wants to throw my arms around him the way I had done as a child, the other part wants to slap him across the face for all the times he's hurt me—for all the ways he's let me down. But I do neither. I just open the door and walk out. Making my way out of the sweltering police station, I slide into the back of my cab, refusing to look anywhere but ahead as we roll down the street. I may not be proud of what I've done, but the one thing I realize is that every day is a gift, every breath is a chance to make something better of ourselves, to create the life we want to live.

And I plan to make every moment count.

BENNY

FORTY-ONE

THE NEXT MORNING, DUTCH'S ARREST IS ALL OVER THE FRONT page of the papers. Everyone is buzzing about the corrupt special prosecutor and the hardworking detective who put it all together, taking down the head of a huge bootlegging operation. Dewey took full credit, as I'd hoped he would, and he's even being considered to fill O'Hara's very tall shoes. I know there should be something, guilt maybe. But all I feel is a deep sense of relief. Ma and the twins are safe. Masie is safe. Even I'm safe, at least for now. Until one of Dutch's partners gets a good look at the ledger JD and I faked, until my part in all this comes out, and I know it will eventually.

Of course, all that had come at a terrible price for both of us.

Tossing the paper boy a new nickel, I take a copy, tucking it under one arm as I make my way toward the train station. Dickey's family home is just a few blocks away, and I pause outside their door to slip a folded note into their mailbox.

It's a lie. A letter from their son telling them he loved them and he's heading off to make his fortune in Chicago working construction for the next World's Fair. I tell them not to worry, but to know he's doing something good with his life.

Of course, he's not doing any of that, and up until his last breath, he'd have said he hated his father and resented his mother. But that's not want they need to hear. And sometimes, a comforting lie is easier to handle than a sad truth. The envelope has a few hundred dollar bills tucked inside as well, more to ease my own conscious than their financial suffering.

I'd have wanted him to do the same for Ma, if our positions had been reversed.

As I walk the final blocks to the station, I say my farewells to the city. The streets that have given me so much, and taken so much in equal measure.

I thought I'd be sadder to be leaving, but every step is taking me toward something wonderful. I can feel it in the marrow of my bones. When I finally look up and see her, my chest swells with joy.

Masie is on the platform, her red velvet cloche hat covering her golden waves, a heavy fur coat draped across her shoulders despite the growing temperatures. I sidle up beside her, blowing in her ear playfully. She smacks me with a gloved hand.

"Benjamin, you scared me silly. What happened to your face?" she asks, cupping my cheek in her hand.

"It's nothing, just a scratch," I tease. "Is everyone here?"

She points to where Ma and the twins sit on the nearest bench, Agnes pushing the bag trolley back and forth while Ma struggles to get Thomas into his new suit jacket. "JD and June picked them up an hour ago."

Aggie releases the trolley and runs to me, wrapping her arms around my waist. She's stronger now, her thin frame finally beginning to fill out.

"I'm gonna miss you, Benny," she says.

I hug her back, holding her for as long as she will allow before she squirms away. "I'm gonna miss you too, sunshine. But I'll visit soon."

"All aboard," the conductor yells over the billowing puff of smoke being expelled from the train.

"Hurry or we'll miss it," June says, scuttling up next to Masie, then taking her in her arms for a quick hug.

"Don't be a stranger now. I expect to see you after the honeymoon. I mean it," June demands, reaching out to grab her bag from JD next to her on the platform.

He holds his hand out to me, and we shake. "You take care of my sister, now."

"I will," I promise. "And you look after them," I say, jerking my head toward my family, who is already on their way to my side.

"Absolutely," he says, picking Thomas off the ground and holding him under one arm like a football.

Ma grabs me, pulling me into a tight embrace. "Benjamin..." she begins, the tears already welling up in her eyes.

I have to cut her off. We don't have time for an emotional goodbye today. "Ma, it's only a few months, then we'll come to Nevada for a visit, I promise. Besides, the dry air will be good for Aggie's condition."

She nods. "I'll miss you," she says, hugging me once more. I lift the leather satchel I took from the club, all the money I managed to skim during the renovations and the take of the door from opening night. It's more than enough to get them settled in a nice place and have a few months before Ma even has to think about finding a job. Besides, JD's going to be taking care of them as if they were his own family. Soon enough, they will be. "Take this," I demand, and she obeys hesitantly.

"What about you?" she asks.

I glance at Masie, who is saying goodbye to JD, and I bite my bottom lip. "Aw, I'll be just fine. Don't you worry about me."

She kisses my cheek quickly, then calls the little ones to her side.

As they load the train, I give the twins a quick, hard hug and kiss them each on the head.

"I still don't understand why you aren't coming with us," Thomas complains.

Squatting beside him, I rustle his hair. "Because there may be people looking for me, at least for a little while, and if they find me, I want them far, far away from you, to keep you safe. Besides," I drop my voice to a whisper, "I gotta have some time to convince this dame to let me make an honest woman outta her."

Masie slaps me playfully. "I heard that."

The train whistle sounds and we quickly usher them all on, waving as the train begins to roll down the track.

The train leaves in a puff of smoke, the whistle silencing our final farewells. Once they are gone, it's just us. I take Masie by the hand, kissing her knuckles.

"Are you ready?" I ask.

Her returning smile is bright, her cheeks flushed. "I've been ready for this since the day we met, Benjamin."

With that, I release her and we grab our own bags, flagging down a cab outside the station.

"To Pier Fifteen please," Masie orders when we slide inside.

I frown. "I thought we were headed north?"

Canada had been our plan, plenty enough open spaces to get lost in, and lots of cold nights to spend beside the fire, tangled up in each other.

Pulling her shoulder forward, she grins. "I have something else in mind, if you're up for it."

Reaching into her purse, she pulls out two first-class tickets to Paris and fans herself with them. I whistle.

"You sure we got enough dough for a trip like that?" I ask, taking mental stock of the few bills still tucked in my pocket.

She shrugs, pulling her small suitcase into her lap and popping it open to expose stack after stack of fresh cash. "Consider it my dowry."

"Why, Masie, are you propositioning me?"

She grins, once more fanning herself with the tickets. "You bet your life I am."

Epilogue

*The chateau is chilly when I wake, so, leaving Masie be-*neath the soft blue quilt, I patter to the kitchen and busy myself lighting the stove fire and ferreting out the last of the biscuits we'd picked up from the bakery yesterday.

I'm still gathering food when I hear Masie shuffle down the hall to the small patio. From Paris, we'd traveled to Switzerland, then finally here to Italy. Dutch's trial has become an international sensation, and news of his conviction and subsequent life sentence had reached even the papers here. Of course, speculation was rampant. Some people report that JD and Masie had been secretly murdered and dumped in the Hudson River by Dutch's enemies, others claim it was the work of a certain corrupt prosecutor. None, thankfully, had come even close to the truth. Soon, it was as if the three of us, JD, Masie, and me, had never even existed.

Alistair kept good on at least part of his promise. He'd re-opened the club only a few weeks later with a new name and a new crowd of shoe shufflers. The club was famous, after all, something of an instant legend, and people came from all over the world to drink his illegal liquor and dance the night away on its once-bloody floors.

When I finally bring out the tray, Masie is sitting on

the edge of the iron balcony, looking down at the sprawling vineyard below.

"Good morning, wife," I offer as I have every morning since I finally convinced her to exchange vows with me in a tiny church in Bern.

Turning to me, she smiles. "Good morning, husband."

There's something about her tone that disquiets me, and I set the tray on the table, rushing to her side. "What is it?" What's wrong?"

With a deep sigh, she lays her head on my shoulder, and I inhale the sweet scent of her honey hair before kissing the crown of her head.

"June sent me a letter," she begins, continuing to stare off into the distance.

"Is everything alright?" I ask, unable to hide my concern. June writes weekly, but none of her letters led me to believe anything was amiss. The twins were doing well, healthy and in school. Ma had taken a position as a seamstress working for a dame who made wedding dresses. JD and June were about to open their own club, with the backing of some local friends. Everything seemed blissful.

"Her letter, it was…off."

"Off how?" I ask.

When she turns back to me, there is worry clouding her grey eyes. "I can't explain it. I have a terrible feeling, Benjamin. I think…"

She hesitates.

"You think we need to go back?" I ask.

She nods solemnly. I don't need to tell her that it's too soon, that there are still people who would do us harm if they found us. Nor do I have to tell her how happy I am here and how reluctant I am to leave, how I don't want to put her in danger once again. I can tell by her expression that she knows all that. And she wants to go anyway.

I set my jaw, grinding my teeth before responding. "Alright. Pack a bag. We're going home."

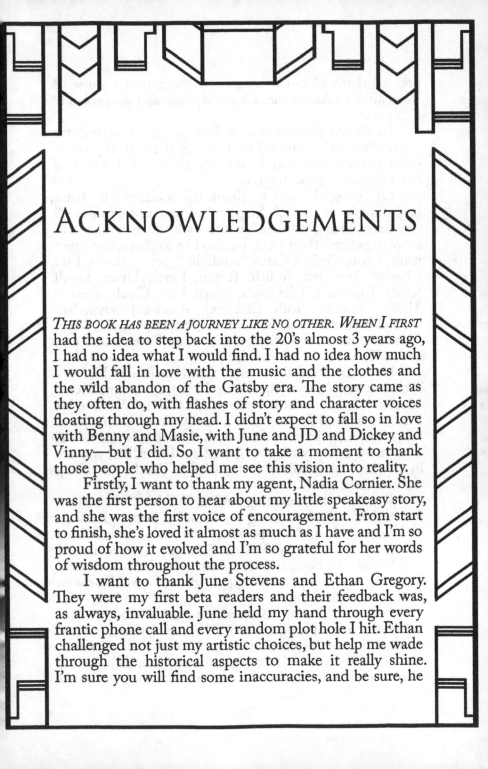

ACKNOWLEDGEMENTS

THIS BOOK HAS BEEN A JOURNEY LIKE NO OTHER. WHEN I FIRST had the idea to step back into the 20's almost 3 years ago, I had no idea what I would find. I had no idea how much I would fall in love with the music and the clothes and the wild abandon of the Gatsby era. The story came as they often do, with flashes of story and character voices floating through my head. I didn't expect to fall so in love with Benny and Masie, with June and JD and Dickey and Vinny—but I did. So I want to take a moment to thank those people who helped me see this vision into reality.

Firstly, I want to thank my agent, Nadia Cornier. She was the first person to hear about my little speakeasy story, and she was the first voice of encouragement. From start to finish, she's loved it almost as much as I have and I'm so proud of how it evolved and I'm so grateful for her words of wisdom throughout the process.

I want to thank June Stevens and Ethan Gregory. They were my first beta readers and their feedback was, as always, invaluable. June held my hand through every frantic phone call and every random plot hole I hit. Ethan challenged not just my artistic choices, but help me wade through the historical aspects to make it really shine. I'm sure you will find some inaccuracies, and be sure, he pointed them all out to me, but I chose to use some of them anyway. Any errors are mine alone and are probably deliberate.

I'd like to thank Camille Ficklin (The Greater) for convincing me not to kill everyone at the end. If your favorite characters survived the book, it's entirely because of her. I do love a good tragedy.

Of course, I want to thank my social media team, beginning with my PA Stephanie Carsten. She does all the heavy lifting and makes me look much cooler and more organized than I am. I'd also like to thank my street team, Katie, Christi/Kathy, Sandi, Jodi, Jenny, Anna, Lisa, Cianna, Ann, Jan, Judith, Regan, Layla, Dyan, Sandi, Kristy, Courtney, Elizabeth, Mary, Lisa, Cindy, Audrie, Alexis, Amanda, Holly, Elizabeth, Amina, Jocelyn, Sariaika, Misty, Brittany, Dee, Sneha, Becca, Angela, Janell, Alyssa, Amanda, Serenity, Amber, Liss, Katie, and Kerry. THANK YOU for all you do!

Huge thanks to the team at Crimson Tree Publishing. Working with Marya (the Cover Guru), Courtney, Beckie, Melanie, and the whole team at CTP is an absolute joy. I've been around the block, and have yet to find anyone as fun, creative, or kind to work with. I hope to write a hundred more books with you ladies! And Cynthia, you are by far the coolest editor on the planet. Thanks for taking my book to a ten!

Thanks to the amazing staff at Wilde's Green Hour in Leadville Co. for letting me dress up in my glad rags and come soak up their speakeasy spirit while researching my novel, as well as well as my Leadville Ladies, Laurel and Stephanie, both talented writers in their own right, for being my own personal giggle girls. Hugs! Can't wait to come see you again!

Of course, I need to thank my family, who are endlessly patient and long suffering. I never would have had the courage or inspiration needed to take this journey without all of you. My original trilogy, Jon, Sidney, and Cami, as well as my bonus edition, Connor—you guys are my whole heart. And to my husband, Jeremy, the inspiration for all the book boyfriends you enjoy, thanks for never complaining and for picking up the slack so I can pursue this crazy dream of mine. I couldn't ask for a better partner in crime or a better friend. Love you to the stars!

And finally, always, and the most, thank you, dear reader, for picking up this book and taking this journey with me. I hope you close the pages a little happier than when you opened them.

XOXP,
Sherry